LILY, MY LOVELY

LENA KENNEDY

Lily, My Lovely

Futura

For my three lovely grandsons, George, Alan and Horatio,
and my friends past and present.

A Futura Book

First published in Great Britain in 1985
by Macdonald & Co (Publishers) Ltd
London & Sydney

This Futura edition published in 1986

ISBN 0 7088 3033 1

Reproduced, printed and bound in Great Britain by
Hazell Watson & Viney Limited,
Member of the BPCC Group,
Aylesbury, Bucks

Futura Publications
A Division of
Macdonald & Co (Publishers) Ltd
Greater London House
Hampstead Road
London NW1 7QX
A BPCC plc Company

Sunset on an evening star,
One clear call for me,
Let there be no moaning at the bar,
When I put out to sea.

BOOK ONE

CHAPTER ONE

Free French

Lily is a familiar character to those who know our London well. If you were to ask Lily what part of the town she lived in, her pretty face would break into a wide smile revealing even white teeth, and her dark blue eyes would light up with humour. 'Cannin' tawn,' she would say with the deep intonation of the East End in her voice. Canning Town was a dreary dockland area, part of the East End which bordered the river Thames. There, long lanes of small tumbledown houses contained the population that drew a living from the thriving industry of the docks on the Thames.

Huge ships arrived from every country in the world, carrying their cargo into the London docks—the Victoria and Albert dock, East India dock, West India dock, the Surrey dock and various others that spread along the riverside for miles, making London seem the centre of the shipping world.

The eldest of six children, Lily in her youth would play down by the riverside with her brothers and sisters. They loved to watch the tramp steamers nosing their way into the docks, or the big liners filling up with passengers, emigrants leaving their homeland for better conditions in the colonies.

These great ships, along with the high cranes that dotted the skyline and the low hoots of the siren, made up Lily's world. It was the only one she knew.

She grew up in one of those tumbledown houses in the same street that her grandparents lived. And when she was eighteen and married to George Brown, she moved into her own little home a few doors down. They would all meet at the local on Saturday nights, having all been shopping in the same market that day and if Mum and Dad went to the pictures, all the kids went too. It was a tight, close community, which provided a roaring, brawling way of life, with plenty to eat and plenty to drink.

Money was scarce but goods and food were easily come by; things fell off lorries as they left the docks and it was well known that the older dockies had hidden pockets in which to conceal their loot.

So Lily grew up happy and healthy, and contented with her way of life. Since she had left school at fourteen, she had worked in the Tate and Lyle sugar factory in Silver Town and would probably still be there but for a certain happening: in September 1939, England declared war on Germany.

On that historic Sunday morning Lily was at her Mum's home with Mum, her four brothers and sister, and old Gran.

Gran's lined face was wan and contrasted sharply with the black clothes she was wearing for Grandfather, who had died only the week before.

At sixty-five Grandfather had still been working when he could. Each day he had waited outside the docks and then fought his way through the crowd in the hope of getting some casual labour. But just last week, he had come home one night, sat down slowly in his little wooden armchair by the fire, and slept his last sleep.

Lily's Dad was a seaman, a ship's cook, who was more away from home than in it. But that day he was in Canning Town. He and Lily's husband, George, were both down at the local enjoying their Sunday pint.

They all ate together on Sundays, and Lily was stringing the runner beans for lunch. Her long auburn hair hung over her eyes, and she puffed a cigarette while she topped and tailed the vegetables with her nimble fingers.

'Well, that's it,' declared Gran, after the first siren went off. 'Anuvver bloody war. Fought it would come.'

'Oh, gor blimey, what're we gonner do nah?' cried Lily's Mum.

Lily calmly sliced the beans and dropped them into the pot.

'Dunno,' she said. 'What're we supposed to do? Nobody's told us so far.'

'I ain't waiting to be told,' said Lily's mother. 'I'm orf tomorrer. I'll go and live wiff me sister in Ireland.'

'Well, I ain't,' said Lily, 'I can't leave George and what abaht poor old Gran?'

'I'll be all right,' growled Gran, 'been frough it af're, I have.'

'Well, it's up to you, but I'm getting aht,' announced Lily's Mum. 'Gahn, kids, gerrup and ger yer fings packed.'

And so, in the first few weeks of the war, the warm little community that Lily had been so happy in, split up. Mum and the kids left for Ireland and, despite her early bravado, the shock upset poor old Gran so much that she had a stroke and became bedridden for a while.

'You'll have to come and live wiff me naw, Gran,' said Lily. 'I expect George'll soon be called up. And how abaht our Mum, then? It beats me how she's got the bleedin' gall to go orf and leave yer, but never mind, I'll look after yer.'

'Yer can put me in the old folks 'ome,' snivelled Gran. 'I don't care. Got nuffink to live fer now, I ain't.'

But Lily was having none of that. 'Now shut up snivelling,' she cried. 'I said I'd manage, and I will.'

So Gran moved into Lily's house and was soon installed in Lily's front room. Now Mum's house and Gran's house stood empty, looking like ghosts of the past with their lace curtains unkempt and doorsteps unwhitened.

'Gives me the bleedin' 'ump,' Lily would remark to George, 'seein' them empty places. I'm used to dodgin' in and aht of Gran's and Mum's houses.'

But George just munched his breakfast toast and sucked his teeth. He was quite unconcerned by the upheaval. Lily cast him a scornful look. After the honeymoon was over, her husband had got on her nerves with his dull outlook and noncommittal ways. All he ever uttered was 'Yes, dear, no, dear,' or 'it's all right wiff me, dear.' At times she could hardly bear his company.

'I shan't be sorry when yer get called up,' she said to him one day, 'sittin' abaht on yer arse all day. I've got meself a part-time job up at the munitions factory so you can give eye to Gran in the daytime.'

George glanced at the old lady dozing in her bathchair. 'Aught ter be evacuated,' he mumbled.

'Mind yer own business, George Brown,' cried Lily. 'I said I'd manage and gor blimey, I will.'

So each morning Lily went off to the factory where she worked in the canteen. Several times a day she pushed a tea trolley down and around the long lines of presses and capstans, where young women in green overalls and caps slaved away on a busy bonus system which ensured that the much needed bullets and gun parts poured into the war effort.

At first Lily was quiet and didn't talk much to the others, but with her rosy cheeks and ready smile, she soon became very popular with the girls. She became a familiar sight, with her hair piled on top of her head, handing out cups of tea or coffee, chatting cheerfully as she moved from person to person. There was one thing Lily was never short of, and that was chat. And it was she who soon spread gossip from one department to another. If a baby was born or someone got killed in the war, it was Lily who transmitted the news, laughing or weeping with genuine feeling. A love note would be passed on with just as much care and concern as the bad news of a husband killed in action. Not only did the hot tea and coffee provide a welcome break to those women who worked like Trojans but so did Lily. She loved her new job and everyone liked her and her habit of diving head first into whatever business was going on at the time. She made the factory buzz with news.

So those first few months of the war were not too bad except for the men who were being called up. One of these was George, but he went off to the army very cheerfully, rather pleased to be getting away from Lily and Gran who had been giving him a dog's life, as he grumbled to his pals as they waited at the station before embarking on the journey of a lifetime into the unknown.

Soon after George had gone, an Anderson shelter was

installed in the small yard at the back of Lily's house where George used to keep his rabbit. Their shelter, a corrugated iron hut sunk half-way into the ground and covered with earth and sandbags, was to be their only means of protection from the bombing. Each night Gran was transferred down there accompanied by Mrs White from next door. With a couple of bottles of Guinness and a pack of cards the two old ladies were quite happy, and Lily felt free to put on her best regalia and go off to the pub with her workmates, regardless of any bombs and blackouts.

While they were on early-morning duty, Lily and her friends' evenings were free, and with the heartiness of the East End Cockneys, they made the most of them. Lily lived nearest to the factory so it was her house that was usually used for the necessary preparations for going out. Their work-day clothes of slacks and head scarves were quickly discarded and replaced with smart suits, little hats with eye veils and plenty of make-up. Hair was brushed out and lacquered stiff, eyebrows were plucked to long, thin lines, cheeks were rouged, and lips painted bright red. They did not have to worry about wrinkles in their stockings because they wore none. Stockings had virtually all but vanished since war began. Instead, the women painted their legs with suntan lotion and drew lines down the backs with eyebrow pencils to represent the seams.

By the end of their careful primping, Lily and her pals looked amazingly smart as they emerged arm in arm from the house and disappeared into the blackout laughing and giggling. 'Look out, boys,' they would laugh. 'Here we come!'

After such nights on the tiles, Lily would chatter about their adventures with her other workmates in the factory. The older, more respectable women were often quite shocked, but Lily's straightforward approach to life and her spontaneous gaiety did much to make a dull day pleasant.

'Don't let your old man catch you, Lily,' they would jest.

'So what?' said Lily cockily. 'What the eye don't see the heart don't grieve for.' And Lily would tell them more about the blokes they had met in the pub.

'Be careful, Lily,' someone would warn her. 'Don't get into trouble. Yer George'll murder yer if he comes back to a ready-made family.'

This kind of remark would instantly get Lily going. 'Don't think I'm that daft, do yer? Have ter be a bleedin' fast worker to get round me.'

'Mean to say yer meet all them blokes and they don't get anything?' The women stared at her in astonishment.

'Of course they don't!' replied Lily scornfully.

Lily's indignation was taken with a pinch of salt and no one believed her. But they all said it was wartime and life was short and sweet. They were tolerant because everybody liked Lily in spite of her randy ways (as they saw them).

Lily's particular pals were Ivy, Mary, and Doreen. Together the girls went out on their sprees several nights a week and they would get the dockland alight long before Hitler managed to. They had a good choice of entertainment for, in spite of the blackout and the blitz, life went on inside the taverns and pubs. Beer was scarce and expensive but the boys on leave were there to live it up—after all, this might be the last leave they'd have.

There was Charlie Brown's pub which was very popular and full of souvenirs brought back from all parts of the world by generations of homecoming sailors. Another favourite was the Bridge House at Canning Town which ran good entertainment every night and was always packed with sailors from the liberty ships, who had just one night ashore before they were off again on the briny.

Lily and her friends would arrive all dressed up at one of these pubs, sit down and buy themselves one drink. Then they ogled the servicemen who would then join them and buy plenty of drinks for them. Then it was off in a cab, if one could be found, to tour the pubs and make it a real night out.

Occasionally, Ivy, Mary or Doreen would feel emotionally attached to one of the men, and would then disappear for the evening with her special escort. When this happened, Lily would sniff and say scornfully, 'Do as yer please. I can mind me own bleedin' business. No one ain't getting me round some dark corner.'

'Oh, you are a hard nut, Lily,' the other girls would say. 'Sometimes a bloke can be very special, you know.'

'Not to me,' retorted Lily. 'Never liked sex, not even with George.'

The first years of the war and the terrible nights when London was blitzed just passed over Lily, making little impression on her. She kept her job, looked after Gran and spent her money in improving her appearance in order to impress the young men whom she would then leave cold.

She and her friends had a lot of fun and a few close shaves, like the night when they went out on a spree in Whitechapel and picked up four Free French sailors who enticed them with promises of luxuries, which they had in their kit-bags, luxuries such as French wine and nylon stockings.

'Come home to my house,' suggested Lily. 'We'll have a party.'

Immediately they all agreed and, after a lot of kissing and cuddling on the trolley bus, they arrived at Lily's house. It had been quiet for a few nights with no bombs, so Gran was still up, sitting in the parlour in her bathchair. 'Fine bleedin' goin's on,' she grumbled when she saw the girls with flushed faces and the excited, foreign-looking sailors.

'We're going to have a party, Gran,' said Lily. 'They've got brandy and wine. You can stay if you like.'

On went the gramophone and as the music filled the room, one of the sailors opened up his kit-bag to produce a box of chocolates which he gave to Gran with many fancy gallant gestures. Gran cackled at him like an old hen. The others opened their kit-bags, producing bottles of brandy and wine and a pair of highly valued nylon stockings for each of the girls. They were all set to have a lot of fun and Lily had just started to pour the drinks when a noisy fracas broke out. One of the sailors was arguing with Ivy in his own language and neither knew what the other was saying but, since he was pushing Ivy towards the stairs, the Frenchman's intentions were pretty obvious. Without a moment's hesitation, Lily waded in and punched him on the nose. 'No bed,' she said loudly. 'We nice girls.'

There was a sudden silence in the room as the meaning of her words sank in. Then almost all at the same time, the outraged sailors grabbed back their gifts. Poor old Gran had just begun to tear the wrapper off the chocolate box with one horny finger when suddenly the box was snatched from her grasp and popped back into a kit-bag.

And with a few angry grunts, the frustrated sailors marched out of the house in a solemn line, taking their nylons with them.

'Oh,' cried Lily, 'talk about Free Frenchmen!'

This made everyone laugh, and they all cheered when Lily produced from under the table a bottle of brandy which the sailors had missed. From then on it was ladies' night as they drank the fiery liquid which had an exciting effect on them. They sang noisily and danced together around the room. When the siren went, with much hilarity Gran was bundled down into the shelter while she continued to complain bitterly about the chocolates that she never got the chance to eat.

Back in the house, the girls finished the bottle of brandy and then lay about so sloshed that they did not care that the windows rattled and the bombs descended around them, causing the whole of the docklands to go up in a blaze. They were too drunk to notice.

In fact, many lives were lost that night, as Lily learned the next morning when, pushing her tea trolley around the factory, she saw so many empty places at the benches. It was a sad day for all. Tears fell down her cheeks and Lily's sorrow was so great that she even forgot about the terrific hang-over she had got from the Free French brandy.

Sometimes Lily tried to explain her relationship with her husband to her friends. 'He ain't no oil painting, my George,' she would say as she poured out tea from the big enamel teapot. 'Suppose you'd say he's kind of homely. But, as I always says, he's mine, and he don't never look at any other bird, so that goes a long way to a happy marriage.'

But Lily's pals protested. 'Yer don't like him in bed and yer keep saying he gets on yer nerves. What's so loving about that?' one of them said.

'Well, that don't bother me,' replied Lily. 'It's all just a lot of pushing and shoving abaht noffink, that is.'

And off she went with her tea trolley, leaving behind her, as she always did, a chorus of laughter coming from the other girls who never quite knew whether to believe her or not.

When George was due for his first forty-eight hour leave, the girls at the factory all joshed Lily. 'Better stop in tonight, Lily,' they laughed. 'Save a little bit up for poor old George.'

'Oh, he'll be well boozed,' retorted Lily confidently. 'He won't be any trouble to me.'

On Saturday afternoon George arrived home heavily laden with all his kit. He stood grinning on the doorstep as Lily gave him a peck on the cheek. She looked him up and down and let out a shrill cry. 'Yer ain't bringin' that bleedin' gun in 'ere! Why, it'll frighten the daylights out of old Gran.'

George sighed. 'I'll hide it in the cupboard under the stairs till I go back,' he said apologetically.

Having got her way, Lily gave him a beaming smile. 'Come on in, then, yer must be dead beat carryin' all them fings abaht.'

George followed her into the small back kitchen and relaxed while Lily buzzed around getting a meal prepared for him. She chatted all the time, telling him about the blitz and the shortages of food and the troubles that old Gran was giving her.

George pulled off his heavy army boots—his beetle crushers, as they called them—and soon his grey woollen socks were steaming in the fire light. The atmosphere was warm and congenial, and he seemed glad to be there, back in his home, with its tiny kitchen and faded wallpaper. He ate the meal Lily put in front of him and in no time he was asleep.

While George slept at the fireside, his ruddy face and knobbly nose glowing in the light of the coals, Lily began to get ready to go out to the local. For this was Saturday night, and no one stayed in on Saturday nights—at least not down in Canning Town they didn't.

As always, Lily's preparations made up a long drawn-out performance, achieved with the help of a mirror propped against the teapot on the kitchen table, two layers of make-up, and plenty of perfume. Her hair was combed and curled and then lacquered until it stuck out like a birch broom.

The bright red lipstick was applied to her mouth and the suntan lotion to her legs. When this runny liquid was finally dry and well smoothed, Lily then had to get into some ridiculous positions in order to draw the seam lines down the backs of her legs with her eyebrow pencil. And it was while she was in an awkward position that George woke up. With a gleeful expression on his face, he reached over and touched her on the bottom.

Lily instantly exploded like a firework. Jumping back, she thumped poor old George about the head. 'You behave yer bloody self!' she yelled. 'I don't want none of yer army tricks 'ere.'

But George was not put out. He just cackled and pulled on his big army boots, lacing them up slowly and meticulously. 'I'm orf to the pub,' he said, getting to his feet. 'Can't wait for you. Could paint the bleedin' 'ouse the time it takes for you to paint yer face.'

'Oh, piss orf!' said Lily ungraciously as she rearranged her hair.

And so Lily and George continued their way of life during George's brief visits on leave as though nothing was different. George's long absences had not changed Lily's opinion of him one bit and George, as usual, was not bothered.

CHAPTER TWO

You and I and a Starlit Sky

One night in September 1942, three years after the war began, it was raining heavily in London. The deserted pavements were shining and wet. Since the sirens had gone off, the city's population had been crouching underground waiting for the rain of bombs that was now a nightly occurrence. All the big air-raid shelters, like the tube stations, were overcrowded but since it was Saturday night there would still be some amateur entertainment laid on somewhere.

When the siren sounded, Lily struggled to get Gran down into the shelter. She was very worried, for Masie White had recently got fed up with the blitz and was refusing to go into the shelter. This meant that Gran was left without a companion, a fact that concerned Lily.

'I'll be all right,' snarled Gran. 'Don't yer worrit o'er me. Had me day, I 'ave. You get out on the booze if yer wants to.'

Lily bit her lip anxiously. It was not often that she felt so disturbed. 'Shut up, yer silly old cow! I'll stop in and that's that.'

'Oh, yes,' grumbled Gran, 'and 'ave the bleedin' 'ump all night? Get me a little drop o' whiskey and I'll sleep like a top, bombs or no bombs.'

'Oh all right,' agreed Lily. 'I'll pop up the pub when it stops rainin', and get you some whiskey. Don't want to ruin me new 'at.'

'Take the bleedin' fing orf,' said Gran. 'Makes yer look like a tart anyhow.'

'Now, shut up, Gran,' Lily cried in exasperation, patting her new hat and rearranging her curls under it.

Lily was very proud of that red velvet hat; it had cost her a
week's wages. It was scarlet with an up-turned brim—the very
latest in fashion. Her pals had all said, 'Oh, Lily, not red, not
with your hair colouring.'

But Lily had been determined to have that hat for some time.
She had spotted it sitting all alone in the window of a West End
shop; it was too expensive to sell quickly in those hard times.
But she had decided then that she was going to have it, come
hell or high water. And as soon as she had enough money, she
went straight to the shop and emerged triumphant, the lovely
red hat in a large paper bag tucked under her arm, a wide grin
on her face.

'Pity you ain't got anything else to do with your money,'
complained Ivy. 'I've got to send my money to help with my
kids' keep now they are evacuated.'

But Lily was so busy thinking how she would create a
sensation when she entered the crowded bar wearing that hat,
she couldn't have cared less about Ivy's troubles.

Lily didn't regret her decision now. She knew she had been
right first time, that the hat really suited her. Her hair lay in
shining curls about her cheeks and the sweep of its brim showed
up her fine straight features and creamy skin. Her wide eyes
shone like stars. Yes, she decided with satisfaction, she did look
good tonight. If only it would stop raining! For having got the
hat in the right position she was not taking it off now. In the end
she solved her problem by finding an old umbrella so that she
could pop down the road to get Gran a couple of tots of
whiskey.

Down in the shelter, Lily tucked Gran in and gave her half the
whiskey. 'Yer can drink the other half before yer drop orf,' she
said. 'Goodnight. Sure yer will be all right?' She still felt uneasy
about leaving Gran all alone.

''Op it,' replied Gran. 'Don't keep on fussin'.'

So at last Lily went out into the blitz. The rain had become a
steady drizzle and there was a stillness in the air. The smell of
acrid smoke was everywhere since a lone raider had flown over
and dropped his string of bombs before heading for home again.

Soon another wave of bombers would come, guided in by the light of the fires of the burning buildings started by the first plane.

None of this worried Lily. Having settled Gran she was now more concerned about not getting her new red velvet hat wet than anything else. She called for Ivy and they went together to meet Doreen and Mary in the Bridge House not far up the road.

When they entered the pub, the huge bar was full. The noise and the cigarette smoke were almost overpowering but to these girls out on the town it was a welcome haven. What went on outside did not matter as long as they clicked tonight and got some blokes to treat them.

'We don't like that bleedin' 'at,' said Doreen as they met up. Ivy and Mary shook their heads in unison.

But Lily tossed her curls disdainfully and ignored them. She felt smart tonight and no one was going to put her down.

In the bar there was a sprinkling of civilians but mostly the men there were servicemen. On one side there were twenty or thirty foreign sailors celebrating their few hours ashore. They were very noisy and sang songs in their own tongue.

'Blimey! What are they?' asked Lily.

The girls all laughed heartily at the memory of the Free French sailors in Lily's house.

A youngish man was singing on the stage. He waved his arms and all his pals joined in the chorus, as he sang of the Transvaal. It was a South African song which had been made popular in wartime by Gracie Fields, but this man sang it in true Afrikaans. He had a sweet melodious voice and as Lily sat down at a table to listen, he broke off and said in perfect English over the microphone, 'Oh my, what a nice hat.'

Everyone in the bar turned to look at her and Lily was furious. But her pals were even more so. 'It's embarrassing,' Doreen said. 'They are all looking at us. Told yer not to wear that bleedin' 'at, Lily.'

'Mind yer own business,' returned Lily, casting paralysing looks at the singer who had continued with his song, 'Sardi Mari'. He still sang in Afrikaans but every now and then he paused to ask, 'Who is she, Sardi Mari? Where does she live, Sardi Mari?' And each time he looked at Lily, which caused a lot of amusement as she actually blushed as red as her hat.

'The cheeky silly sod!' she exclaimed, looking away in embarrassment.

After an encore the young man came down from the stage and came towards Lily who sat up very stiffly as he came nearer. He was of small stature and slim, with brownish-blond curly hair. He wore a neat sailor's uniform with a blue-and-white striped dickey front. Bowing low over her, he said, 'Madame, I really like your hat. May I buy you a drink?'

Instantly Lily burst out laughing. 'Well, if you want to, you can,' she exclaimed, 'but it will cost you four gins—one each for me pals.'

The drinks were ordered and as he sat beside her, Lily had a strange feeling inside her. In a peculiar way she felt as if this man was no stranger, as if she had met him before—but how and where she could not think.

Now he pressed her hand to his lips. 'You are beautiful,' he whispered, 'the most beautiful woman I have seen since I left my country.'

Even Lily could not resist such flattery. 'Oaw,' she said, smiling. 'Turn it up.'

He looked puzzled at her remark. His English was good but Lily's Cockney jargon was unintelligible to him. He sat staring at her in silence.

Lily started to chat freely. 'Where yer from?' she demanded, and without waiting for a reply continued: 'We seem to get a lot of foreigners in here now. Never used to, but can't say I mind. Live and let live, that's what I say. Me, I lives for every bleedin' day. Not much good doin' anyfing else wiff the bloody blitz on all the time.' She paused for breath and finished up her gin.

The sailor ordered more drinks and took her hand with a smile. He had a kind of slow grin that made the corners of his mouth twitch. His serious brown eyes were lit up in humour.

The band struck up a popular tune and in his sweet soft voice, Lily's admirer began to sing again, without taking his eyes off her. 'Some day when I'm growing old/When our love grows cold/I'll be thinking of you/Just the way you look tonight.'

'Romantic, ain't he?' giggled Lily, showing off to her pals.

But the other three girls were getting fed up. 'We're going, Lily,' they said. 'Are you coming?'

Lily looked at the sailor, who clasped her hand tighter. She turned to her friends. 'No, you go. I'll see yer tomorrer.'

Ivy was astonished. 'Don't be silly,' she protested. 'You know we all stick together.'

'Oh, I fancy a change,' smiled Lily, moving closer to this blond suitor so that they got the message.

When the other girls had gone, the sailor plied Lily with more gin and put his arm around her. She felt warm and comfortable, and chatted on to him gaily. He told her that he was called Cornelius, but known as Kasie. He did not understand anything she said, but he continued to stare at her with a strange kind of fascination. He seemed to be entranced by the way two dimples appeared each side of her face as she chatted and smiled, by the lovely red hat perched on her auburn curls and by the carefree manner she had of waving her hands about as she talked, and batting mascaraed lashes over her shining dark-blue eyes.

It had got very late and the bar was almost empty. 'You can't come home with me,' Lily explained. 'I'm married.'

Kasie made no comment but, leaning forwards, he kissed her gently on the lips and took her hand. As if walking on air, and without another word, Lily went with him out into the night.

It had stopped raining at last and there was a clear sky full of twinkling stars. They walked slowly, saying nothing. Soon they came to an old derelict house. Ivy and honeysuckle climbed up the old walls that surrounded a large garden. Kasie drew Lily into the shadow and, feeling in a daze, she went willingly with him into the unkempt garden which smelled so sweetly of honeysuckle and wild roses. Leaning against an old crumbling wall, he drew her to him and held her in a passionate embrace. For a moment, Lily tried to pull away. ''Ere, take it easy,' she said. 'I'm no soft touch.'

Once again, he misunderstood her. 'You are beautiful to

touch,' he murmured softly, and his hand slid up her bare leg. When he pressed his hot dry lips to hers, Lily was lost, her resistance gone. She returned his kisses with warmth. 'You really need me, Lily,' he whispered. 'And, my God, do I need you.'

Afterwards, Lily hung her head in shame. 'Oh, why did I let you? I'm so ashamed—I never saw you before tonight.'

Gently he reassured her. 'Do not worry, Lily. I know enough about women to know that you are not a bad girl. But as from tonight, my *leiblin*, you are my girl.'

'I've missed me bus,' wept Lily, 'and it's a long walk home.'

'I'll walk you home,' he said gently. 'We can go slowly together.'

So they walked back slowly hand in hand. He hummed a tune as they went, a catchy tune from his own country. In no time, Lily had picked it up, and they swung along singing together till they got to Lily's street door. The air-raid warning went off as they kissed goodnight. 'Will I see you again?' Lily asked.

'Yes, Lily, you certainly will,' he replied and spinning round, he sauntered off down the road with that graceful gait.

Lily crept indoors and lay on Gran's bed in the front parlour. She would not disturb Gran in the shelter tonight. As the big bombs whistled down around the docks, Lily lay thinking about the lover, Kasie, who had thrilled her with an ecstasy she had never known before. Never in her four years of married life had she ever felt like that. Perhaps she ought to be feeling ashamed of herself, she told herself, but strangely enough she wasn't at all. She was glad.

At last she nodded off to sleep but was abruptly woken up by the high-pitched whistle of a bomb speeding through the air. Then all the world exploded about her. The parlour ceiling caved in, and her bed went through the floorboards. Screaming in terror, her mouth full of plaster and dust, she crawled out of the smoking debris and lay numb with shock on the pavement outside.

In no time at all, the Air-Raid Precautions men were there sitting her up and helping her into an ambulance. As she recovered consciousness, Lily suddenly cried, 'Where's Gran? Where's Gran? Find Gran! She's in the Anderson!'

But the men shook their heads. 'Sorry, lady,' one of them said. 'It was a direct hit on the back garden. I'm afraid the old lady's done for.'

Lily's legs buckled under her. 'Oh, poor old Gran,' she sobbed wildly. 'Oh, it's all my fault, I'm being punished for being wicked,' she wept.

Old Gran's body had been scattered everywhere. Even her bathchair was hanging down from the lower branches of a tree in the neighbour's back yard. At least Gran couldn't have known what was happening.

The ambulance took Lily off to the hospital where she was cleaned up and given a sedative. The next day, she returned home to see what she could salvage of her belongings. As she wandered about the blitzed house, collecting up anything that was still usable, she wept uncontrollably. She was all alone.

It was at that moment that Kasie arrived and stood in the street, small, clean, cool, staring in amazement at the ruins of Lily's house. And there was Lily herself, her lovely hair badly singed and covered in white dust, her eyes were red with crying, and her clothes dirty as she wandered, dazed, over the debris picking up the few precious treasures that remained.

'Oh, Lily, my lovely!' he cried in dismay.

His was the first friendly face she had seen. Lily rushed into his arms, and he held her close, smoothing the dust from her hair.

'Oh!' wailed Lily. 'I've been blitzed and poor old Gran has been blown to bits. That's her bathchair up there in that tree, and not one trace of Gran can be found.'

She spoke so quickly that Kasie understood very little of what she was saying. But he wiped the tears away with his snow-white handkerchief and said, 'Don't distress yourself, Lily, my lovely. Come along with me. Come, darling, I'll take care of you.'

So Lily, like a bright butterfly now crushed and broken, took the hand he offered and went with him down to Aldgate where they stayed in a hotel, and, even though Lily cried her heart out, they made love all night long.

But the next morning Lily awoke, sat up in bed and yelled out loud: 'Oh, gor blimey! Where am I?'

The figure in bed beside her stirred. 'Whatever is wrong, Lily?'

Lily was in a state of utter confusion. Her mind had been blotted out by a combination of shock and too much Bols gin the night before, and now, at six o'clock in the morning, she found herself in a strange room with a strange man. It was more than she could cope with. She stumbled out of bed and ran to the window. To her relief she saw the familiar sight of Aldgate East station just over the road. 'But what the bleedin' 'ell am I doin' 'ere?' she cried, tears rushing to her eyes. 'What day is it?'

With a quiet smile of amusement, Kasie sat up in bed and lit up a cigarette. 'It's Monday,' he said. 'And you are in the Three Tuns Hotel. Don't you remember? We came here yesterday afternoon.'

'Oh!' cried Lily as her memory rushed back to her. 'Poor bleedin' Gran, blowed up in her bathchair. And Christ, if it's Monday I should be at work or I'll lose me bloody job, and then where will I be?'

She paced up and down glancing around the room with its neat bed and flowered curtains. 'I didn't ought to be 'ere. Only whores come 'ere. The Three Tuns? Why, it's well known for that sort of fing. Oh, Lily, what's happened to yer? Yer used ter be a respectable girl, yer did.'

'Come here,' Kasie beckoned to her very quietly but authoritatively. Lighting a cigarette, he handed it to her. 'Now, Lily my lovely, calm down. You don't want to wake up the neighbours, do you? You came here of your own free will. Remember, your house was bombed and you had nowhere else to go.'

Lily looked at him in shocked silence as her mind cleared. 'But I didn't want to stay in a bloody hotel,' she protested. 'Why, only whores do that.'

He had got out of bed completely naked and was coming

towards her. Lily covered her face with her hands. 'Put yer bleedin' clothes on!' she screeched.

He laughed and twisted the bright bedspread around him so that he looked like a Roman Emperor. 'Hail, the conquering hero comes!' he said with such a dramatic pose that Lily started to smile. Kasie put his arms around her and cuddled her up close.

'You are free to leave me whenever you want,' he said gently. 'I return to my ship tonight anyway.'

'I'm sorry to have made such a fool of myself,' said Lily sheepishly, 'but, honestly, I've never done anything like this before.'

'I know, darling,' Kasie consoled her. 'And I'm the wicked man who has seduced you. Let's get cleaned up and get some breakfast, shall we?'

His gentle tone brought back good memories of the night before, and Lily began to wonder if she did in fact regret her indiscretions. But where should she go now? Back to Canning Town?

As they breakfasted in the buffet at Liverpool Street station, Kasie suddenly said, 'Lily, don't leave me. Come with me to Portsmouth.'

'Oh, I couldn't leave my job, and I'll have to let me mother know abaht poor old Gran, and then there's George . . .'

So Lily chatted on so fast that Kasie hardly understood a word. He gave up trying to and just stared at her, fascinated by the dimples at the sides of her mouth and her lovely auburn hair.

'Can I write to you?' he asked.

'Don't know where I'll be, do I?' replied Lily, but her thoughts were on where she was going to live now that her house was destroyed. So she rattled on. 'I suppose I could get Ivy to put me up, though I don't like her bloody mother-in-law, I don't. Shanghai Lil, was what Gran used to call her—always down Pennyfields with the Chinamen.'

Kasie could understand even less of this but he smiled and gently touched her cheek. 'If we never meet again, Lily, you will have certainly been an inspiration to me. But I promise I'll come looking for you when I next return to London.'

'Don't bother,' said Lily, finishing her cup of tea, ''cause yer won't find me. From now on, I ain't gettin' mixed up with men. Poor old Gran, she didn't deserve that.' She got up and collected her handbag. 'In some way it's my fault,' she continued. 'I ought ter 'ave stayed at 'ome instead of out in the bleedin' pub. That was my punishment. So from now on, Lily is goin' straight.'

He kissed her hand. 'Goodbye, Lily,' he said. But Lily flounced out of the buffet without a backwards glance.

When she arrived at Ivy's house, Ivy's mother-in-law put her long nose outside the door and squinted at her. 'Oh, it's you,' she cried. 'Everybody's bin lookin' fer yer. 'eard abaht yer poor ol' Gran, 'ave yer?'

'Yes, I know,' said Lily wearily. 'Is Ivy in?'

'Not 'ome from work yet, and I can't ask yer in 'cause I'm just goin' aht meself.' She put a hat on very quickly and closed the front door while Lily stood disconcerted outside the house.

'I'll wait for Ivy,' Lily said.

'Please yerself,' said Ivy's mother-in-law as she toddled off towards the market.

As Lily stood in the street, her thoughts went to last night. Kasie had been very nice, she thought. He was so fair, so quietly spoken and so very gentle, he was different from any man she had ever known. Where was it he said he came from? The Netherlands? Lily had never heard of the place. She turned over in her mind all the sweet things he had said to her. Ah, well, she thought, as she saw Ivy coming down the road, no good mooning over him, she'd never see him again anyway.

Ivy was a short stout girl, with shiny black hair that she wore very straight. She had small, dark eyes and a gruff voice.

'Crikey, Lily!' she exclaimed. 'Where 'ave yer been? They're thinking of gettin' up a collection for yer, they all thought yer 'ad been blitzed. I knew where you was of course, but minded me own business. Shame abaht yer Gran.'

Lily's blue eyes filled with tears. 'It was my fault,' she wailed. 'I should 'ave stopped in wiff 'er.'

Ivy put her latch key in the door. 'Don't say that, 'cause if yer 'ad been in the shelter yer'd 'ave copped it, too. Direct 'it, so they say.' In the smelly kitchen she made Lily a cup of tea. 'The old cow's gone aht,' Ivy said, referring to her mother-in-law. 'She does that so's she won't 'ave to give me anyfing to eat.'

'Will I be able to stay till I get sorted aht?' asked Lily.

'Of course yer will, love,' replied Ivy. 'She won't like it, but sod 'er, she can put up wiv it. Come on, let's go down the fish and chippie.'

They went down to the fish-and-chip shop, and then to the pub for a drink where Lily told Ivy all about her blond sailor. Ivy laughed fit to burst. 'Oh, gor blimey, Lily, yer really went orf the rails!'

'That bloody hotel scared the wits out o' me,' said Lily. 'Yer know, yer can easily get a bad name if yer seen in them places.'

'Blimey,' replied Ivy, 'yer was lucky. If I get a bloke they usually are skint and I get lumbered in some dark doorway or over the fields.'

So it was settled that Lily went to stay at Ivy's, sharing Ivy's narrow bed in a gloomy back room. She quickly made the best of a bad bargain, even coping with Ivy's mother-in-law, who was a real tyrant. She spied on them, listened at the keyhole and even pinched their sugar rations. But somehow they survived, going off to work every morning and out on the town at night. Ivy had three children who were all evacuated. She was careful with her money, saving it in order to visit her children every month, so it was back to the old games of knocking the blokes for drinks.

Lily no longer pushed the trolley at the factory. Instead, she had a job behind the counter and was sent on a part-time release scheme to learn to do wartime cooking. Lily enjoyed this. She made meatless pies and stews and did things with spam and soya flour. She began to take such an interest in her new position that she even started to make up her own recipes for things like meatless pasties.

'Wot the 'ell are they, Lily?' someone asked her as she pulled them steaming from the oven.

'U-boats,' she said brightly. 'Let's see yer sink 'em.'

From that day on U-boats were always on the menu.

Lily did not enjoy living with Ivy. There was never enough hot water to wash and the beds seldom got changed. Creatures crawled up the wall and Ivy's mother-in-law would get drunk and shout all sorts of curses up the stairs at them. 'Our boys givin' their blood and yer out on the tiles every night! Dirty cows! Yer'll get yer reward: the pox, that's what yer will end up wiff.'

Ivy took all this abuse in her stride but it horrified the happy-go-lucky Lily.

George wrote occasionally but he was now in Malta which was being bombed day and night. 'Poor old George,' said Lily. 'He was never very brave. I wonder how he's gettin' on.'

Months later, in early spring, Lily and Ivy went straight from work one day to have a drink in a pub in Whitechapel. They were no longer the glamorous females ogling the lads in the bar. Lily wore a coloured head scarf, for hats had gone out of fashion as the war continued, and it was now a case of nose to the grindstone. It was work, work all day and every day. And the shortage of hot water in Ivy's house did not encourage cleanliness.

Lily lounged up at the bar feeling tired and depressed when suddenly two hands came over her eyes and a gentle voice whispered in her ear: 'Guess who?'

'Oh no!' cried Lily spinning round to see the impish face of her blond sailor.

Kasie was grinning from ear to ear. 'I've searched three days for you, Lily. At last I've found you!' Lily pulled away immediately.

'Well, what d'yer want of me?' she snarled, looking very unfriendly.

The Dutch sailor looked hurt and put a gentle hand on her arm. Her flesh tingled under his touch and she did not pull away. 'It is nice to see you once more, Lily. I'm on leave and I thought you might like to help me see the town.'

'Yer welcome to see what bloody Hitler left of it,' sniffed Lily.

Kasie looked amused. The corners of his mouth twitched and the brown eyes twinkled. 'Oh, Lily, Lily, my lovely, we are disgruntled aren't we?'

Unconsciously she leaned towards him and he automatically put his arm about her. 'Come, my darling, let's get out of this place and find somewhere else to eat.'

A sense of weariness came over her. 'What abaht Ivy?' she asked.

'I am sure Ivy can take care of herself,' he said, taking her arm and guiding her out into the blackout.

As soon as they were outside, he took her in his arms and kissed her. He undid her scarf off her hair and gently stroked the hair he loved so much. 'Where is that lovely hat you used to wear, Lily?'

Lily wept. 'I don't get time to dress up now,' she said. 'I'm too busy. And,' she added, 'I'm so bloody depressed.'

Kasie held her close to his chest. 'Oh, Lily,' he cried, 'I could not forget you.'

She put her arms about his neck and returned his kisses. 'That's funny,' she said, more cheerfully, 'nor could I forget you.'

They dined in a small restaurant in the Minories which catered for the foreign servicemen who now thronged London, and Lily livened up. She told Kasie her tale of woe, about Ivy's vindictive mother-in-law and the crummy little house she was living in. Kasie was very sympathetic. 'No wonder, darling, that you have lost that lovely smile,' he said. With a finger he just touched the deep dimples each side of her mouth. 'Now smile,' he said. 'Just one big smile for me.'

Lily felt like a child, he was so calm, gentle and possesive. She rubbed her face on his hand and shivered as she felt a thrill ripple through her. She knew she wanted him to make love to her.

'Will you be mine tonight, Lily?' he whispered eagerly.

'Yer know I will,' returned Lily as an impish grin appeared on her face.

'I know just the place,' he said, pulling a piece of paper out of his wallet. He held it up and read it slowly: 'Smithy's, 22 Apple Square. Do you know where that is, Lily?'

Lily screwed up her nose as she thought. 'Can't say I do,' she finally said.

'Is it in London?' he asked. 'Here it says WC1.'

Lily looked at the piece of paper and burst out laughing. 'Silly sod!' she said. 'That's Argyle Square, not Apple Square.'

Kasie laughed with her. 'Thank you very much. I have worked very hard to improve my English just for you, *leiblin*, I thought you'd appreciate it.'

Lily's spirits had returned. 'Come on, then,' she said. 'Let's go!' She wanted him as much as he wanted her, she could hardly understand herself. No one had ever turned her on like this gentle blond man did. Against him she had no defence whatsoever.

They found Smithy's in Holborn. Mr Smith ran a sort of boarding house for the allied forces and asked no questions and told no lies. The sound of crisp notes was his religion. The big house was warm and cosy, and he never turned anyone away. Folks slept anywhere, even on top of the billiard tables when he was fully booked. Smithy, as he was called, catered for breakfast but most of his guests ate out.

As soon as Lily and Kasie had reached their room and the door was locked, there was nothing more to wait for. Lily removed her shoes and lay on the bed in wait for him. Her heart was thumping like mad, for with Kasie she went to Heaven and did not care about anything any more.

'I still have five days' leave left,' Kasie said afterwards, 'so we will stay here together. This will be our lovers' nest for the rest of the time. Is that all right with you, Lily my love?'

She rubbed her hand over his back, which was smooth and full of freckles, and then up towards his neck where his hair grew in tight little curls. He smelled sweet and clean, unlike

George who sweated like a horse and smelled of beer and shag tobacco.

'Lily, Lily,' he asked, gently. 'Do you want to go out to dinner or shall we make love again?'

'Oh, no,' cried Lily, pulling herself together. 'We had better eat. I can't live long on just love. Well, we can't go anywhere posh tonight,' she said, 'but tomorrer I'll sneak into Ivy's and get my toothbrush and some decent things to wear.'

They walked through the city to London Bridge and queued outside the steak and chips restaurant with other girls and their friends.

'I wonder what makes that place so popular,' murmured Lily after dinner, as they wandered over the bridge to look down at the river.

'I've been told that they serve horse meat,' Kasie grinned.

'Oh!' cried Lily in dismay. 'You mean to say I've been eating some poor bleedin' 'orse? Oh Christ! It's a wonder I didn't gallop out of the place.'

Kasie laughed uproariously. 'You're a real comedian, Lily. The meat will not hurt you—we eat a lot of horse flesh in my country.'

They spent the rest of the evening walking arm in arm around Soho, dropping in here and there to beer-drinking clubs, so Lily was beginning to feel quite tipsy. 'I think I'll sneak into Ivy's and get me gear,' she said, feeling quite bold. 'The old mother-in-law will be out in the pub.'

They got the bus back to the East End. It was a quiet night with no bombing, so everyone was out on the town.

Kasie waited on the corner of the street while Lily crept into the house to collect her belongings. After a while, she came running down the street carrying a small suitcase. Behind her he could hear a lot of screeching going on from inside the house.

'Whatever goes on?' Kasie asked in amusement as Lily, breathless and smiling, came up to him.

'She came in and caught me, the old cow,' Lily explained. 'She cursed me up hill and down dell, and finally I said, "Shut up, you old Chinese whore!"'

'Was that necessary?' he asked.

'Oh, yes, it was!' asserted Lily. 'Had to get that one in even if it was only for me old Gran.'

Kasie sighed. Would he ever understand these Cockneys?

That night they returned to Smithy's to complete the honeymoon. Kasie had a stone bottle of Bols gin to assist them and, alas, morning came all too soon.

Next day they visited the zoo and Madame Tussaud's, Hyde Park and all the tourist sights in the West End. In the evening, footsore and weary, they had dinner in a secluded French restaurant. To Lily, such extravagance was a waste of money. 'It's twenty pounds,' she said in horror when the bill came. 'You sure you 'ave got that much?'

'Don't worry your little head about money,' Kasie told her. 'What I have got we will spend, because when I go back this time, I go back to active service. So let us live, Lily, my love, while we are able.'

Lily's big blue eyes opened wide. 'Yer mean yer might get killed?'

'Not if I can help it,' he grinned. 'But if you care to notice, since we last met I have had promotion.' He pointed to the red cross and anchor on his arm.

'Oh, that means yer an officer.'

'Not exactly but going on that way. Now, if you will be quiet, Lily, and stop butting in, as we walk home I will tell you my story and how I got here.'

'I promise,' said Lily, subdued by her interest.

They strolled hand in hand through the blacked-out streets which Lily guided him through. She knew the way back to Holborn, for this was her own town. As they walked, voices came through the darkness and tiny torch lights twinkled as people found their way around through the night.

In his gentle sing-song voice, he began to tell her the history of how he became a Dutch sailor stationed in England, leaving his home to fight for his own beloved country, now occupied by the Germans. 'I was born on the Zuider Zee, so I suppose you could say I am a born seaman, and that is how I got such a quick promotion. My mother and father, my sisters and brothers are still in Holland under the Nazis. I worry about them all the time and often I think I should have stayed behind to protect them.'

'Don't they write?' quizzed Lily, not quite sure what else to say.

Kasie smiled as he bent down and kissed her. 'No one gets any messages out,' he said softly. 'My country is occupied.'

'I'm sorry,' said Lily, quietly, not really realising what he meant, but sensing that he was sad.

Kasie continued. 'But I have heard through the regular channels that my family have gone ashore, they have left the ship they owned to the Nazis and gone to live on an island in Freisland. For my parents it is the first time in all their married lives they have lived on the land. My mother gave birth to five of us on board a canal boat and she was working beside my father all the time. It's a very hard life but we are a certain kind of people,' he asserted proudly. 'We're like those damned old Boers. We live, eat and sleep on the water; it is our whole life. I owned my own ship, and was saving up to get married. My wife, Jante, was to live on board with me.' He paused and his face seemed to crumple in pain at the memory. 'That night when the Germans came, I was in Amsterdam, Jante's home town. Oh God! it was sheer hell. We put up no defence whatever as wave after wave of bombers came. As people rushed out into the streets, the Germans swooped down and machine gunned them all down. Burning bodies fell out of the buildings and all the harbour was on fire.'

He stopped for a moment and looked down at Lily to see if she was still listening. His face was white and drawn.

Lily was now in tears. She threw her arms about his neck. 'Oh, please, darling, don't talk about it, it all upsets me. I keep thinking of poor old Gran.'

Kasie held her tight and nuzzled her soft hair. 'Yes, perhaps you are right,' he said. 'It does not seem good to look back. But I did want to let you know how I came here in England. We had better leave the rest for another day, it would be wrong to spoil this lovely night. Come, we will sing a song and the next pub we come to we'll go in.'

Pushing bad memories aside, they skipped along, singing a saucy sea song, which was in Dutch but Lily knew it well, too, having heard it sung so often in the East End taverns.

Sadly, Lily's second honeymoon had to come to an end. A few days later, she sat forlornly beside Kasie at Victoria Station. 'Are you sorry?' she asked. 'Do you care if we don't ever meet again?'

Kasie took her face in his hands and kissed her full on the lips. 'I will live for our next meeting,' he murmured.

'Don't fancy goin' back to Ivy's,' said Lily. 'That old cow of a mother-in-law will probably turf me aht after what I said to her the other day.'

Kasie looked thoughtfully at her. 'How would you like to come with me to Portsmouth?' he asked, as he had the first time he had left her. He still lived in hope.

'Gor blimey!' exclaimed Lily. 'I couldn't do that. I ain't never been aht of London.'

'The blitz is not quite so bad down there,' Kasie reassured her, 'and I expect you could get a job. I won't be ashore much now I am assigned to the mine sweepers but I am based down there, and I'm likely to get some time ashore.'

Lily was thinking about the problems it would cause and began to chatter nervously. 'I suppose I could go out to me muvver in Ireland. At least then I'd be out of the bloody blitz. Mind you, she's no picnic to live wiff. She left old Gran for me to look after, she did. Bound to blame me, she is, for what happened. And then there's poor old bloody George being bombed to 'ell out there in Malta. Life ain't worf livin', it ain't.' As she gave vent to her feelings, she started to weep, heartbroken, her head on his shoulder.

'Oh, Lily,' Kasie cried, almost in tears himself, as he got up from the bench quickly. 'Sit there. Don't move, and take care of the kit.' And off he went with his swinging sailor's walk.

'Where are yer goin'?' Lily tried to call after him but as the sound did not come, it dawned on her that she had never called him by his real name. She had just used dear or darling, and this thought amazed her and she wondered why it was.

He returned soon afterwards, grinning mischievously. The corners of his mouth curled up and his brown eyes, which were usually stern, shone with humour. 'Up you get, Lily,' he said. 'All aboard. I got you a single ticket on the train.'

'I won't go,' Lily stated obstinately, but her heart was hovering and in a strange way she was pleased that he was leaving her little choice.

He held both her hands. 'Trust me, darling. Let's take a chance on some happiness while we are still young, and you are so beautiful.'

That did it. Lost in a daze Lily held on to his hand tightly as they went through to board the train to Portsmouth. Kasie suggested that she sit on her own in first-class. 'It's better not to be seen together,' he explained. 'My shipmates are on this train and I don't like them to know my business. Besides, they might pinch you from me.'

Lily stared at him suspiciously. 'I don't think I'll come,' she said half-heartedly. 'I've changed me mind.'

Kasie shrugged and looked at his watch. 'That is entirely your own decision,' he said. 'But you had better be a big girl and make it. The train will soon be leaving. Trust me,' he whispered, looking down into her eyes. The steady gaze in those dark-brown eyes seemed to hypnotise Lily. She calmly took his arm and allowed him to escort her to the first-class compartment. 'I'll hang about in the corridor and keep my eye on you,' he told her. 'When we reach Portsmouth, go into the buffet in the station and wait for me. Promise me, *leiblin*?' he pleaded.

Lily nodded dumbly and sat in a remote corner of the carriage well away from the other passengers—two well-dressed women and a petty officer. The rest of the train was overcrowded. Hundreds of servicemen sat on their kit-bags in the corridor; women in naval dress walked up and down the corridor, back and forth to the toilet, laughing and jesting with the service personnel as they pushed past them. Throughout the journey south, from under the brim of her smart black felt hat,

Lily kept an eye out for her lover who came and stood a while
by the window smoking a cigarette and giving a whimsical grin
in her direction. And all the while, the wheels of the train
seemed to be saying: 'Lily, Lily, what are you doing? Go back,
Lily! Go back while there is still time.' But Lily knew she was
trapped and did not really care about it any more.

At Portsmouth the sailors poured out of the train pushing and
shoving and talking. Two of them had a fight right on the
platform and they kept on fighting even when they rolled over
the edge and onto the line. Then two members of the Military
Police patrol jumped down and hooked them up. Lily watched
all this in fascination. She had seen many a dockside pub brawl,
but this was truly exciting. As the soldiers were led off by the
MPs, she found the buffet and ordered a cup of tea. She sipped
the tea and watched the Military Police patrolling the cleared
platform.

Soon Kasie arrived. He quickly looked around him and then
hurriedly approached her. 'Made it,' he said jubilantly. 'Got rid
of my kit and found someone to sign me in. Now I'll be able to
spend the whole evening with you—and we must find somewhere for you to stay.'

'Dunno as I am goin' to like it here,' grumbled Lily. 'Seen
these chaps fighting on the railway.'

'Oh, bloody Englishmen!' exclaimed Kasie. 'They're always
fighting.'

'Do you mind?' asked Lily, pretending to be insulted. But he
took her hands and kissed them.

'Come now, Lily. You belong to me. I knew you would not
stay in an hotel so I made a few enquiries. One of those lady
sailors said you should go to the Y.W.C.A. I've got the address.'

'What's that?' asked Lily.

'It's a sort of ladies' hostel. You tell them you came down
here to look for a job and they give you a room and help you to
find a job.'

'All right,' said Lily, blithely. 'In for a penny, in for a pound.'
But her conscience suddenly crept upon her again. 'I must be
bloody mad. Gawd knows what Ivy will be thinking.'

'Lily, Lily, my love.' Kasie's gentle hand on her arm restrained her, and so, pushing her conscience back, she gave a hearty laugh.

He picked up her suitcase and they walked down into the town. Kasie waited in the pub while Lily booked into the hostel.

'Hope you don't mind sharing,' the lady behind the desk said to Lily, who shook her head. The mood Lily was in, they could behead her and she wouldn't care.

After she was all booked in, she met Kasie in the pub where they had a drink. Later, they said goodnight outside the hostel. The rain was pouring down on them and she clung closer as they said goodnight.

'Don't leave me, Lily,' Kasie pleaded. 'Be here when I return.'

'How long will you be gone?' she asked.

'Four days, that's all. My duties are four nights away and two ashore. Isn't that something?'

'I suppose so,' said Lily, without enthusiasm. 'But what I'm goin' to do in this bloody strange tawn all alone, beats me.'

'Don't worry, darling,' he said. 'We'll think of something.'

The small, spotlessly clean room in the hostel, with its two white beds and stiffly stretched sheets, rather scared her as she came back into it. Her room companion lay stretched out on the other bed. She sat up as Lily shut the door.

'Hullo,' she said. 'Want a fag?' She offered Lily a packet.

Small and fair with short cropped hair, she looked Lily over, surveying carefully the neat green suit, smart shoes and nylon stockings. 'Civvies eh! London, ain't you?'

Lily nodded and began to unpack her night clothes.

'I'm Rita Harris,' the other woman said, 'but everyone calls me Budgie.'

Lily sat down on the bed and stared at her. 'Why?' she asked.

The young woman giggled. 'Look!' She turned so that Lily could see her profile. 'Can't you see the nose? Makes me look like a budgie, someone once said. So that's how I got my nickname.'

Lily looked closely at the fair, good-humoured face with its little hooked nose. Budgie explained that years before, her nose had been broken and flattened out at the base. 'Oh, yes,' cried Lily in amazement, 'it does make you look like a budgie.' And they fell back on their beds in peals of laughter.

Budgie sat up again on her bed and chatted gaily to Lily. 'I'm going into the forces,' she informed Lily. 'Tomorrow I've got my medical. I'd like to get into the w.r.e.n.s, but I might not make it—they're very particular.'

'Don't think I would like the forces,' replied Lily, 'but I might get a job down here.'

'What's your trade?' asked Budgie. Lily liked her quick, lively manner.

'I'm a cook,' said Lily.

'Easily get in the Naafi,' said Budgie. 'I'll scout round with you tomorrow if you like. I don't go for my medical until the afternoon.'

'Thanks,' said Lily, pleased to have made a new friend. 'I don't know this place at all. Never been out of London in me life, but that ain't much of a bloody place to live in now.'

'I heard it's been blitzed to hell,' said Budgie. 'It's not so bad down here now. We get an occasional raid but that's all, and there's plenty of life—lots of pubs and lovely men,' she added with great satisfaction.

The two women lay on their narrow beds long into the night exchanging life stories. Budgie told Lily how she had hiked half-way across the world starting off from Canada. Lily told Budgie of her lover and of her husband, who was overseas.

'I don't blame you, Lily,' Budgie said sympathetically. 'We only live once, but if I was you, I'd keep the fact about your lover boy under your hat. Folks are funny about those things; it's better to keep your business private.'

'I suppose so,' said Lily doubtfully. 'Kasie always says I chat too much.'

'Yes,' said Budgie. 'And believe you me, pal, I know what folks are like, I know the world, 'cause I have bloody well lived.'

So, on her first night out of London, Lily got her first lesson in diplomacy from Budgie, the out-going worldly Canadian.

In the morning they had breakfast together, and Budgie explained to Lily how to get the best out of the crummy Y.W.C.A. while she was here. Afterwards they walked around the town, and Lily registered at the Labour Exchange. Later, they had coffee in a cafe which faced the wind-swept promenade, a mass of tangled barbed wire, for no one was allowed to go near the sea.

When Budgie went for her interview for the W.R.E.N.S Lily sat in the park watching couples walk by arm in arm. She suddenly felt very lonely, so she went back to the hostel and wrote a letter to Ivy. She told Ivy that she was having a holiday and would be back in London in a few weeks and asked her to take in any letters which arrived for her from George. An inexplicable feeling of gloom swept over her, and she lay on her cold hard bed feeling very down-hearted until Budgie came back. Budgie was very drunk and staggered about everywhere throwing her clothes on the floor while she sang: 'All the nice girls love a sailor!' She danced in the middle of the room. 'I made it, Lily!' she shouted joyfully. 'I got in the W.R.E.N.S—ain't it super?'

Lily was not sure what to say. She was feeling cold and homesick, and longed for London, and the frivolous gaiety that had survived in that well-blitzed town. Unable to share Budgie's delight, she fell asleep wondering why she had come down to Portsmouth at all.

In the morning, the Labour Exchange telephoned Lily at the hostel to tell her to go for an interview at the Ministry of Food where there was a job vacancy for an assistant cook.

As Lily got ready to go out for her interview, Budgie came back dressed in her new uniform. The little sailor hat perched on her head made her nose look more ridiculous than ever. 'Bye, love,' she said. 'I'm off. I'm going to Wales to training camp, H.M.S. Glendower, I think. Here's my address. Write to me.'

'I'm in two minds whether to go back home or not,' confessed Lily.

Budgie gave her a terrific blow on the back. 'Stay here, and go and have a good time,' she said, and then off she went with many farewells to the staff in the hostel.

Lily felt a little bucked up by Budgie's attitude, and tripped off to the job interview in a better frame of mind. Perhaps it showed, because she was surprisingly successful.

'We run canteens for civilian workers,' the manageress told her. 'We are short of good cooks and you seem to have the right amount of qualifications. We like our girls to live locally, so suitable lodgings will be provided. I hope you will be happy with us.'

Lily came out of the Ministry of Food building feeling a lot more cheerful. The wages seemed good to her and it would be a change of scene, so why not?

She had not heard from Kasie for days. It occurred to her that she might never see him again, but she wasn't going to worry. She would wait till Monday before she left the hostel, and he might turn up before then, she told herself.

On Sunday night Lily was sitting in the hostel lounge reading the local paper, when she heard the familiar tune that Kasie always used to whistle, 'Mejsie song'. She grabbed her coat from the chair, and dashed off out to meet him outside.

Kasie looked tired and as Lily kissed him, she noted that his chin was rough and needing a shave. Not a word did they utter, they just walked hand in hand up the dark cliff and lay in the long grass at the top. His body was hot and urgent. Lily shivered with inner passion. Her need of him was so great that she could not control herself, and she let herself go.

'Lily, my love,' he said when it was over. 'We must never do that again out here. We must find a place to live together, you and I.'

They fell silent again as they lay on their backs looking up at the starlit sky. Every now and then a searchlight swept across the sky and the stars twinkled brighter.

'You and I, Lily, and a starlit sky . . . Why, I'm getting quite poetic,' Kasie laughed. 'But I will always remember this particular moment, for you have become part of me, my whole existence, and I am never going to let you go.'

'Don't be silly,' said Lily, giving him a playful push. 'I'll have to go back when George comes on home.'

Kasie rolled over and pressed her tight against his chest. 'Oh, Lily, my love,' he murmured, 'must you spoil this wonderful moment? Forget George! Forget him and think only about you and me, nothing and nobody else.'

CHAPTER THREE

The Love Nest

Lily liked her new job even though it was hard work. She was a pastry cook in a large kitchen working with all sorts of aliens—French and Dutch, and even Italian prisoners-of-war. It was a bright, lively and cosmopolitan kitchen with plenty to eat.

She liked her lodgings, too. She had a nice room with a clean bed and a bathroom down the hall. It seemed like a palace compared to Ivy's home. Her plump, jolly landlady woke her at six in the morning with a cup of tea. Lily would go off to work and sometimes she finished work at three in the afternoon, when she would go to the pictures or window shopping.

Kasie was back at sea again. He had told her that he might not be around for a couple of weeks.

'Why?' she had asked.

'We are not supposed to talk about our jobs at all,' he said, 'but if you insist. If you sit on the promenade at about five o'clock in the evening, you will see our fleet going out. We sweep the mines from the channel to keep the sea lanes clear. That's all I am going to tell you, Lily, my lovely. Now, promise you will wait for me. Be here when I come ashore—that's all I ask.'

'I might stay for the summer,' announced Lily. 'I like my job and it's nice and peaceful down here. I never lived at the seaside before, and I hear that the blitz is worse than ever in London.'

'I don't think I possess your heart, Lily, but willingly I give you mine. Say that you truly love me.'

'You know I can't talk a lot of slosh like that,' scoffed Lily, 'but I give you everything else, don't I? So I suppose I must love you,' she added more gently.

'It's not enough, Lily.' Kasie's eyes grew cold and he held her tight, almost viciously. 'I swear I'll kill you, Lily, if you let me down while I am away at sea.'

'Lot of bloody time I get,' complained Lily. 'I'm up at six in the morning, and on me bleedin' feet for six hours at a time. Can't see me gettin' it away with anyone. I ain't got the bleedin' energy.'

Kasie put his head on her shoulder and his whole body shook with laughter.

'Oh, Lily, sometimes I don't know if you are good for me or bad for me, but you amuse me and that makes me love you more and more.'

She slipped her hand inside his jacket and pressed close to him. 'I wish you and I were in a nice warm bed together,' she whispered. 'It's cold out here.'

'We will be, Lily, next time I am ashore, I promise you.'

The next evening she sat on the bench on the promenade and watched the fleet of small ships move swiftly across the harbour knowing that Kasie was off to sea once more. She waved her hand at them and whispered, 'Goodnight, Kasie, come back safely.'

She went home early to bed to dream of her lover. That night, Portsmouth harbour was badly bombed.

As the bombs fell all around her, her landlady screeched up the stairs. 'Come on, quick, Lily! Come down the cellar!'

But Lily stayed in bed and called back: 'No, it's all right, I'm used to it. I've been through worse than this!'

The next morning when she walked to work she had a strange melancholy feeling. The boats in the harbour were still smoking and fire engines were everywhere.

'That was a bad night last night, Lily,' said the boys she worked with in the catering. 'They say there was a big sea battle on as well.'

'Who cares?' said Lily. 'If you gotta go, you gotta go.' She rolled out the big wads of dough into long strips and punched these into round rings to make those meatless pies. She moved very quickly, her touch so light and her movements so expert.

'One thing about Lily,' said the head cook, 'she's a worker. She don't down tools, she just keeps going, whatever's going on. Could do with a few more like her.'

'She's a Cockney,' said another. 'Hard as nails but as loyal as they come.'

So Lily earned her popularity among these strangers and did her bit for the war effort cheerily and willingly. Two weeks passed and still there was no sign of Kasie. Then three weeks passed. Lily strolled nonchalantly about the town hoping to catch a sight of him. Other men tried to pick her up, but she would not be tempted. Sometimes she even walked down to the dock gates and although she often saw batches of his country-men coming out of the bars in town she never had the courage to ask about Kasie. 'I'll give him another week,' she told herself, 'then I'll get out. I've had enough and it will be nice to see old Ivy again.' She made these plans to console herself and made up her face and ironed her blouse to while away the evening hours.

She went to the cinema one Saturday afternoon and when she returned her landlady said; 'A note came through the door, Lily. It's for you.'

Her heart missed a beat. He was back! She read the note quickly. 'I am looking for you, Lily, my love. Will be down at the Victoria, K.G.' She rushed upstairs, brushed out her hair, put on a nice dress, and dashed off to meet him.

Kasie was wearing a new uniform with brass buttons, and he looked very spruce as he stood up at the bar ordering drinks for them both. She stared at him with his mop of fair hair and those clean features, and noted again the way his hair receded from his forehead just a little, and grew thick and curly at the nape of his neck. A pang in her breast made her realise how much she had missed him, and that she really loved him. All thoughts of George or London were driven from her mind completely.

When Kasie returned to their table, she snuggled close to him. 'I really missed you,' she said warmly. 'Where have you been?'

'I lost my ship; I have been away in hospital.'

'You mean it was sunk?' cried Lily in alarm. 'Why, you might have been drowned.'

'I nearly was. I was two days on a raft, Lily, thinking all the time that I might never see you again.'

'Oh, poor darling,' wept Lily. All her pent-up emotions came seeping through.

'Oh, please, hush, no crying,' begged Kasie. 'We will have a long weekend of love to make up for my absence. Just to please me, Lily, let us stay in a hotel tonight. I will wine and dine you, *leiblin*. I have my pay, so nothing will be too good for you this weekend.'

Lily looked at him anxiously. 'Do I look all right? I don't want to go into a posh place looking like a tramp.'

'In my eyes, you are always beautiful,' he reassured her, 'but tonight you look lovely in that blue dress. It suits you very well.'

She gave a wide grin, her vanity appeased. 'Like it?' she asked. 'I bought it in town at the summer sale.'

Kasie raised his hand to her lips and hummed a tune: 'Some day when I'm growing old, when our love grows cold, I'll be thinking of you, just the way you look tonight.'

'Oh shut up,' said Lily coyly, giving him a playful shove.

They strolled along the sea front. It was a bright moonlit night and the sea was smooth, calm and peaceful as they made their way to a country inn further out of town.

'Now, Lily,' he warned her as they reached the door, 'I want you to be calm. There's nothing to worry about. Our apartment is booked and our dinner will soon be served. I am very much in the mood to celebrate.'

They dined by candlelight in the bright little restaurant and made love in the clean warm bed. Lily had no reservations about anything any more.

'Oh, Kasie,' she exclaimed. 'I don't think I could turn back now. I feel I really belong to you.'

'And I, my love, will make you my wife when this bloody war is over,' promised Kasie. 'That is, if we survive. Meantime, let us go on living for each day. Next week I'm going back to school to a ship ashore for a while. It's in Devonport, not far away. I'll get back here weekends, so you be good and wait for me.'

'I'm a little lonely here,' she said, 'but I do like my job, so I'll stay.'

'You had better not desert me now,' he threatened. His tone was mocking and affectionate but Lily sensed that underneath it, Kasie was deadly serious. She giggled. It was great to be loved and made such a fuss of. She had not had much attention in her young life.

So on Sunday afternoon they said goodbye once more as he got on the train for Plymouth, and Lily returned to her lodgings to get ready for work in the morning.

The next months flew past. Every weekend they went to the country inn out of town, and during the week Lily worked hard and looked forward eagerly for Fridays.

One dark cloud on the horizon came in the form of letters from Ivy, that is, the ones from George which Ivy collected and sent on to her in Portsmouth. They were two air-mail letters with much crossed out by the censor. From his tone, George seemed very down-hearted and Lily suddenly felt very guilty about what she was doing. Still, she consoled herself, George was still very far away, so he could not come between her and Kasie. By now she had decided that she would die if she had to return to London and dull old George. She knew she had to answer so she scribbled a quick letter to George, using Ivy's address and putting it in the envelope for Ivy to post in London. Then, in her letter to Ivy, she wrote: 'Hope you don't mind but I don't want old George to know I've left the old place.'

That weekend Kasie arrived looking very jubilant. He had brought Lily some presents—a navy-blue sailor's jersey, and a gold anchor on a chain. This jewellery he placed around her neck with great care and whispered, 'Now you are anchored to me forever, my love. Say you'll never leave me!' He held her very tight.

'Whoa!' gasped Lily. 'All right, I'll never leave you.' As she spoke she felt as if poor old George's letters were burning a hole in the pocket of her mack.

Rain was pouring down now and they walked through the park swinging their clasped hands. Kasie began to sing in that sad sweet voice that Lily loved so much: 'The leaves of brown came tumbling down that September in the rain, With every word of love I hear you whisper and the rain seemed to play a sweet refrain.' Lily joined in at the end as her spirits seemed to soar, but then Kasie's mood seemed to change abruptly.

He stopped singing and turned to look at her. 'Lily, my love,' he said, 'you are very beautiful but I have to say that you cannot sing.'

Lily was wounded by his words. Losing her temper she struck out at him, trying to hit him with her fists, but Kasie caught her wrists and laughed.

'Why do you do that to me?' she cried, boiling up in her temper.

'I'm sorry, darling,' he cuddled and soothed her. 'But you do have a very flat, tuneless voice, Lily, and no one can argue about that.'

Lily calmed down. She knew that what he said was true but no one had ever had the nerve to say that to her before. She loved Kasie all the more for being so frank, and that Saturday night was as blissful as the others.

'Oh gawd,' said Lily the next morning. 'If I go on like this, you'll be giving me a baby.'

'I'll try not to, Lily,' he said. 'We both have enough to live with at the moment. I leave Devonport next week and come back to base. By then I will have further promotion—I will be the equivalent of your English Petty Officer.'

'No kidding?' said Lily. very impressed.

'So if I am stationed here we'll get a flat and I will live out. How do you like that idea?'

She did not reply. Summer had gone and there was still George to consider. Perhaps, she thought to herself, it would be better to go home now.

'What are you thinking about?' he asked.

'Nuffink,' said Lily, shaking her head. 'Will we be able to do that?'

'Do what? Live together? Who says we cannot?'

'I dunno,' replied Lily. But she knew that their relationship could not be permanent and she was afraid of getting further involved in it.

The following weekend when Kasie arrived he said: 'I've got a big surprise for you, Lily. I've found us a flat. I'm back in the mine sweepers, so I will be able to live out and get an additional allowance for doing so and now you can give up your job and take care of me.'

This news filled Lily with dismay. The trap had sprung so now she could not escape. But she still remained silent about it.

The flat Kasie had found had belonged to another Dutchman who was married to an English girl, so Kasie informed Lily. It was five miles out of town in a very nice suburban district, and was large and comfortably furnished. Lily loved it from the moment she saw it. There were big windows with velvet curtains and very highly polished old furniture. There was a big Victorian sofa and comfortable deep armchairs.

'Crikey!' she said. 'Ain't it posh.'

'Well, it's ours for three months,' said Kasie. 'I shall be spending two days at sea and one ashore from now on. How's that? I shall make you into a real *hausfrau*, so that when I take you home I will be really proud of you.'

'What's that?' she asked.

'It means a good housekeeper, that's all. English women are not so house proud as our women.'

'You ain't makin' no skivvy out of me,' Lily warned. 'I can't stand all that spit and polish, there are other things in life 'sides polishin' up the 'ouse all day. That's what me and me muvver used to row abaht. Always at it, she was, dustin' and polishin'. There was no peace in the 'ouse when she was in it.'

Kasie stared at her in amazement, and then put his hand over her mouth. 'Oh, what am I going to do with you?' he cried, laughingly.

'I'll give you three guesses,' she said taking his hand and leading him towards the bedroom.

The months of September, October and November of 1941 were the most wonderful of Lily's life. Kasie was so kind and patient to live with. Having given up her job, or at least told them that she was off sick, Lily had very little to do and, for the first time in her life, she did not have to rush out to work early in the morning. Instead, she would lie in bed looking out into the olde worlde garden. Their flat was on the second floor of a tall, well-built Georgian house which had been turned into three self-contained flats. A large pear tree stood under the window and now, in late autumn, it was heavy with big juicy pears. Kasie would lean precariously out of the window and then present Lily with a pear while she lay in bed. With much ceremony, he would say: 'A gift, my darling, from the Gods of love.'

The days when Kasie was away at sea, Lily would polish the furniture until it shone like glass. When he was there, she could cook exciting meals for them, laying the table with china, glasses and the huge candelabrum.

'Who does all this lovely stuff belong to?' she asked Kasie one day.

'To a very nice lady whose husband went down at sea. He was my officer and lost his life just recently. His wife has gone home for a while to Scotland and I am taking care of it all for her.'

'She must trust you a great deal. It's all valuable.'

'We've known each other in peace time,' he replied, 'but after all, what value is china and glass in the days of war? It is hearts and minds we should be concerned about.'

And so they lived like man and wife out in the village of Eastleigh. Lily was so happy. She never wrote to Ivy or George and, in fact, she completely forgot her past life. All she cared about was her blond lover, her true lover.

When Kasie was ashore they would go down to Hayling Island to the roller skating rink and have lots of fun, then into the town to tour the bars. Often she met his shipmates and their wives and he was now very proud to show her off, and no longer insisted on furtiveness or secrecy. And when the young boys gathered around Lily, Kasie got extremely jealous, for there was no doubt that Lily had some special quality that attracted people to her like magnets. Her open smile and her vivacious manner made her the star of every party.

Occasionally Lily would hear a gossipy whisper when one well-dressed lady would say to another, 'She's not his wife, you know. He just brought her down from London.'

But Lily did not care. For in her eyes she was more a wife to Kasie than she had ever been to George. And now she had burned her boats behind her and had given up worrying.

CHAPTER FOUR

Jealousy

As the year drew to an end, the weather became very cold and Lily got bored. 'I am going back to my work,' she told Kasie. 'I'm supposed to be off sick, so I know I'll get my job back.'

'I would much sooner you didn't,' replied Kasie, 'but perhaps it will be just as well, for there are plenty of changes on the horizon.'

'What do you mean?' she looked keenly at him. Deep in her heart she had always felt that this tranquil life she had been living could not last forever. And now she was being proved right.

He took her on his knee and they sat beside the blazing coal fire. 'You know that I am in the Dutch navy and the English navy has only borrowed me. I am working hard to improve my position and because I speak both German and Dutch and a little English—which is improving every day—I got this position as an instructor in the mine school. It is now certain that we will have war with Japan and she will for sure try to take our colonies, so it is possible my next ship will be sailing to the Far East.'

Lily leaned against him feeling relaxed by the heat of the fire and his caressing hands. She understood half of what he was saying.

'Lily,' he complained, 'you are not listening.'

'Oh, I was,' she insisted, 'but, honestly, I don't understand it. I was never one to get bothered about politics, and history was my worst subject at school.'

'Oh *mein Gott*,' he sighed, 'you are a hopeless person, Lily.

You have so little sentiment, yet I love you. I was just trying to prepare you for our parting.'

'Oh, that don't worry me,' she quickly said. 'I knew it would come.'

Lily was welcomed back to work at the canteen. She made excuses for her long absence and said that she had had to go back to London for a while.

Kasie had changed his duty roster and came home less often, and sometimes only one night a week. Even then he would bring his study books with him and sit reading far into the night. This always made Lily a little disgruntled and she would sit cracking peanuts, of which she was very fond, and scatter the shells around on the floor.

Kasie would give her paralysing looks and get up to sweep up the bits of shell with a little dustpan and brush. His disapproval made Lily feel that their love was growing cold.

In December the whole of Portsmouth was disturbed by the sinking of the *Repulse* and the *Prince of Wales* out in Singapore. The Japanese had fitted torpedoes to their planes and the British ships had no air cover. The casualties were immense, and most of them were men from the south coast because Portsmouth was their home base. At work, women fainted and even grown men cried. Lily felt empty, as if she did not belong. In the East End during the blitz there had been a similar kind of tight community, but down here it was different. These were sailors' wives and mothers, fathers and brothers, and they felt the strain of that long wait for news of the dead and injured.

Lily tried to explain all this to Kasie when he came home that night looking very pale and exhausted. But he shook his head. 'Lily, you have no idea what it is like when there is such a great disaster as this. One family in three will have lost a son or a husband, or a brother. I have seen such sights as that when I was on the destroyer escorting the troop ship. The sea swarms with black, oil-covered bodies. It froths and boils like the fires of hell, and the cries and screams of the wounded and dying ring in your ears long after you have been rescued.'

'It sounds terrible,' whispered Lily. 'I'll try to understand, Kasie.'

He shook his head again. 'I don't think you ever will, really, Lily. Sorrow rolls off you, but then you are just my happy-go-lucky *leiblin*, and perhaps that's all a fellow needs.'

His voice was so sad it was as if he was overwhelmed by some secret sorrow and Lily felt that she could not get through to him properly.

In January as Lily waited for the bus home from work, she spotted a familiar face. There was the short, fair figure in uniform, a small round sailor cap on top of her head, and that pointed face with high cheekbones, and the odd squashed nose. It was no other than Budgie, the little friend she had made the first night she arrived in Portsmouth.

As Lily touched her arm, Budgie spun round. 'Why Lily!' she cried with a great grin. 'You still here? Come on, let's have a drink.'

Lily went off to the bar with Budgie who was already a little drunk. 'I lost my boyfriend,' she told Lily. 'He went down with the *Repulse*.'

'I'm sorry to hear that,' returned Lily.

'Only got into the w.r.e.n.s to be near him and then he got posted. And he'd promised to marry me when he came back.' Two large tears rolled down her funny-looking face.

Lily squeezed her hand. 'Don't cry, love,' she said.

Budgie ordered two more gin-and-tonics and cheered up a little. 'Didn't think you would stay here.' She looked Lily over. 'Must say, you look very smart in those civvies. Did you shack up with that guy you was telling me about?'

'I went to live with him.' replied Lily.

'In the forces, was he?'

'Yes, the navy, but he's not English, and he's really in the Dutch navy.'

'Oh, the Free Netherlands Navy,' nodded Budgie. 'Got a lot of those chaps out at *H.M.S. Drake*. I'm in Communications now.' she said. 'It's not such a bad job.'

'Where's that?' enquired Lily just for the sake of continuing the conversation, for all this Forces jargon bored her.

'It's in Devonport. It's a ship ashore. You must have heard of it.'

Lily nodded. Wasn't that where Kasie was stationed? 'I think my boyfriend is there,' she said.

'What's his name?' demanded Budgie.

Lily hesitated. 'It's, well, I call him Kasie.'

Budgie rubbed her funny nose as she thought. 'Karl Cornelius De Fries, that right?' she asked. 'He's the instructor in the mine school. We call him Kasie Cop.'

Lily looked at her in amazement.

'I'm on the switchboard and have to know these guys,' explained Budgie. 'Fancy you shacking up with him, Lily. Taking a chance there, he's a proper ladies' man.'

'I'm not sure what you're gettin' at.' Lily felt quite annoyed.

'Oh, don't kid me, Lily. Why! I saw him in the town a little while ago. He was with one of our officers—Dutchie Jan, they call her. She's young and good looking. Kasie Cop was not wasting his time.' There was a hard bitchiness in Budgie's tone as if she was at last beginning to enjoy herself. She drained her glass. 'Shall we have another one?' she suggested.

This time Lily got the drinks but she was feeling a little riled. 'I'm sure you are mistaken,' she told Budgie when she returned. 'And why should they give him that strange name?' she asked.

Budgie cackled. 'It means cheese head. You know, he's got that dome-shaped nut with not much hair in front. Looks like a Dutch cheese.'

Lily choked on her gin, she was so horrified. 'Well, that's not my Kasie,' she replied defiantly. 'He's very good looking.'

'Could be,' replied Budgie nonchalantly, 'but that's how they are out at *Drake*. Everyone gets a nickname. K.C., get it all in Kasie.'

The gin had begun to affect Lily and now her face glowed red. 'Well, where did you see him, then?' she demanded.

'Over the road in that hotel. Wanna come and take a peep?' asked Budgie.

They finished their drinks and a little unsteadily they walked across the road. 'We'll go round to the side bar,' giggled Budgie, now really enjoying herself. 'Then you can see into the lounge. Like that you'll see him before he sees you.'

Lily was angry and regretted that she had ever shown Budgie so much sympathy for her own troubles, but she stood at the bar counter while Budgie ordered more gins. She looked into the hotel bar and there behind some discreet palms sat her Kasie talking in a very interested manner to a lovely fair girl who had a fresh complexion and golden hair wound round her head in a plait. Lily's heart almost jumped out of her mouth and the hand that held her drink trembled.

'Don't make a scene here,' Budgie warned Lily. 'She's my officer and I'd get into trouble.'

They went and sat in the corner. 'Don't take on so, Lily,' said Budgie, who seemed almost pleased by the trouble she was causing, 'there's plenty more fish in the sea. I don't know if he shacks up with her—she's very toffee-nosed—but he's always hanging around her.'

Lily swallowed her gin but did not answer. She felt an almost overwhelming desire to get up and tear that blonde hair out by its roots.

Suddenly Kasie and the girl got up. Kasie handed her a gas mask and she put on the three-cornered w.r.e.n.'s hat and they then left the lounge.

Budgie held on to Lily's arm. 'He's going to the station, she's got to get the train. Don't make a fool of yourself out in the street, Lily, this is a funny town full of bloody Military Police.'

Lily was unable to decide what to do. Kasie was probably going home, so she would tackle him there. 'I'm going, Budgie,' she said, getting up. 'The bus is due any minute now, be seeing you.'

As she stood in the bus queue, Lily saw Kasie come out of the train station and make off down the street towards the more sleazy end of town. She let him go. She would not run after him.

She stood with hands in her pockets huddled up against the

strong wind. The gin was beginning to affect her. Fierce emotions ran through her brain, and suddenly she decided that she would find out where he was going, after all. She ran across the road but he had already disappeared into a street where there were several pubs. It was beginning to get dark and this was a very shifty area. Sailors in groups lurched past her. Dare she go into one of these bars? Why not? But which one? She hesitated for a moment and then chose the fourth one. Inside it was crowded with women and sailors. As she entered all eyes turned towards her. Not to be beaten, Lily ordered a double gin. She swallowed it neat and stood looking around this sleazy establishment, which was obviously some sort of pick-up joint. But she was an East Ender and used to such atmospheres, so why should she let it worry her? Her anger was mounting within her. Kasie was not there, so she crossed the road to another bar.

The moment she walked in she spotted him. He was standing talking to the pianist, his back towards her. Lily strode forward, doubled up her fist so that her knuckles shone white, and landed him a swift punch in the face. 'You lying bastard!' she shouted.

Kasie spun round, holding his hand to his face in shock. He stared at Lily as if he was having hallucinations.

But Lily's temper had broken its bond and with one hand she swept all the empty glasses off the piano onto the floor. They landed with a resounding crash and everyone looked in their direction. 'You swine!' she screamed at him, 'You two-faced bastard! I'll kill you!'

Suddenly Kasie recovered his wits. Grabbing hold of her, he pulled Lily outside into the now blacked-out street. She fought and kicked and screamed like a street woman but he forced her into a dark doorway and put his hands around her throat. Even in the darkness he looked as pale as death, and his eyes were cold and hard. He held her still and squeezed hard. 'Be quiet, Lily,' he ordered, 'or by God I'll murder you.'

From the fierceness of his tone, Lily knew he meant it and for the very first time, she really felt afraid of him. She suddenly dissolved into tears.

Kasie loosened his grip and cuddled her. 'Now,' he said,

more kindly, 'what's all this nonsense, Lily? And you stink of gin. Whatever is wrong with you?'

'I don't know,' Lily sobbed uncontrollably. 'I wanted to hurt you. I saw you with that lovely young woman.'

Kasie shook his head. 'Oh,' he sighed, 'so that's what it's all about. Well, I can assure you, Lily, that you're going the right way to lose me by disgracing me in front of my shipmates. I'm a very proud man.'

'Oh, I am sorry,' sobbed Lily. 'It's just because I've been drinking. I met a girl I knew.'

'I was on my way home to you, Lily. I stopped for one drink.'

'But who was she?' sobbed Lily. 'I saw you in the hotel lounge.'

'She was, as you called her, a lovely young woman who is a great friend of mine,' explained Kasie. 'She was only a little girl when I left Holland and is now a liaison officer and brings me news from home. Now, does that satisfy you?' He was obviously still very angry for his voice was cold and a little – sarcastic as he uttered the last few words.

Lily shivered violently with fear—or was it love? She was not sure but she clung passionately to him, her face wet with tears. 'Oh, darling, I'm truly sorry. Kiss me! I can't bear the thought of losing you.'

'Come on, Lily, let's get you home. With a bit of luck I'll find a cab around the corner.'

Once back home, he made coffee and Lily bathed away her tears.

'I cannot stay tonight,' Kasie told her. 'I'm supposed to be on duty. Now, you'd better get to bed, Lily.'

Lily lay crying into her pillow as he prepared to leave her. When he came to kiss her goodnight, she clung to him desperately and forced him to lie down beside her and love her. And Lily loved him in return with complete abandonment. It was as if this terrible passion she had for him was growing stronger and stronger.

He left at five the next morning. As he opened the door, he

turned to her. 'I don't know when I will be back,' he said in a surprisingly cold voice. 'There's going to be hell to pay. I was supposed to be on duty last night.'

'Oh,' Lily exclaimed huffily, 'and I suppose that it's my bloody fault.'

'Yes, Lily, I'm afraid it was,' he replied severely. And Lily began to weep once more.

He left quietly and she heard him whistling down some navy transport as it passed the house. She got up and looked out of the window. As she watched him climbing into the jeep, she wondered if she would ever see him again.

CHAPTER FIVE

Back to the Smoke

That day, Lily did not go to work. Instead, she hung about the house, gloomily thinking about how her relationship with Kasie was going to end. She did her best to console herself by telling herself that she would get by without him, that she had been a fool to get so involved, that Kasie was a womaniser, and Budgie was right about him all along.

And she thought about how he had forgiven her for her jealous outburst in the pub but made her feel afterwards like a naughty child. She decided that she had better go back to the East End of London where she belonged. It would be nice to see Ivy once more, she told herself, and get down to the Bridge House on Saturday nights again.

That night, Portsmouth had another bad raid. Lily hid under the blankets as planes swept low over the house dive-bombing the harbour and, for the first time in her life, she was really scared.

In the morning she went off to work. The street had a depressed look of the aftermath of an air raid. Flags still flew at half-mast for the loss of *Repulse* and the *Prince of Wales* and their missing crew members.

'The Germans are after the floating docks being built out there,' one youth told her as she started work.

'Out where?' she asked.

The boy pointed out to see where two shadowy shapes rose up out of the waves.

'I thought they were a funny shape for a ship,' said Lily. 'What are they for?'

'We're not sure,' he replied. 'Some say they're for the Second Front when we invade France.'

Lily pulled her overall over her head with a disgruntled snort. 'Christ, ain't this bloody war never going to end? And we never know who's winning. They don't tell us, do they?'

She pulled her work tools from the wooden drawer in the table. 'I thought I'd get a bit of peace and quiet down here,' she grumbled. 'I might as well be up London in the blitz.'

Suddenly a lone fighter flew over the town spraying it with gunfire. The windows blew in and dust and glass showered Lily's pies. 'Oh, you German bastards!' she cried shaking her fist. 'That's me bloody lot! It's back to the bloody smoke for me tomorrer.'

The fact that she had no news of Kasie depressed her further. When she got home she found a letter on the doormat. It was from Ivy. 'Wonder what Ivy's been up to,' she muttered. A second later, she gasped open-mouthed with shock. For inside the envelope there was another letter from the War Department: 'We regret to inform you that your husband, George Brown, 7456977 2nd Royal Fusiliers Regiment, has been wounded in action and is now at the Military Hospital in Manchester. A railway pass will be issued if you wish to visit him. Apply . . .' With it there was a note from Ivy, saying: 'Thought I'd better post this off to you, Love Ivy.'

Lily's head swam. No, she was in no doubt about her staying in Portsmouth any longer. Kasie would understand. Sadly she packed her pretty undies that he had bought her and the little souvenirs he had given her. Tears streamed down her face as she wrote him a note and propped it up on the dressing table: 'Sorry, my love, I must go. I'll not forget you ever, but my husband has been sent home wounded, so he needs me. Love you always, Lily.'

At eight o'clock the next morning as she sat on the station waiting for the London train, she did wish that she could have seen Kasie just once more. But she did not dare contact him at his base; he had always been very adamant about that. So that was it: it was goodbye.

Back in London, it was strange to walk down the old familiar street once more. Her house had been pulled down and there was just a wooden hoarding where it had stood. There were derelict houses all around and large empty areas as if whole blocks had been swept away. She could hardly believe her eyes.

Now she had to find somewhere to stay. She decided to make for Ivy's house.

Ivy's house was in not much better condition. The windows were boarded up, the chimney pot hung lopsided from the roof, and boards held the street door together. She bent down and called through the letter box: 'Are you there, Ivy?' Soon she heard soneone trotting downstairs and the door opened to reveal Ivy looking slick in a navy blue uniform and peaked cap.

Ivy stared back at Lily in amazement. 'Oh, thank Gawd you turned up,' she said in her true Cockney manner. 'I was worried out of me bleedin' life when that letter came from the War Office.'

Lily followed her up the narrow musty stairs to Ivy's bedroom which seemed to be still intact. A kettle sat on an oil stove in the middle of the room.

'What's the outfit?' Lily asked.

'I am on the buses,' replied Ivy. 'It ain't bad. Clippies, they call us. Money's good and there's plenty of life. Take your coat off. I'll make a cup of tea. I'm piggin' it here all alone now since we got blasted. The poor old cow downstairs got herself evacuated. Blew her out o' bed, it did. She really got the bleedin' wind up, still.' Ivy lit a fag and offered one to Lily. 'I'm better orf on me own 'cause what the eye don't see the heart don't grieve for.' She gave Lily a cheeky grin and handed her a cup of tea.

They sat on the bed and chatted. 'Poor old George copped a packet,' Lily said.

'Yes,' said Ivy. 'That will stop your larks. They've sent him home. What happened to your boyfriend?'

'Oh, I was fed up with him anyway,' said Lily, gratefully sipping the tea.

'Suppose you ain't got anywhere to stay,' said Ivy.

'No, I hoped you'd put me up.'

'Well,' said Ivy, 'it's all closed up downstairs. You wouldn't want to stay there. Mind you, it was filthy. One thing old Hitler did was kill off some of the old cow's bugs.'

Lily smiled. It was good to hear Ivy's patter once more. 'If I can stay with you till I find a place, I'd be grateful.'

'Course you can,' said Ivy but she bit her lip and looked anxiously at Lily. 'But you see, Lily, it might get a bit awkward. I shack up with me driver some nights—might be once a week. It's when he's supposed to be firewatching. He's got a right old bag of a missus and he's terrified of her.'

Lily's wide smile had returned and she began to giggle. It was the same old Ivy. Blitz or no blitz she still liked her sex life at regular intervals.

'Tell you what,' Ivy suggested, 'when he comes over, you can go down on the deck in the sleeping bag. He won't mind if you don't.'

'No, Ivy,' laughed Lily, 'I won't mind.'

'Well, there ain't bleedin' room in that bed for three of us, is there,' cackled Ivy. 'Here, I've got something to drink,' she said, producing half a bottle of gin. 'We'll have an early night. I'm on duty at five and you got to go and see your poor old George in Manchester. What the bleedin' 'ell did they want to send 'im up there for?' complained Ivy.

By midday the next day, Lily was on her way to visit George. She had felt a little apprehensive about how he would look after all this time, but she was quite unprepared for the shock the sight of him gave her. George was lying in a crowded ward of the hospital, his head completely encased in bandages with just one eye showing which peered out at her with great hostility.

'Hello, George,' said Lily, bending down to kiss him. Her lips pressed onto the rough bandages which smelled of disinfectant.

George made a grunting noise and tried to utter something through the bandages. It sounded like, 'eff orf.'

The nursing sister bent over him saying, 'George, your wife is here.'

But the only response from George was another swear word, and then he began to toss and thrash about the bed shivering and shaking, crying out in fear. Lily turned away, unable to look, and the nurses hurriedly put the screens around George's bed and told Lily to go into the rest room while they calmed him down.

'He has shrapnel in his head and is badly shell-shocked,' said the sister. 'But he will improve, time is young yet.'

Sobs slipped from Lily's stiff lips as she tried not to cry. 'I won't stay,' she said miserably. 'He doesn't know me. I'll go back to London.'

'You must please yourself,' the sister said. 'But we'll keep in touch with you and you must ring us anytime if you want to know how he is.'

With weak and trembling knees, Lily found her way to the station and took the next train back to London. As she sat on the train, her mind was in a whirl. Was George going to die? Oh, she felt so guilty! 'Poor old George, he had not asked for that. Please, God, let him recover,' she prayed, 'and I'll not let him down again.' Lily's Sunday School training as a child, forgotten for so many years, came back to her now as she sped back to London, and her mind dwelt on the spiritual plane. 'Make him better. I'll always be kind to him. I know I'll be happier if he dies and then I'll go to Kasie, but oh, dear God, I'll never be able to live with myself if he does.'

It was midnight when Lily got back to Ivy's. Ivy came downstairs to let Lily in. Her hair was in curlers and she wore a flowing nightie. 'Thought you'd stay up there for a while,' she said, looking surprised.

Lily didn't say anything and when they went upstairs, she noticed in the bed the huge shape of a man pretending to be asleep.

'It's me driver,' Ivy whispered. 'Get down in the armchair and the sleeping bag and have a kip. I'll be gone early in the morning. By the way, how's George?'

Lily began to weep. 'Just a bloody mess, that's what. He didn't even know me, and he's all wrapped up in bandages. Oh, Ivy, it was horrible!'

'Never mind, love,' comforted Ivy. 'You done all you could do. Now, have a good sleep,' and she climbed heavily back into bed beside the big mound of her man. 'Ger over, bleedin' sod,' she said, giving him a push. And Lily spent the night curled up in the armchair.

Those first two months back in London were a great trial to Lily who had to sleep crouched in the sleeping bag and perched on two armchairs several nights a week while grunts and groans came from Ivy's bed while this huge, shapeless man made love to her. But Lily had nowhere else to go so she had to endure it.

Ivy's man—Big Ben, as he was called—was really too much for Lily. He was so gross and so unaffected by anything around him. He spent his off-duty time swallowing gallons of beer and dodging his wife in order to go to bed with Ivy. He did not mind Lily sleeping in the same room at all. In fact, he seemed positively to like having her for an audience. But Lily hated it. He often got bouts of wind during the night which kept her awake and once, Lily awoke to see him using the chamber pot in the full light of the window. He disgusted her and she knew she had to leave.

After a few weeks, Lily went to the council offices to try to get a house. She sat there for a very depressing hour amid the other war-weary and the homeless.

'We'll put you on the list,' the clerk told her, 'but seeing as you have no children and at the moment your husband has little hope of leaving hospital, it will be quite a long wait.'

'Thanks very much,' muttered Lily, and walked to the Labour Exchange to register for work. All this made her feel so alone. 'Oh, Kasie, why did I leave you?' she sighed as she wandered home.

'Try and get on the buses,' suggested Ivy, 'so we can be together. You can count, can't you?'

'Course I can,' snapped Lily. 'You should know, you went to my school, didn't you?'

'Well, yes,' replied Ivy. 'I'll bring home an application form tonight and help you fill it in.'

While she was out of work, Lily lived on her savings, and hoped that they would last until she got a job. After a few weeks, she went again to see George who was slightly improved, but confined to a wheelchair.

'Where the bleedin' 'ell you been?' he grumbled. 'Was waiting to see you.'

'I did come, George,' Lily explained, 'but you were too ill to see me.'

He looked at her rather vacantly. 'Crafty lot of cows here,' he said. 'Pinch yer bloody fags, they do.' He then suddenly relapsed into a coma which he had not come out of by the time she had to leave.

'Don't worry,' said the sister reassuringly. 'We are pleased with his progress. He will need an operation sometime later, but we're waiting for the right moment because the shrapnel moves around.'

That night back in London, Lily got really sloshed with Ivy and Big Ben in the Red Lion at Aldgate. Afterwards, all three of them struggled home, arms linked, singing at the top of their voices, 'Roll me over, in the clover.' When they got in, Ivy immediately fell into bed and was asleep instantly. Ben lurched around the room. 'If you're a bit short of a bit of the other, Lily,' he muttered, 'I'll always oblige.' Then he too collapsed on the bed and was asleep in no time.

Lily hid in the sleeping bag laughing her head off. Oh God, what would her precise and proper Kasie think of a set-up like this? How she missed him. She decided she would write to him the next day. And one thing was sure, she could not go on living this way for much longer.

Having passed her first test, Lily went to train as a clippie. She rather liked the work. It was very interesting and it kept her busy all day. She had her meals in the canteen and saw little of Ivy who was on late duty.

She wrote to George a few times at the hospital. She knew that although he could not read the letters the nurses would read them to him. And it was in those long love letters to Kasie that she poured out her heart and true feelings. For some reason she did not tell him about George. She did not want him to know, but what she did tell him was of her love for him and her recollections of those nights of passion down in Pompey.

Six weeks passed and she still had no reply from Kasie, but she was happier in general, because she was now working on the 80 bus that passed through the East End to the West End. She looked very smart in her navy blue uniform, her bright hair tucked up under the peaked cap. Her good humour had returned and in her happy-go-lucky manner she would shout: 'Full up!' or 'Upstairs only!' in her Cockney manner. Lily was a great success as a clippie.

London had become full of Yanks. All along Oxford Street they strolled with young English girls hanging onto their arms. Sometimes they would try to get aboard Lily's bus blind drunk, but she would stand no nonsense and simply chucked them off with plenty of back chat. So the old Lily had returned to form, the affair with Kasie practically forgotten.

She had managed to get herself a one-roomed flat in a back street near the Minories. It was provided for her by the London Transport, and it was handy being near the bus garage since she often started work at four o'clock in the morning and some-times finished as late as midnight. At the end of the day, her legs always ached from trotting up and down the bus stairs, yet she was happy. There were lots of laughs to be had and, although there were still air-raids, the population of London had begun to return from evacuation.

Cinemas re-opened and the West End theatres opened up with big musical productions. Piccadilly was always full of young service folk on leave, and never a day went by when a young serviceman didn't get aboard Lily's bus and want to make a date with her. Sometimes she would go to lunch or the pictures during the day with a lonely lad on leave but that was where it ended. No one had yet taken Kasie's place in her heart.

In the hospital, poor old George deteriorated. He lolled in his invalid chair, with his mouth open. His one sightless eye was always covered with a black patch.

'How I dread those visits to the hospital,' Lily confessed to Ivy.

'Don't go, then,' said Ivy. 'He don't know you, anyway.'

'I can't help meself,' said Lily, 'but I get so depressed afterwards.'

'Gawd knows how I'll get on when my old man gets home,' pondered Ivy. 'He'll beat the living daylights out of me if he ever finds out what I've been up to.'

'In some ways I wish poor old George could,' said Lily.

'Well, I certainly ain't looking bleedin' forward to it,' sniffed Ivy.

The year 1942 progressed very slowly for Lily. It was all work and no play. The war out East had intensified. Our soldiers were fighting in Burma and many had been taken prisoners. Still the G.I.s poured into London.

The first week in December, the streets were wet and shiny with rain and it was very cold. The sky was dark and heavy with snow. Lily held onto the rail and looked solemnly out at Oxford Street as her bus slowly manoeuvred its way through the heavy traffic. Selfridges had made some sort of show for Christmas and dressed the windows with tinsel. Bells and lanterns swung from the lamp posts outside. They would never be lit up because of the blackout, but it was still nice to remember that it would soon be Christmas. This would be the fourth Christmas since the war began. Lily was in a pensive mood wondering what she would do for the festive season. Everyone seemed to have some sort of family but Lily. Would she be all on her own this year? At that moment, a slim figure in uniform jumped aboard the bus and, as Lily put her hand up to push the bell, he grabbed her by the shoulder and swung her round to face him.

'Hey!' roared Lily. 'What's your game?' It took a moment for her to realise that she was face to face with Kasie.

'Oh, Lily my lovely!' he cried, laughing and putting his arms about her.

'Hey, don't do that!' said Lily, disentangling herself from him. 'The driver will see you. Go upstairs! I'll come up with you.'

Kasie ran upstairs and Lily followed him keeping a wary eye on the driver.

Kasie had taken a seat at the back of the bus and he caught hold of her hand as she came up. 'I've searched all London for you,' he said, pressing her hand to his lips.

'Hey, turn it up!' cried Lily. 'Someone might see you. I'll have to go downstairs again, someone's getting on the bus. Stay on till we get to Aldgate. I'm getting off duty then.'

Lily punched tickets and pushed the bell all down Oxford Street, and through the City to the Minories in a kind of dream. Her lover was sitting upstairs. What should she do? Run off and leave him? It was no good getting involved again, she thought, yet her heart thumped in the way it used to at the very thought of his kisses, the hard dry mouth and his tongue that entwined with hers. She shivered with ecstasy at the very thought.

When the bus neared Aldgate, Kasie came downstairs and stood with her on the platform. A mischievous grin curled his lips.

'Wait for me while I check in,' said Lily breathlessly, yearning for his arms to engulf her.

Ten minutes later, they met outside the bus garage in the darkness. Kasie swept her into his arms so close that Lily shivered with love. 'Oh, Kasie, how I've missed you,' she whispered, clinging tightly to him.

'Lily, Lily, my lovely, why did you leave me?' he cried as tears wet his long fair lashes. 'Don't ever go away again.'

They walked hand in hand to Lily's lodgings. Without a sound, she unlocked the door. 'I'm not supposed to do this,' she whispered to him. 'Keep very quiet.' They tip-toed into her room.

The room was small and box-like with one single bed against one wall, a wardrobe and a wash basin. This was Lily's home. Since she ate in the canteen, she spent very little time in this room, though it could have been the Ritz or the lowest hovel for all Kasie cared at that moment. Entwined in each other's arms, they fell onto the narrow bed together.

Lily quickly kicked off her slacks, and soon the hunger that had mounted up within them was realised, as once, twice, and then three times, their emotions were released together.

'Oh, Lily,' cried Kasie, nuzzling her neck, 'how have I lived without you?'

'You were well worth waiting for, my darling,' whispered Lily. And with their arms clasped about each other, they slept the sleep of exhaustion and did not wake until someone thumped on Lily's door calling her for her five o'clock bus which was ready to go out.

'Oh, Christ!' said Lily, waking with a start. 'Don't make a sound! Get under the bed!'

Lily dragged on her slacks, rinsed her face in the hand basin and put on her peaked cap. 'All right, I'm coming,' she shouted. 'Don't knock the bleedin' door dahn.' She whispered to Kasie who lay grinning under the bed. 'Here's the key. Creep out and lock the door. See you in Lyons of Oxford Street at twelve midday.' Straightening her cap, she strode out of the door.

All through that shift, Lily hummed a little tune and wished the passengers a good day. She was the ideal clippie that morning. The world seemed a brighter place to her now that Kasie was back. Her body felt buoyant and happy; she was a real woman again.

At midday she was off duty until three. As she approached the Lyons Corner House, her good mood evaporated. Suddenly, she had misgivings about it all. He might not be there, she told herself. She had been terrible last night and she felt ashamed. She hadn't cared what she did. Oh, she must be mad! And surely she couldn't go through another traumatic affair with him after the dramas of last time.

But Kasie was there. His peaked cap was set at a jaunty angle on the back of his head while he patiently waited for her. She went to the self-service counter and filled a tray with her lunch of spam salad and coffee. She came and sat down at his table and ate her food.

Kasie smiled fondly at her as she hungrily devoured her meal. 'Still the same good appetite, Lily,' he jested.

'Yes,' she nodded, 'in several things . . .'

'Oh, you were wonderful last night, Lily,' he exclaimed enthusiastically. 'It was almost worth that long absence and all the worry you have caused me.'

'Worry? What worry?' demanded Lily, a forkful of spam salad half-way to her mouth.

'Why, the worry of going off and leaving me.'

'I explained that my husband had come home,' she said.

Kasie's face whitened and jealous anger flashed in those stern brown eyes. 'Where is he now?' he demanded.

'Gone back,' she said nonchalantly.

He grabbed her wrist. 'I don't believe you, Lily,' he said earnestly. 'There is something very wrong with your marriage.'

'Well, if you say so,' said Lily evasively.

'You are mine, Lily,' Kasie said firmly, 'and have been since we first met. Write and tell your husband it is finished with him. I will face him and let him know he has lost you.'

Lily put her hand over her eyes so that he could not see the tears. 'You don't own me. I can make up me own mind,' she mumbled.

He pulled her hand away. 'Lily, don't play around with me! What is it? I swear I'll be true to you. I'll take you home after the war. Come back with me to Scotland now, it's lovely up there. I've been away to the deep sea, but now I am on the corvettes, we can live ashore as we did in Pompey.'

'Oh, please, please Kasie!' cried Lily brokenly. 'Don't ask me to do that. I can't leave my husband, I haven't got the courage.'

'I don't believe it, Lily,' Kasie argued. 'I remember you when you were absolutely void of sentiment. What brought all this on? And why do you live in a hostel if you have a home with your husband? Is he really in England?'

'Yes, he is,' lied Lily, 'and I go home at weekends.'

'So, you and I are no longer lovers,' he said coldly. 'What was all that about last night?'

'Just sex, I suppose,' she muttered.

Kasie banged his fist down hard on the table. 'That is not what I expected of you! Sex? I can get that anywhere, but I love you, Lily, I need you with me. I could never forget how happy we were. Please, *leiblin,* put me out of my misery.'

'Let's go for a walk in the park,' Lily said, getting up. 'We can't talk here with everyone looking at us.'

They sat in the park kissing and cuddling. 'I'm such a fool with you,' said Lily. 'You've only to touch me and I want to go to bed with you. I don't understand meself.'

'Well, you have your choice,' Kasie said firmly. 'You can come to me in Scotland—I'll leave you the address when I go tonight—or stay here. But remember, if you leave this husband, you belong to me. Do it any way you like.' He looked down at her long slim legs and frowned. 'Did your husband make love with you when he was home?' he asked. 'No, of course not,' she replied. 'He wasn't fit enough.' Kasie smoothed his hand longingly down her nylon-clad legs. Nylon stockings had come back with the Yanks. 'Oh, darling, don't let him touch these lovely legs,' he begged. 'They are mine.'

'Oh, shut up!' said Lily. 'And be careful. You'll ladder me bloody stockings.'

He began to laugh.

'Also, I have to get back to work,' she continued. 'It's all right for you laying about all day, but I got to get me living. Now, where's me key?' she demanded. 'Let's have that back. I don't want you creeping in on me late at night. I got enough on me plate without losing me job.'

Kasie handed her the key with a grin. 'Well, you've not changed much,' he said.

Just a week before Christmas, Lily sat in the bus canteen chatting to Ivy who was a bit depressed.

'Might go down and stay in Wiltshire with me kids for Christmas,' said Ivy. 'Don't suppose Big Ben will be able to lose his old woman at Christmas time.'

'I've got five days off,' said Lily. 'I get a very lonely feeling when I think abaht it. It's not going to be a picnic stuck in my one-roomed flat all alone.'

'What abaht lover boy?' asked Ivy.

'Nothin' doin',' shrugged Lily.

'I suppose you could go and see old George in Manchester.'

'Oh, I don't know, he still don't seem able to hold a sensible conversation. It gets a bit frustrating.'

That morning a telegram was slipped under her door. It was an order for ten pounds and the message with it read: 'Lily, my love, be with me at Christmas. Here is your fare. Love, Kasie.'

Lily gave a deep sigh and kissed the paper. 'I'll be there, darling,' she whispered.

On Christmas Eve, well wrapped up in a heavy coat and with a beret pulled down over her ears, Lily braved the bitter cold and caught the Flying Scotsman from Kings Cross station. It was a long, tiring journey in an overcrowded train full of service personnel. Several times the train stopped and blacked out because of air-raid warnings, but all the time Lily sat very quietly thinking of her lover.

At Stirling she changed on to the slow local train to Oban on the west coast. By now she was really tired having travelled through the night without any proper sleep, but the early morning beauty of the Scottish countryside held her spellbound. 'I never knew there were such places,' she exclaimed out loud, much to the amusement of an old man travelling in the compartment with her.

'First time in Scotland?' he asked.

Lily nodded. 'It looks really beautiful,' she said, 'and nothing like poor old blitzed London.'

'I hear it's been really bad down there,' the old man said.

'Well, some of us survived,' said Lily flippantly.

'You're travelling to the west coast, I presume.'

'Yes, to visit my husband,' Lily lied easily.

When the grey ocean came into sight and she saw the wide bay in which all the flying boats were anchored, she was very surprised. It was such a sudden contrast between the dark mountains and the wide, grey expanse of sea. It amazed her and there, on the platform as the train drew in, was the small, neat shape of Kasie. She could have recognised him a mile away.

As she got off the train, Kasie came up and gave her a swift kiss. Taking her suitcase, he hustled her out of the station and into a waiting taxi. Once inside the cab, he swept her into his arms. 'Happy Christmas, darling,' he whispered. 'Oh, I thought you might not get here.'

After that long passionate kiss, Lily gasped for breath. 'Blimey!' she said, 'this must be the last place God made.'

'It's great up here,' said Kasie. 'There's lots of fresh air and lots of things to do. We're going to have a wonderful time. I am off duty till New Year.'

Their room was over the top of a bar-cum-restaurant, known as Riley's. It was clean and comfortable with a grand view of the bay, and Lily and Kasie wasted no time in getting to know each other again.

'You are more lovely each time I meet you,' whispered Kasie.

'I dunno abaht that,' said Lily, tidying up her hair. 'I'm getting bleedin' older all the time.'

'We'll grow old together, Lily, you and I,' said Kasie sentimentally. 'And after the war, I will buy a ship and we will travel through the canals of my country and along the Rhine, for that is where you see really lovely scenery.'

Lily frowned. 'I don't want to think about the future,' she said. 'I feel I will just live for each day.'

'That we will do, my darling,' he said, 'Now let's go down to dinner.'

They dined in the cosy restaurant where a big log fire was burning brightly. They ate fresh salmon and fruit pie with cream, and drank a bottle of white wine and several Scotch whiskies. Lily felt so warm and mellow inside.

'It must be nice to eat lots of good things all the time,' she said. 'I get so bloody fed up with dried egg and spam sandwiches.'

'Come up here to live,' insisted Kasie. 'You would be surprised how easy it is to get luxuries up here.'

'Oh, it's all bloody black market,' she said dismissively. 'That's what money does for you.'

'Could be,' replied Kasie. 'But it's a naval town and a lot of the v.i.p.s are evacuated up here.'

'Never mind abaht the poor sods in London queueing for grub then,' cried Lily in a loud, rather angry voice.

'Hush!' he warned, looking about as if there might be someone listening. 'Now, you must try to behave yourself up here. I want no swearing. I've a good position now and my own crew—I'm first mate on the corvettes.'

'Good for you,' said Lily without humour. She gave a little yawn; the long journey had tired her.

'Come on, my love,' he said tenderly, rising from the table and taking her hand. 'I can see you need an early bed.'

The next morning Lily rose and stood for a while looking out of the window and watching a flying boat land on the water. Kasie came up behind her and put his arms about her. 'Merry Christmas, darling,' he said.

'I'd forgotten it was Christmas Day,' she said gently. 'It's so quiet up here.'

'This is my Christmas gift to you,' Kasie said as he draped a lovely silk scarf over her head and then turned her around to face him. Taking her hand he pulled off the thin gold wedding band that George had put there, and replaced it with a wide gold ring. Engraved on it were two little love birds kissing.

'You and I, Lily,' he said. 'Now you are mine and I shall throw away that other ring.'

Lily struggled to retrieve her wedding ring. 'Oh, no, Kasie,' she cried. 'Let me keep it.'

'Promise me you'll not ever wear it,' he demanded.

'All right,' she said, taking George's ring and putting it in her purse. Two big tears ran down her cheeks as she thought of poor old George in that hospital. And this was Christmas Day.

'Let's go back to bed, Lily,' said Kasie, pulling her to him. 'Let us celebrate our honeymoon.'

Lily wanted to say no but she knew it was not possible. His hand on her arm and his brown eyes looking into hers made her tremble with emotion. 'Oh darling, darling,' she gasped, 'love me, make me forget.'

The rest of the festive season was great fun. They went to a special ship's dinner on Christmas night and there were a lot of little brown men who gathered about Lily jabbering like monkeys. She could not understand a word they said. 'This is my crew,' explained Kasie. 'All of them are brave Dutchmen but they are now fighting the war with us again for England and home.'

'I thought they were Japanese,' whispered Lily.

'Silly girl,' he said with a laugh. 'The Japs are on the other side.'

Many songs were sung and speeches were given. Kasie sang 'I dream of Jeanie with the light brown hair,' which was very popular with the Scottish guests, and Lily blushed scarlet with emotion as Kasie looked at her, his fine voice caressing her ears. At times it almost felt as if his hands were caressing her body.

They were very drunk that night and a big fellow in a kilt put Kasie over his shoulder and humped him up to bed. Lily wavered along behind very unsteady on her legs, and they both slept very heavily.

The next day they stayed in bed for a long time, each with a terrific hang-over.

'It's that damned Scotch whisky,' declared Kasie. 'I should have stuck with my Bols gin.'

'Tomorrer it's over,' said Lily, holding her throbbing head. 'I have to go home.'

'Oh, Lily, don't leave me,' Kasie cried. 'Stay up here! It's easy to get accommodation and I'll apply to live out. I'm only at sea a few days at a time.'

Lily sat up in bed, feeling very dejected. As she put her hands over her eyes, the heavy gold ring which Kasie had given her gleamed in the light of day. 'Kasie, I can't stay,' she said gently. 'I'd lose my job.'

'You don't need a job,' he said quickly.

'Oh, yes I do. I must have an income.'

'I'll make an allowance over to you,' he said eagerly.

'No, don't ask me,' she almost wept. 'Please, Kasie, let me go tomorrer. I'll come up again when you need me, I promise.'

He suddenly looked angry. 'I always need you,' he said. 'I

swear I'll kill that damned husband of yours if you try to leave me for him.'

Lily's lips twitched. Poor old George. That wouldn't take long, she thought. But she replied cheekily: 'You got to bleedin' find him first.'

'That I will do, I promise you,' he said very coldly.

In spite of his fervent pleas, the next morning Lily was on the train travelling back to London. Grim and white-faced, Kasie had stood on the station platform looking after the train.

His last words to her still rang in her ears as she headed south. 'Get rid of that husband and come back to me. Do you hear me? This time, I do mean what I say.'

CHAPTER SIX

Surviving

During the long winter of 1943, Lily was not quite as lonely as she had been. She kept up her correspondence with Kasie because he had said to her, before she left Scotland, 'Whether you hear from me or not, still write to me, darling, for eventually the letters do catch up with me and when I'm at sea they are particularly welcome.'

Lily went back to her job on the buses and was very busy most of the time. On her free evenings, she would sit writing her heart out to Kasie. Since returning from Scotland, she had felt on top of the world. She was able to visit George every weekend, and she felt no sense of guilt whatever. She could not understand herself for this; it was as if she now belonged soul and body to Kasie.

Often she met Ivy for a drink after work. Ivy was a trifle disgruntled nowadays because her route had been changed as had her driver, after Big Ben's wife had complained to the supervisor of the bus garage on account of Ben's nights out with Ivy. 'Miserable old cow,' muttered Ivy. 'Sent poor old Ben to Stamford Hill, they have. I'm gettin' very fed up. I've applied for a council house, though, and if it keeps quiet like this, I'll get my kids home.'

'Might keep you off the tiles,' Lily said with a grin.

'Bloody sauce!' said Ivy without any ill feeling at all.

George now limped about his hospital ward and was beginning to be able to make some sort of conversation but was always extremely aggressive to Lily no matter how nice she tried to be to him. He just pushed past her and sat with his pals in the ward watching them play darts or dominoes.

Lily would sit very forlorn watching the rest of the wounded men as they limped about. Some were badly scarred and had lost their limbs, these big, tall, strapping men now crippled for life. She felt very sad about it all and because she usually was smiling, her sadness now showed up on her face as she sat waiting for George to acknowledge her. Not that George noticed anything. He just snatched the sweets she brought him and then left her.

One weekend, a tall, well-built man came and sat beside her. 'Hallo, Lily,' he said in a broad north country accent. 'I'm Norman Clegg, old George's pal when we was in Malta together. That's where I left this . . .' He put out his left arm of which half was missing.

'Oh, I'm sorry,' murmured Lily quite taken by surprise at his straightforward approach and friendly manner.

'Don't look so downhearted,' Norman said kindly. 'George is doing well, and when they get that shrapnel out of his head, he'll be back to normal.'

'I hope so,' said Lily. The tone of her voice was flat.

'I'm teaching him to play dominoes, and he's doing fine.'

'He seems not to want to talk to me,' Lily told him.

'Well, this place can do that to them,' he replied. 'And George is relatively lucky. There are some real bad cases here but we're all fond of old George. Look!' He opened his shirt. 'Had me lungs full of shrapnel, I did.' A long red scar ran all the way down his chest. 'I'm fine now, and I'll be going home soon. Come on, I'll take you to get a cup of tea. Old George won't even miss you.'

Lily had a cup cf tea with Norman and they became good friends.

'I live up here in Stoke-on-Trent,' he told her. 'Used to work in the Potteries but I won't be doing that anymore.' He put out his half arm.

'Never mind,' said Lily, 'There'll be other things you can do.'

'I'm going to be fitted up with an artificial arm later on, but meanwhile I get by.' He smiled and his pleasant face crinkled and his blue eyes shone. What a nice, kind man he is, Lily thought.

On her next visit, George was not so good, and Lily and Norman pushed him around the grounds in a wheelchair chatting about this and that. Occasionally George would break into their conversation. 'What about the Arsenal? Who are they playing?' he asked in a demanding voice.

'I don't know,' Lily would reply irritably, but Norman would obligingly turn the conversation to football and tell of the times he went, 'Oop for the coop to London.'

So with the tension eased by Norman's presence, a fairly pleasant afternoon was passed and, after that, Lily actually began to look forward to her weekend visits to George.

In May Kasie wrote to say he was now stationed in North Wales and to ask if Lily would like a week or two in Rhyl. Immediately, Lily applied for leave, packed her bag, and was off once more to meet her lover.

Rhyl was a bright seaside town on the north coast of Wales where everything went on as if there was no war on at all. The big touring theatre companies put on plays and amusements, and the Food and Environment Ministries were all there in full force. Lily thought that the town folk were very smug and announced to Kasie that this must be because they had never even had an air-raid.

Kasie would not agree with her. 'I think the folk here are charming and most obliging to us foreigners,' he said.

'After your money, I suppose,' replied Lily cynically.

Kasie sniffed. 'We are becoming a little shrew,' he said drily.

Summer had come early that year and May was a glorious month. Every day they lay on the hot sandy beach with the sun beating down on them. In the smartest of swimsuits and with her long legs spread out, Lily lay beside Kasie and argued with him. 'Oh, it might be because I work on the buses,' she said, 'but I see life a little different to the way I used to. It's all corruption, now, with the black market and all those G.I.s spoiling our young kids with chocolates and nylons, and all the things they've been deprived of for so long.'

Kasie stroked her bare shoulders and looked lovingly at her. 'Don't get bitter, Lily,' he said gently, 'for the war will soon be over and then I will take you to my country where it is beautiful and so peaceful. We will drift along the canals and soon forget the horrors we put up with.'

'It sounds wonderful, Kasie, but it won't happen,' said Lily flatly. 'It will be like London, in your country—never ever the same again.'

Kasie nodded reluctantly. 'I suppose you are right, my lovely,' he said, 'but I've always been the dreamer.' He paused for a moment and added sadly, 'I yearn so much for news of my parents. I wonder what occupation has done to them.'

'Don't you ever hear from them?' asked Lily.

'Not now. When I was in Portsmouth I knew that young liaison officer and she had been in my village.'

'What happened to her?'

Kasie winced. 'She was caught by the Nazis. Who knows what happened to her?'

They both remained very quiet for a while until Kasie got to his feet. 'Come on, let's move over to the dunes so that I can cuddle you close.'

They spent the rest of the hot afternoon in the sand dunes, so close and so silent as if they were the last people in the world. Kasie went into the water for a swim when the tide came in, but no power on earth would get Lily near the surf.

'You must learn to swim, Lily,' Kasie said. 'How are you going to live with me on the water if you cannot swim?'

'Not me,' said Lily. 'I hate water.'

'When I was a baby I fell overboard into the swift flowing Rhine, and right away my mother jumped in after me and my sister after her.'

'Well, that's all right if you like it,' replied Lily. 'But I was born and bred beside the Thames and got hell knocked out of me if I put one foot in the water. So I'm now afraid of it.'

During those two weeks in Rhyl, Lily and Kasie became very close again, and their relationship matured. They told each other of their parents and their young days. Kasie told her of how he escaped from Holland. 'The Germans commandeered my ship and forced me to work for them. We used to sail to Sweden and bring back timber. But one night, four of us killed the guard and we sailed for England. It was not an easy voyage. The Germans caught up with us and they bombed and machine-gunned us. Luckily a British ship came to our aid, and I landed on this shore without a bean and only the clothes I stood up in.'

Every evening, they danced at the Palais and often went to the bars where Kasie would sing in his sweet low voice the most popular songs with the inhabitants.

Lily was so proud of her blond sailor. She loved his fresh, fair complexion, his gentle but firm manner and, most of all, his loving. Of this they had plenty. She bloomed with health. Her skin got very tanned and her auburn hair shone like burnished gold.

'Each time we meet, you are more beautiful,' Kasie would often say. 'You have become a very neat dresser and you never wear too much make-up. Oh, I really love you the way you look now!'

Lily would toss her head proudly. 'Oh, yes, but I don't talk posh, do I?'

Kasie would always laugh, for this was a bit of a bone of contention between them. His English was now very good and his accent perfect. 'It does not matter,' he would say reassuringly. 'You will have to learn a complete new language when you come home with me anyway.'

'Oh, gor blimey!' cried Lily. 'I couldn't never do that.'

Soon that lovely furlough flew past and once again they found themselves kissing goodbye at the station. As always, Lily wept.

'Have you sent that letter to your husband, Lily?'

'Not yet,' she answered. 'I haven't had time.'

'Find the time, Lily,' he said firmly, 'because one day you've got to face up to him.'

In fact, Lily had no intention of ever letting Kasie know the truth about George. She just could not face the future. She went back to London to her one-room flat, and back at work she laughed and joked with the passengers as her big red bus progressed each day back and forth through London.

The city still thronged with overseas servicemen who frequented the underground cellars, beer clubs and all the other dens of vice that wartime had brought to the big city. Shop windows were all boarded up and sandbags hemmed in the historic buildings. Here and there were glaring empty spaces left from the early blitz. But this summer it was fairly quiet. Londoners poured back to their broken-down homes and the parks were full of sun bathers and courting couples. This was Lily's town and she was glad to be there as she dashed up and down the stairs of the bus, her figure slim, lithe and healthy, demanding the fares in her loud Cockney voice and settling disputes in her no-nonsense manner.

'Come on, part up,' she would say to some fare dodger. 'This ain't bleedin' Dr Barnardos, yer know.' Generally, she felt fairly settled. With her sex life catered for by Kasie, she never felt the need of other men and frequently had to fight off the advances of Mac, her driver, when on late duty. He had failed his army medical because he was a diabetic. 'Blimey!' he would say, 'why are you so stingy, Lily?'

'Bugger orf,' Lily would tell him firmly. 'That's all you bloody men fink abaht. Me, I'd sooner have a cup of tea during break time.'

On her days off she would travel to Manchester to visit George who now seemed to have made a little progress. He was well institutionalised, and never asked to go home. He loped around the hospital doing odd jobs. He liked sweeping the path and fetching and carrying for the very sick patients. Everyone liked George and he liked being liked, but he still remained aggressive towards Lily.

'We still can't operate,' the doctor told Lily. 'It's better that he stays here for the time being and then later we'll send him up to London.'

Lily had begun to accept George as he was and talked to him like a child. Sometimes Norman came on Sundays to visit George, too, but really it was to see Lily. He was now out of hospital and fitted with a false arm. When it was time for her to leave, he would take Lily to the station, and hold her arm looking down so sincerely at her.

'I'm working on a farm near my home town,' he told her one day. 'I'd like to buy a small holding after the war, you know the kind of thing—with big greenhouses and grow tomatoes and cucumbers, things like that.'

'Be nice to see a cucumber again,' murmured Lily, 'and one of those nice big tomatoes. Used to like them when I was a kid, used to eat them like apples, I did.'

Norman's eyes twinkled and he smiled that crinkly smile at her. He loved Lily's directness of manner. 'You and George will be welcome to come up and stay with me after the war,' he said.

'Gawd knows when that will be,' said Lily, shaking her head, 'and do you really think George will ever be himself again?'

'Well, not quite, but if they operate he will improve.'

'Don't seem much of a bloody future, does it?' complained Lily.

'Well, there is an alternative,' suggested Norman.

'Can't do it,' said Lily, knowing exactly what he meant. 'Don't know why. I never loved old George all that much, but I can't let him down now.'

Norman bent down and kissed her on the cheek. 'I know, Lily, and I understand. But remember that I have grown very fond of you both and will remain your friend whatever you decide.'

'Thanks, Norm,' replied Lily. 'Here's my train. See you soon.'

Lily sat in the train as it rattled along towards London, listening to the noise of the wheels which seemed to echo her thoughts: 'After the war, after the war.' The end of the war was all there was to look forward to, yet without Kasie it would be no life at all. For Lily knew that her heart was Kasie's forever, but still she could not desert old George.

CHAPTER SEVEN

The Bus Clippie

But the war still did not end and there was no end in sight. For the next year, Lily spent all her leaves with Kasie, and each time she stayed with him they got to know each other better and their love grew stronger. In between these occasions, she worked hard as a clippie. London's bus services were kept going by those indomitable clippies, the working women in their uniforms who got to their destinations whatever was happening on those red buses which glided out early in the morning and late into the night.

In the New Year Kasie wrote to say that he would be coming to London. Because of her aversion to hotels, Lily rented a bedsitting room in Hampstead. It wasn't very nice, being in a downstairs basement and damp and smelly. A whole procession of lodgers had obviously passed through it during the war years. When Kasie saw it, he turned up his fastidious nose. 'Couldn't you find a better place than this, Lily?' he asked, looking around in disgust.

'Oh, don't be so stuck up,' retorted Lily. 'It was hard enough to find any place with the blitz knocking everything down.'

Kasie looked at her very sternly, and then those brown eyes began to twinkle and his white, even teeth showed through the blond frame of the beard that he now sported.

'And cut that bleedin' beard orf,' cried Lily. 'I hate hairy men!'

But Kasie just swept her into his arms. 'What am I to do with you?' he laughed. 'Come on,' he said, leading her to the bed, 'let's make the best of it.'

'It's a roof over our head, ain't it?' Lily was annoyed by his ingratitude but allowed herself to be taken to bed.

During that leave Kasie often got curious bouts of depression. News had recently begun to leak out to the newspapers of the extent of the Nazi persecutions. Sometimes when he read the paper, huge tears rolled down his face. 'Darling, darling!' Lily would cry, snatching away the newspaper. 'Don't do that!'

'I'm so ashamed,' he wept one day. 'Here I am spending money that I should be saving to help my old folk after the war. They are starving out there. I just can't bear it.'

'Well, that's not my bloody fault,' snapped Lily, her temper rising. 'I don't ask you to spend the money on me.'

'I care very much for my family,' said Kasie.

'So what?' returned Lily. 'Blame old Hitler, not me.'

But Kasie was offended. He got up and stalked out of the house.

'Oh, well,' sighed Lily when he had gone. 'Must be this bloody dump that's depressing him. Let's face it, he's cooling off. When this war is over, he'll go home and forget me, so it might as well end now.'

She thought about poor old George in that loony hospital. He had recently had a second operation on his head, and was now in a hospital in Surrey. It was time she thought about making a home for him. 'Ah, well, all's well that ends well,' Lily thought philosophically. 'He might have left me in the family way.' She brushed her hair and stared at her reflection in the mirror to try to cheer herself up. She looked okay, she thought, she was still good to look at, and there were plenty more fish in the sea after Kasie. Then two soft arms crept around her and the blond beard brushed her face. Kasie was back, with a bottle of Bols in his pocket and plenty more inside him.

'Sorry, darling,' he whispered into her ear, and, because Lily loved him so much, she put her arms around him, too.

'It's all right, love, it's this gloomy dump getting on our nerves,' she said.

They sat in front of the battered old gas fire with its broken bars and drank the Bols gin until, very sloshed, he began to sing in his soft sweet tone, sea shanties and songs from his home-land. They lay down close together on the dirty old rug and the world was theirs.

Later he told her of the wide rivers and the canals that he had sailed on in his youth, of the magnificent tulip fields and the little barges where whole families were reared, of his mother and his father who had worked side by side and how his mother's shoulders were bowed from humping the sacks of grain as they loaded the cargo from that little ship they had all been born in.

'Oh, Lily,' he said, 'it is because you have no family that you do not understand my love for mine.'

'I've got a family,' said Lily in a husky voice, the gin taking effect. 'But me muvver's shacked up with another bloke in Ireland and me Dad went missing in Singapore. And poor old Gran, she got blowed up,' she wept. 'Now I ain't got no one and nobody loves me.' She was quite overcome with emotion.

'Hey there, pipe down!' said Kasie. 'I can't get a word in.'

She smiled and cheered up a little. 'I do go on, don't I?' she said sheepishly.

'Let's get matters straight,' Kasie said firmly. 'So, nobody loves you, but what about this mysterious husband of yours?'

'You mean George?' mumbled Lily.

'Yes, I mean George,' Kasie said slowly and deliberately.

'Oh, he's gone back abroad,' lied Lily.

Kasie's lips twisted into a mischievous grin. 'But where, Lily? What unit?'

'How do I know?' replied Lily irritably.

'But you must know,' he persisted.

'It's the Fusiliers, I think,' said Lily.

'Be honest with me, Lily,' he said, 'this husband who you choose to ignore has left you for another, I think.'

'What?' cried Lily, completely trapped. 'Not my George, he would never do that!'

Kasie looked at her quite exasperated. 'What are you hiding from me?'

'Nuffink,' said Lily in pure Cockney. 'What the bleedin' 'ell are you beefin'abaht? I'm here, ain't I?'

'Okay, let's forget it,' he sighed, 'but soon I will be able to correspond with my family and I want to tell them I am bringing home an English wife.'

'Please yourself,' replied Lily nonchalantly, 'but let's get divorced first.'

'I don't believe you are married,' he told her. 'I have loved you now for two years and I'll not let you go easily.'

'Oh, don't let us quarrel again, Kasie,' pleaded Lily. 'Let's go to bed. I'll always love you whatever the future brings.'

Soon that last leave was over; they kissed a passionate goodbye.

'I get this strange feeling each time I say goodbye that we will never meet again,' said Lily.

'Thank you very much, Lily,' he said a little sarcastically.

'Oh, I didn't mean it like that. I mean that you will go home and forget me, not drowned in the sea.'

He held her tight and looked down into her eyes. 'Lily,' he said, 'I've no intention of getting killed or ever giving you up, so remember that, will you?'

Lily left the station feeling very cold and gloomy. She went to find Ivy in the Red Lion in Aldgate. 'It's those bloody damp lodgings,' she complained to Ivy. 'Feels like I got the flu' coming on.'

But Ivy was also full of woe. Her husband had been home on leave and had given her a black eye. 'It was that old cow, me muvver-in-law,' she complained.

'Blimey! Is she still around?' asked Lily.

'Yes, and she got a new bleedin' lease of life now she's in an old ladies' 'ome. She filled me old man in with all me misdemeanours, and some of yours, too, so you'd better stay out of sight when me old man's 'ome.'

Lily returned to her one-roomed flat at the hostel and decided to rest because she had a bad cold coming on. But there was little rest to be had at the hostel. She could hear the constant whine of the huge trolley buses as they pulled in and out of the bus garage just behind. People came in and out banging doors and talking loudly, and she could not even get anything to eat unless she got up and went down to the canteen.

On Monday morning, even though she felt like sleeping in, Lily got up for work at half-four as usual. It was a sort of cold misty morning.

The inspector said, 'Sure you feel like work, Lily?'

'I'll be all right,' she said. 'I think I'm over the worst of it.'

She stood on the bus platform taking fares from early morning travellers through the City along to Waterloo Station. As they approached the bridge, the warning siren sounded. The few passengers on the bus scurried off to seek shelter. Then the driver yelled, 'Hang on, Lily! I'll try to make it over the bridge.'

Lily, still feeling poorly, hung onto the rail while Mac revved up the engine and sped onto the bridge. Then to her horror, she saw a buzz bomb cruising like a bird ten feet above the river heading straight for the bridge. Screaming out a war cry like a real highlander, Mac drove the bus frantically across the bridge and just got to the other side as the buzz bomb struck. The whole world seemed to turn upside down. Lily was thrown out onto the ground and struck her head. She knew no more until she regained consciousness a few minutes later and saw the burning wreck of her bus down in the street below the bridge. Blood dripped into her eyes from the cut on her head. As the ambulance men lifted her up, she managed to gabble, 'Where's Mac?'

'Down there.' One of the ambulance men jerked his thumb towards the wreckage. 'Done for, poor sod,' he told her in a gruff Cockney voice.

Lily's heart missed a beat. By sheer luck she had been thrown off before the bus had hurtled down into the road. Poor Mac, and she could have easily been with him.

The hospital cleaned her up and stitched the wound on her head and she was put on the sick list for a while.

The following Sunday, she went out to Surrey to visit George. He had improved immensely and was most happy to see her. With a black patch covering his injured eye, he shambled along and was in good humour because he had been told that he was going home at last.

The doctor took Lily aside. 'He has brain damage,' he informed her, 'and it will re-occur, but his shell-shock has left him. A holiday will do him a lot of good. It will help to rehabilitate him and build him up for the major operation he must face later on.'

Lily looked alarmed. 'I live in a hostel, I can't look after him,' she said.

'We'll see what can be arranged,' said the head sister. 'I'll get in touch with Welfare.'

Lily shot the sister a sullen look.

'We've done all we can,' said the sister. 'It's up to you now.' With that she walked away.

'Old cow,' muttered Lily. 'What does she know about my circumstances?'

Nevertheless, the authorities wrote to Lily to tell her they had accommodation to offer her. Reluctantly, Lily went to see them and not for the first time, sat waiting in a long line of war-weary people who had lost their homes.

When her turn came, the clerk offered her a house. 'It's half a house,' he told her. 'The bottom half is habitable but the upstairs isn't. The house is in Sewell Street, Limehouse, No 13.'

'No, thanks,' returned Lily immediately. 'Not Pennyfields with all those Chinks. Not me, thank you. I came from Cannin' Tahn and I want to go back to Cannin' Tahn.'

'We've done our utmost for you, Mrs Brown, because of your husband's disabilities. We hear he is being sent home and you must make the best of it. These are hard times with so many homeless.'

'Well, I ain't living in Limehouse,' protested Lily.

'The Chinese population left with the coming of the war and the house has been redecorated,' the clerk tried to persuade her. 'The place is ideal for your husband, being downstairs, and it's all we have, so you'd better take it.'

'Ah well,' Lily sighed. 'I suppose it's any port in a storm. They'll be calling me Limehouse Lil pretty soon.'

Accompanied by Ivy, Lily went to inspect her new home in Sewell Street which was next door to Limehouse Church, a huge, run-down church surrounded by an ancient graveyard and with a square tower that was a landmark for East Enders. Sewell Street ran alongside it. It was made up of a long line of three-storey houses, most of them now empty having been badly blitzed when the docks just across the road were bombed. A high wall separated the street from the river.

'It's not too bad,' said Lily to Ivy.

'It's pretty dreary,' replied Ivy, 'but you'll get used to it. At least, it's sort of home from home, being so near the river. And there's a pub nearly next door—that should be useful.'

'I don't like that bloody graveyard quite so close to my back door. It gives me the creeps,' said Lily.

'Shouldn't worry,' said Ivy. 'They're all dead in there. It's the live ones you have to worry about.'

Lily spent the day cleaning the basement kitchen and Ivy's sons, now returned from evacuation, brought lots of items of furniture on a coster barrow. Ivy had scrounged what she could from the other bus clippies.

Lily cleaned the old gas stove, scrubbed the bare floorboards, put down the rugs that Ivy had sent and reluctantly began to build her nest once more. The war damage authorities sent her a cheque for her old house, so she was able to buy a second-hand bed for George and a big old-fashioned three-piece suite, but nothing could dispel the cold gloom from this house.

'Number 13? It's a bloody unlucky number,' complained Lily. 'And it stinks of those foreign spices that the Chinks used to use. Still, I suppose it's no good grumbling.'

She consoled herself and Ivy with a couple of gins in the pub next door, and then spent a lonely night listening to the mice scampering around in the empty rooms upstairs. Morning never came too soon. Lily was very unhappy. The prospect of living with George in this miserable house really scared her.

CHAPTER EIGHT

Coping With Life

It was very difficult for Lily to settle down in Sewell Street when George came home from the hospital. She couldn't go to work because she had to care for George since he needed her so much. Stuck at home, time hung heavy on her hands. There was always Ivy and the Blue Anchor, the pub next door, but without a wage packet, she could not always afford to go drinking of late.

Ivy had many problems now. Her husband had been invalided out of the army with stomach ulcers and was, in Ivy's opinion, 'like a bear with a sore arse' to live with. Her three children had now all returned from evacuation, two boys and a small girl called Trudy whom Lily was very fond of. They had all recently moved into a council-owned property that used to be the old Guinness buildings in the Mile End Road—a pre-war dwelling with small, pokey rooms and lots of stone steps. It was like a concrete jungle, with a backyard strung with lines of washing, for the kids to play in.

'It's bloody awful,' complained Ivy at one of their now infrequent meetings in the pub. 'Nuffink like the old street in Cannin' Tahn. It's all bleedin' foreigners. Don't know where they all come from.'

Lily agreed that their own little communal life had once been great before the war.

'Not a shop to get anyfin',' continued Ivy. 'Got to go all the way up the main road if yer only need a packet of tea. Yer remember old Mrs Appleby on the corner of our street? Also, there's me old man to contend with,' she complained. 'Oh, he's a rotter! I miss old Ben—at least he was kind to me.'

Ivy's moaning made Lily think of Kasie and his warm, clean body, his sweet-toned voice. 'It will never be the same, you know, Ivy,' she said. 'We have had the good times so now we had better try to cope with the bad ones.'

'How's old George?' asked Ivy.

'Well, I manage, but it's no picnic. He's up one day and down the next. I have to go with him every time to the toilet and sometimes it's in the middle of the night and bloody freezin'. And then there I am hangin' abaht outside asking "Are you done, George?"'

This tickled Ivy's fancy. 'What's he say, then?' she giggled. '"No, just wiping."'

They both began to laugh heartily as they used to. 'I'd really miss you, Ivy,' said Lily. 'You've been a good pal to me.'

'Well, I ain't goin' nowhere,' replied Ivy. 'At least, I don't think so.'

They said their goodbyes, and Lily watched Ivy's short, plump figure walking quickly down the road as she went to collect her little girl from school. Lily went back home and was only in her house a minute when she heard the frightening sound of London's latest hazard, the German rocket bomb, exploding in the distance. She shivered and hoped that Ivy had reached home safely, for these rockets gave no warning and were even deadlier than the earlier buzz bombs, and destroying huge areas and killing many.

In May that year, a Second Front was launched, a big invasion army to France. There was a hint of victory in the air but, as Lily listened to the reports on the wireless, she wondered if it would ever end.

George was very fond of the wireless, so Lily had spent almost her last few pounds to buy him a second-hand set. When he listened, he was often very bright and took in all the news with gestures and grins, but he still could not hold a conversation. Occasionally when he was angry, an obscene word would burst from his lips and he cast nasty looks in Lily's direction. At such times she would wonder how she was going to live a lifetime with him, when he was not even grateful for the care she gave him now.

Every two weeks Lily would put George in his wheelchair (she was still very strong and could pick him up like a baby), wrap a blanket around him and wheel him through the streets up to the London hospital for his treatment which seemed to be doing him good. He was much quieter than he used to be and did not toss and turn, or scream out in his sleep very often any more.

It was the lively, extrovert Lily who seemed to fade during these first few months when George came home. She also looked shabby in an old blouse and skirt, and shoes that were very run down. In spite of the extra allowance she got for looking after George, money was short. Food was still scarce and money was spent to get black market meat and cheese, and goods that were badly needed, such as coal. Coal was very expensive so a lot of money went into trying to keep the big, gloomy house warm. But somehow Lily survived.

She felt sad about Kasie. She had written several letters to him since George had come home and received no reply. Very disheartened, she decided that he was either lost at sea or else trying to forget her.

That was a really cold winter. The troops out in Holland were snowed in and the earlier promise of victory had come to a halt. Everyone seemed depressed.

One bright spot that dull December was a visit from Norman Clegg. There he was one day on the doorstep loaded with parcels. He was so well wrapped up in an overcoat, hat and scarf that Lily hardly recognised him and, thinking he was some kind of intruder, almost closed the door in his face.

But she recognised him the moment he opened his mouth. 'Halloo, it's me, your old chum, Norman.'

George was overwhelmed to see Norman. He giggled and slobbered, and held onto his hand and wept.

'Now, now, lad,' said Norman gently. 'Mustn't get excited.'

Lily stood watching them. Apart from herself, no one else had ever bothered about George, and it was heart-warming to see the fuss he made of Norman who was a genuine friend. He came over and put his arm around Lily and cuddled her close. He looked about the poverty-stricken home, at the little coal fire, now almost out, at George's narrow bed in one corner and the old settee where Lily slept in the other, at the square kitchen table covered with an old linoleum tablecloth. On the table was Lily's and George's pitiful meal—a half-cut loaf, a packet of margarine and two mugs filled with weak tea.

Apologetically, Lily moved to clear the table. 'Sorry about the mess,' she said. 'We find it's better to eat and sleep in here because it saves fuel.'

But Norman held her tight. 'Why didn't you let me know how bad things were with you, Lily?' He was shocked by the sight before him.

'Well, we was all right,' said Lily. 'It's the bleedin' snowy weather what got us dahn, and this miserable bloody street with its damned high wall over there. There's nuffink to see, just the rotten churchyard out the back.'

Norman sat on the old settee and pulled her down beside him. Lily put her head on his broad shoulder and wept.

Watching them with his one eye, George started to cackle. 'Fancies you, Norm does,' he blurted out.

Ignoring George, Norman patted her back. 'Now, have thee cry out, lass, and you'll feel better.'

As Lily felt the warmth and comfort of a real man's arms about her again, she realised just how lonely she had been.

'Right, then,' said Norman, when all had settled down. 'What's it to be, lad? Fish and chips?' he asked George. George nodded eagerly and pointed to his mouth as he always did when he was hungry.

'Right thar, lad,' said Norman. 'Thee be good while Lily goes with me t'get the supper.'

Together, Lily and Norman walked along the dreary street. The snow had turned to brown slush and there was a biting wind blowing over the high wall from the Thames on the other side. The street was deserted and, as they reached the corner, the huge shape of Limehouse Church loomed out of the mist which hovered over the graveyard that she hated.

''Tis certainly a gloomy spot, Lily. I think it'd kill me to be penned up here,' announced Norman.

'It's not doing me a lot of good, either,' said Lily drily.

'Never thee mind, lass, as soon as the snow has gone, you will bring George up and stay with me for as long as you wish. I've got a nice plot of land and a small wooden bungalow, and am doing very nicely with me plants. I'll build a nice brick place there one day.'

As Lily listened to Norman's account of the life he'd made for himself, she really envied him. He was such a contented man. 'How could I get George all the way up north?' she complained.

Norman brushed away her objections with a wave of the hand. 'It'll be easy, lass. Put him in his wheelchair and wheel him to the station and I'll be there waiting at t'other end.'

Lily began to smile. 'Sounds all right,' she said. 'But will it work?'

They had reached the fish-and-chip shop and were standing in the queue. The savoury smell of the chips and fish surrounded them. 'Makes you feel hungry, doesn't it?' said Lily.

Norman squeezed her arm. 'Lily, you will never go hungry, not while Norman has a penny in his pocket.'

Lily stared at him, thinking how strange he was. He took everything so seriously; she had never known anyone like that before.

On the way back they stopped at the pub next door for a drink and brought home beer for themselves and lemonade for George. In the end, they had quite a merry supper even though the fire burned low and the room was cold. At one point when George made complaining gestures about the cold, Lily got up and went to the cupboard out in the hall. Coming back, she produced George's old army boots and put them on the fire. 'He ain't goin' to need these bloody boots any more,' she said firmly. 'Might as well have a warm up.'

The boots blazed brightly and they huddled around the fire, holding their chilled fingers out towards it. Sitting with Norman on the settee, Lily could almost feel his body burning for her, and she knew he really needed her.

When George dozed off, Norman's and Lily's lips met, and his big hands fondled her breasts. 'Oh, Lily, I want you so much,' he whispered.

Lily felt the urgent need of a man, but she pulled away. 'Oh, no, Norman, not with George in there. And it would be such a pity to spoil a good friendship.'

Taking her rejection well, Norman got to his feet. 'Well, better go, lass, I'm booked in at the servicemen's club, and they lock you out after midnight. I'll call in the morning before I leave.'

They kissed good night on the doorstep and Norman said, 'You know I love you, don't you, Lily?'

She nodded.

'It won't be easy for you to neglect George for that's the kind of great-hearted lass you are,' he said before he left. 'But you are going to need a man and someone to care for both of you.'

When George was in bed, Lily lay alone on the settee tossing restlessly. Her need for Kasie was bad. Over and over in her mind she turned the wonderful moments they had shared down in Pompey and those two weeks in Rhyl—passionate moments that would never come again. In misery she pressed her face into the pillow and wept real tears of self-pity.

Next morning, Norman came to say goodbye. 'Just a little Christmas box from me, Lily,' he said, putting an envelope on the mantelpiece.

Lily's face flamed a guilty red as she wished she had earned the money by giving him her body. She would have felt much better if she had.

The cold weather went right on through until early spring, and with each heavy snowfall, Lily grew more depressed. By now she was quite convinced that Kasie was dead and that George would never be normal. The only bright spots in her life were the letters from Norman with ten pound notes in them. 'Have a drink on me, Lily, darling,' he wrote. 'Don't forget, see you up here in the spring.'

So when the snow had finally cleared and April brought

sunny days and buds on the trees in the park, Lily was restless for a change.

'I've a good mind to take Norman up on his offer,' she told Ivy.

'Why not get away for a holiday? Looks like you need it,' replied Ivy.

'It's so strange. I just can't commit myself to Norman. All the time I feel that eventually Kasie will come looking for me.'

Ivy looked doubtful. 'Wouldn't bank on it, Lily. Men soon forget,' she said authoritatively. 'Tell you what, I'll go around occasionally to your house when you're away and if there are any letters I can send them on to you.'

Lily smiled gratefully. 'Thanks, Ivy, I think I'll take a chance. It's not that I don't like Norman, because I do, and he is so good to old George, it's something else but I'm not sure what that is.'

It was a fresh spring day when Lily packed a suitcase, put George in his wheelchair and set off for the mainline station where they were most kind and considerate. For in these sad times so many disabled servicemen were on the move that people were always ready to help. They got George into the railway carriage, folded up his chair and told Lily to collect it from the baggage car on arrival.

George was like a small boy looking out of the window with a kind of satisfied grin on his face. 'Souff End,' he mumbled as if boyhood memories still remained in that damaged brain.

'No, no,' said Lily, 'we're going to see Norman.'

George nodded excitedly but then went off into one of his deep sleeps and did not wake up until they reached Manchester where Lily saw the big broad shape of Norman waiting at the barrier. He came on to the platform and helped Lily get George into his chair, and without much fuss, Norman wheeled George out of the station, a beaming smile on his pleasant face.

'I think this is the happiest day of my life, Lily,' he announced. 'I've got an old truck outside. It's not much to look at but it does to take my produce to market. I hope you won't mind travelling in it,' he said apologetically.

'I'm so tired,' said Lily, 'I'd travel in a hearse if I had to.'

Norman grinned. 'Ah, tha's great, lass,' he said with admiration.

With George wedged in between them, they rattled along in the old truck. Soon they were outside the busy town and on their way up north. All around they were looked down upon by sombre hills which cast brown and purple shadows, and in the distance they could see tall chimneys belching out long lines of smoke which floated away to form little grey clouds.

'It looks so nice up here,' said Lily. 'I can see right down the hill. All those houses look like little boxes.'

Norman smiled proudly. 'Yes, Lily, this is our Northern land, my home sin' I were born. It's not pretty, with all the industry that goes on, but it's kind of peaceful. And once you get to know the moorlands, you will love it.'

Norman's village was called Hill Drop. It was aptly named, for the land behind seemed to drop straight into a green valley. Norman's home was a kind of wooden shack at the edge of the pretty village. The shack was quite quaint. Honeysuckle grew over it, and it was hemmed in from the road with rough fencing. There was a big garden in the front full of daffodils, and a wide blue border of forget-me-nots lined the path to the front of the house where Norman had placed a rustic bench to sit on.

'Oh,' cried Lily as they drew up outside, 'it's so pretty!'

'It looks great but it's small,' Norman said with some pride. 'It's a pre-war place, and not modern. The old fellow I bought it from was more interested in the land around than the house itself. And I have to admit that that's basically also the case with me, but I've made it as comfortable as I can.'

'Give over, Norm.' said Lily, as he helped to get George from the truck. 'It'll be heaven for me after that bloody old house in Sewell Street.'

Norman's 'shack' was big and roomy with high beamed ceilings and plain white walls. But it was carpeted and properly furnished. There were two bedrooms and a big kitchen with a huge old-fashioned wood-burning stove. The whole place was scrupulously clean.

'Oh, I love this,' said Lily, warming herself at the big stove.

'I cook on that and it also heats the bath water,' Norman announced, glad of her approval.

'You have a bathroom!' cried Lily. 'Well, I never did.'

Norman opened a small door and showed her the bathroom. 'Put it in meself,' he said, 'I'm getting very good at doing odd jobs in spite of this bad arm.'

'It's marvellous,' said Lily, 'And you have all this warmth and clean air.' She looked out over the hills at the white sheep that dotted the hillside.

'We'll have a meal first, Lily, and then I'll take you out to see my greenhouses.'

'Shall I cook?' asked Lily.

'No, love, it's all ready. But you can lay the table.'

Lily put a nice clean cloth on the table and laid the shiny cutlery. 'You've got some nice things, Norm,' she remarked.

'Most of it belonged to me old mum. She died when I was in the army. Thought a lot of her, I did. I suppose that's why I didn't marry.'

Lily paused in her task of setting the knives and forks and looked up at him. 'I often wondered if you had ever been married,' she said.

'No,' Norman shook his head. 'I never did, but now I'd like to.'

'Well, better find yourself a nice North country girl,' jested Lily.

But Norman came and put his arms about her very shyly. 'No, Lily, you'll do me nicely,' he said.

Lily looked at George asleep in his chair, and a cold shiver went through her. She did not love Norman and had a sudden feeling that she was trapped.

The meal was roast beef, baked potatoes, and fresh vegetables from his garden. It was all well cooked by Norman.

'Well,' said Lily in admiration, 'it's the first time I ever knew a man to cook as nice a meal as that. Old George, when he was well, couldn't even fry an egg.'

They sat around the open fire in the sitting room and chatted of the things they knew—Lily of London and Norman of his own Northern scene.

They put George to bed and Norman said, 'You can have the other bedroom, Lily, I'll settle down in here in the sitting room.'

Lily shot a quick look at him. 'You can share with me, if you want to, Norm,' she said resignedly.

'Oh, Lily!' Norman got up like a big bear and crushed her against him. 'Blimey, Norm!' she gasped. 'Don't squash me. I'll go to bed and wait for you.'

Ten minutes later, Lily sat in the small room in the clean double bed. The blankets were covered with an old-fashioned bedspread which was made up of small squares of crochet all joined together. She examined it carefully, thinking as she did so that someone had worked very hard with dainty hands to make it. Perhaps it had been Norman's mother. She realised that she was feeling quite strange, rather unemotional about what was about to happen, as though it was something inevitable.

Norman crept shyly into the bedroom and turned out the light before he undressed. He was a little clumsy and the weight of his body almost crushed her, he felt so heavy. But he was kind and gentle and ever so grateful afterwards. But as Norman snored beside her, Lily lay restless and unhappy. Unsatisfied, she longed for the hot embraces of Kasie, and she wished she could shut her ears to the moaning and groaning of old George in his sleep, which came through the thin wooden walls from the bedroom next door.

Yet that next week had its compensations. The early spring weather was lovely, and the moors were fresh and green. Norman spent a lot of time working. He had two huge greenhouses filled with cucumbers and tomato plants, and a lot of young bedding plants that he was growing for the summer.

In her active manner, Lily took care of his chickens and turkeys, cleaned the house and, in the evenings as the sun set over the hills, she sat potting up young plants. It was a nice peaceful scene.

George seemed very happy there, too. He ate all the good food that Norman provided and in the late evening would try to play cards and dominoes with Norman. He never had much success but Norman was patient with him, and when necessary, would pick him up and carry him to the lavatory. Once he even gave him a bath in the little bathroom he was so proud of.

Although Lily felt relaxed, she was also unhappy because she knew that Norman was growing used to her and that it would be difficult to leave him. But she made the best of a bad bargain, and tried not to worry too much about it.

In no way could she educate Norman about sex matters. Sex to him was a slow comfortable act that was necessary but not everything to him. Often after a hard day's digging he would kiss her and say, 'Good night, Lily. Got to be up early in the morning, it's market day.'

Then Lily would lie awake beside him hot and restless, needing to be loved. Often even when they did indulge, she would try to persuade him to repeat the act, but he would say, 'Go to sleep now, Lily.'

'It's better the second time,' Lily would say, remembering Kasie and his ardent lovemaking. But once was always enough for Norman.

Yet together they all lived in comparative harmony right through the summer. Lily helped Norman pick blackcurrants and strawberries and water his greenhouses. Afterwards she cooked huge meals. Her skin grew tanned and her body filled out so she was very fit and healthy.

Yet often a feeling of loneliness welled up inside her when she took Norman's old dog for long walks beside the river. She would be happy here, she would think to herself, but something was missing. Norman was so kind and considerate and took such good care of George. What more could she want? What was wrong with her? She knew deep in her heart that she ached for the loving caresses of Kasie, but she also knew that she did not have the courage to leave Norman now that she had well and truly burned her boats.

·The war news was good. The Allied forces had entered

France, and now it looked as though it would soon be over at last.

Norman was very happy about it all. 'I'm going to get building plans from the council as soon as the peace is signed. Then I'll build a nice cosy house for you, Lily.'

Lily gave him a stiff smile. The post had just arrived with a bunch of letters from Ivy who had collected Lily's mail from Sewell Street and sent it on to her. There were two blue-edged overseas envelopes that could only be from Kasie. Lily had pushed these into her apron pocket and was now sitting looking at the other two.

'Why don't you read your letters, Lily?' asked Norman from behind the newspaper. But Lily continued to feed George his porridge, leaving the letters unopened as if she was afraid to know the contents. But eventually she did read Ivy's depressing letter in which Ivy complained about her husband. Much to her fury, she wrote, he had got her pregnant and now she was swallowing all sorts of concoctions to get rid of it. The other letter was from the medical authorities who wanted to know why George had not attended the hospital for treatment for the past two months. They explained that it was necessary to continue the therapy treatment to prepare George for his final brain operation which would be carried out in August at the new clinic at the London Hospital. Lily was asked to report to his doctor immediately.

'Oh, blimey!' she burst out, after she had read the letter. 'That's put a stopper on it.'

'What do you mean?' asked Norman, looking alarmed.

'Read this!' She passed him the letter. 'That means I'll have to go home soon.'

Norman's face paled a little and he stared at her. 'No, Lily,' he insisted, 'all you have to do is have his treatment transferred. There are good hospitals up here, you know.'

'No,' she said. 'I can't do that to him. He has waited two years for this operation and if we transfer him up here it will mean he will have to go to the end of the list again. That wouldn't be fair, Norman.'

'Well, if you say so, Lily,' Norman said, bowing his head, 'but I can't take the time off just yet to go with you. This hot weather will ruin my crops if I'm not here to do the watering.'

'No one's asking you to, Norman,' replied Lily. 'I never came up here on any permanent basis, you know that.'

'What you're telling me is that you want to leave me,' Norman said in dismay. 'I can't believe it, Lily.' His nice blue eyes stared at her appealingly.

Lily's kind heart got the better of her, and she went over and put her arms around Norman's neck. 'As if I'd want to go away from you,' she said, nuzzling him fondly. 'It's been wonderful up here and I promise I'll come back to you as soon as George has had his treatment.'

Norman held her hands. 'I wish I could really believe that, Lily,' he said sadly.

'Now stop fussing. I'll go and get my things ready. I must go in the morning if I'm to take him to the hospital on Monday.'

Once she was in the bedroom she closed the door and quickly pulled Kasie's letters from her apron pocket. She sat on the bed to read the first.

Darling,
   I did at last receive your letters and also your new address. I cannot tell you where I am but I will soon be seeing you and holding you in my arms again. I will always love you no matter how long we are parted. The news is good, so we have our future together to look forward to.
                                   Love Kasie.

Then she read the next letter:

Dear Lily,
   Did not hear from you, darling, is everything all right? Wrote to your new address. Did you get my letter? Won't be long now. I am longing so much to love you, darling.
                                   Kasie.

Tears poured down her cheeks as she read these words. 'Oh, Kasie, Kasie,' she cried, pressing the letters to her lips. Then, pulling her suitcase down from the top of the wardrobe, she started to pack her things.

Next day she took a very sad departure from Norman who hugged and kissed her. Sitting in his wheelchair, George started to snivel. 'Stay with Norm,' he mumbled.

'No, old son, got to get you on your feet again,' said Norman bravely. And turning to Lily, he said: 'I'll always be here waiting for you, come what may.'

Lily's heart seemed very heavy for she felt so sorry for him. But she smiled and said brightly: 'Get up to London in time for the Victory parties. They'll really go to town up there.'

With George settled in the compartment, Lily gave Norman a final wave and sat back in her seat. She was really looking forward to going home. 'The countryside's all right for those that's used to it,' she muttered. 'Me, I come from Cannin' Tahn.'

CHAPTER NINE

V for Victory

As the train pulled in at Liverpool Street Station, Lily breathed a sigh of relief. The smoky buildings and the familiar scene suddenly felt very important to her, and she delighted in the sound of the Cockney porter's brash voice as he helped get George off the train. 'Gor blimey, mate, ain't you an armful?' he said as he put him into the wheelchair. Then he whispered to Lily, 'Good luck, mate—ex-service, ain't the poor sod?'

Lily choked up inside but she replied brightly: 'Thanks a lot, mate. Blimey, it's great to see the ol' tahn again.' Then, ignoring the taxis, she pushed the chair out of the station towards home. She was not one to ride in cabs, that was an expense she was quite unused to.

So with her suitcase on the back of the bathchair, she pushed it on through the back streets of Aldgate, and along the West India Dock Road to Limehouse. It was a long haul and now her legs ached. George was whining and grizzling, and showing that he wanted to pee by pulling down his rung and pointing to his lap.

'Shut up!' yelled Lily. 'You got to wait, we're nearly home.'

As she strolled down the road, passers-by stole glances at her. She was always a big strong girl and the holiday had done wonders for her. She looked very fit and she was dressed in a white dress that fitted her hips very tightly. The scooped neckline showed her golden tanned skin, and her long, burnished mane of hair hung down over her shoulders, making her look very dishy. The fact that she was pushing a small wizened figure in an invalid chair made people notice her more, particularly when she yelled at George above the noise of the East End traffic.

As they reached the sailor's hostel near Rotherhithe Tunnel she paused to cross the road. The sudden breeze whipped George's rug up from his lap. Lily leant her full-bosomed body over the back of the chair to put the rug straight and said to George: 'Now, shut up! We've just got to cross the road and in five minutes we'll be home.' As she straightened up she felt someone's eyes staring at her so intensely that a cold shiver ran down her spine.

On the wide steps of the seaman's hostel stood Kasie. He was dressed in a navy blue raincoat which hid his uniform and he had no hat on, so his bright curls waved in the breeze.

Lily's heart gave a lurch and she nearly jumped into the air. Controlling herself as best she could, she pushed the chair over the road and pretended not to see Kasie at all. But he was soon walking beside her, nimbly dodging his way through the traffic to get to her. Walking beside her, behind the wheelchair so George could not see, his hand caressed her arm.

'Lily, darling,' he whispered. 'Don't say you don't want to see me.'

'I do,' Lily replied in a trembling voice, 'but it's not convenient at the moment.'

As she slowed her pace, George gibbered like a monkey. 'Piss, piss,' he cried, more clearly than usual.

'Who *is* that?' cried Kasie.

'Be quiet, George, we're nearly home,' said Lily.

Kasie stared at her in amazement. 'Don't tell me that's George, your husband,' he whispered.

Lily nodded.

'Oh . . .' He uttered a foreign swear word and put his hand to his head. 'Why did not not tell me?' he asked.

'Go away, Kasie,' Lily almost sobbed.

'Not until you promise to see me later,' he replied. He put a hand on the handle of the chair. 'You look all in, I'll push it,' he said.

Lily was forced to let go and allow Kasie to push the wheelchair. They walked along in silence. George had dropped off into one of his odd dozes. With his mouth agape, he looked terrible.

White and grim-faced, Kasie pushed the invalid chair to the street beside Limehouse Church and they halted at that dreary slum with its ragged curtains and dirty windows.

'Please, Kasie,' begged Lily, 'Let me see to George and then I'll be with you. Wait in the pub,' she pointed to the drab bar next door.

She opened the front door of the house and Kasie pushed George's chair into the passageway. Then without a word, he turned and walked away.

With mounting excitement welling up inside her, Lily got George on the toilet, gave him his tea, undressed him and put him to bed. The house was very cold. She filled a hot water bottle and put a sleeping pill into his hot milk. After a moment's thought, she popped in another one, and put on the radio while he drank it. In no time at all, George was alseep snoring.

Lily went to the tap, rinsed her face and hands and brushed her hair. Glancing out of the window towards the grim graveyard, there, in the misty evening, she saw Kasie propping his neat shape against the wall and smoking incessantly. He had got fed up with waiting in the pub. With a swift move-ment, Lily opened the back door and stepped out into his strong loving arms. Her troubled mind and aching body were swept away in the passion of their meeting. Kasie held her tight and collapsed against the wall, his body so urgent with love.

Almost fainting from Kasie's caresses, Lily led him towards her house. Her body was shot with that shivering of love that she could never control when with him. Putting her finger to her lips, she pushed open the back door and together they almost fell down onto that battered old settee that served as Lily's bed.

So heaven had opened its gates once more for Lily as she went there with Kasie. Norman's cold caresses were forgotten now that she was in the arms of a real man once more.

Afterwards, as they lay exhausted, the sirens began to wail

and the guns roared. London had begun its victory celebrations. Out in the street, voices were raised. The street party had begun.

'What's that?' asked Kasie, sleepy from their lovemaking.

'It's Victory Night. We should be celebrating,' said Lily. 'Let's go to the pub.'

'But what about him?' asked Kasie in a worried tone, glancing at George.

'He'll sleep till the morning,' said Lily. 'Let's go, darlin', we have so much to make up for.' She smoothed down her dress, but did not worry that her hair was tousled and her lipstick smudged. Proudly, she took her lover's hand and danced out with him into the crowded street.

A huge bonfire burned in the middle of the road. Sailors sat up on the high wall, jumping down every now and then to grab hold of the girls and dance with them around the fire. Fireworks exploded and an old fellow banged out tunes on a piano outside the pub. Flags and bunting festooned the dreary old street. At last London was alive again after years of war, bombs and food shortages. There was nothing but goodwill in the air. As soon as Lily and Kasie reached the pub, they were handed a bottle. ''Ere sailor,' someone said. 'It's on the house.'

Until three in the morning, Lily and Kasie danced and drank with the neighbours. It was certainly a night to remember! By the early hours, the bonfire burned low and most of the parties had moved indoors where they were still going strong. But Lily and her Kasie fell over the church wall, too drunk to get back home. There they lay on an old flat gravestone, as the fireworks still exploded about them and vociferous voices roared out the victory songs.

'Kasie,' said Lily, trying to pull herself together. 'Get up! We'll go indoors.'

'No,' he mumbled, pulling her closer, 'this tonight is our marriage bed under the stars. It's just you and I, Lily. And here tonight you will conceive my son and we will take him home to his grandparents.'

'Don't be so silly, Kasie,' said Lily, pushing against him and trying to rise. But to no avail. Kasie's body covered hers and she was lost. Victory night was certainly one for her to remember.

In the pink light of the dawn, Lily, now cold and stiff, rolled over and tried to wake Kasie. He did not stir but went on sleeping like a baby, with a gentle smile on his face.

Lily went indoors and made some coffee. While the water boiled she had a look at George, who still snored. She took a cup of coffee out to Kasie and finally managed to rouse him. He sat up, for a moment bewildered until he recognised her squatting beside him. A wide smile creased his face. 'Oh, my lovely,' he said, reaching out to her.

'Come on, Kasie,' said Lily. 'Bleedin' 'ell, yer can't stay here in the graveyard, it's five o'clock in the morning. Come in and freshen up. George is still asleep.' She pulled him up and guided him into the house where he sat for a while with his head in his hands and then silently lit a cigarette. He looked around in horror at his poverty-stricken surroundings which had dust and cobwebs all over the place, gathered during her absence.

'Lily,' he said severely, 'why did you not tell me? And is this your home?' He wrinkled his fastidious nose in disgust.

Lily, suffering from a big hang-over, snapped back at him. 'All right, you needn't turn your nose up. I know it's a bleedin' mess but I haven't been here for weeks. I was staying up North to be near the hospital with George.' She was glad that her quick brain could assist her so easily. And Kasie clearly believed her.

'I'm sorry, darling,' he said, pulling her onto his knees. 'Is that wretched creature really your husband?'

Lily nodded.

'Well, it will make it a lot easier for us once we've got rid of him,' he said.

'I'm not so sure about that,' replied Lily.

'But surely, Lily, there is nothing to hold you to that poor wreck.'

'There's such a thing as loyalty,' she said firmly. 'Perhaps you don't quite understand that, Kasie.'

A mischievous grin appeared on his face, as it always did

when Lily got on her high horse about something. 'Don't start making any more excuses, Lily,' he said. 'This man is no longer your proper husband. I am. Why . . .' he held up two slim, supple hands, 'I could put him out of his misery in two minutes.'

This last remark made Lily lose her temper. 'Why, you rotter! You bloody beast!' She lunged at him but his strong hands grabbed hers and his firm smooth lips covered her mouth. As Lily succumbed, she began to weep. 'Oh, Kasie, Kasie, don't make life worse for me than it already is,' she sobbed. 'I have suffered enough.'

He cuddled her close. 'I know, darling, and you have been very loyal and very brave. But now the war is over and we have to think of ourselves. So, my darling, do as you wish but I tell you, in no way will that poor old thing come between us, remember that.

'Now for the good news,' he said brightly. 'Guess where I'm stationed? At Shadwell Dock, just down the road, so for a while you'll see a lot of me, darling.' He looked around the room. 'And I hope to make things much better for you.' He tightened his grip on her again. 'Lily, you are mine and nothing and no one will come between us. You will return home with me and raise my children or I'll cut my own throat—and maybe yours, too.'

'I think you have become very cruel,' said Lily quietly. 'It's not like you.'

'War does strange things to a man, Lily,' Kasie said rather flippantly. 'Anyway I'm off. I've got to get some air; this place smells like a sewer.' Giving her a parting kiss, he put on his cap, pushed his arms into his raincoat pockets, and wandered off.

Lily did not know why, but she just put her head down on the table and wept bitterly.

The following month was filled with frequent battles between Lily and Kasie over what to do with poor George. The arguing wore her out, as did Kasie's greed for sex, and his attitude to Lily's way of life. He seemed to have become quite arrogant and bitter, and was not a bit like the sweet gentle young man she had met in the middle of the blitz.

Every night George got an extra ration of sleeping pills while Lily went out on the town with Kasie. Lily was beginning to get quite guilt-ridden about George, who slept all night and most of the day and seemed to be having some sort of mental set-back as though it were too much trouble to rouse himself even to eat. It made her feel bad.

At least there was no shortage of food. Kasie was very generous and every evening he brought meat, cheese, wine and chocolates specially for Lily. He was back on his old home ship now and discipline was very relaxed as the Dutch sailors waited to sail back home to their country.

One night Lily went aboard Kasie's ship to have dinner. Kasie had bought her an evening dress for the occasion, and she had a fine time wining and dining with those very pleasant people on board the ship. She particularly enjoyed being treated as Kasie's legal wife.

Even in the street now, the neighbours nodded respectfully to her. As far as they were concerned, this very nice blond naval officer was Lily's man.

Poor George seldom left the house these days, while Lily went off on various jaunts with Kasie. He was quite popular at her local pub, too. He had got a concertina and often sang in his sweet tone and played sea shanties for the regulars who liked him a lot. Sometimes they went to Petticoat Lane where Kasie, who had plenty of money, bought presents to take home to his family and this sometimes made Lily feel very jealous.

So, in spite of the good times, life was not carefree and Lily's heart was often heavy, as she told Ivy, who was very disgruntled at being three months pregnant now.

'Tried everything to get rid of it,' said Ivy, 'but so far no luck.'

'Oh, Ivy,' Lily said with concern. 'Don't do that. If you're now three months, you should stop.'

'Oh, who wants to be saddled with a baby? It'll all be washin' bleedin' nappies over again. Yer can't get out for a drink,' complained Ivy.

But Lily looked very sad, for she had begun to feel very sick in the mornings and was almost a month overdue. It had been Victory Night, she was sure of it. And if it was true, she had little alternative but to cling to Kasie, although she still felt that it was a very uncertain future with him. 'You know, Ivy,' she said. 'I do love him but I'm afraid of his way of life.'

'He's bleedin' good to yer, if yer ask me,' said Ivy, noshing the huge lump of Dutch cheese that Kasie had provided.

'But what am I goin' to do abaht George?' asked Lily.

'Put 'im in a 'ome. Don't reckon he'll ever get better,' replied Ivy.

'What? Go away and forget him? Leave him to rot in some loony bin?' Lily was horrified. 'Don't think I can do that.'

'Well, it's certain you can't take 'im wiff yer,' said Ivy, still unconcerned. 'I'm orf, goin' dahn the Mile End. I 'eard abaht a woman who does the job there. I ain't goin' to tie meself dahn, not wiff that bastard husband of mine, I ain't. Can I take some of that cheese?'

'I'll wrap it up,' said Lily, 'and half a pound of butter.'

'Good,' said Ivy, 'ain't seen much butter in our 'ouse for a long time.' Heaving up her short and extra-tubby shape, Ivy breezily departed.

A strange feeling came over Lily, as Ivy left. 'Take care, Ivy,' she called after her. 'Look after yourself.' Ivy turned and gave a cheeky signal before going on her way.

Lily then began to wash up and tidy the kitchen, before Kasie arrived. She didn't really care what it looked like, for she was not houseproud, but Kasie often looked astounded at the sink filled up with dirty crocks, and the littered table, and he would never take a meal in the house. 'Come on, let's get out of the hovel,' he would say. 'It stinks of poverty. When I give you a house it will be on the water, and be clean and fresh, and our children will grow up strong and healthy.'

Lily wondered if she would like living on the water. She could not even imagine what it must be like. She could not swim, and was too old to learn, she thought. And how did one get on with a small baby? Suppose it fell overboard . . . Small worries obsessed her but she did not share them with Kasie because so far she had not told him of her condition and she didn't know when she would.

CHAPTER TEN

Wise Child

Those last few days before Kasie sailed for home were very hectic ones for Lily. She was now almost certain that she was pregnant but still she could not bring herself to tell him.

Kasie was very full of himself and, with money to spend, he took her on long tiring shopping expeditions in the West End shops. The victory flags still fluttered overhead as London slowly came back to life after six years of war. Down came the wooden hoardings and the blackout blinds, and the sandbags disappeared. The streets thronged with servicemen home from France getting a good time in the big city before they returned to their small towns and villages in the countryside.

The little stalls and suitcase traders came out onto the pavements and vendors hollered out about their wares. The air was tense with hidden excitement as the civilians, who had stayed huddled in the air-raid shelters for four years, came out into the sunshine. Some could be seen lying on the grass in Hyde Park cuddling and kissing. Mums and Dads queued up for the Zoo at Regents Park and Madame Tussauds in Baker Street. This was Lily's London, the one she loved. So with Kasie, she threw herself whole-heartedly into the swim of the victory celebrations, and in spite of the fact that her legs ached and she was feeling very much under the weather, she rouged her cheeks and put on a nice dress each day, and off they went.

Poor old George languished at home getting thinner and thinner and sort of dopey. Lily would leave his food near him but it seemed to be too much trouble for him to eat it. One day he fell out of bed and lay on the floor all day until Lily came home to find him. He had wet himself and was weeping like a child. Lily got very angry, and nagged and slapped him. But then her conscience pricked her, so she cleaned him up, and fussed over him but then sat down and resorted to tears herself.

George's one good eye always seemed to stare at her accusingly. He only ever said a few words, one of which was 'cow', and others, 'where's Norm?'

After that incident, when Kasie saw her eyes red with weeping, he said he was very worried. 'What's wrong, *leiblin*?'

When Lily explained what had happened, he looked contemptuous. 'For God's sake, Lily, put that poor fellow away where he will be properly looked after. Now you are mine. Forget about him and put on a pretty dress. We're going to a party,' he informed her.

The party was being held at Charlie Brown's pub, a well-known tavern in the West India Dock Road. Lily hated going there because she didn't like the owner who was a woman called Elsie Potts. Elsie was dark-haired and had snow-white skin which she loved to display. She also had a deep, sultry voice, and she played the piano and sang to entertain the customers. On many occasions, she would ask Kasie to join her and together they sang duets of popular songs to a very appreciative audience. Lily hated Elsie because she was jealous of her; she knew that Elsie fancied Kasie and it hurt to see him pay attention to another woman, for she did not actually trust him.

'Don't think I'll go,' she said. 'I hate that sexy cow. One day I'll punch her on the nose.'

'Now, now, Lily, behave yourself,' grinned Kasie, taking a brush and brushing her long hair nice and smooth. Reluctantly, Lily finally agreed to go.

She wore a dark-blue dress which suited her well. It was tight-fitting and had a heart-shaped neckline.

From his pocket, Kasie pulled a bright scarlet rose. 'Look, I brought you a posy to wear.' His hands smoothed her breast as he was about to pin the flower on her.

'This is our last night, my lovely, let us be happy together. Now, I'll put this rose on your beautiful hair. That's where it will look best.' He slipped the flower on to her hair.

'Oh, blimey,' cried Lily, 'I can't wear it down in that pub. They'll all think I'm a senorita from Spain.'

'Leave it there, Lily, don't spoil this moment for me,' pleaded Kasie. 'Get your purse and we will go.'

As she quietly closed the door she thought she heard George call out. The sleeping pills did not seem to be as effective as they used to be. She turned to go back, but Kasie put a firm hand on her arm and quickly closed the door behind them.

The party turned out to be great, for Elsie was a famous East End character and well known for her hospitality. There were famous stage and screen personalities and all kinds of men from the Allied Forces. The whole bar was draped in red, white and blue, and upstairs a buffet was laid on with smoked salmon rolls, jellied eels, cockles and winkles, and all the other favourite dishes of the East End.

Lily got sloshed very easily and before long was sitting with her elbows on the table watching Kasie having a good time. He was very popular with everyone there and she felt very much alone. She could not get into the mood for this gaiety, for this fantastic crowd who drank, sang and danced as if the end of the world was coming. Elsie Potts was in her element, and had gathered all the young sailor boys around her. Lily watched bitterly. The red rose in her hair glowed in the bright lights, as did the tears in her dark blue eyes.

Kasie was well oiled and getting up on the stage and looking in Lily's direction, he began to sing in that sweet tone: 'When I grow too old to dream, I'll have you to remember, So kiss me my sweet and so let us part, For when I grow too old to dream, Your love will live in my heart.'

As she listened to these words, Lily let out a deep sob. Getting to her feet, she rushed towards the stage. Kasie leapt down and they clasped each other in a long embrace, his lips on hers. The red rose fell to the ground and was crushed under foot.

The audience roared with laughter at this unusual display of affection but Kasie, with his tears mingling with Lily's, took her hand and together they left the party and walked as if in a trance, staggering a little, down the West India Dock Road. Eventually they arrived at Limehouse Church.

'Do you remember Victory Night, Lily?' Kasie held her to him.

'I do,' replied Lily. 'We made love in the churchyard. But not tonight, Kasie. Tonight you come indoors with me.'

He had always refused to stay in the house before, and had made it a policy to return to his ship each night. He used to pretend that he did not have an over-night pass but Lily knew it was because George's presence in the next room embarrassed him.

Tonight, however, she was not going to let him go, and they slept huddled up on that old settee too much in love and too drunk to care. For this was their very last night. Lily was convinced that Kasie would go home and forget her.

But Kasie assured her that this was only a furlough. 'I'll be back in two months, Lily,' he said. 'I'm still in the navy, we're not released yet. The war still goes on,' he said, 'the Japs have not stopped fighting.'

But Lily closed her eyes and kept them shut. 'Please go, Kasie,' she said. 'I'll not open my eyes until you are gone.'

When he had gone, Lily went next door to rouse George who was very cold and hard to keep awake. She made him a hot water bottle and boiled some milk. She felt so guilty she was afraid to look at him, wondering how much of her lovemaking with Kasie he had heard the night before. Overwhelmed with guilt, she tried hard to rouse George all that day, but he kept slipping off into a kind of coma. The next morning, she dressed him, put him in the wheelchair and pushed him through the early morning streets to the London Hospital. They would know what to do about him. And she felt bad that she had not taken him for his treatment for two months.

As she walked along, she began to feel very queasy, and she ached from head to foot. The wheelchair seemed heavier than usual, though it was made worse by George's dead weight as he lolled back in it with his mouth open wide.

At last she reached the hospital gate but as she pushed the

wheelchair in through the door and along the wide corridor, a red mist suddenly swam before her eyes, and she pitched forward onto the floor. The wheelchair carried on down the corridor without her until it hit a wall and threw George out on to the floor. Two nurses, seeing this, ran to help and someone else picked up George who seemed scarcely aware of anything, and put him back in his chair. Soon the emergency services took over and Lily woke up in a cubicle in the Casualty Department. A young nurse was bathing her head and passing smelling salts under her nose.

'Oh, my gawd!' cried Lily. 'Where am I? What's happened to George?'

'He's all right,' said the nurse. 'We're taking care of him. I'll get you a cup of tea and then Sister wants to speak to you.'

As Lily sipped her tea, the sister, a big, aggressive lady, stood over her. She was stiff and starchy and very unfriendly. 'We have admitted your husband, Mrs Brown,' she said. 'He has sadly deteriorated and it is pretty obvious that in your condition you are no longer able to give him all the care he needs.'

Lily's blue eyes stared apologetically at her. 'My condition?' she stuttered.

'There is no need for naivety, Mrs Brown,' replied the sister in a severe tone. 'The fact that you are pregnant is the reason for your fainting spell. You should have sent for an ambulance and not pushed that heavy chair all the way here.' She stared at Lily as if she was some kind of viper. 'I don't know your circumstances, but if you need aid, go to the Welfare. We cannot be expected to believe that the child is your husband's.'

'That's my bloody business,' snapped Lily. She got up unsteadily and flounced out.

Once outside in the air her head cleared. So it was true after all. This time Kasie had left her pregnant. Why hadn't she told him about her fears? She must be mad, she thought. Now she had to talk to someone. 'I'll go and see Ivy, I haven't heard from her in weeks . . .'

As she waited at the bus stop to get a bus to visit Ivy in Mile End Road, a funeral passed by. It was very simple—just a hearse and another car going to the East London Cemetery. She looked away, funerals depressed her. The bus came and she got off at Mile End.

Outside Ivy's flat in the old run-down Guinness Buildings, stood Trudy, Ivy's little girl. She looked very tidy for once and was dressed in a black-and-white gingham dress and a white bow in her hair. She seemed very disconsolate with her head down and one foot scraping the ground.

'Hallo, love,' said Lily cheerfully. 'Is Mum in?'

'Mum's dead,' Trudy said flatly. 'Everybody's gone to the funeral, 'cept me.'

Lily could not take in the child's words. She stood open-mouthed, and speechless with astonishment. Ivy's front door was open and a neighbour came out sniffing and wiping her nose. 'They've gone,' she said to Lily. 'Were you supposed to go to the funeral?'

'What funeral?' cried Lily.

'Poor old Ivy's funeral. Don't say you didn't know.' The woman began to weep. 'Come in,' she said and Lily followed her into Ivy's small parlour which smelled of flowers. Stray blooms littered the floor. The table was laid with a white cloth and jars of pickles and plates of sandwiches.

'Just gettin' the tea ready,' said the woman buzzing about. 'It's a terrible thing. And not yet forty. Poor dear, it gave us all a shock, I can tell yer.'

Little Trudy rushed in and climbed onto Lily's lap. Putting her arms around Lily's neck, she clung to her like a limpet. 'Mummy won't never come back no more,' she whispered in Lily's ear.

Suddenly the truth hit Lily hard. She began to shake, and held the little one close. Not noticing Lily's state, the neighbour began to chat. 'Silly girl she was. I told her not to, but she was much against having another baby. It goes on all the time around here. Someone ought to report it. That's the third woman I know what's lost her life that way.'

Lily could not believe what she heard. The woman put the

finishing touches to the table. 'Oh, well, they won't be long, be back soon. I'll leave you, that all right, dear?'

After she had left, Lily sat cold and forlorn with Ivy's little girl on her lap. She could not shed a tear, she felt so numb. This had been her old mate, the only loyal friend she had ever made. And now she was gone forever to a cold grave, and leaving behind her a lovely family.

She was not sure how long she sat there but soon the room was full of people dressed in black. One of them was Ivy's mother-in-law who, when she saw Lily, came up to her and said, 'Well, of all the bleedin' cheek! Our Ivy would be here today but for you, you dirty cow.' She snatched Trudy from Lily's lap. 'Pat,' she called out to Ivy's husband. 'Look what we got 'ere, Lily Brahn, Ivy's best mate.'

Ivy's husband lumbered over, red-faced and boozy. 'Get aht,' he roared, ''fore I bash yer bloody face in!'

Lily got up without uttering a word and ran down the road as swift as the wind. Sobs were tearing at her throat when she reached the main road, and she collapsed onto a park bench and let loose those hot tears. The shock and horror of it all was more than she could bear. So Ivy had got a back street abortion. Oh, poor Ivy, she never deserved such an end. She was only thirty-nine and leaving behind those two boys and that lovely little girl. Lily could not bear the thought of it.

That evening she sat in the pub next door to her house swilling down gin and tonics. Now she was really alone. Kasie had gone. George had gone and now she had lost her one and only friend. What would she do now? A strange twinge inside her made her put her hand on her stomach. No, she was not alone, she reminded herself. There was a life within her, a child of love. Even if Kasie never came back, that part of him would remain with her. And with her hand resting on her stomach, she sat dreaming of a little girl with fair curls just like Kasie's.

'Got the bellyache, Lily?' asked an old man sitting nearby.

'Shut yer cake 'ole, nosey ol' sod!' replied Lily. Finishing her drink, she then went home to her lonely bed to dream of Kasie.

A month later, the early morning sunshine showed up the

dark, untidy kitchen. Lily got up and opened the back door to get the full benefit of the warmth and light. She felt strangely buoyant that morning. She had not been sick and had enjoyed her cornflakes. It was as if someone else had taken her over. She cleaned up and washed up humming a little tune, an old song that Kasie had taught her. As she hummed, she thought about Kasie. He was home now over in Holland, no doubt in the bosom of his family that he loved so much. He had probably taken up where he had left off, so it would be very easy for him to forget her, she thought.

She went into George's bedroom, threw open the window and stripped the bed. The smell of urine always hung about this room, so it needed some fresh air. Poor old George, she thought, he was only a vegetable but somehow she missed his company. She decided to go up to the hospital later on that day. They might let him come back to her.

She looked out at the lonely churchyard with its graves, and thought that even that did not seem so fearsome this morning. It was on one of those flat old gravestones that she had conceived, on Victory Night amid the booming of the guns and ships' sirens. She would remember that night forever . . .

But now she must face the future and think of this child within her. Soon it would be a living, breathing human being, whom she would love and care for. The exciting thought made her catch her breath.

Before he left, Kasie had given her about twenty pounds. But it was not enough. The rent and bills had to be paid and she had to eat plenty as there were now two to feed. She sat in the kitchen thinking about what to do. She knew that she had to work, not just for the money but it would also help her forget poor Ivy. Later that day, she went out and bought the *East End Recorder* and looked down the list of jobs. There was a vacancy for an assistant cook in a cafe in Aldgate. That was just the thing; she had always been good at cooking.

The next day Lily started work in the Red Lion Cafe. She peeled potatoes in the sleazy dark kitchen, made lots of little steam puddings and fried buckets of chips. The owners, a couple called Mr and Mrs Frank, were Welsh-Italian, a strange mixture, but they were kind and pleasant folk and were extremely good to Lily.

She worked wearing old slippers and a blue overall. The heat in the kitchen was intense; sweat poured down her face, and her lovely hair hung in greasy strands. But she was good at her job. She turned out hundreds of meals for the lorry drivers and factory workers and, because the time went by quickly, she never minded the work. Every evening she got home very tired and ready for bed.

In her pregnant state, Lily developed a very healthy appetite and now it seemed that she was always eating. She particularly liked cream pastries and lots of pudding with custard.

Mrs Frank would look at her curiously. 'Have you always had such a good appetite?' she asked.

'Yes, I love me grub,' said Lily, not daring to admit the reason for this gluttony. The loose overall she wore covered up her crime, if crime it was, as her stomach slowly swelled and the child began to move inside.

On those lonely evenings back home, Lily would sit and talk to her unborn babe. 'It will be nice if you are a girl, me darling, because we'll have a lot in common. And when you're born, I swear you'll not want for a thing. I'll dress you in silks and satins and you shall have everything that I can give you. I will love you all my life because you really belong to only me.' In this way Lily passed the first five months of her pregnancy and never worried about it.

One day she had a letter from Norman asking how she was and if George was all right. Lily wrote back to tell him that George was back up North in the Military Hospital and they were considering a final operation which meant life or death to him.

Immediately Norman wrote again, sending Lily a ten pound note and asking her to come back to him. But Lily put the letter in the fire. In no way was she going to share her lovely baby with him. The baby was hers and she would provide for it.

At six months Lily was quite a size but she still did not slow down. She was cutting slices of bread for sandwiches one morning, holding the bread close to her, when Mr Frank called out: 'That's right, Lily, it's good you have something solid to cut the bread on!' He and his wife now knew Lily's secret and had not shown any sign of disapproval.

Lily stopped, looking down at her belly and laughed outright. 'Oh well,' she said, 'I still do my job, don't I?'

Both Mr and Mrs Frank agreed at this but they were a little concerned about her. 'Better give it another couple of weeks, Lily,' Mrs Frank said, 'and then take a rest. You can come back later, and really you ought to be attending a hospital.'

'What for?' demanded Lily. 'I feel fine.'

'That may be, but for the baby's sake, Lily, you should get advice.'

'Perhaps you are right. I'll go to the clinic tomorrow. But me Mum had five and never went anywhere. She only had the midwife.'

Mrs Frank smiled kindly. 'Times are changing, dear. If you need help, we'll advance you some money.'

'No, I am all right,' said Lily, putting on her coat, 'but thanks. Tata, then.'

As she walked out of the cafe she suddenly felt sad and alone again, and it was with weary steps that she walked towards home. She dreaded that empty house and wondered what she was going to do with herself until the baby was born.

With a heavy heart she reached home and opened the back door. A shadow crossed her path and a gentle voice said: 'Don't be scared, Lily, it's Kasie.'

She spun round to face him, and he stared at her body in open-mouthed astonishment. 'Oh, Lily, my lovely, what happened to you?'

Her stomach was so extended that her dress was taut across it, and her hair awry. Recovering from her initial shock, she backed away from him. 'You should bloody well ask,' she cried, and then ran into the house.

But Kasie caught her. Putting his arms about her, he held her tight. Lily dissolved into hard passionate sobs.

He stroked her tummy. 'Tell me he's mine, darling,' he begged.

She nodded.

'Why did you not tell me before I left?'

'I didn't want to hold you. You were so anxious to go home,' she said.

'But I told you I would be back.'

'Yes, in two months,' grizzled Lily. 'It's now been four months and I'm six months pregnant.'

Kasie kissed her hard on the lips and then bent down to listen to her tummy. He kissed that, too. 'Oh, Lily, my darling, what a lovely welcome. You are the mother of my son.'

'It's a girl,' sobbed Lily defiantly.

'Nevertheless, I'm its father, that I am quite sure,' Kasie said proudly. 'It was Victory Night, was it not?'

She nodded again, and Kasie began to laugh. 'Come on,' he cried. 'Where's that lovely smile? I'm back and stationed in London. What about that? I'll be able to take care of you both.' He paused and looked around the room. 'Where is he?'

'You mean George? They took him away from me,' she said.

'Best news I've heard in ages,' said Kasie with a grin. 'Now, darling, let us sit and plan our future. And I've brought lots of presents for you.'

Out of his kit-bag came a hand-knitted woolly cardigan, sweets, wine and cheese. 'My family were all pleased to hear about you and have sent you these,' he said. 'My parents are looking forward to meeting you, and now I have to tell them the news that they will be grandparents.'

He was so sincere and happy that Lily snuggled close to him. 'Oh, Kasie,' she cried. 'I could love you so much.'

With the return of her lover, the happy times began again for Lily. She still felt unhappy about poor Ivy but she knew that nothing would bring her back.

'Can't live with the dead, Lily,' Kasie said when she told him about Ivy's death. 'And in this war I have discovered how close we are to death each moment we live, so I get all I can from every day I survive.'

His good-hearted way of dealing with problems did Lily a lot of good, and soon she stopped worrying over George, and even the baby. Live every unfulfilled moment, she told herself.

They were also soon back to the nights in town, with the boozing, and the parties. At first Lily objected to Kasie's constant lovemaking, but he had laughed at her. 'It won't hurt my son. It will do him good.'

'I would hate to lose this child now,' said Lily, 'even though in the early days, I sometimes thought of doing what Ivy did.'

When he heard this, Kasie's face whitened in temper. 'Forget that foolish woman,' he hissed fiercely, 'because if you tried to hurt my son I would strangle you with these bare hands.' He spread out his small, tough-looking hands before her.

Lily was frightened. 'Don't say that,' she protested.

'Oh, I'm quite capable of it, Lily,' he grinned. 'That's what this lousy war has taught me—how to kill.'

But most of the time now it was a carefree existence for her. Lily would meet Kasie sometimes in the West End, where he had landed himself a soft job at Headquarters, in Marble Arch. He had plenty of money which he spent very easily. He bought lovely things for her baby, indulged her with candlelit dinners, and they went to lots of shows. But still he did not want to live with her in that gloomy house. Still he always made excuses that he had to get back to his billet.

'I could not live in this dump,' he would say. 'I don't blame you, but you are not a domesticated woman. If you are going to look after me when we are married, you must change your ways.'

Lily stared at her sink full of dirty washing-up and sighed. George would have soon cleared that up, but Kasie wanted a servant as well as a bedmate. Oh well, she thought, she would cross those bridges when she came to them. At the moment life was great. She felt so full and blooming with good health. Her body was swollen with pregnancy, her hair was bright and shiny and her cheeks glowed pink.

Together they would walk hand in hand through the park and kiss and cuddle. Life with Kasie was still full of romance. He talked of his plans for the future once he was released from the navy. He would take her home to his own land, he told her. 'I have applied to buy a ship from the navy,' he said. 'They must compensate me for the loss of my own ship that the Germans bombed out of the water. And when the war is officially over—and it will be soon—I will try to buy a ship from them.'

Lily was a little taken aback by it all. She was not sure she wanted to live in a ship, especially with a young baby.

Kasie refused to listen to her reservations. 'It will be wonderful, darling. We will sail along the Rhine right through to the Danube, and I will make a fortune doing a bit of smuggling.'

'Isn't that illegal?' asked Lily.

Kasie grinned. 'Of course it's illegal,' he said, 'but I can assure you that, having discovered that the whole system is very corrupt, I will never sit down and let them ride over me again.'

It was during these conversations that Lily began to get a true idea of Kasie's character. He was brave and loving, as she knew, but he was also not truly honest. Still, who was she to complain? Didn't her old dad regularly nick from the docks? So in some way they had something in common. And she felt events taking her over. Kasie was so full of plans and dreams for the future that she felt she could not turn back now.

Lily had booked up at Bancroft Maternity Hospital to have her baby. She went as Mrs Brown, and no questions were asked since these were strange times and it was a wise child that knew its own father.

'I wish you would stay with me at night,' she complained to Kasie. 'I get very nervous in case I am taken bad in the night.'

He put his arms about her and looked thoughtful. 'All right, my lovely,' he agreed, 'but I will not sleep in that room where that dirty old man slept. I'll arrange my own sleeping quarters.'

That evening, to Lily's surprise, Kasie arrived carrying a huge bedroll, sailor fashion over his shoulder, and two big hooks which he screwed into the ceiling. He slung up his hammock over the old bed-settee where Lily slept, and jumped into it, holding out his arms. 'Come on, my lovely,' he said, 'come aboard.'

Lily just sat giggling and declined the offer.

So for the last remaining weeks of Lily's pregnancy this was where Kasie slept when not on duty. He would often put out his bare toes and tickle her nose just as Lily was dozing off to sleep and they would lark about together, like two small children.

Feeding Kasie proved to be a problem. He did not like anything that Lily cooked for him. He also hated tea, and she had to make coffee in the special way that he liked. 'You'll be a good *hausfrau* by the time I've finished with you,' he would tell her.

After several disasters, Lily finally lost her temper with him. 'Wot the 'ell do yer eat, then?' she cried in exasperation. She had time on her hands and was determined to please him.

'I don't mind fish,' he replied. 'In fact, I love fish.'

Praying that she was going to solve this problem at last, Lily went down to the market and bought a very large smoked haddock. It was an enormous fish and still had its fins and two holes on either side where it had been hung up at the market. She fried it in a pan and when Kasie came home, she placed it in front of him.

Kasie stared at this fish in amazement. Poking it with a fork, he asked: 'Whatever's this, Lily?'

'It's 'addick,' replied Lily, annoyed that he was being choosy again. She was near her time and very short-tempered. 'You can eat it like that or have some spuds with it.'

Kasie poked the fork in the little holes. 'What the hell are these?' he cried.

'Those are its bleedin' ear 'oles,' snapped Lily, losing her temper.

'Oh, my God!' cried Kasie, going into fits of laughter and waving the fish about on his fork.

In a rage, Lily snatched the haddock off the fork and smacked it into Kasie's face. It instantly disintegrated all over the place.

'*Mein Gott!*' Kasie cried, placing his hand on his head. 'What did you do that for?' He stared down at his uniform trousers which were swimming in fish. Grease dripped down the front of his snow-white shirt.

''Cause there ain't no bleedin' pleasin' yer,' yelled Lily, dashing off to the settee where she threw herself down and wept very loudly.

'Well, that was a disgusting exhibition, Lily,' Kasie said. 'I will get cleaned up and go. If I stay I will only lose my temper and with you in that condition, it is better that I don't.'

Minutes later, she heard him wash under the tap and then the back door close behind him. She was all alone again, and absolutely terrified. Pains had started shooting across her back, but she was not due for another three weeks. 'It might be wind,' she consoled herself and drank some hot water. Kasie would be back when the pub closed, she did not doubt.

Ten o'clock came, then eleven, and then twelve o'clock. Still there was no sign of Kasie. Lily was devastated, and the pains were getting worse. He might have met another woman, she thought. This idea made her hot and sweaty. He might have gone to Charlie Brown's and that Elsie Potts would have soon snatched him up. Overwrought with pain and jealousy she rolled about on the settee until one very sharp pain took her breath away. This was it. She must go to the hospital. She picked up her little case which was all ready packed with baby things, and went painfully out into the dark lonely street.

It was two in the morning when she almost fell into the waiting room at the Bancroft Maternity Hospital. At six o'clock she gave birth to a tiny golden-haired babe who weighed only six pounds.

'She'll be all right,' the nurse said. 'She's well covered but sort of tiny.' She held the minute bundle and handed her to Lily, who could not believe her luck. This was hers, really hers, her own lovely baby.

Now everyone can go to hell, she thought defiantly—Kasie, George and even Norman. For she would never be alone again.

After lunch the sister came up to her bed. 'You've got a visitor, Mrs Brown, but it's not usual to let other visitors in until the husband has seen the child.'

'He's abroad,' Lily said quickly. 'Who's out there?'

'He said he was your brother,' said the sister tactfully. 'I'll let him in but he mustn't stay long.'

Kasie came in carrying a bunch of flowers and a parcel under his arm. Although he was grinning that mischievous grin, his dark eyes surveyed her with true concern. 'I told them I was your brother,' he said.

Their hands clasped together. 'Why did you desert me?' Lily asked.

'Oh, Lily, how was I to know it was time?'

'Well, I made it,' she said triumphantly. 'Walked all the way here and I had the little girl that I wanted.'

Kasie's lips twisted. 'Please, Lily, don't rub salt into my wounds.'

'Go on, get sorry for yourself,' she jeered.

As he put his head down on her hands, she could feel the hot tears that fell from his eyes. She bent over and kissed the back of his neck whispering, 'Now, Kasie, don't let me down, love, will you? I'll be home next week.'

He placed the parcel on the bed. It contained a beautiful, expensive shawl for the baby. 'Goodbye, Lily,' he said softly. 'Thank you for my lovely child.' Then he walked dejectedly down the ward and disappeared through the doors at the end.

Lily lay back in bed looking dreamily at her baby. She had that same kind of fair hair as Kasie, Lily noted. She felt so happy, overwhelmed by that wonderful feeling most mothers never forget when their first-born is placed in their arms. And it was an extra special feeling for Lily, for this tiny golden-haired babe was hers alone. So right from the beginning she was very possessive of her.

'I've always wanted to call my baby girl April,' Lily said to the nurse attending her.

'Well, why not?'

'She's born in January, so how can I do that?'

'Well, it's your choice,' replied the nurse patiently. 'Not every April is born in that month.'

'I'm called Lily May because I was born in May,' said Lily, vaguely wondering what Kasie would like to call his daughter.

'What about Avril?' suggested the nurse. 'Now, that's a pretty name and quite like April.'

A bright smile lit up Lily's dark-blue eyes. 'Yes, that is nice and rather unusual.' She looked at her babe. 'Yes, darling, you will be called Avril. I hope you'll like your name.'

With her baby wrapped in the beautiful shawl that Kasie had brought, the following week, Lily went home in a taxi. She was disappointed at the cold, empty gloom of her house, for she had hoped that Kasie would be there, but still she was very happy and contented with her lovely new baby. Lily set about making her home warm, and to buy a cot and a pram, she drew out her savings.

No one came to see her beautiful child but Lily did not care. She had no friends left, few relations and her neighbours knew very little about her. Lily nursed her babe, rocked her to sleep and wheeled her out in the pram, all the while wondering why Kasie had not arrived but not caring too much. Sometimes she tried to analyse her feelings for him. Did she love him truly or was it just sex that held them together? She did not know, any more than she could define the sudden contentment that possession of this lovely baby gave her.

After she had been home two weeks she received a letter from Kasie.

> Darling Lily,
>   I was sent back on duty. Sorry, my lovely, I was not there when you needed me. I am back on the mine-sweepers but not for long. Why don't you and the baby come down to Portsmouth and stay with me? It would be nice to live here like we used to. I am ashore three nights a week.
>
>   All my love, Kasie.

'In no way,' declared Lily to her baby as she threw down the letter. 'You and I, Avril, will stay here. You do not need a father, not while you have a mother.'

Lily did not answer Kasie's letter, but the next day she went off to register her baby as Avril Brown, whose father is George Brown, then on to the Social Welfare to collect her dues as an ex-serviceman's wife whose husband was permanently disabled. She returned quite pleased with herself finding that she was not going to be too badly off, with the rent paid, free baby food and money for living expenses.

'I've got plenty of clothes,' she told Avril. 'He was pretty generous, that way. And we don't need much in the house—one room will do us, love.'

Avril's little face creased up with wind.

'Oh,' cried Lily, 'bless your little heart, there's a nice smile for your mum.'

So with a wide charming smile she would walk her pram along the high road and sit in the Tunnel Gardens and, for quite a while, was content with her lot.

One day she wrote to Norman asking him if he would visit George in the psychiatric ward of the Military Hospital in Manchester. She told him that she was unwell and unable to travel.

Norman responded with a long letter begging her to come back to him. 'This is your home, Lily,' he wrote, 'and always will be. We will take George from that lousy place and he will settle down nicely here with us.' And he had enclosed another ten pounds for her fare.

Lily tore this letter up in small pieces, too, saying: 'But now there are two of us, ain't there, Avril?' She put the ten pounds in her purse. 'That will be handy. You shall have one of those lovely fluffy bonnets off the stall down in Crisp Street,' she promised her baby.

For some time, Lily continued to live in her dream world which included only herself and her baby. Three more angry letters arrived from Kasie demanding to know what the hell was wrong with her, and why she did not write to him. But Lily only smiled at his words and muttered: 'Leave me alone, you bloody devil. I'm free of you all.'

One evening as spring approached and the evenings were getting lighter, Kasie arrived pale of face and very unsteady on his legs. He stood at her back door like either an avenging angel or a devil—Lily was not sure. She tried to shut the door but he put his foot inside and said sternly: 'Lily, open up or you'll be sorry.'

She left the door and ran inside. Snatching up her child, she stared defiantly at him across the room.

Kasie put down his gear and emptied his pockets on to the table—the main item being a bottle of Bols gin. He then strode across the room and took the baby from Lily's arms, holding her up to look at her. 'Hello, hello?' he cooed. 'Papa's come home.'

Lily began to cry. 'She's my baby. I don't need you now. Why didn't you stay away?'

He put the baby in its cot and his arms went around her. 'Lily,' he said, 'you will always need me, and I, you.'

Her head rested on his shoulder as she sobbed, 'Oh, Kasie, I can't go through all that with you again.'

He grinned into her hair. 'Why, was it so terrible, Lily—all the love we had and the lovely child that resulted from it?'

'Oh, but I can't stand the indignation of it all,' wailed Lily. 'I'm afraid for her, I don't want her to be a bastard.'

Kasie took possession of her lips, murmuring, 'Lily, my lovely, how I have missed you.'

She gave a feeble struggle but knowing it was a losing battle, she put her hands up to feel the little nest of curls at the nape of his neck as she used to do, and let her body lean towards him. 'I know I'm a fool, but love me, darling, I really need you.'

After they had made love, Kasie became very serious again. 'Now,' he said. 'You and I have to face the future. I want no more nonsense from you about that poor afflicted husband. Now that you are rid of him, you must sue for a divorce. You'll get that easily. Then you and I will go home together, now that the war is over and the Japs are finished. So I want no more trouble with you.'

Dressed in a long blue dressing gown, Lily was making Kasie his coffee. It was quite a task and had become a work of art for her, he was so hard to please. She was concentrating on this and so she did not reply at once.

'You were listening, I hope?' Kasie said sharply.

'Yes,' she said, 'but it's not an easy decision because George and I need to stay together. For one thing, he's officially registered as the baby's father and I live on Social Welfare money.'

'Well,' Kasie said decisively, 'you can stop that welfare money. I will take care of my wife, and as soon as your divorce is made official, I will take you and the baby home to stay with my parents.'

Lily looked surprised. 'You mean you'll stay here till we are married?'

Kasie nodded. 'If possible, yes.'

'Well, you have had a change of heart,' she jeered. 'I thought you couldn't wait to be back with that wonderful family of yours.'

He looked sad. 'You could be right there, Lily, but circumstances have changed, so I want us to be married when I take you home. I have already told my parents of my plans, and they are expecting you.'

Lily was puzzled. Something was different. Kasie had never seemed to bother too much about the legality of marriage, being twenty-nine years old and so far not settled down. Yet suddenly he was prepared to stay in this country, which he hated, and wait for her to be divorced. Was it the baby? Or had something else happened, something she did not know about? Her astute Cockney mind turned these things over cautiously, for she was not going to jeopardise the happiness of her lovely Avril for anything in the world.

'Well, it's up to you, Kasie,' she said. 'But I'll not do anything until you're out of the forces and working in civvy street—I'm not that sort of mug.'

He stared at her in astonishment at her words. 'Why are you always so mercenary?' he asked.

'It's the way I was brought up, I expect,' replied Lily with a casual grin. 'Where I come from, we know how to survive and I'm not putting all my eggs in one basket.'

'Please yourself, Lily, but I think I'll be out of the Forces in a few weeks. Then I will have to go home and return when I get a work permit.'

For the next month or so, Lily went on in her same old way, looking after her baby and sleeping three nights a week with Kasie when he wasn't at his billet. They settled down together with surprising speed.

'We're like an old married couple, Lily,' he jested.

'As long as you don't put me in the family way again, you and I will get on fine,' threatened Lily, but with humour.

One day Kasie brought all his personal possessions to Lily's house and left them for her to look after. They consisted of a suitcase full of letters and documents, and an old banjo.

'I'd like to leave these here, Lily,' he said. 'I cannot trust anyone in that billet.'

When Kasie was out, Lily would often open the suitcase and try to decipher Kasie's letters from home. She had always felt that there was some mystery about Kasie's family, and she hoped to find some clue. But the letters were all written in Dutch so she couldn't understand a word. There was, however, one little note which intrigued her. It was just a square of pink paper with two lines on it, and signed Wrenska. This seemed very significant to Lily, and she went over it so many times trying to make some sort of sense of it. She could not stop thinking about it so finally she decided to ask. 'Who's Wrenska?' she said casually after supper.

Kasie went quite pale. Collecting himself, he said, 'Oh, Lily, I see you pry into my property.'

'Well, what have you got to hide?' she demanded, on the attack.

Getting up from the table, Kasie got the letter from the suitcase and held it in front of her as he translated it into English. 'It says . . .' His voice sounded very emotional. '. . . I never want to see or hear from you again. Wrenska.'

'Well, then,' said Lily. 'What's it all abaht?'

He looked seriously at her and sighed. 'It seems that I must tell you the whole sad story,' he said. 'Wrenska was my girlfriend, the one I was going to marry who disappeared the night Amsterdam was bombed. As you know, I was working aboard my own ship bringing timber from Sweden for the Nazis—it was not of my choice that my ship was commandeered—so I never saw her again. And, as you know, I escaped to England.'

'So this person's not dead after all,' said Lily brightly.

Kasie shook his head. 'That's right, but it's not the end of the story. I discovered later that Wrenska ran from the Germans and found my mother and father who had gone to Friesland and were living in a house on the land for the first time in their lives. But Wrenska was left pregnant. I hadn't been sure but we had suspected it for some weeks, which is why we were anxious to be married. My parents took her in and took care of my son, who was born in their home. He is now a fine strong boy almost five years old. When I met him I was very proud of him . . .'

Lily had gone deathly white, and a strange, sickly grin had appeared on her face, for this was not at all what she had been expecting to hear. For a moment after he had finished his story, she was speechless, but then her quick temper came to her aid. 'Oh, gor blimey!' she cried. 'Don't tell me you've put two bastards into this world . . .'

'That is so,' he replied with a guilty nod.

'Well, of all the bloody nerve!' she yelled. 'And here's me sitting and listening to that bloody tall story about you taking Avril and me back home with you.' Suddenly her blue eyes flooded with tears. She rushed over to the baby and swept her up in her arms. 'Oh, darling,' she cried. 'Please forgive me, I called you a bastard. Oh, my gawd, what am I going to do?'

Kasie put a gentle hand on her to restrain her. 'Calm down,' he said. 'I have no intention of deserting you. I love you. Wrenska has gone with the past—that is what that little letter is all about. She has fled with our son to another part of Holland because I told her I would not marry her. I told her I would not marry her because I love you.'

Lily stared at him wide-eyed with disbelief. 'Oh, please, Kasie, don't try to destroy me,' she begged. 'I don't care about going to your God-forsaken country, I like it here, but don't say that our love and our beautiful baby were all for nothing.'

Kasie almost ran at her. Grabbing hold of her, he held her tight. 'Lily! Lily!' he cried. 'Try to understand. I have upset my family. I let down the mother of my son just for you. So, darling, try to understand my love and my need of you. I did all that for you.'

'Oh, Kasie,' cried Lily, melting into his arms.

Although she gave herself to him then, it seemed that a dark cloud had arisen over the horizon. For the rest of that day she thought about this girl who had waited all this time for Kasie. Part of her wondered if she could face the situation bravely and tell him to go back to her, but white hot jealousy of this girl rose within her. Her legs trembled at the thought of another girl having shared Kasie's love, and of that sturdy son he was so proud of.

'That Wrenska woman won't get him, Avril, I swear to gawd she won't,' Lily hissed under her breath to her sleeping babe. 'Kasie is your daddy, and that's how it shall remain, even if I have to go to that damned unknown land. I'll make sure of that, I swear by all that's holy, I will.'

CHAPTER ELEVEN

The Final Decision

A difficult period followed Kasie's confession about his ex-fiancée and son. Lily would often taunt Kasie and provoke him into a terrible row, whereupon Kasie's usually calm and gentle temperament would change, and an inner hardness would bring a murderous glint to those dark-brown eyes. When that happened, Lily knew it was time to withdraw and shut up, for she soon learned that all that yelling and shouting of insults would get her nowhere. In some ways she was a little afraid of him.

Yet through all these times, their lovely child held them close. Kasie adored Avril and he would play with her, petting and fussing her like some would a young kitten. He would strum quietly on his old-fashioned banjo and sing old sea shanties to lull her to sleep. His voice was so sweet as he crooned, 'Oh, Shenandoah, I love your daughter.' Lily would sit and listen and at such times her heart would soften and she felt she just loved him more and more.

Kasie drank fairly heavily while he was off duty, but he seldom went out to the pub, preferring instead to bring his rations of Bols gin home with him. He was also very strict about not allowing Lily to go out and leave the baby alone—though there was little need for him to worry; Lily was an excellent mother.

'We must make plans for the future, my lovely,' he tried again to raise the subject.

But Lily still did not want to face the future. She was happier now than she had ever been in those first post-war days, willingly sharing her lovely child with Kasie. Occasionally the spectre of that woman in Holland who had Kasie's five-year-old son haunted her.

'I love only you, Lily,' Kasie would insist when she raised the subject. 'I have fallen out with my parents because of you—what more do you want of me?'

Lily would stare at him suspiciously and declare, 'Why don't you go home and marry her? Avril and I will get on all right, we have each other.'

One day when she said this, Kasie grabbed her arm in a brutal manner. 'Listen, Lily,' he said firmly. 'Don't try to provoke me. I have made plans for our future life together, so behave yourself.'

'Oh, that's what you tell me,' was Lily's terse reply. 'Besides, how do I know that she won't come and try to get you back? How do I know what she is like?'

'She is a very lovely woman,' returned Kasie, that mischievous grin hovering about his lips. 'I am most particular, I choose my women with care.'

Overcome with jealousy, Lily struck out at him. 'You swine! You lousy swine!' she yelled.

He held on to her wrists and laughed. 'But it's still you I will marry, my lovely,' he said.

The briefest physical contact with each other always led up to the ultimate thing: they would make love and the quarrel would be over. A fight always brought the same results. Kasie would slide his hand up her leg to find her lips and, in spite of Lily's efforts not to give in to him, she always did. Each was always hungry for the other's body. And as time went by, this passion never waned.

Soon 1945 made way for 1946. Avril was now one year old. Her hair had grown quite long and was a mass of flaxen curls. She had Lily's dark-blue eyes and terrible temper and often screamed and held her breath until she was blue in the face, just to get attention. Kasie spoiled her rotten and frequently bought her lovely presents, including a silver rattle with "Papa to Avril" engraved on it.

Some days Lily would dress up Avril very prettily and go on

the bus to meet Kasie in the West End where they would all have tea together. Surrounded by his countrymen, Kasie would show Avril off to them, for he was still a very popular figure with his shipmates.

Lily no longer wrote to Norman or bothered to visit George. She had become completely bound up with Avril and her lover Kasie. Although she had promised that she would make some arrangements to get a divorce from George, she hadn't actually managed to get round to it yet.

A few months into 1946, Kasie began to make extra money. He was determined to get a stake, to get some money to start them off on their new life. He needed enough money to make an application to the English navy to buy an old ship. 'They are due to compensate me for the loss of mine during the war,' he explained, 'so I should get it cheap. I have seen one I fancy—an old landing barge they used in the Normandy invasion. At the moment it's laid up, down in the docks at Southampton.'

Lily tried to be interested in his plans but in her heart she did not like the idea of living in a ship. 'Suppose the baby falls in the water?' she asked cautiously.

'Well, you, my lovely, will just have to learn to swim,' grinned Kasie.

'I'm scared of the water,' cried Lily. But Kasie just laughed.

One day Kasie told her that he was going away for a week or so. 'Try not to miss me too much,' he said, 'and do not in any circumstances go out and leave the child alone.'

'Oh, shut up!' snapped Lily. 'You know I won't. But where are you going?'

Kasie grinned and from his pocket, he produced a small string bag. 'Look, see these? Guess what they are.'

'Onions,' said Lily.

'No, they're bulbs, Dutch bulbs, Dutch anenomes.'

'Well, what abaht them?' demanded Lily.

'These little bulbs, Lily,' he said proudly, 'are going to make us rich. I have twenty thousand of them.'

'Where did you get them?' Lily was suspicious.

'I have good comrades who bring them over when they

return from leave. These are the first bulbs to reach England since the war and they're worth a lot of money. I intend to go up the north-east coast where there are big nurseries and make big money selling them.'

'But that's illegal, isn't it?'

'Yes, *leiblin*, but extremely profitable,' he grinned.

'Well, do be careful,' she warned. 'I don't want you to end up in the nick.'

Kasie swept her into his arms. 'Don't worry, my lovely, we'll be rich and very happy together.'

Lily smiled but she felt a little disturbed about it all.

After a week's absence, Kasie returned jubilantly waving a bundle of notes in his hand. 'Well, here's to the next assignment. I have to pay the boys to bring the bulbs over but it's still a hundred percent profit.'

'It's smuggling,' cried Lily. 'Suppose you get caught?'

'Well, darling, you'll have to say a prayer for me then,' he grinned.

A few days later, he made his application to buy the old landing barge he was so keen about, and he came home very excited. 'Now, we own a ship,' he said proudly. 'We'll call her *Avril II*. So now at long last we have a home of our own. You and I will sail the Rhine and the Danube. I intend to have *Avril II* converted into a deep river barge: she'll be ideal for that.'

'Can I see it?' asked Lily, not really sure if she wanted to.

'Yes, but not yet. First I must go to Southampton and get her out of dry dock. I'll arrange for some tugs to tow her to a steady harbour and get her a complete refit. All that will cost a lot of money but still at the moment I have sufficient.' He paused as though unsure of going on, but he did. 'By the way,' he said rather shiftily. 'My comrades were forced to dump the last bulb consignment in the sea. The Customs had got wind of them. But no matter, we'll find something else.'

Lily sighed and laughed. 'I think you're a bit of a crook,' she said affectionately.

'Maybe,' laughed Kasie holding her in his arms, 'but also an excellent lover!'

Kasie was as excited as a schoolboy about his ship and talked of little else. Now on release from the Forces, he spent the weeks down at Southampton making arrangements to take *Avril II* back home to Amsterdam harbour. He only came home at weekends, but he always brought Lily presents. One day he gave her a little silver butterfly on a chain. It had a centrepiece of blue china with a painted windmill on it, and was exceedingly pretty. He put the chain around her neck. 'This is for you,' he said. 'It's a present from my mother. She has at last agreed to take you into her home as my wife and the mother of her granddaughter.'

'Well, that is good of her,' Lily returned sarcastically.

Ignoring her comment, Kasie fastened the chain clasp and kissed the back of her neck. 'That is a piece of Delft china in the centre. It comes from a place not far from our home.' And Lily was very pleased with the gift and her irritation soon subsided.

One Sunday Kasie asked her to go down to Southampton for the day to see his ship before it was towed out across the Channel to Holland. 'I will have to travel with her,' he said. 'You can come, too, but only to the two-mile limit. Then the tug men will bring you back.'

Lily looked very dismal. 'So will you be going home?' she asked.

'Only to prepare us a home, Lily. In the meantime, I'll make arrangements for you to live with my parents until the ship is afloat.' He was so happy and so enthusiastic about it all that Lily did not have the heart to argue with him.

'Now,' he continued, 'you must come to Southampton because Avril must be there to launch her ship.' His eyes flashed with excitement. 'This is just the beginning,' he said. 'There will be many more ships that we own in Avril's lifetime . . .'

'I'm not sure that I want to go to Southampton,' grumbled Lily.

'But you must come,' insisted Kasie, 'otherwise I will be so disappointed. And you'll like it down there—there's lots of fresh air, which will do you both good.'

As always, Lily gave in to Kasie's wishes, and on a bright

spring day, she travelled down to Southampton with Avril who was dressed all in white with a fluffy white bonnet covering her flaxen curls. Sitting on the train, Lily kept wondering why she was going, but the sight of the sunlight gleaming on Southampton Water cheered her up. 'Look, Avril!' she said. 'It's the seaside.'

There was the huge shape of the Queen Mary looming out of the water with her hundred port holes and huge funnels. 'Oh, my,' said Lily in awe. 'Just look at that, Avril, that's the biggest ship in the world.'

On Kasie's instructions, she took a taxi from the station to the coal quay, where he was waiting for her. As usual, she felt a warm inner glow when she saw him. It was nice to belong to someone who loved you, she thought.

Kasie was wearing his funny little skipper's cap on the back of his head and some baggy blue overalls which made him look short and dumpy. She was surprised to see her normally neat, smart Kasie in these working clothes. He kissed her warmly and showed her a small row-boat which was weaving back and forth at the dock side. Holding Avril, he jumped in very nimbly and then put out his hand to Lily. But she hesitated. Staring down at the cold grey water, her face was as white as death.

'For God's sake, Lily, come on, jump in!' Impatiently, Kasie caught hold of her and roughly pulled her off the dock side into the boat.

Huddled on the seat, Lily clutched Avril close as Kasie's strong arms rowed them out to sea where a huge, derelict-looking ship was anchored. When they reached the ship, Lily froze with fright when Kasie tried to persuade her to climb the ladder to get aboard the landing barge. She squealed with terror as the tugmen leaped into the boat and hauled her up the side.

Kasie cursed her under his breath, but then yelled at her. 'Must you make a complete fool of me? I told these men that you are my wife, but whoever heard of a skipper's *frau* who cannot even get into a row-boat without that big performance?'

Lily was trembling too much to reply. She stared in horror around the rusty old ship which smelled of coal dust.

Kasie led her into a small cabin and put Avril on the bunk. Lily felt so depressed that she was on the edge of tears. He suddenly cuddled her tight. 'Sorry, *leiblin*,' he whispered, 'but I have been working hard to get her afloat and I'm a bit short-tempered.'

'I'm also sorry, Kasie,' she said, 'but sorry that I came.'

'Now, Lily, it's a fine ship, I know it's dirty but it has been lying in the coal quay for a year. Once it is painted and repaired you will not recognise it. And there is so much room, we can turn it into a grand home for us and our many children.'

Suddenly there was a loud banging on the side and shouting.

'We're getting underway,' explained Kasie. 'Won't be long, I'll take you up on deck when we are out of the Solent.'

But Lily was not even listening. She sat wiping the coal dust from Avril's hands and face.

Ten minutes later, Kasie was back. He picked up Avril, covering that lovely white pram suit with black grease. 'Come on,' he said, 'let's go up on deck, Lily. Bring that bag—that is our lunch.'

They sat on some oil drums at the prow of the ship as she went slowly out to sea. The white-topped waves broke over the bows and the sun shone down from a very blue sky, warming Lily's long, bare legs. To her surprise, she began to enjoy herself as they ate their sandwiches and drank a bottle of wine. When it was finished, Kasie smashed the empty bottle against the side crying out, 'I name this ship *Avril II*, and God bless all who sail in her.'

Avril chuckled with glee, and Lily smiled at the sight of her man, with his bright curls blowing in the wind, his bare feet and the wind blowing out those baggy overalls. He came and sat close and cuddled her. 'Come on, Lily,' he said. 'We'll go down into the cabin.'

There on the small bunk, they made passionate love, and afterwards Lily cried, overcome with love and nerves, for today Kasie was leaving her.

'I'll be back soon, Lily,' Kasie assured her. 'But I will send you your fare if I cannot make it myself. Promise you won't let me down . . .'

Lily got off the bunk, put on her knickers and pulled up her stockings. 'Let's hope those bloody workmen weren't peeping through the port hole,' she laughed.

The thump of the engines had ceased and the ship that earlier had rolled from side to side was now steadier.

'We are out at sea now, Lily,' said Kasie. 'You are only allowed to go the two-mile limit, and as much as I would love to take you with me, it is not possible. Goodbye, my darling and take care of our baby.'

With a final passionate embrace he helped her into the boat with the two workmen from the tug company. This time she was a little calmer but she was afraid to look the tugmen in the eyes.

So ended Lily's sea voyage. Once back on the train to London she began to think about what life would be like aboard that dirty old ship, and she was not entranced. Little Avril's new pram suit was filthy and God only knows what she looked like with all the rust and coal dust. And the strange smell of engine oil lingered on her hands. No, she was definitely not impressed.

She stroked Avril's head of hair. 'You know, love, I don't think we want to live on that mucky boat, do we?'

But the baby cooed and said, 'Papa! Papa!'

Lily smiled sadly. 'I know, darling, you love him too. What are we going to do?'

That night a terrible thunderstorm blew up and the rain beat on the windows of the house in Sewell Street as Lily, still feeling slightly sick, thought of that rocking and rolling boat with Kasie on board braving the stormy sea. She prayed that he was safe.

As the weeks passed and she thought about what it would be like to live in a foreign country, she liked the idea less and less. She felt trapped and wondered how the problem would be resolved. Then she had a depressing letter from Kasie in which he said that he had had a bit of bad luck with the ship which lost its rudder in the night of the storm. This meant there would be a much longer wait to get it into dry dock for a refit.

Lily did not care about the ship's problems and she felt she had got a reprieve for a while. Shortly afterwards, another letter arrived from him urging her to sort out her divorce. 'We can be married out here,' he wrote. 'I have in the meantime made arrangements for you to live with my parents in Friesland. I love you and miss you, so do not let me down.'

An angry flush came up on Lily's cheeks as she read it. He seemed to be stalling, she thought, and irrational thoughts rushed through her mind. Was he trying to put her off? Had he met that other woman and had a change of heart? As she fed Avril with a spoon, hot tears of jealousy rolled down her face. 'He's your papa, Avril, and I won't let her have him.'

Kasie was so well involved with his own troubles, that he had sent her no money. The rent had to be paid, so it was back to the Welfare for Lily, as Lily Brown, wife of a disabled service man.

Although this made her feel bitter, she tried to be philosophical, too. 'Let him go, Lily,' she told herself repeatedly. 'He will soon forget you.'

She wrote to the hospital to ask how George was, and then she wrote to Norman asking him to visit George. The hospital wrote back, stating that with the aid of a new drug, George was vastly improved. They were now considering rehabilitating him.

Lily was betwixt and between when she heard this news. She did not want George home while she had Avril to care for but she did not want to desert him entirely, either. Her guilty feelings about George made her suddenly hit upon the idea of moving to a new address where Kasie could not find her. She went to the Housing Department telling them she wanted to move, but they told her that she could not yet. They said her area was due for development, but it would take time before they could give her a council flat.

'Well, that puts the kibosh on that idea,' Lily said to Avril as she went home. She wasn't really sure what she wanted at all at that point.

Kasie finally did send her money for her fare, with a note. 'I cannot come and fetch you but will be waiting at the Hook for you both,' he wrote. 'Don't forget to get a passport. Looking forward to seeing you. Love, Kasie.'

'He'll be bleedin' lucky,' said Lily, putting the money in her purse. 'Let's go down to the market, Avril, and I'll buy you a pretty dress.'

So Lily spent Kasie's money on toys and sweets for Avril. She found that she was living for each day, trying to put Kasie out of her mind.

As time went by, Kasie began to write her long, angry letters, demanding to know what date she intended to sail, and whether she had got her passport. What was wrong? Why did she not write?

But Lily ignored these questions and just went her own merry way. For a while, she lost all sense of reality, allowing the love for her daughter to surmount all her other commitments. She went about just living for each day. She would forget to pay the rent, and with the money indulged Avril with sweets and ice lollies, expensive toys and pretty clothes. Half-way through the week she would have spent all her welfare money but Lily did not worry, she just muddled along till next pay day.

Throughout this strange time, she often thought about her love for Kasie. Her passion for him had not subsided even though he was absent from her bed, but deep in her heart she knew that theirs was a self-destructive love affair. He was inclined to be selfish and often cold and cruel and she could not live up to his expectations. Sometimes she was overwhelmed with jealousy. She would think about that woman in Holland whom Kasie had obligations to and then she would be convinced that there must be several more women around the world, if she knew the truth. Knowing that she had never completely trusted him, she often wondered if some other woman was sharing his bed at night. Kasie was so hot-natured he gave all for love. It could not be easy for him to be alone.

Then she would wonder if she could really cope with a lifetime of him. He seemed determined to load her up with children and that was one thing she now knew she did not want. No one, she vowed, was to come between her and Avril.

One day, she was wheeling the baby in her pushchair along the West India Dock Road feeling a trifle despondent. She had spent all the rent money, her feet ached and her long hair blew untidily across her eyes. She eased the pushchair in order to push the hair from her face, when it jarred to a sudden halt. There stood Kasie with his foot on the brake. She stared at him in amazement.

'Well, Lily,' he said with his usual grin, 'Don't look so pleased to see me.'

'Oh, blimey!' cried Lily. 'Where the bleedin' 'ell did you spring from?'

'Not from the air, I can assure you, my lovely, but from the river. I came over on a Dutch potato boat now unloading in the dock.' He bent down to kiss Avril.

Despite his apparently easy manner, Lily noticed that Kasie's face was very white and tense. He needed a shave and that wild mop of curls had grown long. Dressed in an old navy blue Guernsey sweater, baggy pants and old plimsolls, he certainly did not look like her smart, neat Kasie.

'But why this sudden appearance?' she demanded. 'What's wrong?'

'You know perfectly well,' he said quietly. 'You and I have plenty to discuss, but I haven't got much time. I have to be back aboard the ship before six o'clock or I will be arrested for illegal entry into your country.'

He took hold of the pushchair and wheeled it away from the main road down through the back streets beside the river. Lily said nothing but she walked dolefully along beside him feeling very apprehensive.

'Now, Lily,' he demanded, 'why haven't you answered any of my letters? What exactly have you done towards getting a divorce? And why did you not get a passport and the sailing tickets?'

'I don't know what you're gettin' so het up about,' complained Lily. 'I said I'd come, didn't I? It's just not convenient at the moment.'

'Lily,' he said sternly. 'Don't play games with me. What date are you planning coming to me—the year 2000?'

'No need to be sarcastic,' complained Lily. 'You know it's not easy for me.'

They had reached a lonely spot where the Regent Canal wandered into the river under an old iron bridge. They stopped and Kasie pulled her around to face him, looking down at her very seriously. 'I am tired and very frustrated,' he said. 'I've been working night and day to make a home for you and Avril, and you never replied to any of my letters. So what am I to think? That once more you have changed your mind?'

Lily stared at her feet feeling very guilty.

He held on tight to her wrists. 'Tell me what you're thinking, Lily,' he said. 'It's now or never.'

Lily looked up at him dubiously. 'I don't get a lot of time,' she said lamely. 'Avril takes all my day up.'

A dark murderous glint came into those brown eyes. 'For God's sake, Lily,' he cried, 'for once in your life tell me the complete truth! Do you love me? Do you want to spend the rest of your life with me or not?'

Out of sheer bravado and feeling trapped in a corner, Lily went on the attack. 'Bleedin' 'ell!' she cried. 'I'm 'ere, ain't I? Wot else d'yer want of me?' But she knew she didn't have a leg to stand on.

'You know I've had bad luck with my ship,' Kasie said, ignoring her outburst. 'So I have taken a job as mate aboard a Rhine barge. This is not only for myself, but to get extra cash for you and Avril. And now what thanks do I get? You gradually back out of our bargain.'

Lily had begun to cry. Kasie moved forward and held her in his arms. 'You have to decide,' he said. 'Otherwise I will lose myself in the world. An old sailor can easily do that.'

She put her head on his shoulders. 'I can't do it, Kasie,' she sobbed. 'I don't really know why, but I think it's because I am afraid to take Avril to live in that dirty old ship.'

Kasie sighed and gently pushed her away from him. 'This is the last thing I wanted to do to you, Lily,' he said, 'but our baby goes with me.' He put his hand on the handle of the pushchair in which Avril slept peacefully.

'Oh no, you don't!' Lily yelled, making a grab at the pushchair. 'She's mine! Go away and leave us alone!'

'No,' he said grimly. 'It's now or never.'

Lily tried to strike out at him but he pushed her violently against the iron wall of the bridge. She cracked the back of her head and was for a moment stunned.

His eyes glared as he put his hands threateningly about her throat. 'I have only to crack your neck and toss you into that canal,' he warned, 'and I will be out at sea with Avril before they even find you.'

Lily gasped at the pressure on her neck. 'Oh, Kasie, don't hurt me.'

His grip tightened and she knew he meant what he said. Her legs went weak and she was on the point of collapse when suddenly he released her, swearing loudly in his own language. Then he crashed his fists against the iron wall of the bridge. 'God, how much more can a man stand?' he cried brokenly.

The backs of his hands were split and blood squirted everywhere. Bright red splashes appeared on Avril's little white silk dress.

'Oh, Kasie,' screamed Lily, 'look what you have done to your hands!'

He stood weeping, and tears poured down his face. Snatching the white sheet from the pushchair, Lily tore it in half and bound his wounded hands with it. He stood white and submissive as if all the fight had been drained out of him.

'Pull yourself together, Kasie,' she begged. 'Come, let's go to the hospital and get your hands attended to.'

'Oh, Lily, Lily,' he sobbed. 'How can I let you go?' Blood was seeping through the bandages. He glanced down at his hands. 'A little blood-letting will not hurt me,' he said. 'I must get back on board that ship or I'll be in more trouble.'

Very subdued and looking weary and devoid of all emotion they walked along side by side in silence to the West India Dock.

At the dockside he hailed the skipper who gave him the signal to come aboard. Turning to her, he said in a quieter voice, 'I am going home, Lily, but if this is goodbye, it must be forever. I'll never come back again.'

She threw her arms around his neck crying, 'Oh, Kasie, I love you, I will come to you, I can't live without you.'

He stood looking at her. He was so pale and the bandages on his hands were still seeping blood. 'Be sure, Lily,' he said. 'For God's sake, be sure, because it's life or death to me.'

'Oh, darling,' she clung to him desperately.

His stern face softened as he bent over and kissed her. 'I am truly sorry, Lily,' he said. 'I tried to hurt you, but I am at the end of the road.'

'I swear I'll come to you,' she wept.

'All right, be there next week, I'll send you the sailing tickets this time. Don't let me down, Lily, I cannot face life without you.'

There was a movement aboard the ship and a hoot of the siren. 'I had better get on board,' Kasie said quickly. 'She's due to pull out.' Releasing Lily's grip, he ran lithely up the gang plank and, without a backward glance, disappeared below deck.

Forlorn, Lily pushed the baby in the pushchair back to Limehouse. Her neck felt stiff and her eyes sore and red with weeping. 'Oh, Avril,' she wept, 'what are we going to do now?'

After a week she received a long love letter from Kasie.

. . . You are my life. Without you I cannot go on. I swear I'll be good to you and Avril. Go and get a passport in your maiden name. It will avoid complications, I am sending the sailing tickets for May 6 and money for travelling expenses. I will be waiting for you at the Hook when you get off the boat. This is the very last time I will ask you. I swear to God that if you let me down we will be finished forever.

With love, Kasie.

Lily read the letter very forlornly, but she knew that she did not have much choice. 'Oh, well,' she sighed. 'I suppose we'd better do as he says.'

The next day, Lily set off to get herself a passport. If she had known how complicated it would be she would never have tried but after an afternoon of climbing over red tape and shouting at those officious clerks at the Passport Office, she finally emerged with a passport in the name of Mrs Lily Brown and Avril Brown, having been forced to produce her marriage certificate. She also had her visa, which was just a visitor's permit lasting only two months. She knew that Kasie would not be too pleased about the short-term visa, but she couldn't help that. 'At least if I don't like it there, I can come home again,' she told herself. For still she had an uneasy feeling, a fear of crossing the sea and leaving behind all the familiar things that made up her world.

However, on May 6, 1946, Lily began her journey to join Kasie across the sea. She had packed a few clothes haphazardly the day before and had not bothered to pay the rent which was already in arrears. Nor did she notify the council that she would be absent for two months. The long train journey to Harwich tired her. Avril was very lively, and jumped around the train compartment, drawing the attention of the other travellers who admired this bonny child dressed all in white, with her rosy cheeks and blonde curls. Still very gloomy, Lily got aboard the night ferry, which was very crowded. With Avril cuddled in her arms, she lay in her cabin trying not to think about the cold grey North Sea which she had caught a glimpse of as she came aboard. Avril was tired after her performance on the train and slept peacefully. Luckily it was a smooth crossing and, although Lily's tummy rumbled in fear, she was not sick. At dawn, she stood waiting on deck holding Avril in her arms as the ferry anchored.

As they docked, Lily saw two well-shod feet walking up and down the dockside and she knew that Kasie was there waiting for her. Despite her weariness, it gave her a warm comforting feeling inside. And going through the Customs was made easier with Kasie on hand; he had wheedled his way onto the dock side, because he knew someone in charge.

The warm embrace and his delight at seeing Avril made Lily's heart miss a beat. Avril was very excited and called out, 'Papa, Papa.'

'At last, Lily,' Kasie said. 'Today I am the happiest man in the world.'

He picked up her suitcase and carried it while Lily pushed the baby along in the little blue pushchair. The early morning breeze was fresh and invigorating and Lily suddenly felt light-headed and carefree. Perhaps it had all been worth the worry, she thought, delighted to find herself back in a happy-go-lucky frame of mind.

Her first impression of Holland was one she never forgot. 'Blimey! It's all bleedin' bikes and boats,' she exclaimed as they crossed a hump-backed bridge over a very wide canal, and cyclists peddled madly past them. Down in the water, there were literally hundreds of boats—big ones, little ones, sailing boats, row-boats and some nice big house boats with net curtains and red geraniums in the windows.

Kasie grinned. 'It will be very nice when you learn our language, Lily,' he said. 'Then you might even avoid all those swear words.'

Lily was now in a relaxed mood. She giggled. 'Not me,' she announced defiantly, 'I'll never talk all that bleedin' foreign stuff.'

Kasie sighed indulgently and kissed her on the lips. They stood on the path in such a long embrace that passers-by stared curiously at them.

'I intend to educate you, my lovely,' he said, drawing away. 'And what I cannot accomplish, my mother will complete.'

'She'll be bleedin' lucky,' retorted Lily, quite unabashed.

'Maybe I will be sorry I made you come to me,' he said suddenly very seriously, 'but today I am exceedingly happy.

And my mother will go crazy over Avril. She has three grandsons already. This will be her first granddaughter.'

Lily felt a jealous twinge, uneasy about the fact that he was so anxious to share Avril with his mother. She could not understand it. Watching him now as he folded a blanket over Avril's chubby legs as a protection against the cool breeze blowing in from the sea, Lily noticed how tender and gentle he was with the child. Surely she had not made a mistake. He did love them, so surely he would cherish and protect them, she told herself. But still within her, this anxious feeling about pulling up her roots nagged at her. Well, she told herself, the visa was only for two months, and she had already decided that if it became impossible in Holland she would return home. But her own common sense told her not to let Kasie know about this just yet.

'I have got us some lodgings at the Hook just for tonight,' Kasie explained, 'and in the morning we will travel north to my parents' home in Friesland.'

The rows of houses in the town were very high and overlooked the harbour. 'That is because the land is below sea level,' explained Kasie, 'so there is always the danger of floods.'

Lily stared out at the grey cold North Sea and wondered silently if it would sweep in and flood the town that night. What a place to live, she thought.

The room that Kasie had booked for them was high up on the top floor of one of these strange-looking houses. There were some flagstones outside the entrance and a number of children ran in and out of the building, their wooden clogs making a terrible clatter. Inside it was clean and homely. The landlady was a big, blonde, jolly woman with wide plaits of hair wound about her head and a starched white apron tied around her thick waist. She wanted to delay Lily to gossip about the war. As she chatted away, Lily listened politely without understanding a word, and the landlady laughed loudly when Kasie finally explained that Lily did not speak the language.

Lily felt rather numb as they climbed the five flights of uncarpeted stairs to their big bare room which was also very clean. There was a double bed against one wall and an old-fashioned carved cradle for Avril in the corner.

The landlady brought up their supper on a tray. It was very welcome, and consisted of two kinds of bread—black and white—cold meats and cheese, and a bottle of wine.

When they had finished eating, Kasie put out the tray and locked the door. 'Now,' he said with a twinkle in his eye, 'we're back in our own little love nest . . .' They kissed and cuddled and larked around for a while. But before they went any further, they had to put Avril to bed. Kasie bathed her in the big sink in their room and finally managed to persuade her to settle down in the little wooden cradle. He sat on the floor beside her rocking the cradle and crooning a German cradle song in his sweet low voice.

Lily undressed and lay on top of the bed listening to him. Strange inner stirrings excited her as she remembered Kasie's lovemaking, and she put out her hand and stroked his smooth, fair, freckled neck as he bent over the now sleeping baby.

'Won't be long,' he whispered.

She got in between the cool white sheets and in no time his sweet-smelling naked body was beside hers and they were back in that passionate ritual of love that bound them so close.

In the morning they said goodbye to their hostess and all her many children who stood outside their home waving and smiling. Kasie had generously distributed coins among them.

'My, what a family!' said Lily. 'Seven kids.'

'We have big families in Holland,' Kasie explained. 'That lady's husband is still a prisoner in Russia and she has to struggle to feed them. We have very meagre rations here; the Germans stripped our land bare and it will take many years to recover.'

But Lily did not worry about such things. She was more concerned about her appearance. Determined to look her best when she met Kasie's parents, she had dressed carefully in a smart grey suit and a burgundy-coloured hat with a neat brim.

'How do I look?' she asked.

'Fine,' grinned Kasie. 'Just like a Dutch *hausfrau*.'

Lily was slightly annoyed, and not quite sure of his meaning. 'I wish you wouldn't take the mickie,' she said.

Immediately Kasie looked sad at having offended her, for there was always a slight verbal misunderstanding between them. Kasie had learned his English from books, and often Lily's choice vocabulary puzzled him. And so it was the other way round, too.

The journey across Holland to Friesland was very stimulating. From the train window Lily stared in wonder at the miles and miles of tulip fields. The variety of colours astonished her, she could not believe such sights existed. As they travelled on Kasie pointed out all the things of interest—the wide rivers, the cool, slow-moving canals, and the windmills along the flat, green countryside. Lily was fascinated. It was so different from anything she'd seen in England.

At the end of the train journey came the long trip on the ferry across the stormy Zuider Zee to Friesland. Now Lily did not feel so good, she was very queasy and wanted to stay below decks in the saloon. It horrified her to see Kasie staggering about the sloping deck carrying Avril shoulder high, their fair hair blowing in the wind. However, Avril seemed to enjoy it, she was chuckling with delight.

'Oh, be careful,' cried Lily. 'You might trip and fall into the sea.'

Kasie returned Avril to her arms. 'Avril must learn to know the sea and its changing elements,' he said severely. 'After all, she is a skipper's daughter—even if I do have a landlubber for a wife.'

In the early evening, when the sun was setting and cast a golden sheen on the water, they reached the small island of Heeg, one of a series of small islands in the middle of lakes. There stood a picturesque house made of red brick with tall chimneys and paved courtyard. It was a welcome sight to the travel-weary Lily, though her heart suddenly thumped hard, for she was a little afraid to meet Kasie's parents.

Yet there was little need to worry. As they came to the door a blonde, blue-eyed woman of comfortable proportions came to greet them. She embraced Lily and then took Avril from her arms with soft, loving words which Avril seemed to understand. The baby grasped the enamelled crucifix which hung on a thick gold chain about her grandmother's neck.

'*Or zat is mio,*' laughed Grandma.

Those were the first words of Dutch that Lily ever understood and she laughed too. Avril responded to this warm affection and went willingly into the house in her grandma's arms. Then Kasie's father stepped forward to greet Lily in a gruff voice. He had a big bushy moustache and stern eyes, which like Kasie's lit up when he smiled.

Lily took his offered hand and knew instantly that she liked him. That was the start of a happy association that was to be evergreen. He nodded his approval to Kasie and then embraced Lily in his strong, muscular arms.

The room they had walked into was bright and warm with white-tiled walls and a white-enamelled stove that threw out a welcome heat. The table was laid for supper with shining cutlery and a snow-white tablecloth. In the centre there was a huge bowl of red and yellow tulips.

They sat down to a merry supper with well-cooked meat, lots of vegetables and a pudding to finish. After supper Oma (Kasie's parents were to be known as Oma and Opa, meaning Grandma and Grandpa) whisked Avril off to get her ready for bed. Lily was about to protest when Kasie put a gentle hand on her arm. 'Let my mother do it, Lily,' he said. 'She will look after her.'

Opa opened a bottle of cognac and they all sat around the big table. The red-shaded light suspended from the ceiling on a chain was pulled down to give Oma better light for her sewing. Kasie and his parents chatted non-stop, but not one word did Lily understand. The room was so warm and cosy, she soon felt her lids drooping and tried desperately not to doze off to sleep.

They all laughed at her, and Kasie took her for a walk around the lake to help her wake up. A large moon cast a silver gleam on the still water.

'You know, Lily,' said Kasie, putting his arms around her, 'my parents really like you, but then I knew they would.'

Lily smiled. 'I like them, they're nice, but I can't talk with them.'

'Oh, it will come to you,' he reassured her. 'Soon you will be gossiping all day long with my mother. She is wild about Avril. You realise that mother is the boss. That is how it is in Dutch homesteads—the hen rules the roost,' he jested.

Lily had an uneasy feeling that Avril would be taken away from her, but she did not say anything.

When they returned to the house, Opa and Oma had discreetly disappeared to their bedroom which was on the ground floor and had low windows looking out onto the water. The room which was set aside for Kasie and Lily was upstairs and had a big double bed in a deep recess with doors. 'It's just like a cupboard,' said Lily. 'How funny.'

The mattress was stuffed with feathers and was so soft. With Kasie's warm body beside her, Lily felt sleepy and very comfortable. He pulled her towards him under the sheets. 'It's so good to bring you home, Lily, and this is our own place of love.'

'I've never slept in a cupboard before,' murmured Lily as she dropped off to sleep in his arms.

The orderly way that Oma ran her house on the island of Heeg impressed Lily and the peaceful way of life quickly relaxed her. But Kasie told her that his mother was not content. 'Mother does not like it here,' he informed her. 'She will not mix with the people, the farmers, for she is one of the water folk and considers herself superior. I am glad you are here, Lily, for her sake. For even though she will never admit it, when Opa is working, as he still does out on the sea wall, my mother is very lonely.'

'Why don't she leave, then?' asked Lily.

'Well, they came ashore because the Nazis commandeered their ship and now they are too old to buy another. It is my ambition to make a home for them aboard my own ship one day.'

Lily felt a little impatient with Kasie's mother. When she thought about that lovely house, so beautiful and clean, and then compared it with her own East End home, she thought that Oma had very little to grumble about.

Every day was ordered by routine. Each day, they did the same things at the same time. In the early morning by the time when Lily rose, Avril was already dressed and sitting up at the table waiting for her breakfast of thick, milky cereal and buttered rusks which she loved. The adults' breakfast was always plain—even on Sundays—and consisted of hot rolls and coffee and home-made preserves. It was all very nice but sometimes Lily really fancied some eggs and bacon with fried bread and tomatoes, the kind of breakfast she was used to back home.

After the meal, Lily would help Oma to wash the dishes and make the beds. Then there was another break at eleven, when Oma made a pot of tea which she kept hot on a thing called a tealight. The tea was served without milk but with a sort of plain cake known as 'coken'.

In the afternoons they did little chores like preparing fruit to make jam or peeling the potatoes for the evening meal. All this was done in a very leisurely manner, mostly sitting out in the courtyard facing the big blue stretch of water where little boats went sailing by. Oma would chat to Lily in her tongue and between them they did eventually develop a kind of sign language which enabled them to communicate.

All this time, Kasie lazed about doing very little except repair and paint a little sailing boat and, when it was eventually finished, he took little trips across the lake. He insisted that Lily try and conquer her fear of the water and learn to swim.

To her surprise, Lily found that she began to like sailing. Kasie taught her how to move the little sail back and forth at his signal. Sometimes he terrified her, by jumping out of the boat into the water and then hauling her in behind him. Lily would kick and scream and he would laugh and say, 'Lily, one of these days I think you will drown me!'

There was no way to get away from the water; it surrounded

them. Although she still did not swim, in some way, Lily began to get used to it. Then one day Kasie's eldest sister arrived in her ship which was anchored almost outside the front door. She had brought her two young boys with her. They were to stay with Oma so they could go each day to their new school, and Lily was pleased that Avril would have some other children to play with after being alone for so long.

CHAPTER TWELVE

On the Island of Heeg

The slow peaceful existence on Heeg, the regular cleaning, and washing and the three substantial meals each day continued to amaze Lily. Her way of life had always been so haphazard, she could only marvel at the smooth running of this home. Oma was never still, but never really busy either, with her wide smile and spotless apron and her terrific sense of humour. Lily was well aware that never in her whole lifetime had her life been so untroubled.

Avril settled down happily and played with her two young cousins out in the courtyard. She was always anchored to a long rope when outside so that she would not stray near the water.

Lily had been most indignant about this at first. 'I'll not have my child tied up like a dog,' she had protested. But Kasie in his firm but gentle way had persuaded her that it was all right. 'Lily, this is our way of life,' he said gently. 'It's how we protect our young until they can swim and take care of themselves.'

Every morning she watched the children of the island gather at the water front and take off in small row-boats to school on the mainland. Tiny tots rowed their even smaller brothers and sisters. High winds often washed the water over the boats, and Lily looked on terrified that one child would fall out of the boat into the water and drown.

'Our children learn from an early age to travel the water,' explained Kasie, 'so you must conquer your fear and encourage Avril.'

But Lily was quite sure that she never would trust her child in one of those school boats.

Each day Lily learned more of Kasie's way of life but was not yet able to converse. This business of talking in a foreign tongue was quite incomprehensible to her. Whenever she tried, she would end up in a fit of giggles. Luckily, the sign language she had developed with Oma was sufficient for her and they got on very well together.

Every weekend, the members of Kasie's family gathered at the house on Saturday night when a huge supper was served with beer, and cognac was opened up after the meal. It was now late summer and they would all sit out in the courtyard, watching the glorious sunsets which made the huge lake shine with a myriad of colours. Kasie would strum on his little banjo and they all joined in the singing. Feeling part of this group in some ways but an outsider in others, Lily would think how far away all this was from the East End pubs and the roar of London's traffic. It was a completely different world.

Kasie's sister, Rica, was tall and homely. She had braved the inland seas in her small boat and hard living had made her look much older than her years. She spoke some English and she seemed keen to tell Lily of her own adventure in love. It seemed that her husband had been imprisoned by the Allies for working with the Nazis. So alone aboard their ship and anchored in a garrison town, Rica had done the soldiers' washing to earn a living and had apparently taken a lover. His name, she said, was Harry, and he came from Hounslow in England. In excited broken English she would whisper to Lily about her secret affair, and Lily would nod and smile and pretend to understand.

'You know Hounslow?' Rica would ask. 'Harry from Hounslow,' she would tell her repeatedly.

When Lily asked Kasie about Rica and her lover, he snorted scornfully. 'Bloody bitch. Harry! There's probably Tom, Dick and Harry, if I know my sister!'

So perhaps life was not so different out there, after all, Lily would reflect. When the Allied Forces had arrived in London, plenty of girls made fools of themselves, including herself.

Lily often wondered about Rica's two little boys she had brought home with her on her last trip. They were both very close in age—one being seven and the other just turned six, and they looked very unlike brothers. Cornelius was very fair and Fritz was very dark. But then hearing about Harry from Hounslow, Lily thought one might belong to some man other than Rica's husband. But she was not very bothered and with her inborn love of children, she got on very well with both of them.

Kasie often took them all on fishing trips. He sailed the slow moving canals in his sailing boat until they found a cool backwater where he would dive and lark about with the boys and threaten to pull Lily out of the boat into the dark-green water. A deep fear of water still persisted within Lily and she had no intention of learning to swim.

One morning at breakfast when Kasie had already left, Cornelius turned to Lily and said: 'Why is your name Mrs Brown and Avril's Avril Brown? Why aren't you called De Fries, like I am?' He was learning English at school and from Kasie, and was becoming remarkably good at it.

An embarrassed silence descended over everyone until Oma got up and told the boy to leave the room. Although she did not understand exactly what Cornelius had said, she got the gist of it.

The boy went unwillingly, but had the last word, 'If she was married we would all have the same name.'

Lily was puzzled by Cornelius' remark and although she couldn't be sure, she thought that Oma and Opa had started arguing about it.

When Kasie returned from Amsterdam that night, the arguments were still going on.

'There seems to be a lot of trouble going on,' Lily said as she prepared for bed. 'What is it?'

Kasie sighed. 'Cornelius poked his nose into your handbag and found your passport. He's in disgrace for such behaviour.'

'Oh, is that all?' said Lily, 'but then why does he say that his name is De Fries? I thought he was Rica's son.'

The look of guilt on Kasie's face confirmed the suspicions she had had about the boy's identity. 'He's your son, isn't he?' She spoke slowly and deliberately, without taking her eyes off Kasie's face.

For a few moments, Kasie hesitated, but he could see that he had to face the truth. He dropped his fair head. 'I cannot pretend any more,' he said. 'You had to find out one day.'

Lily gasped and stepped back in horror at his words. Perhaps she had guessed the truth but Kasie's bluntness shocked her. Eaten up with jealousy over Wrenska, the boy's mother, she screamed at Kasie, 'How dare you do this to me? How dare you? I'll not have my Avril in the same house as Wrenska's son. I don't want to have anything to do with Wrenska!'

Kasie grabbed her tightly by the shoulders and held her.

'Lily, listen!' He was firm again. 'Cornelius is my son, yes, but he is just a little boy and part of our family, you must never forget that. Oma has taken care of him since his birth, they have fed and nourished him all through the bad times of the Nazi occupation. Wrenska took him away for a short time but she did not really want him—she took him to spite me. So when she abandoned him, Rica took him in as a brother for Fritz.'

But all this meant very little to Lily. She was so eaten up with jealousy of the boy's mother that each time Wrenska's name was mentioned a burning hate went through her and already she began to think of Kasie's frequent trips to Amsterdam, supposedly to check on the progress of his ship. 'How do I know that you are not still seeing his mother when you are in that town?' she said suspiciously. 'Why was all that secrecy necessary?' she demanded. 'Why wasn't I told he would be living here?'

Kasie shrugged. 'I don't know, really. My parents thought you should know but I was afraid that you might reject the boy if you knew the truth about him. I was thinking of Cornelius. This is his home and the idea of someone else rejecting him was too much to bear. Now I see it was a mistake to keep it a secret.'

'But how do I know you don't still see his mother?' returned Lily sullenly. 'How do I know you're not lying to me about her?'

'His mother hates the sight of me and would not cross the

road to see me,' Kasie replied a little sadly. '*You* are my woman, the one that I have chosen for a wife. That we are not yet legally married is your fault, not mine, and I have no regrets, at least not so far,' he added a little sarcastically.

Lily resented this and flew into a quick temper. 'Well, I'm *not* tied to you, thank gawd, so I'll go back where I belong, home to England.'

Kasie went quite white and his eyes glowed, but he controlled himself. 'Well, Lily,' he said coldly, 'that is your prerogative. Do it if you must.' With that, he walked out of the door and left the house.

Lily watched him from the front door as he strolled along with his hands in his trouser pockets. He went to the village inn, where he stood outside awhile, chatting to the lads of the hamlet, who lounged about there. Soon they were all chatting and laughing.

A white hot jealousy consumed Lily at the realisation that she could not completely share Kasie's life, and she sat down on the wooden steps in the entrance, put her hands over her face and wept heartbroken tears of home sickness. How she longed for the noises of London—the chatter of the Cockney voices and the roar of the traffic!

After a while, Oma came and put a comforting arm about her. 'Come,' she said softly. 'Coffee time.'

So Lily went inside and dried her tears. For a while she sat with the old couple at the oval table. Oma served coffee in small dainty cups with small squares of dark chocolate, and Opa shared his bottle of cognac with her. Their concern and gentleness warmed her just as the cognac did, and for a while she forgot her troubles. She did not understand much of the conversation between the two of them but she guessed that Oma nagged Opa about Kasie's behaviour, while Opa was inclined not to take it very seriously.

Kasie came in at midnight very drunk. With a grunt, he lay down on the rug in front of the stove and promptly went off to sleep. Oma got up from her chair and put a woollen wrap over him. There was not much more to be said or done that night, so they all retired to bed.

Lily spent a restless night, lying in bed and waiting for daylight to arrive so that she could get up and find her way back to England. She would forget Kasie, get away from him and forget him, she vowed.

She must have dropped off to sleep in the end because she was woken up in the morning by Kasie who came in with his hair all wet from a swim in the lake, and a sweet smile on his face. He was carrying a tray. 'Good morning, my lovely,' he said cheerfully. 'Look, I have cooked you an English breakfast.' He put the tray on her lap, and there was a large plate of eggs and bacon, rolls and a pot of coffee. It all looked very appetising. Recalling how she had grumbled so much about the plain breakfasts she usually got Lily couldn't help smiling.

'I couldn't get a newspaper,' said Kasie, bending down to kiss her forehead.

Lily started to giggle. All her anger had disappeared. 'I'm sorry, Kasie,' she said, putting her arms about his neck.

He stroked her hair. 'Now, eat first, Lily, and we will make it up afterwards.'

He sat on the end of the bed watching her enjoy her breakfast, a sad smile on his face. When she had finished, he took the tray and placed cool dry lips on hers. 'Seeing as I spent last night on the floor, I think we'll sleep late, you and I . . .' he murmured.

His arms went around her and Lily almost sobbed, 'Oh, Kasie, how can I leave you?'

'Stay, darling, I have no wish to live without you.'

That evening a grand family discussion went on for hours after supper. Lily could not keep up with what was going on and having hardly slept the night before, kept dozing off. At last she was woken by Kasie shaking her. 'Wake up, Lily, we have at last reached a decision. We are a close family and always discuss our problems in this way. My mother has explained how unhappy you are when I am away and does not think we should be apart so much. I agree with her. Now, since I am needed in town so much to take care of the ship, I think that we should go and live on her now until I can get her into the proper dock for the shipwright. This plan will also mean that I shall no longer have the expense of paying a watchman to look after her. How does that suit you, my lovely?'

'As long as I am with you and Avril, I don't care where I live,' said Lily, full of feelings of love.

So with all the arguments settled at last, Opa brought out his bottle of brandy and they sat around the table chatting and finally singing. Lily held Kasie's hand under the table, and tears of happiness flowed down her cheeks.

The day they left Heeg for Amsterdam, Opa rowed them across the lake to the railway station on the mainland. Lily watched his strong arms pulling the oars and thought how sorry she was to be saying goodbye to Oma and Opa. She had grown very fond of them during her time in their house.

By evening, they were in Amsterdam. From the station, they took a taxi to the harbour. There was the old landing barge lying at anchor amid a whole colony of boats. Lily thought it looked just as rusty and dilapidated as ever.

Kasie heaved Lily up the ladder and, on reaching the deck, she stood looking about her in dismay at the slippery iron deck, the ply ropes, pots and boxes all over the deck. She wondered if she was doing the right thing by taking Avril from that nice comfortable home on Heeg.

'Welcome home, Lily,' grinned Kasie, carrying Avril on his shoulder. 'Look out there,' he said, pointing to the water. 'There's no need to be lonely in Amsterdam harbour.'

Lily stared down at the other boats. There were rows and rows of them, of all shapes and sizes with lines of washing strung up across the decks and waving in the breeze. 'People live here all the time,' he said. 'These are our neighbours.'

Like most Dutch people, the neighbours turned out to be very friendly. They called out greetings as they passed by and soon Lily always waved back to them. There was constant activity in the harbour, with boats coming in at night and going out in the morning. During the day, Lily's neighbours would come aboard to chat and there would always be farewell drinks when one of them pulled up anchor.

Kasie wasted his time away down at the water front with Avril sitting on his knee while he chatted to the other skippers all dressed in their flat caps and wide trousers.

In the evenings Lily and Kasie would go down to the tavern to eat and spend a very merry evening with plenty of drinks and a sing song. And there was never any worry about Avril since, unlike in England, children were allowed in the taverns.

Gradually, Lily began to get used to life on the water. She usually wore slacks, a sailor's jersey and white plimsolls, and felt very comfortable. But she still complained about the ship being a 'dirty old tub'. For it had lain in a coal quay in Southampton for nearly a year and very little had been achieved during its three months in Amsterdam. The coal dust still lingered everywhere and got into Avril's nice white woollies. It made Lily furious that she was always having to do the washing because this had to be done up on deck in an old tin bath and in salt water which was hauled up in a bucket. Then the soap would not lather in salt water, so Lily would have to sweat all the harder over her task. But she insisted on doing it. If there was one thing Lily hated, it was to see Avril in a grubby dress. When she got really fed up, she would nag. 'Why can't we get a flat in town?' she would ask Kasie. 'Why do I have to live on this dirty old tub?'

'This dirty old tub, as you call it, cost good money,' Kasie would reply. 'And she is still eating it up in harbour fees so I cannot afford to rent you a flat, Lily. And in any case, you must get used to this way of life, for it is how we will live until I make a lot of money and then, darling, I'll give you anything you ask.'

'That'll be the day,' replied Lily scornfully. 'What do you do all day, you lazy sod? You hang about down on the water front and drink gin all day and fill up with beer at night.'

Kasie would look downcast at her words. 'Oh, Lily, give me a little time, and if I cannot get into the shipyard, we'll put her up for sale and I'll get a job.'

For Lily there were so many hazards about living aboard ship. For instance, the milk boat came each morning to deliver milk which was poured into a big jug. This milk, Kasie insisted, had to be boiled but Lily either burned the milk or forgot to boil it altogether. 'Oh, what's the difference?' she would declare when Kasie scolded her.

'It must be boiled, Lily,' he would say. 'It came straight from the farm and we have had no direct sterilisation of milk since the war. If it's not sterilised it might carry disease—and you want to protect your child, don't you?'

Lily could hardly argue with him then.

She and Kasie also argued about the drinking water, which was delivered by boat once a week. Lily was always very extravagant with it and inevitably, they would run out before the next delivery arrived, causing arguments between them.

But despite all the aggravation Lily had plenty of fun in Amsterdam harbour and made many friends. One of these was a little coloured girl called Easi who came from the Dutch East Indies. Easi lived aboard a ship with a white man, who, some said, was a German. The couple had sailed this ship from the Indies but it had broken down so, like Kasie, they awaited their turn for the shipwrights. Easi's man was a brute and often beat her. On these occasions she would flee over to Lily, weeping as she hopped across the decks from boat to boat, her arms a mass of bruises.

Lily would shout at Easi's man, 'You bloody German bastard!' But he would only laugh at her.

Lily would comfort Easi who would then return to her man until the same thing happened again. It made Lily quite exasperated but there was little she could do about it all. It made her angry that Kasie was friendly with the man, too. 'How can you talk with that swine after the way he beats his poor little wife?' she demanded one day after Easi had been over.

Kasie gave a nonchalant shrug. 'He's all right,' he said. 'He is not a Nazi, and besides, she's not his wife. She's only a coloured girl.'

At that, Lily exploded. 'Oh,' she gasped, 'I think that

comment is despicable. Sometimes I don't understand you at all.'

And so they went on, quarrelling, making up, and making love. Their lovemaking never subsided.

With time, Lily conquered her fear of water. Kasie had his sailing boat brought down from Heeg, and they often sailed across the harbour on lovely bright windy days. On Sunday mornings races were held on the water between members of the harbour community, and it was at one of these impromptu regattas that Lily crewed for Kasie, and was surprised by her own skill at manoeuvring the small sail. Kasie, who was very competitive, had trained Lily especially for this day and they crossed the finishing line first.

After the race, a party was held in the tavern and the organiser, a very genial gentleman who liked to show off his knowledge of the English language, came over to Kasie and, smiling at Lily, he said, 'The English zeefok. The English *frau* she is zee good on zeefok.' Lily got up and smacked the man across the face. Kasie grabbed her and led her off, trying not to laugh. He explained between chuckles that the small sail that she had manipulated so well was known as a "fok".

Lily was deeply embarrassed. 'Shall I go and apologise?' she blushed.

'No need,' replied Kasie. 'I don't suppose they'll invite us again.'

'Oh, what a silly bloody language!' she said.

Lily was always very nervous of being left alone on board the ship when it got dark. She insisted that she had seen the ghosts of soldiers walking about down below.

Kasie scoffed at her. 'Oh, don't be so silly, the only spirits that I know of are in the bottle of Bols.' He was quite unsentimental about such matters and showed no sympathy for Lily's fears. She often felt very lonely, and longed for her own kind to talk to. Once she took a walk along the shore and as she wandered she looked up at the tall houses. In one street she looked in through the big windows and saw some women sitting in them. Two of them called out to her and Lily acknowledged their greetings with a wave and a smile. Then to her delight she saw two young British service men coming timidly along the road. Delighted to see someone from home, she stopped to greet them with a cheerful smile. 'Hallo,' she said, 'where you from? London?' But the soldiers hurried on past and ignored her. One did seem inclined to stop but his pal dragged him quickly away. Lily felt very hurt by their behaviour, and she told Kasie so later that evening.

Kasie looked shocked. '*Gott auf Donner*, Lily!' he cursed. 'What am I going to do with you? You not only prowl about the red light district and get friendly with the prostitutes but you actually stopped those boys. They thought you were soliciting. I'm lucky you weren't arrested.'

'Oh, Kasie,' said Lily in despair. 'What a bloody fool I am! I should have known, I lived in the dock area all my life in London—what the 'ell is wrong with me?'

All these small incidents upset her and in her heart the longing for home grew. She had now been away from England for more than ten weeks and it seemed a lifetime.

One day Kasie came in looking very white and tired.' 'Lily,' he said, 'it's no good. I have to give in. It will break my heart but I have put the *Avril II* up for sale. I cannot wait another three months for a refit as there is very little money left in the kitty.'

In some way Lily felt a sense of relief. 'Let's go home to England,' she suggested. 'Maybe you'll get a job there on the docks or something.'

Kasie looked surprised. 'Is that what you really want? I had hoped you were happy here.'

'Yes, I am, Kasie, but I'll never feel really at home. I miss my own kind of people.'

'Well, I will not give in. I will sell the ship and we will live it up a bit and then I will go as a mate on a Rhine barge. You'll like that, Lily. We'll get posh quarters and I'll have a regular wage.'

But Lily did not answer.

The following Sunday morning, two tugs came to pull the

Avril II to her new home. Kasie had sold her and she was to be a ferry boat in Sweden.

Lily was in a very bad mood, as the ship had been sold much more quickly than she had expected and she wasn't yet ready to move. She was on deck doing Avril's washing and told Kasie that she had no intention of being hurried. When Kasie tried to reason with her, she yelled and swore loudly and said that no one could make her go until the next day.

The tugmen and the shipping agent came aboard and they all joined in the argument. Little Easi came skipping over the decks to help Lily and to take care of the baby. Other harbour folk just stood on the boats and stared as the argument got heated. Kasie and Lily were shouting in English and the tugmen in German, Swedish and Dutch; it was like the Tower of Babel. Kasie dragged the washing from the bath and threw the water overboard. Lily picked up a bucket of water and threw it at him. The baby screamed and the shipping agent, who spoke some English, endeavoured to calm her down. He apologised for the short notice, and explained that while the tugs waited, money was going down the drain.

Kasie packed suitcases and threw them into a small boat. But Lily folded her arms defiantly. 'If I have to leave this boat like this without any time to pack,' she said, 'I'll go straight back home to England.'

'Please your bloody self,' snarled Kasie. He was almost at the end of his tether and aiming to throw kitchen pots and pans overboard.

Easi brought Lily's coat to her and put the baby in her arms. Tears fell down her face at the thought of losing her friend. 'You have to go, Lily,' she said. 'You can't keep the tugs waiting, it's not advisable, it costs too much money.'

So Lily finally gave in and allowed Kasie to help her into the little boat. Then without a backward glance they rowed across the bay to the railway station—Lily, Kasie and Avril, along with the pushchair, a pile of suitcases and a little stray dog that Lily had taken in. The waves washed over them, and they did not speak a word. When they landed they were wet and gloomy and stood side by side watching *Avril II* being towed out to sea. She looked good from the distance.

'Well, Lily,' Kasie said glumly. 'There goes our first home.'

Lily threw herself into his arms. 'Oh, I'm sorry,' she cried.

'Could well be,' he muttered, 'but it's the last time you'll ever show me up with all your tantrums. I warn you, I've almost had enough.'

So had Lily but she was too upset to reply. She just held the little dog by the lead and stood by Avril in her pushchair, while Kasie went into the station to book their tickets back to Heeg. 'We'll go home,' he had said, 'until I find some other way for us to survive.'

CHAPTER THIRTEEN

The Parting of the Ways

Lily waited for Kasie to return with the tickets, still wet and shivering from the spray of the waves which had washed over the small row-boat when they crossed the bay. Standing there on the shore, she thought she had never in her life been so forlorn. Her hair was a damp, tangled mess and blew across her eyes, and her wet plimsolls stuck to her cold feet. She felt dirty and distraught. She hadn't even had the time to wash before she left. She looked down at Avril whose poor little nose was red and her hands very cold. The child was grizzling miserably. A big lump rose in Lily's throat but her pride would not allow her to weep.

Kasie came out of the station looking white and tired. 'There's no train until the morning,' he said. 'You all look so cold. Come on, we'll find a place to eat and get warm.' He put an arm around her and gave her a sweet, gentle smile. 'Come on, my lovely, it's not the end of the world.'

They found a small cafe and had hot onion soup, Bols, coffee and brandy. It was not a luxurious meal but a very satisfying one. They sat with heads close together, Avril on Kasie's lap and the little dog on Lily's.

'Cheer up, my lovely,' he said. 'At least we're not broke even if we are homeless. I've got twenty thousand gilders for the ship. I've got the cheque here in my pocket.'

'I'll bet the whole of the harbour inhabitants were laughing at us,' said Lily dolefully.

'They are of no importance,' he replied. 'We'll go back to Heeg until I find a suitable ship.'

Lily looked very miserable. 'I don't want to go back there,' she said. 'Let's all go to England. We have enough to live on till you get a job.'

He sighed. 'Lily, my darling, I will not give in. This is my country, the one I fought for. I'll get a good living here even if it kills me.'

'But what about me?' she asked. 'I can't stand this way of life.'

'Darling,' his voice was cold, 'it was your own choice. Do not expect me to change my way of life, will you?'

She knew it was hopeless and didn't know what to do except fuss and kiss the little dog.

This made him angry. 'For Christ's sake, Lily, why did you have to bring that stray hound along?'

'It's not a hound,' said Lily defiantly. 'It's a she and her name is Mimi.'

'*Gott auf Donner!*' he cried. 'It has the name of a French whore! Let it free, it will find another home.'

'No, I won't,' said Lily obstinately. 'Mimi stays with me.'

'Well, Mother will not be very pleased. She has already got three dogs.'

'I'm not going back to Heeg,' said Lily defiantly.

'But why not, Lily? I thought you liked my parents?'

'I do, Kasie. Can't you understand? I'm used to having a home of my own and looking after Avril myself.'

'I can only do my best for you, Lily. If I take a flat in town it will be expensive and I shall never own a ship of my own.'

'Who wants to live on a bloody ship?' Lily almost yelled at him but then the tears began to fall.

'Don't cry,' Kasie pleaded. 'I'll think of something. We have to find a place to sleep tonight, but where and how with a stray dog and a baby, I am not sure.'

'I won't part with Mimi,' said Lily, cuddling the small dog whose coat was of many shades and whose tail now wagged with excitement.

'Okay, you win,' he said. 'I'll ring the harbour master. I believe that Rica and her husband, Jan, they will be in port tonight, so we can stay with them. I hate that Nazi bastard, it really annoys me to have to ask him for a favour. Let's get a taxi, she is on the other side of town.'

So once more off they went, baby, pushchair, dog and suitcases, to the other side of Amsterdam, to where his sister's ship, the *Helga*, was anchored. Now they had to contend with Jan, Rica's husband, who had just been released from detention camp.

Rica welcomed them both with open arms. In her excitement, she gabbled at them in her own language. Her husband, a dark, moody man, said in perfect English: 'Welcome aboard our ship, English Lily.' And Lily was quite sure he meant it.

The ship was warm, bright and comfortable, as those little Dutch cargo ships often are. After her short spell of living aboard the landing barge, Lily could not believe she was really on a ship. The supper table was laid with an embroidered table cloth and lovely china. There was a real kitchen with a big white enamelled stove and shining utensils. When Lily remembered the dark galley in the *Avril II* lit with only an oil lamp, she thought there was no comparison. There was also a small washroom with a portable shower. It was great to wash herself all over and put on a clean dress.

Rica helped her bath the baby and then they all sat down to a grand supper of roast chicken and a sweet pudding made with almonds. It was delicious. They sat drinking and talking till after midnight.

'I can't believe this place,' said Lily. 'It's like a real home.'

Rica smiled proudly, but Kasie turned to Lily and said: 'We do not all live like pigs, Lily, just because we live afloat. I know you had to rough it a little on the landing barge but one day when I get my own ship we will also make it a comfortable home like this one.'

Later, Kasie got a little drunk and argued with his brother-in-law about politics and the war, and talked to Rica between bouts. The conversation was mainly in Dutch and Lily was not able to follow it very well. However, she understood enough to hear Kasie ask Rica where the children were, and Rica's reply.

The meaning of the latter was very clear: 'They are with Wrenska in Rotterdam.'

Lily froze. So, Wrenska was still around and very involved with the family after all. Jealousy gnawed at her heart. She also worried about the fact that Jan had announced that they were sailing to Rotterdam the next day and she and Kasie had agreed to go along. But now she knew that Wrenska was in Rotterdam.

When they went to bed, Lily turned to Kasie. 'Is *that* woman in Rotterdam? I heard Rica say that the boys are with her.'

He got angry. 'Lily, will you let well alone? The boys have started at another school and Wrenska lives in the town near the school, so they stay with her. We have to do these things otherwise our children will not receive a good education. Why don't you try to keep out of the family affairs?'

Lily was a little hurt and that woman called Wrenska haunted her dreams all night. In the early dawn, she awoke to hear the engines beginning to throb as the little ship got underway. There was a heavy swell and the ship rocked from side to side. Lily hugged Avril very close.

Kasie rose and got dressed. 'Better go up and give Jan a hand. He's mad to sail in this weather—a storm is coming up.'

The little ship began to rise high in the air and then down again. Lily felt her stomach heave, it was like going too high on a swing. By dawn the small ship was rolling from side to side as Jan fought his way across the Zuider Zee in the face of a bad storm which sometimes can be much worse in an inland sea. Huge waves crashed over them, the wind howled and the crockery came crashing down and rolled about the floor. Lily was terrified.

At Rica's suggestion, a terrified Lily, holding Avril very tight, staggered up the companionway to the small housing where Jan stood at the wheel with a grim-looking Kasie beside him. The white-topped waves raced towards them like a line of soldiers into battle. Lily was petrified and quite sure she would never see dry land again.

Rica seemed quite calm, and comforted her. 'Soon over,' she

said. But Lily closed her eyes and actually prayed that they would soon be on dry land.

By daylight they had sailed into calm water, and the sun shone. Cuddling Avril, Lily was at last able to fall into a heavy exhausted sleep on the seat in the steering house.

When they dropped anchor in Rotterdam, Lily awoke to see the sun shining on the big town. She heaved a sigh of relief, so glad was she to see the shore and the roofs of the buildings. She had had enough of the endless raging sea.

Over breakfast they talked about the future. Kasie insisted that he and Lily would return to Heeg and Lily insisted that she wanted to go home.

'Why not get a job aboard a Rhine barge?' suggested Jan. 'The offices are in the town.'

'I don't want to live on a damned old barge,' complained Lily.

But Kasie liked the idea. 'It's very comfortable. And if I get a mate's job, you will have nice quarters, the river is smooth and the scenery is fine.'

Rica could see the tension rising. Tactfully, she suggested to Kasie: 'I will mind the baby. You take Lily into the town and cheer her up a little.'

Lily jumped at the idea and immediately dashed to the cabin and dressed up in her nice grey suit and little felt hat. Together they went into the town, holding hands and feeling a little sad because they both knew it was coming to the parting of the ways, and neither of them would give in.

'I'll go in the bank and put my money away and draw just enough for us to have a big spend-up, like we used to do in London,' Kasie told her.

So they lunched in a posh restaurant and afterwards toured the big shops. On the main street they found a lovely shop where he bought her a grey silk dress and a cute little hat. It was burgundy red with an eye veil and fitted close to her head like a bonnet. He put it on her head with a smile. 'Remember, Lily, how you wore a red hat the first time we met? That was what attracted me to you.'

She smiled wanly. 'That seems such a long time ago now.'

'Oh, cheer up, my lovely,' he said, 'I will book us into an hotel tonight and wine and dine you and make love to you. It will be just like old times.'

They had a candle-lit dinner and danced close together. Full of wine and good food, the old magic returned and Lily and Kasie were as one again. They made love that night as never before, and they arrived back on the *Helga* at Sunday lunchtime, both looking radiant and ready to face the world once more.

On Monday morning, Kasie went off to the shipping office and got himself a job on a Rhine barge. He was very pleased with himself. 'I was lucky,' he explained. 'The mate got sick so I have replaced him temporarily.'

Lily said goodbye to Rica and Jan who sailed off to other parts taking with them Mimi, the little dog. Rica had been quite taken by her and insisted on keeping her. Then Kasie took Lily and Avril to another part of the harbour where the huge Rhine barges were docked.

Lily had not realised that Kasie would be working on such a big barge. At one end of the flat deck were the Captain's quarters, at the other end were the crew's quarters.

Kasie told Lily to be wary of the Captain's wife. 'She does not speak English—only Dutch and German—but that is just as well, because she is bound to be very nosy—these Dutch *fraus* often are.'

'Well, why should I care?' said Lily.

'Because, my lovely, your papers are not in order. You never told me that you only had a two month visa. You've already out-stayed your visit by three weeks.'

Lily looked dismayed. 'I'd better go home,' she said quickly.

'No, I did not mean that,' Kasie assured her. 'The Captain is my friend and an old shipmate of mine. We were in the navy together. He speaks good English and will protect us. But be careful of his woman. It will be all right, but unfortunately you cannot go ashore and we will have to hide you when the Customs or military come aboard.'

'Oh, crikey!' shrieked Lily. 'That don't sound too bloody good, does it?'

'Don't worry. On the next trip I will have my own ship and we need not hide you then.'

Lily's new life aboard the big flat Rhine barge was something new. She had her own quarters which were very nice and just like a big flat with bathroom, sitting room and bedroom.

The barge delivered skimmed milk in tins from Basle in Switzerland to Rotterdam harbour, where it was reloaded onto the bigger ships. It went back and forth, back and forth. Kasie worked very hard and did not bother Lily much. She, much to the amusement of the crew members, would like sunbathing on the deck.

Lily quite enjoyed herself but she did not like the Captain's wife at all. The first time she had visited the Captain's wife, she had pointed down at Lily's feet and had yelled something in a guttural voice, which clearly meant that Lily had to remove her shoes before entering the Captain's clean living quarters. From then on, Lily disliked her and avoided her as much as possible.

Gradually the novelty of life on the barge wore off. Whenever they were in port, Kasie went ashore to drink with the crew, leaving behind a lonely Lily. Avril got bored, missing the company of the other children, and was often difficult.

Lily longed to go ashore herself, for the scenery everywhere was lovely, with miles of dark green forest and bright little towns with quaint church steeples. She would have loved to explore them but she had strict instructions from the Captain not to go ashore until her papers were in order.

When they were in Basle she saw the snow-capped mountains in the blue distance and the huge boats full of tourists. She wondered if they were English tourists and thought how surprised they would be to know that she was trapped aboard this bloody great barge. And so, during the voyages they made back and forth along the wide Rhine, resentment slowly built up in Lily, and she quarrelled incessantly with Kasie. 'I want to go home,' she would say. 'I am a prisoner on this thing, and I hate that old rat bag down the end. Also, Avril is miserable, I can't seem to amuse her.'

To her surprise, one day Kasie did not argue with her. 'In

Rotterdam next week, we will leave this barge,' he said. 'I do not like it any more than you do. I have just heard from the shipping agent that he has a ship which he thinks I might like. Then I will go to the burgomaster and beg for an extension on your visa. Then I'll be able to get rations for you and Avril. But, Lily, you *must* write to your husband and start divorce proceedings so that we can legally get married. Once we've done that, life will be a lot simpler.'

Lily looked worried. 'I don't know whether poor old George is alive or dead.'

'Well then, you had better find out,' he replied abruptly.

For the last few days of the voyage, Lily's mind was in a turmoil. She fought with the Captain's wife over the washing line, and annoyed Kasie by refusing to cook for him.

'I can't bloody please you whatever I do,' she yelled and swore at him. 'I am going home, whatever you may say, Kasie. I've really had enough.'

When they were docked in Rotterdam, Lily decided to creep out and go on her own. She took her belongings and put Avril in the pushchair one quiet afternoon when the Captain and his wife had gone shopping in the town and Kasie was down in the big warehouse loading up cargo. Wheeling the pushchair quickly, she left the ship, looking furtively from side to side, and headed for the big bridge that crossed the river. There were several entrances to the bridge, a wide road for traffic and two small paths on either side. Without hesitating, Lily pushed her baby along up the slope onto the bridge. Suddenly a crowd of cyclists came riding at her. One crashed into the pushchair, knocking it over sideways, and then the cyclist, a young boy, fell off his bike. Lily ran to save her baby who was still strapped in the pushchair but was unhurt. Reassured that her baby was all right, she turned and charged straight at the boy who had caused the trouble. 'You silly sod!' she cried, beating and kicking him. 'You bloody square-headed bastard!' She rained violent blows and insults at the poor bewildered lad who crouched on the ground, terrified of this foreign woman and her fierce brutality towards him. A passer-by tried to restrain her and a crowd gathered around her, gabbling in Dutch so Lily never understood a word. Then along came two policemen who tried to talk to her. Lily was quite incoherent with temper and they led her off to the police station where a kindly officer who spoke English explained that she had been in the wrong place, that the path she had been on was reserved exclusively for cyclists. Had she looked at the notices, he told her, she would have seen that not only was she in the wrong place, but also that she had been going the wrong way. So the boy had been surprised to see her there and had been unable to avoid her.

Realising that it had been her fault, Lily finally calmed down.

'Now, tell me where you are staying, and I'll send for your husband.'

Kasie arrived within the hour. His shirt sleeves were rolled up, and he looked hot and grubby, and far from pleased with Lily. 'I told you to stay on board,' he said.

'I'm not a bloody prisoner,' cried Lily. 'And I'm going home.'

Kasie seemed to agree with her. 'I think that is the best thing that you can do, Lily,' he said. 'Get your affairs in order and then return home, for I am sick of all the embarrassing situations you create.'

At the Ferry Ticket Office in Rotterdam, they still argued. Kasie had changed his mind yet again. 'There is no reason why you should not go home with Avril to my mother until I have settled my affairs,' he told her.

Lily looked at his pale face and his wild unruly hair. He was obviously under great strain and she felt very sorry. But she knew what she wanted. 'No, I'll go home and then come back to you,' she said.

His mouth twisted in a bitter grin. 'I swear by all that's holy, I will never run after you again, Lily.'

She softened and held up her lips to kiss him. Kasie pulled her to him and held her very tight. 'Lily, don't leave,' he whispered in desperation, 'we will get by.'

The ferry's siren sounded. It would be sailing soon.

With big tears falling down her cheeks, Lily wheeled the pushchair up the gangway, unable to turn around because she knew that Kasie was crying. He was standing against a brick wall, his arms over his face to hide his misery.

CHAPTER FOURTEEN

The Gipsy Camp

Lily did not remember very much about that long journey home across the North Sea. She spent most of it crouched disconsolately in a dark corner of the ship's saloon. The boat was full of young tourists off to visit England for the first time since the war had ended. They argued and sang, got drunk and very seasick. Then the ferry broke down at ten o'clock in the rough misty sea. It was all one to Lily. She never noticed anything. With Avril in her arms, she huddled down in the big seat trying not to show her tears. Mentally she recalled all the wonderful moments she had shared with Kasie, and thought about how happy they had been during all their time together.

The ferry engines had stopped and the big boat had stopped dead. All the kids shouted and sang. Some got nervous and spread rumours. 'There's a live mine floating ahead of us,' said one young man. 'I've been up on deck and seen it.'

His words reminded Lily of Portsmouth and the time when Kasie would speed out to sea in those fast moving mine-sweepers. How great it was when he came home to her! Yet now she was leaving him. Why? She would probably never know why but some force pulled her back to England, to her own grass roots however poverty stricken they had been.

About an hour later, the engines started up again and the big ferry moved on at last. It got into Harwich very late and it was two o'clock in the morning by the time Lily was pushing her sleeping child through the dark East End streets to Limehouse Church and Sewell Street.

She was coming home at last, she thought joyfully. And how good to feel the solid London pavements under her feet!

Arriving at her house, she tried to insert the latch key into her front door, but it would not move. Puzzled, she went round to the back door, past the old graveyard that held so many memories. Just as she began to try to force the back door, it opened and a huge black man wearing only a pair of short pants stood there. His big body shone in the moonlight. Lily gave a gasp of surprise.

'Wha' yo want, missy?' he asked.

'I want to come in. This is my house,' said Lily.

The man shook his head emphatically. 'No, no, thees is owa house. Yo come wrong place,' he told her.

Behind him appeared a big coloured woman enveloped in a long flowing nightie. 'Go away,' she said. 'Thees middle of night. We lives here.'

Gradually they pushed the protesting Lily out and slammed the door.

'Oh, gawd!' cried Lily to the night. 'It *is* the right house, I must be going mad.'

Slowly she walked back to the main road feeling very downhearted and weary. The old coffee stall still stood under the arch. Well, that was at least a familiar sight, she thought with relief. This was where the down-and-outs lurked and the all-night revellers stopped for a cup of coffee. Usually it was a place to be avoided, but tonight, thirsty and exhausted, Lily stopped and got a cup of coffee.

She sat on her suitcase sipping it and wondering what was happening to her. Around the stall lounged a few drunks and the layabouts who eyed her curiously. A short, stumpy man in baggy trousers and rolled up sleeves, and a trilby hat on the back of his bald head, came towards her. In a loud Cockney voice, which had a kind of guttural accent, he shouted at the man serving the coffee: 'I'll 'ave a cuppa and a hunk. How's tricks, Tom?'

The proprietor nodded and said, 'Evenin', Dutchy.'

Lily was dolefully drinking her coffee when Dutchy turned round and spotted her. 'Gor blimey!' he exclaimed. 'What yer doin' awt 'ere wiff that babe this time o' night?'

'Got nowhere else to go,' Lily said miserably.

He came and stood next to her. 'Bin chucked awt 'ave yer?' he asked sympathetically.

'No,' replied Lily. 'I was travelling abroad and came back to find me house full of bloody blackies.'

'I know, cock,' he said kindly. 'Bloody East End's full of 'em now and more arriving every day. Where yer bin?'

'In Holland,' she replied.

'Oh, wiff the army?' he asked. 'That's my side of the world but I've bin 'ere twenty years.'

Lily let him think she was a soldier's wife from the Allied Occupation Forces.

'You could go up the dosshouse,' he suggested. 'Dahn the Mile End Road. 'Ave yer got any money? There's an 'otel in Aldgate.'

'Nope,' said Lily, 'only got guilders, I forgot to change my money when I got off the boat and it got in two hours late.'

'How many yer got?' he asked.

When Lily produced the bundle of notes that Kasie had given her from her handbag, Dutchy's eyes gleamed greedily. He flicked his fingers through them. 'I'll give yer a fiver for them,' he said. 'Don't know as I'll be able to change 'em, but can't see yer wiffawt a light, and that little babe as well.'

Lily wallowed in his sympathy and gratefully accepted the fiver, not realising that she was being robbed.

'That will get you a bed and a bit of breakfast,' said Dutchy a little apologetically. And when little Avril awoke and began to grizzle, he said, 'Give us 'er bottle, I'll get 'er some warm milk.'

The stall proprietor warmed up some milk and put it in the bottle but still Avril went on wimpering.

'Tell yer wot,' suggested Dutchy, ''ow would yer like to stay the night wiff me missus? She won't mind. Got a big family of me own, I 'ave, it's just dahn there under the arch. I'm all right, bin around 'ere a long time, ain't I?' He turned to the proprietor, who said, 'Nothing to worry about, love. Dutchy's okay.'

Wearily Lily got up from her suitcase, Dutchy took the case

and they trundled the pushchair through the arch into complete blackness. Suddenly Lily felt very panicky.

'It's all right, love,' said Dutchy. 'See that light ahead? That's me billet. We'll be there in a minute.'

They went through a pair of big iron gates and an alsation dog ran out at them. 'Lay dahn,' said Dutchy, kicking out at the dog with his boot.

Lily then suddenly realised that she was in the gipsy camp. It had always been there, the crowd of caravans and the herd of piebald ponies in the huge yard under the railway arch. In the past she had never bothered about them. Gipsy people were different to East Enders, and they lived on their own side of the fence. Now her heart missed a beat. What was she getting into? But from a caravan, and carrying a lighted oil lamp, came a lovely looking but faded woman with a black shawl around her shoulders. 'Who's that with you, Dutchy?' she said. Her voice sounded nice and sort of friendly, and Lily felt herself relax a little.

'It's a gal got stranded,' replied Dutchy. 'Got a baby wiff 'er. Fought you'd take 'er on, just fer t'night,' he whispered in a low voice.

The woman came and put an arm around Lily. Then she picked up the sleeping child and said: 'Come, love, it's all right, nothing to be afraid of.'

Dutchy slouched off into the darkness. 'I'll kip in the old van,' he said. 'See yer in the mornin'. Goodnight.'

In a daze, Lily climbed into the clean, bright and very warm caravan. The gipsy woman wrapped the sleeping Avril in a blanket and laid her on the bed. Turning to Lily, she said, 'Have a warm around the fire, love. Would you like a hot drink?'

Lily, now more relaxed, said, 'I'm sorry to trouble you so late at night but I've been shut out of my house.'

'Council was it?' she asked. She looked shrewdly at Lily with her big hazel eyes. 'Probably commandeered it for the immigrants,' she said. 'It's going on all the time about here.'

'I wonder what they did with all my furniture and belongings,' murmured Lily.

'Put it all in storage, love,' replied the gipsy. 'Don't worry, I expect they'll give you another house, maybe even a new flat. Now, get some sleep, we'll talk in the morning.'

She took off Lily's shoes and helped her onto the bed, covering her with a bright woollen patchwork cover. 'Sleep, darling,' she said, 'it cures all ills.'

Exhausted, Lily slept very peacefully until the morning. When she awoke she found Avril sitting contentedly on the strange woman's lap sucking at her bottle. Outside a great hullabaloo was going on with the children playing and the dogs barking.

'That's all the kids making that racket, but they're not all mine.' The gipsy opened the door and called out, 'Shut up! Stop all that noise and get ready for school!' Closing the door, she said, 'Dutchy and me, we got four children. The rest are cousins. I'm a true gipsy but Dutchy is not. They call us Pikeys in the East End. You seem like a Cockney gel, so I expect you know us.'

'Well, yes,' Lily said, with inner caution. 'But I've never been inside this camp before.'

'We've been here twenty years. Dutchy owns this yard and we keep ourselves clean and respectable, so they leave us alone. But there is always talk about moving us on, yer can't never trust these bloody councils.'

As they chatted, Lily felt a great sense of warmth which emanated from this woman, who was called Maria. She had the sort of earthy motherliness that Lily had been without for a long time. 'It's strange,' said Lily, 'but you remind me of my gran. She got killed in the blitz.'

'Oh well, I'm as much an East Ender as I am gipsy,' replied Maria. 'When I left my family and came to live with Dutchy, they disowned me anyway.'

Soon all the kids came in washed and dressed ready for school. There were two boys and two girls. One girl was a lovely fair child of about ten with blonde, curly hair. The other was dark with long plaited hair.

'That's my girl, Marlene, and Maureen, her cousin. Maureen

belongs to Dutchy's sister who buggered off to Ireland with a bloke. Still, the kids is all right with me. That's Maureen's brother, Steve, and Jamie is my boy.'

The two sturdy lads stood grinning at Lily.

'Go on, off you go and mind the road,' said Maria, and off the children went, their little legs running towards the big iron gates with the alsation dog running with them. 'Got two older boys,' explained Maria. 'One works with Dutchy, and the other boy is doing his National Service. Got a nice little business, has Dutchy. Collects scrap iron. Never had no regrets, and always gave me a good living, did Dutchy.'

All conversation was carried on in this slow, relaxed manner. Maria moved very little, and when she did it was slowly and carefully.

The bright caravan was full of knick-knacks—big old-fashioned cases, gilt mirrors, paper roses, pretty bits of china and silver candlesticks. Sitting beside the little fireplace, Lily thought it was all delightful.

'Like to have me bits and pieces around me,' said Maria, noticing Lily looking around. 'This is my own caravan. I don't let Dutchy in here unless he's behaved himself, and the kids have got their own quarters and spend most of the day outside.'

Quietly Maria made the tea, boiled eggs and cut and buttered wafer-thin slices of bread. She then served it all up on a little table with a lace cloth on it, all with a quiet, efficient manner. A peaceful feeling came over Lily, a very comforting feeling. Suddenly she did not feel so lonely; it was as if she had known Maria a long, long time.

In the same manner, Maria took Avril and washed, dressed, fed and fussed over her. Nothing was too much trouble for this woman.

Dutchy came and stood in the doorway of the caravan but made no effort to enter. 'How goes it, gels?' he asked in a loud voice. He looked just the same as he had the night before, dressed in a striped shirt and braces and the greasy trilby hat perched on the back of his head.

'We're getting along very nicely,' replied Maria in her soft voice.

'Right, then,' said Dutchy, 'I'll leave yer to get on wiff it.' Off he went across the yard calling, 'Come on, John!' Whereupon a long-legged lad with auburn hair appeared trundling a coster barrow, and they both headed for the gates.

In this cosy little caravan the only noise came when the trains rattled over the arch above, disturbing the tranquillity of the yard which was full of old lumber that Dutchy had collected on his rounds. After they had eaten, Maria took Lily on a tour of the camp to show her the bigger caravan which the children slept in, and another which was shared by Dutchy and their son John. There was also a huge hut in which there were tables and chairs, a big, old-fashioned wood stove, an old piano, toys, old plane models, paintings, finished wicker baskets and half-made artificial flowers strewn around the place.

'This is where the kids play when the weather is bad. They don't get under my feet,' said Maria.

Lily was impressed by how each little unit of family seemed to fit one with the other. This family had a kind of freedom of loving when no one had to conform.

'Dutchy drinks a lot,' explained Maria, 'and I am a teetotaller, so he don't get in my van unless he is sober. But we get on together well enough.'

The yard was big and there were several showman's caravans being stored there. 'Brings in a few pounds,' Maria told her. Piles of rubbish lay all around—old iron and old cars. There was also an outside toilet which was quite clean.

'We ain't got such a bad camp here,' Maria said proudly. 'I've brought my children up well and they are getting a good education. That's more than I got because we were always on the move. And you can stay as long as you like, Lily. I expect your husband will come over and get you settled once he knows where you are. They do look after the soldiers' wives, I know that.'

But Lily did not reply. Maria was so nice, and so open-hearted that Lily did not want her to know the truth. She felt quite safe inside this camp. Outside was the teeming London town, and not far away, the market where she used to shop. It was all so warm and comforting that Lily decided to stay.

In the early evening, Maria would put on a black shawl and with a basket of paper roses and bags of spring lavender, she went off to work, saying, 'Well, Lily, I can rest easy with you giving an eye to the little ones. It used to worry me, leaving them—it's a rotten stinking world out there.'

Lily thought so too, and hid herself in the warm security of these London Pikeys, as they called themselves.

When Maria went off to her mysterious work, Lily sat by the camp fire and played games with the children. They were very happy children and it did not take a lot to amuse them. They baked chestnuts and potatoes in their jackets, and Lily invented stories and taught them songs she had learned from Kasie. One song was 'Lili Marlene' and Maria's little girl, Marlene, would be thrilled when Lily sang it, and would jump up and dance, her blonde curls bobbing in time with her feet. While the chestnuts and potatoes baked in the red-hot embers of the fire, Avril was content to sit on Lily's lap and watch the other children cavorting about in the twilight.

Marie would come home at about eight o'clock with her big bag full of food, and the two women would have a good chat after the children had gone to bed.

The only sign of Lily's anxiety was that she spent a lot of her time watching the main road, with a worried expression on her face.

'Lily, what is wrong? Why do you continually watch the road?' asked Maria one morning as they sat plucking chickens and preparing vegetables for a meal.

'Just a habit,' said Lily dreamily. 'I suppose it's because I used to live over there.' She pointed towards the church. 'In that street beside the church.'

'Well, you are welcome to stay here and you earn your keep, but if you want another home you must go to the Welfare or write and ask the army to send your husband home on compassionate leave.'

Lily sighed. 'That's not possible,' she said quietly. Because she now trusted her, she told Maria her story. 'My husband is in a mental home somewhere, I don't know where,' she added as a final detail.

'But why did you go abroad? Was it a lover?' Marie questioned her.

'Yes,' replied Lily. 'Avril's father but it didn't work out.'

Those shrewd gipsy eyes surveyed her. 'Is that who you are looking for when you look to the road?'

'Oh yes,' cried Lily, glad to be able to tell the truth at last. 'I know he will come looking for me, I'm really sure about that. But I'm now afraid he won't be able to find me.'

'Never be so sure, Lily,' said Maria. 'Life has too many twists and turns. Show me your hand.'

Lily held out her hand, palm turned upwards. Maria took hold of it and closed her eyes. 'You will end up with the man who first bought you a ring,' she said.

'No, no way!' cried Lily, pulling back her hand. 'Poor George is finished, the bloody war did for him. Besides, I never really loved him. Since I have known Kasie, I've realised how stupid my marriage was.'

'Well,' said Maria, 'take heart, another man is on the way to claim you.'

Lily laughed outright at that. 'No thanks! No more men for me. If Kasie deserts me, I've finished with them.'

'Oh well,' sighed Maria, 'it's all in the hands of fate.'

'I was thinking,' said Lily, 'I ought to try to draw my army pay. I've not used that book for four months.'

Maria's eyes gleamed greedily. 'If you get your back pay it will be quite a lot, and it would be better to do that than sit mooning after this lover.'

As Lily pushed Avril in her chair along the main road to the post office, her eyes still looked out for Kasie. Perhaps she should write to him, but where was he? If she wrote to his parents they would know but could they read her letter? All these thoughts and dilemmas crossed her mind as she walked along.

At the post office the clerk was quite incensed when Lily produced her Army Pay Book. 'This is out of date,' the man said officiously. 'A new department handles Social Welfare now. Why didn't you hand your book in at the end of the hostilities?'

'I wasn't here,' Lily replied flatly.

'Well, we will keep the book now. You must go to this address and they'll sort out your financial problems,' the man said coldly, handing her a piece of paper with an address written on it.

In a daze, Lily went back to the gipsy camp to tell Maria that her army book had been taken away. It was her only means of support. Tears filled her eyes. 'Oh, Kasie,' she wept, 'how could you desert me?'

'Well, it looks to me like you deserted him,' said Maria sensibly. 'Cheer up, why bother? If he loves you, he will find you. In the meantime, why not come out with me and I will teach you the ropes. Then we can take turns to mind the kids. How's that? Come on, Lily, don't cry, you're a big girl, and men are not worth the tears we shed for them.'

So, dressed in an old black shawl and with her hair hanging loose down her back, Lily went with Maria to stand outside Mile End station with a basket of paper flowers in one hand and little sprigs of heather wrapped in tinfoil in the other. At every passer-by, she would hold up a sprig and ask, 'Like some lucky heather, sir?'

'You look like a gipsy,' Maria had said. 'Just con them a bit, pretend to read their palms and charge them a pound a time. It's easy when you know how.'

So they took turns on Maria's pitch, down by the station. Sunday morning was usually Lily's turn. She liked that time for the crowds of travellers came out of the tube to go down Petticoat Lane, and the air was full of excitement. In no time at all, she had become quite good at this fortune-telling.

'Use your loaf,' Maria had said. 'If it's a woman she will have love worries and money worries—it's all in the game.'

Six weeks passed and Lily stuck out her new job. Sometimes

she took Avril with her, and held her by the hand as she walked the East End streets, always hoping that Kasie would appear looking for her. Her face became thin and wan and she had an increasing number of sleepless nights when she yearned for his warm body beside her.

Marie was concerned about Lily's health and mental well-being. 'Try the old house,' she said one day, 'maybe there's a letter there from him to you.'

Lily did try to find out but the response she got from the black family was most disheartening; they would not even open the door to let her talk to them.

Finally, she sat down and wrote to Kasie at his parents' house telling him that she was staying with a friend. She gave him Dutchy's address as the Scrapyard, Railway Arches, Dock Road. It was not a very prepossessing address, but Lily did not care. She had become desperate to know her fate.

Two weeks later a long letter arrived. It was five pages long and Lily guessed that Kasie was probably drunk when he wrote it. There was no address, just a Rotterdam postmark. The lines of writing slanted across the page and there were smudges where his tears had fallen.

'Lily, my lovely,' he wrote. 'Do you realise how I have waited to hear from you and wondered how Avril was? Having reached the conclusion that you no longer cared, I faced my responsibilities and married my son's mother, Wrenska. I have now my own small cargo ship along the Rhine. Our paths lay in different directions. God knows I'll never love another as I loved you. So farewell, my darling. I hope you are well. I'll never forget you.' And so it went on and on, accusing her of using him, and of never having any intention of staying with him.

As she read it, Lily gave one great heart-broken sob. Throwing the letter on the ground, she snatched up her baby. 'Oh, darling, darling,' she cried. 'We have lost your lovely papa—what are we going to do?'

The gipsy children crowded around her. Maria picked up the

letter, read it and then gently took Avril from Lily. 'Come in,' she said gently, 'let's go in the van and have a cup of tea.'

Maria gave Lily love, comfort and understanding, so Lily clung to all that was left—her baby and her friends.

The winter came cold and snowy. Lily trod through the slush of London streets to sell her wares. She had no stockings and no make-up. Her hair was long and straggly, her face thin and pale. Sometimes the noise and the squalor of the gipsy camp got on her nerves but at least there was warmth and love there.

Dutchy was often very drunk and would shout and swear a lot about the yard. His eldest boy, Jim, was now home from the army and stared at Lily in a strange way. 'Got on ald banger, goes well. Come out for a ride, Lily?' he asked one day.

'No, thanks, Jim,' said Lily, reading his mind.

Yet in spite of this harassment, she still hung on to the gipsies' mode of living in a kind of hopeless manner as if the world she knew did not exist for her any more.

With plenty of food, Avril grew big and strong. She chased around with the other children on her sturdy little legs, her silver-blonde hair hanging down her back. She was nearly three years old, bonny, and just a little aggressive. One day, she put out her little foot and kicked an old bucket that was lying in the yard. 'Det dat pucking bucket awt 'f it,' she shouted in her child's voice.

For a moment, Lily was speechless with shock. 'Naughty girl!' she scolded her. 'Bad word.'

'Dushy say,' Avril replied in her baby way, hanging her head down in shame.

Lily had now a van of her own. Dutchy had bought it, since he bought and sold caravans as a sideline. Young John and the two small boys had painted and cleaned it, and fixed it up very nicely for her.

'Naw, yer a real Pikey,' said Dutchy with his wide grin.

Lily was not sure at that point if she wanted to be a Pikey. Each day she was less in love with this life.

'Why don't you take young Jim into your van?' suggested

Maria. 'You need a man and we be very proud. I can see from the way he looks at you that he fancies you.'

Lily thought with horror of that shy, lanky, ginger-haired boy with his patched jeans and oil all over his shirt. Besides, he was only nineteen and she was twenty-eight. 'Oh, Christ,' she laughed off the suggestion. 'I ain't no bleedin' cradle snatcher.'

Unable to make any decisions, Lily remained cloistered with them adapting to their way of life which was dubious and unsociable to all who were not Pikeys, making a living from collecting scrap and telling fortunes, and living in the big old yard underneath the East End railway arches.

That first winter passed and with the spring Lily thought more about Kasie and worried about Avril living this harassed and embarrassing way of life. She was standing outside Mile End station one Sunday morning with a basket on her arm and holding Avril by the hand, when out of the underground station charged a huge noisy crowd wearing big rosettes and coloured hats. They were all shouting and yelling. They were the football fans, for this was the morning after the Cup Final. Lily held tightly to Avril's hand and moved towards them. Crowds meant business, and she did not want to miss this lot. Suddenly a huge figure grabbed her arm, and a big, red-faced man stood looking down at her.

'Oh, dear God!' he cried, 'it's my Lily. Doan't thee know me, lass? I'm oop for t'coop,' cried Norman Clegg. He was wearing a red-and-white rosette in the buttonhole of his jacket.

Lily tried to rush past him in horror but he held on to her tight. Even when she tried to wrench her arm away she could not escape.

'Lily, for God's sake! What are thee doing begging?' he hollered.

Sensing danger, Avril began to scream and Norman's fellow football fans all stopped to stare.

'Let's get away from here,' he said, pushing Lily ahead of him till they came to a cafe. Inside he stood looking down at her. 'I knew there was no mistake, Lily. I'd know thee anywheer. Whose is the child?' He patted those blonde curls and handed

Avril a chocolate biscuit. He then ordered some teas and they slid into a quiet spot at the back of the cafe. Lily was too shocked to even say a word.

'What's thee been up to, then, lass?' asked Norman, stroking her work-worn hands.

Lily turned to him with a defiant look in her blue eyes. 'It's a way of earning a living,' she said. 'It's not considered to be begging. I live with the gipsies so I do in Rome what the Romans do,' she retorted.

'I've searched everywheer for thee, Lily. I always hoped thee would come back to me.' Norman looked at Avril, who, with chocolate round her mouth, had begun to enjoy the situation. 'Is that the reason why?' he asked.

'Well, yes,' stammered Lily.

'Who was it?' Norman demanded. He looked angry.

'No one you know,' said Lily wearily.

Norman did not really want to know, anyway, so he put his good arm around her and Lily put her head on his big comforting shoulder.

'Lily, you have got to come home with me,' he said softly. 'I will be father to your child. I'm doing well with my nurseries and have built me nice brick bungalow. Come home with me, love. I haven't forgotten how happy we were when George and you came to stay with me.'

George! The very mention of his name brought fresh forebodings to Lily. 'Have you heard how he is?' she asked.

'Yes, I have,' said Norman, 'and often he comes up for a little holiday. You would never know him, Lily, he is so greatly improved.'

A lump came into her throat and she wanted to cry. But whether it was from pleasure or sadness, she was not sure. 'Where is he?' she asked cautiously.

'Still up North,' replied Norman, 'in what they calls a rehabilitation centre. Come home with me, Lily, and I promise you faithfully that I will give your baby and poor George a good home.'

She stared at him with disbelief in her eyes. It was all too good to be true.

'Now,' said Norman, picking up Avril. 'We'll go and collect your belongings and get on the train home.'

But now Lily hesitated. They were a rough lot in the gipsy camp. What effect would Norman have on them?

'Well, will you come?' he begged.

She took off the black shawl and put down the basket outside the station. 'I've very little to bring with me,' she said, 'nothing of any value.' Most of Lily's good clothes had been sold by Maria and Lily had never argued. She always thought she owed the gipsies so much. 'But I'll come,' she said, 'if, that is, you will have me, Norman,' she added shyly.

He held her tight as they went into the main line station and booked tickets back home to Norman's place in Hill Drop village, high up on the Yorkshire Moors.

Norman sat beside her with Avril on his lap. Lily looked vacantly out of the window watching the train slide past the gipsy camp. She could just see the children playing in the yard and the smoke curling up from the camp fire in the middle.

'Sorry Maria,' she whispered softly, 'but I have to think of Avril. But I will not forget you.'

Avril chatted with Norman in her baby way. 'Puff, puff,' she said, referring to the train. Then later on she said, 'Papa, Papa.'

'No, darling,' Lily said with a sense of warmth inside her. 'Say Daddy.'

'Yes, lovey,' said Norman, his eyes shining as he turned to Lily. 'Thanks, lass, you have made me a very happy man.'

BOOK TWO

CHAPTER ONE

Hill Drop Village

On the long journey to the village of Hill Drop in the north, Lily's mind was very active as she sat in the train compartment with Norman and Avril. With a wan smile on her face, she thought of Maria. What had she thought of Lily when she went looking for her and found only the basket of paper roses abandoned outside the station? It had not been very kind to drop everything like that—perhaps she should drop a note of explanation.

Norman was jovial and extremely happy. 'We'll get poor old George out of that terrible institution,' he told her. 'He'll be handy to me because he likes to work. He was always busy when we were in that military hospital.'

Lily closed her eyes and pretended to doze. Before her mind's eye, Kasie's gentle smile hovered close to her and she heard his voice whispering, 'Lily, my lovely . . .' She had lost him to that other woman, and she knew it was her own fault. She had been so sure that he would come searching for her, it hadn't occurred to her that anything else could happen. She would have held on to him then so that they could have settled down in the East End and been happy together, as they had been in the wartime.

Deep despair seemed to envelop her. Was she doing the right thing now? She was entering another cage. It was not the rusty old one that Maria had provided, but a nice, clean, comfortable one. It was all for Avril's sake, she told herself repeatedly. She, at least, must be adequately provided for, and this was the only way.

The train stopped at Barnsley and outside the station Norman proudly presented his old car. 'I had it painted and cleaned, and put special gears in it so I can drive it easily. It's just like a new car, it is.'

It was then that Lily suddenly recalled that Norman was disabled.

'How's your bad arm?' she asked.

'Mean to say you never noticed?' Norman grinned.

Lily looked directly at him and realised that he had an artificial arm. He wiggled his gloved hand at her and Lily shuddered. The sight of it repelled her. Again she thought of her lively, active Kasie, and his fair, freckled body, and the way he used to swim underwater and of all the physical things he did. But he was gone forever.

Norman had made great improvements to his home since she had been there two years earlier. The old shack had disappeared and in its place stood a red-bricked house. It was built in the rural style with a high sloping roof and mullioned windows. Neat net curtains hung at the shining windows and in the front garden early daffodils bloomed. The green of the lawn and the gold flash of the flowers caught Lily's eye immediately.

'Oh, this is very nice,' she exclaimed with pleasure.

'It's all yours, dear,' replied Norman sentimentally, putting his one good arm around her waist.

The large modern kitchen thrilled her and she liked the living room which was full of highly polished old-fashioned furniture. The smell of lavender polish pervaded the air.

'The furniture is mostly old,' Norman informed her. 'It belonged to me own folk. I brought it over from their cottage. It's all good stuff, too good to throw away.'

'It looks so well cared for,' said Lily.

'Old Strawberry, she does that.' Norman sat Avril in a chair and went to put the kettle on.

'Strawberry!' quizzed Lily. 'Who's she?'

Norman did not often laugh outright but this time he did. 'She's an old body what does the 'ousework. She has known me sin' I were a lad, looked after me mother in her last days. Ev'ryone calls 'er Strawberry 'cause she has this red eye condition, but I warn you she is a reet old beezy body, so we will not tell her too much. She won't be far away now . . .' He looked out of the window. 'Reet, 'ere she cooms,' he said in his strong northern accent.

A small thin elderly woman bustled into the house wearing a bright crossover flowered overall. Her Yorkshire accent was so thick that Lily hardly understood a word she uttered, and those red-rimmed eyes roamed over Lily in strong disapproval. They glanced at her grubby, stockingless legs, over her washed-out cotton dress and her long, tangled hair, and made it obvious that Lily was not welcome.

Strawberry snatched the teapot from Norman's hands, saying in a cracked voice, 'I'll wet the tay.'

Norman escorted Lily back into the comfortable sitting room and said sympathetically, 'Sit down, dear, we'll have a cup of tea in here.'

Yet Lily felt quite stunned by the old hag's reception and was just beginning to realise how awful she must look. That dreadful old woman's red eyes had condemned her, and she was so relieved when she heard Strawberry leave after a long debate with Norman in the kitchen.

He brought in a tray of tea and biscuits. 'Well, she's gone straight down t'village to let the residents know that you are back, Lily,' he said. 'But if you don't care, Lily, nor do I. This is your home and old Strawberry will not enter it again wi'out your permission.'

At that moment a warm glow of affection for Norman came over Lily. She moved closer to him, and he bent his head and kissed her. His lips were warm and comforting, not hard or demanding, as Kasie's had been. They gave her a feeling of contentment that she had not felt for a long time.

'I will not force myself on you, Lily,' Norman said. 'It will be up to you but I sincerely hope that we will get back to our old relationship. I know it will take a little time. I do not wish to pry into your past but I am hopeful that you will be my wife, legally or otherwise, and that I will become Avril's father. What more can I say?'

Lily put her arms about his neck. 'No more, Norman. You

have said it all. I will love you and be faithful to you, I promise, on my honour.'

So Lily prepared to settle down with Norman, quite happy for the time being to accept the warmth and security he offered. They did not actually make love for a while, for Norman was cautious and Lily did not encourage him. The first time was one Saturday night after they had been down to the local pub.

'I'm not much of a drinking man, Lily,' Norman had said one day, 'but I do like a couple of pints after my day's work is done. I go down to the village inn because that is wheer I meet the folks I knows and wheer I gather all the information needed about the rural life up here on this wild moorland. Next Saturday we'll go into town and I will buy you some of the things you need, and we'll then go together to the Hill Drop Inn and face the locals. Then we'll let them know once and for always that you are my chosen wife. By the way,' he added sheepishly, 'I lied about us, I told them that I was Avril's father and that you and I had met and married down in London during the war.'

'Suits me,' replied Lily, who was gradually coming back to her old cheeky self. The fresh air gradually took away her listlessness and her form filled out from the good, nourishing diet of newly laid farm eggs and fresh milk.

That Saturday, they went into town and Norman bought Lily a tweed suit, a white blouse and underwear. For Avril he bought some little white dresses and some woollies and pants to wear around the farm.

In his spending habits, Norman was so different from Kasie. Kasie used to throw his money around in a boastful manner and give the impression that he had plenty even if it was his last pound. Norman, however, asked the price before purchasing anything and counted out the notes very carefully. He only shopped at the nice, old-fashioned clothes shop because, he said, 'It's the best value as the clothes are of good quality.'

Lily thought that they were very much out of date, but she did not complain. Her fighting spirit had died a little since she had left Kasie. Still, she looked very nice in the brown tweed suit with the white blouse and sensible brogues, and her hair was well brushed and rolled up neatly.

In the evening, Norman escorted her to the village inn, which looked so nice and cosy when they entered. There was a big log fire glazing and a very congenial landlord who greeted them. 'Good evening, Norman. Good evening, Mrs Clegg.' He called to them in a loud voice as if imparting the news to the grapevine.

'Well, fancy old Norman getting himself hooked,' someone said, looking up.

In a little side bar Lily caught a terrifying glimpse of old Strawberry. She was wearing a black monstrosity of a hat which was perched on her sparse hair and her hoarse voice with its thick Yorkshire accent and strange dialect rolled off her tongue as she described to her drinking cronies the day that Lily arrived. 'No stockings, dirty feet, just like a bloody gypo, and not a stick of luggage. God only knows where he got her from.'

'I heard that they have a nice little girl,' someone remarked.

'It's a wise child what knows its own father,' returned Strawberry viciously. 'I've known Norman sin he were knee high and there is plenty of nice clean lasses in this village. He must be bloody mad.'

Lily, trying hard not to listen to this conversation, swallowed up her drinks greedily and by the time they were ready for home she and Norman had both had enough.

'Police sergeant was in t'other bar,' said Norman in a slurred voice as he struggled to start up the old car. 'It's a good job he knows me.'

But Lily was too woozy to care. All she knew was that she never wanted to enter that place again.

When the young babysitter had left, Lily pulled Norman down onto the sofa and spread her legs wide. 'Come on, Norman,' she said, 'let's make love. Sod that lot down in the village, it's me, you and Avril, now.' She slipped off her blouse and put her full breasts against his lips. 'Go on, Norm,' she urged. 'Do that, it always gets me going.'

Lily's hot young body was so hungry for a man. She used her

tongue and her warm body to give Norman little sex thrills that
Kasie had taught her. Norman was having the time of his life.
When he fumbled to enter her finally, she closed her eyes and
thought to herself, 'Kasie, love me, darling.'

After a while they left the sofa and got into bed. Norman was
still wearing his vest. Lily giggled. 'For Christ's sake, strip off,
Norm,' she teased him. 'That's the right way to do it, and the
more you do it, the more you'll get to like it.'

It did not take too long to settle down with Norman. Those
wild, undulating moors never ceased to thrill Lily. The miles of
space and silent peace of it all, entered her very soul, making her
want to run and gambol like those young lambs high up on the
rocky crags. Because Lily was alive again, her young body
thrilled to nature and her sad memories almost disappeared.
Norman was no longer the shy man he had been and although
their sex life had cooled down rather quickly, she was at peace
with life. Avril was happy and the three of them often took long
walks on the moors with Norman's two labrador dogs, Pip and
Peter. Clear cool springs ran down the hillsides. Avril liked to
dabble her feet in them and Norman would point out features of
the countryside from high up there on the hill.

'See that black cloud over there? That's the smoke from the
potteries outside the town. It's nice and fresh up here, and the
child will grow up reet bonny.'

Lily knew she had not one regret about Avril being here, for
Norman was completely devoted to the child and she to him.
She was always calling him Daddy, which made him really
proud. But one morning, right out of the blue, she put down
her spoon and pointed at Norman. 'That Daddy. Where Papa
gone?' she asked.

Norman didn't understand. 'What did she say?' he laughed.

But Lily swept Avril up and carried her outside. 'Go and play
with the ducks,' she said, pushing the girl into the yard, her face
white and strained as memories came racing back.

But apart from such episodes, it was a good life up there in
that wild, lonely place. Lily became very useful to Norman,
helping him with his horticultural farm. She was soon taking

cuttings, sowing seeds, learning to supervise the huge green-houses and taking care of the chickens.

Norman worked from dawn to sunset and never seemed to cease working. Planting and harvesting in the spring, he took the boxes of bedding plants to sell at the market. In the late summer, he took lettuces, cucumber and tomatoes. In the autumn it was apples and pears. He worked hard and although he did employ some casual labour, most of his concentrated energies went into the running of this self-built business very successfully. Norman had few interests other than Lily and Avril, his dogs and his farm. And his one treat was to ride down to the local on his bike for a last minute drink; that was all he demanded from his social life. He was not ungenerous but was very careful. He paid all the bills, bought most of the food and gave Lily a little pocket money which she was supposed to make last, though usually she would spend it all in one day on a trip into town, where she would buy sweets and toys for Avril, and eat high tea or go to the cinema. Lily had very little need for money there. All the home comforts were there including the modern, well-stocked kitchen that Lily loved. She had never had such a nice cooking stove and so much hot water at her disposal before.

On market day Norman would go off to sell his produce, and he always brought back little presents, like a white rabbit for Avril or a nice cooking pot for Lily. They were usually small useful items that gave him a lot of pleasure to present.

Lily was quite content to work beside her man all that summer and autumn. When the winter came the hills were covered with snow. They sat about the big log fire, Avril with her story books and Norman with his farm catalogues and the wireless. Lily had always been fond of cooking and now tried out new recipes from an old cook book she had found in the loft.

'It was me mother's,' said Norman. 'She was very careful with her property, so I am glad you have found a use for it.'

'Who the bleedin' 'ell is Mrs Beeton?' yelled Lily from the

kitchen one night. 'Put twelve eggs in one cake? She must be potty!'

Norman roared with laughter. 'I don't think you'd better use that recipe,' he yelled back, 'that was written when eggs were two a penny.'

Lily often borrowed Norman's old bike and wearing mud-splattered slacks and Wellington boots, cycled into the village, where she would dash into the village shop-cum-post office for stamps for Norman's business correspondence. In the shop there was always a cold atmosphere, a barrier she could not crack. One day when she rode down to the post office, she saw Strawberry there with another of her terrible hats on. She stood nattering with her cronies. They had all been to some afternoon affair.

'That's her!' Strawberry said in a very loud voice. 'She never wed him, you know. She came here looking like a tramp, I saw her, you know.'

Lily was feeling very dishevelled that day, having been shovelling up fertiliser all the morning. Hearing Strawberry made her lose her temper.

'Hey, you, lousy red eyes!' she yelled. 'Shut yer cake 'ole or I'll shut it for yer!'

All the old ladies scattered out into the street and Lily strode past them furiously. When she got back home, she burst into tears.

Norman comforted her. 'Those old busy bodies have nothing else to do, but you do draw attention to yourself.'

'What do you mean?' demanded Lily.

'Well,' he said nervously. 'Now, don't get upset, but when you go down to the village you should dress nicely and not go down in those muddy old pants.'

'Well, of all the bloody sauce!' cried Lily, pulling away from him.

'Look here, Lily, I'm a man of property, so they expect it of me and you.'

'It sounds bloody daft to me,' cried Lily. 'I certainly am not going to put my best suit on to go to the post office for a few stamps.'

'I know that you have not got all the nice clothes that you used to have to look so smart,' said Norman. 'But upstairs there's a sewing machine. It was my mother's—she was the village dressmaker, you know. I'll get it serviced for you, and you can make some clothes. There are patterns and even several rolls of material up there, too.'

Lily sighed. That was just like Norman. If you wanted anything you were supposed to work for it. But that old sewing machine was a Godsend that winter and kept her occupied. She made clothes for herself and little nighties from some old red flannel for Avril. She liked them so much that she made one for herself. It was huge and billowed out like a tent when she danced around the living room in it one night.

'Ee by goom, Lily,' said Norman, 'you'll have all the bulls after thee.'

Lily's eyes twinkled. 'Never mind the bulls, what about you, Norman?' With a wide grin, she lifted up the nightie to display her long, well-shaped legs.

'Now doan't thee start, Lily,' said Norman, 'I've got a busy day tomorrow.'

Lily giggled but her mind was suddenly on Kasie. He would never have missed out on that invitation. Even after all these months, he was still engraved on her heart.

Earlier that year, they had gone to Birmingham to visit George in the hospital for the mentally disturbed. Even now, after the end of the war, it was still a very dreary and overcrowded place. Lily had been quite dismayed at the sight of George—a small, bent figure with a black patch over his eye where the shrapnel had entered his brain. Yet mentally he had vastly improved and was very pleased to see Norman. But as before, he eyed Lily with suspicion. She handed him a bag of jelly babies, which he was so fond of, and he grabbed them and gobbled them up greedily without a word of thanks. Then he went off to find a wastebin to put the wrappers in, instead of throwing the paper away as he used to. They strolled around the hospital grounds admiring the winter-flowering shrubs and well-kept lawns, but George did not say one word. He just kept stopping to pick up dry leaves and twigs and putting them tidily under the trees.

'Whatever's the matter with him?' cried Lily, quite disturbed by this behaviour.

'Nay, Lily,' Norman tried to explain. 'It's nothing to worry over, he's just got a mania for tidiness. It's being in this place for so long.' He put an arm on George's bent shoulder. 'Want to come home with us, George?' he asked.

'Not now, too busy,' replied George with a slight hesitation.

'It's nice high up in the moors, and Lily will be there,' cajoled Norman.

George's one eye looked directly at Lily, and with an evil-looking grin, he shook his head. 'Too busy,' he said again. Lily shuddered.

That visit was not a success, and Lily said afterwards, 'He's scared the wits out of me. I don't want him staying with us, it might not be good for Avril.'

Norman looked sad. 'It takes all kinds to make up this lousy world, lass,' he said quietly, 'and I feel responsible for George. I know you don't, otherwise you would never have deserted him.'

This was the first time since she had come to live with him that Norman had criticised her, and she did not like it. 'Well, surely we are not going to quarrel over that barmy old bugger?' she said emphatically.

Norman looked rather shocked. 'Surely there is some human kindness in you for poor old George. Have you forgotten that he got his injuries in the war and there but for the grace of God go I?'

Lily flushed guiltily. 'Oh, do as you please,' she said, 'but if he gets dangerous, then back he bleedin' well goes.'

Norman sighed. 'All right, we'll wait till the spring. He'll be useful here, I know. I can find him little jobs to do—that's what he needs. I'll spend the time until then converting the loft into a bedroom for him, that'll help the winter to pass more quickly.'

That first winter passed by fairly peacefully, and Lily got quite interested in her dressmaking. She sent off to a glossy magazine for up-to-date patterns and bought nice material in the town. Soon she was very proud of her achievements.

Norman was impressed. 'You are not exactly brainy, lass,' he remarked, 'but you have very clever hands and perhaps that is just as well.'

'Thank you very much, old clever clogs,' returned Lily.

So while the snow lay thick on the moorland Lily made herself a two-piece suit for the spring and several smart day dresses. Very pleased, she often held a lone mannequin parade in front of the dressing-table mirror matching up beads and rings with each new dress. Then sometimes she would examine the lines under the eyes and suddenly feel a little disillusioned. 'I don't know why I bother to dress myself up,' she would say to herself. 'There's nowhere to go and no one to see me, and no one bloody well cares how I look.' Then she would put down her head and those dammed-up tears would come pouring out. 'Oh, where are you, Kasie, my love? And do you still think of me?' But the howling of the wind over the moorlands was no answer.

After Christmas and when the snow had begun to clear, Lily was soon back at work beside Norman, sitting at the kitchen table sowing seeds in boxes with monotonous regularity. They sowed box after box, poking a tiny hole in the soil and pushing in a seed to germinate and give fruit in the spring.

She also did a lot of cooking. Norman was very fond of his food and Lily was well able to please him, delighted that he was not as fastidious as Kasie who had been so hard to please. Norman loved plain cooking, and she made lots of big steak-and-kidney puddings with plenty of spuds and cabbage, and big joints of roast beef served up with Yorkshire puddings. Norman began to put on weight but Lily, whose appetite was good, fortunately still remained slim.

Little Avril was now a chubby four-year-old with fat legs and rosy cheeks. She ruled both Norman and Lily with her tantrums, yet she was charming when she was in a good mood.

Norman spent a lot of time with her patiently teaching her the alphabet and reading stories to her. Avril was bright for her age, intelligent but strangely perverse.

As he promised, Norman converted the loft into a small bedroom for George. 'He'll be nice and warm up here,' he said, displaying his handiwork. The walls were wood panelled, there was a small bed, a wardrobe and a rush mat on the floor.

Lily stared at it all apprehensively, thinking how strange it would be to have her real husband sleeping just over her head. The bedroom she shared with Norman was directly below.

One Sunday afternoon on a lovely spring day, Norman brought George home.

'Who is he?' demanded Avril, before the men had arrived, 'this man who is going to sleep upstairs?'

'He's called Uncle George,' explained Lily. 'He's just a poor man who has been ill.'

'Oh, is that all?' said Avril, losing interest immediately.

However, when George did arrive, Avril took one look at his eye patch and screamed in terror. She ran to Lily hiding her face in her apron.

Norman, a little flustered, sat chatting to George in the sitting room, making jokes about the old army days. George seemed completely relaxed, and chatted and giggled freely.

Feeling very much on edge, Lily prepared the evening meal while Avril sat in her wicker chair in the kitchen looking very sulky. 'Don't like him,' she said, 'he's a wicked pirate.'

'He's a what?' asked Lily.

Avril went off to fetch one of her story books. 'Look,' she said when she returned, pointing to the picture on the cover. It was of a pirate complete with an eye patch with a skull and crossbone on his hat.

'Silly ninny!' said Lily. 'Uncle George had his eye shot out in the war, that's why he wears that patch.'

Soon Avril began to lose her fear of George and began to take an interest in him, peeping around the door at him. Whenever George noticed her, he pointed at Lily and then at Norman. 'George, Norman and Lily, he! he! he!' he would cackle.

That night when George had been settled in his bed, Norman said: 'You know, Lily, it's very sad, George thinks that child is yours and mine, and he doesn't seem to mind. He knows I always fancied you.'

'Who bleeding well cares what he thinks?' returned Lily irritably.

'Don't forget that he can put two and two together, will you?' said Norman, puffing casually at his pipe.

Things were never quite the same after George arrived. Lily could not put her finger on the problem exactly, but the peaceful atmosphere that had helped her to forget the heartbreak of losing Kasie was now disturbed. George was always on the go, tidying up the yard, or fetching and carrying for Norman. Norman had an old farm truck and George would go with him to the market to sell the products. They always came home very happy together, and Norman would tell her about some amusing incident that George, in his dim way, seemed to think funny, too, while Lily would never see the joke.

George's behaviour towards her was strange. If Lily passed anything to him he would snatch at it like some kind of animal, which really annoyed her. Or he would get up from the table and start clearing the plates before she had finished eating her lunch. At midday Norman would eat his meal quickly before going straight back to work, but Lily liked to laze awhile and smoke a couple of cigarettes before she cleared away. George would get up and clatter about around her. 'Sit down, you dozy sod,' she would yell at him. But George would just ignore her and carry the plates into the kitchen and start washing up.

When Lily complained to Norman about this, he just said placidly: 'Leave him be, Lily. He thinks he's earning his keep. That's the way he's been trained in the hospital, it's work for him and that's all there is in his life.'

So Lily took Norman at his word and became quite lazy, leaving the housework to George while she popped off to the Ladies' Club down in the Hill Drop Village after taking Avril to the small preparatory school run by the nuns. She would dress up in her latest creation, paint her nails and put on big earrings to match her dress. Recently she had had her hair cut short and had it permed and then put a red rinse in it. Norman disapproved of the rinse but he knew that there was no point in trying to make her wash it out.

When Lily first joined the Ladies' Club, she was rather apprehensive about it, convinced that all the other members would be a lot of old fogies. But she was getting so fed up with not seeing anyone, it was actually Norman who suggested that she join at first.

'Go and have a good natter, lass,' he had said, 'it will do thee nerves good.'

To Lily's surprise, the other ladies had turned out to be quite young and friendly. The recent post-war building programme had brought estates of bungalows and council houses to the village, and the women who moved into them were young and a little lonely, missing the town and looking for the warmth of a community life. They liked to spend their afternoons having tea and gossiping or organising jumble sales to raise money for the outings. Lily began to look forward to those afternoons, and she would plan her outfit so as to make the best impression on the other members of the club.

'You do look so nice, Lily,' someone always said to her when she arrived each time.

Lily would smile casually and say: 'Just a little thing I knocked up. Would you like the pattern?'

And so Lily gradually became part of this community. Strawberry had passed on, and few of these newcomers knew Lily's business; she was just accepted as a respectable farmer's wife. So our Lily came into her own and was quite popular in the little Yorkshire village. Norman was very proud of her.

Norman was still working very hard and George continued to help on the farm. He would follow Norman about like a faithful hound, and as each day passed, George seemed to improve mentally.

Avril was growing big, strong and healthy. She was still at the prep school where the nuns had taught her to round off her words very carefully.

'Blimey, ain't we getting posh!' Lily would declare. She herself never made any effort to change her Cockney habits. If anything, she would revel in them and liked to shock the ladies at the club with an outburst of her perverse Cockney humour.

Lily was basically happy living with Norman. She had only faint stirrings of remorse now when she looked back over her past life, and occasionally she thought it would be nice to have more children, but her sex life with Norman had dwindled to almost nothing.

'It would be nice to have another child, company for Avril and we might get a son and heir,' she did suggest to Norman one night.

'Not wi' me, lass,' he replied. 'If you can recall how badly I was injured in the war, after that last big operation, they told me although my sex life would not be impaired, I'd never reproduce.'

'So I've got a couple of old crocks,' said Lily, bitterly, referring to both Norman and George.

Norman winced. 'Sometimes, Lily, you can be most callous and very cruel.'

Lily blushed guiltily. 'Sorry, Norm,' she said. 'I never meant it.'

Yet life was not really so bad up at Hill Drop. In fact, she was more secure and happy than she had ever been before. She asked no more from life except the right circumstances to bring up her child.

CHAPTER TWO

The Comfortable Cage

In that comfortable cage Lily lived for the next three years. Avril was now seven years old and attended a convent school nearer the town.

In the meantime, Lily had learned to drive. Norman's old Ford had been replaced by a Mini, which gave her the freedom of being able to go to town whenever she had the inclination. Yet the comfortable life had made her lazy. Once Avril was taken to school, Lily would return to the village or drop in on a friend to discuss the doings of the Ladies' Club or some other social event. Then she would return back home to cook the lunch.

George still did the housework and kept the bungalow spick and span, while Norman's nursery prospered.

The house looked very cosy. Lily had put plant pots outside the front door and had splendid rose bushes growing in the front garden. The lawn and hedge was very trim. The golden labradors sat on the stone-flagged path browsing in the summer sunshine. The red and white roses rambled up the yellow brick walls. Just inside the porch there was a black-and-white tub full of tiger lilies whose bright speckled blooms Lily often stopped to admire when she returned from the village. She loved the feelings of peace she got whenever she came into the carpeted hall to look in the old brass letter rack for the day's correspondence. She had filled out and seemed taller. Her hair was now rinsed to a glowing red. It shone after she had brushed it well and set it in a modern style. This was a different kind of woman to the weary, bedraggled girl who had arrived here four years earlier. She seldom thought of her past life and had even begun to get used to George who was known to most of the local inhabitants as Uncle George. For the secret of the farm at Hill Drop had never been divulged.

Norman set up a shop in the nursery selling fresh eggs, fruit and vegetables to the new council tenants who lived in a huge development which had sprung up just half a mile away.

On Saturdays and Sundays Lily worked in the shop, where she was quick, bright and pleasant, serving the customers in her cheeky Cockney manner. 'Right, cock, 'ow many taters yer want?' she would ask the amazed kids who came to do their mum's shopping. Lily had never lost the flat London intonation in her voice and the Yorkshire locals found her hard to understand.

Norman was still very kind and good to her. He had grown big, fat and florid in the face. He had also slowed down physically as well as sexually, but Lily did not mind. There had never been such great excitement in his lovemaking, so she could well do without it.

Although she was more used to him, George still aggravated her. He was sly and very greedy, but Norman still managed to communicate with him when others had failed, and wouldn't hear a word said against him. He just told Lily to be tolerant of George.

One day Avril came home from school looking rather puzzled. 'Mother Superior thinks I should turn Catholic,' she said. 'She asked me if I was baptised and I didn't know. Have I?'

Lily looked annoyed. 'Of course you have,' she insisted.

'What religion?' asked Avril.

'In my own religion,' announced Lily.

'What about Daddy, is he Catholic?'

'Look here, Avril,' Lily said tersely, 'I pays good money for those nuns to give you a good education, so you can tell them to mind their own business.'

Avril looked a bit disturbed. 'Really, Mummy, I can't possibly do that,' she said in her posh tone.

'Oh, then I bloody well will,' declared Lily.

When she consulted Norman about this matter, he said:

'Leave well alone, Lily. We pay for her, and there's no compulsion for Avril to be a Catholic, but I do think it's time we put our house in order.'

'What do you mean?' snapped Lily.

'Well, dear, I think we should get around to getting her legally adopted by me and getting you to divorce George and marry me.'

Lily was really annoyed. 'I don't see why I should have all that bloody upheaval just because of them nuns,' she declared. 'And I'm going to make a right fool of myself if we get married after living together up here for five years.'

'Please yourself, dear,' said Norman amiably and turned to his accounts which he always did in the evening after they had eaten dinner. He was so placid and easy going he did not attempt to argue with her.

That summer, Avril developed whooping cough. She had always been such a strong, bonny child that when that persistent dry cough wouldn't respond to any medicine, Lily was almost distraught with anxiety. The whooping cough lasted for weeks, leaving Avril pale and listless, and Lily a bag of nerves.

Finally, Norman suggested a holiday for both of them.

'Dunno,' said Lily. 'Ain't been anywhere for years.'

'I can't come with you, I'm afraid,' said Norman, 'as this is my busy time with the harvesting. You and Avril go on your own. I'll book it all for you. I used to go to Lowestoft when I was a boy, it's got lovely stretches of sands. My mother had an aunt there, I believe her daughter still runs the boarding house. I'll write and find out.'

A week later, Lily set off with Avril for two weeks in Lowestoft. Once on the train and free of Norman, she had a strange, exciting sense of freedom.

'It will be so nice to be together all day, just you and I, Avril,' she said.

'Why?' Avril was sulky. 'Won't there be no other kids to play with?'

'Oh, I expect so,' said Lily. 'I've never been to Lowestoft before.'

Lily soon discovered that Lowestoft was a bright little seaside town but extremely boring. She put on a different dress every day—part of the stock of summer dresses she had made during the winter—and she and Avril would walk along the promenade together. Avril was also bored and worrying about her pony and her school friends. She played on the sands for a while but Lily would not allow her to go in the sea. 'I'm afraid of the sea and I can't swim,' she told her. 'If you fall in, you'll drown.'

Avril stared scornfully at her. 'But I can swim,' she protested.

But Lily would still not trust her out of her sight.

Sometimes they would go to the ice-cream parlour down at the harbour from where Avril liked to watch the boats as the herring fleet sailed out. Lily would sit over her cup of coffee and dream of the days she spent aboard the old landing barge. Visions of Kasie would come sweeping back to her—his blond head wet and curly when he used to shake the water out of his hair after his morning swim, just like a puppy. She wondered how he fared.

At the end of the first week one afternoon, she was walking along the quayside holding Avril's hand. A large cargo ship had dropped anchor just that day, and Lily's gaze roamed over its name on the bows. It was called the *Lykilire*. That was a strange name, she thought, and something told her it was Dutch. Her eyes followed on to the big bulky bows and there just below was the word *Amsterdam*. She paused momentarily and looked up. A man in a peaked cap was hanging over the rail shouting at another figure on the shore. She nearly fainted as a shiver went through her. There was no mistake; she would know that voice anywhere.

'*Gott auf Donner!*' Kasie swore. Then in English, 'Flaming hell, can't you tie her up properly?' His small lithe figure came running down the gang plank.

Lily grasped Avril firmly by the hand and hurried on, hoping that he wouldn't see her. But it was too late. Kasie always looked at every woman, and he had already seen her.

She heard him as he ran up behind her just before he caught

her arm. 'Oh, it cannot be true—my lovely Lily!' His arms went about her.

Thinking that her mother was being attacked, Avril screamed, and rushed at him, kicking him on the shins.

He let go of Lily and knelt down beside Avril. 'Baby, baby,' he cried. 'Look at me.'

Avril's expression immediately changed. A wide smile crossed her chubby face. 'Papa?' she cried in wonder, putting her arms about his neck.

'Oh, dear God, she remembers me,' he said with great emotion. He held the child tight, tears pouring down his face.

Lily stood with trembling knees praying to God to give her the courage to grab hold of Avril and run. But it was no good, she was like a rabbit trapped by the light of a torch.

'I want ice-cream,' said Avril, making the best of her opportunities.

'So you will, my *leiblin*.' He took her hand, then Lily's, and they crossed the road to the ice-cream parlour.

While Avril got stuck into the huge ice-cream she had ordered, Kasie brought two cups of coffee and sat facing Lily with a whimsical expression on his face. Lily was pale as death with a hard lump in her throat. She sipped the hot coffee unable to utter a word.

He put her hand to his lips. 'I believe you are more lovelier than I ever remember,' he said. 'You're a real fine figure of a woman.'

Lily tried hard to smile. 'That's right,' she said glumly. 'Tell me I've got fat.'

He smiled that lovely gentle smile and his fingers caressed her arm. An exciting shiver went down her spine, Lily knew it was a losing game but tried to keep her cool.

'Fancy finding you in this God-forsaken harbour, I can't believe it,' he said. 'I only got here by accident myself. I was on my way to Gravesend and ran short of fuel.'

Lily's resolve went. 'Oh, Kasie,' she said brokenly. She bent her head forward and their lips met in a long kiss.

'What's he kissing you for, Mum?' Avril asked, looking up.

Under the table his hands fondled her knees. 'How are my lovely legs, Lily? Oh, how I have longed to find you again! I've wandered around London day after day looking for you.'

'But you deserted me,' Lily challenged him. 'You married someone else.'

Kasie looked down at his hands sadly. 'To my regret, Lily, you were my love and still are.'

Lily was trembling violently. Kasie still had this extraordinary impact on her. Unable to stop herself, she put out her hand and touched his cheek. A thrill went through her as she felt the fresh pink skin and tiny golden bristles on his chin.

'Oh, darling,' she said. 'I can't believe you are really here.'

He held her hand tightly and pressed his lips to her palm. As hot, violent emotions ran away with them, they forgot about Avril.

'I've finished my ice-cream,' she yelled. 'Would you like to come and play on the beach with me?'

'Yes, darling,' said Kasie, with tears in his eyes.

They got up and walked hand in hand along the promenade. Avril dashed along in front of them, and they sat on the warm sand watching the girl build a sandcastle. They were so close together, so hot and restless.

'Now that I've found you,' said Kasie, 'I'm not going to let you go. Come aboard my ship and sail home with me, just you and Avril. I have my own line of ships now—that old cargo boat and two passenger ships which sail down the Rhine.'

But Lily was not listening. All she could think of was the heat of his body beside her. She pressed closer and they lay embracing in the hot sun.

'Oh, Lily,' Kasie said, gripping her tight. 'Let us go aboard my ship. You need me—it's still the same with us, that is why I can never forget you.'

'I mustn't,' gasped Lily, 'not with Avril.'

Avril had got bored with her sandcastle and was now coming towards them. They got up. 'I must go home, it's lunchtime,' said Lily. 'I'll meet you tonight at the harbour.'

Lily walked back to the boarding house in a daze. Cousin

Edie served a nice cold lunch. She was sweet and pleasant and reminded Lily of Norman in her ways. She wore very staid clothes and around her neck hung a long chain with a cross at the end of it, and her silver hair was piled high up on her head. She had never married and spent her time between the boarding house and the local church.

Lily sat at the table feeling hot and flustered, hoping that Avril was not going to say anything. 'You must not tell Cousin Edie that we have seen Papa,' she had warned her on their way back from the harbour, 'because if you do she'll get cross.'

In fact, that was sufficient for Avril because she liked to manipulate people, which was not easy if they got cross.

After lunch, while Avril had a nap, Lily lay out on the veranda and stretched out her long legs. As she thought of Kasie and his caresses, a voice deep within her said: 'Go home to Norman while you're safe. Get back to that cosy cage for Avril's sake.' But commonsense would not prevail. She ached for Kasie. That old magic was still there. Her body needed him, and she knew she must go to him.

At five o'clock that evening she said to Cousin Edie: 'Will you give Avril her supper and see that she goes to bed?'

Cousin Edie was only too eager to have charge of Avril for the evening. 'Oh yes,' she said, 'I'd be delighted—she's such a charming child.'

'I thought I would like to see that film—you know, the one with Bob Hope in it.'

'Oh, yes. I never go to the cinema but it will be nice for you. Mind how you go. I'll see that Avril goes to bed. Take the front door key, dear, in case I'm asleep when you get back.'

Jubilantly, Lily fled upstairs and had a bath and made herself look nice for Kasie. Wearing her beige suit with a pink frilly blouse, she walked briskly down to the harbour. It was still fairly light and she could see his slim shape pacing up and down on the quayside, his peaked cap on the back of his head. His hair had receded from his forehead which was shining and bare but otherwise he had changed very little.

The moment she reached him, his strong muscular arms went

around her. 'Oh, Lily, my lovely,' he cried. Already his body was stiff as he pressed her close to him, and they stood lost in a world all of their own in the dim light of the evening by the harbour wall.

He caught hold of her hand. 'Come on, Lily,' he urged, 'just for a while, and then we'll go out and celebrate.'

Clutching her tightly, he guided her up the gang plank of his ship and over the iron-clad deck to his small cabin. They literally fell onto the bunk together.

'Oh, God, how I have longed for this moment,' he whispered. He slid his body into her and they were as one, as they had been years before.

Afterwards, Kasie turned on the light, and got out a bottle of Bols. Lily shared the fiery liquid with him and pressed her body to him as they sat together on the bunk, her mind awhirl with emotion and memories.

At midnight, Lily said, 'I have to go, Kasie, I cannot stay out all night. I am staying with a cousin of my husband's and she is very strait-laced.'

Very happy and a little boozy, Kasie looked at her in his whimsical manner. 'So we begin again,' he sighed. 'You are about to leave me and now I hear about this other man. What husband? Not that poor deranged old fellow, George, is it? Tell me who my rival is this time?' He gave her a twisted smile.

'Oh, give over, Kasie,' said Lily. 'I married again, and so did you. What do you expect of me?'

'Well, did you divorce that old fool, or did he die? Come clean, Lily.'

'I did not divorce him,' said Lily, 'so I did not legally marry again, but Norman is good and kind to me and takes care of Avril. It was for her sake that I did it.'

'So, you are just this man's mistress,' Kasie assessed the situation. 'Well, that's better. Where is George now, still in the asylum?'

'No,' said Lily. 'He lives with us and we take good care of him.'

Kasie began to laugh a little drunkenly. 'Oh, what a set-up—husband and lover in the same house. Maybe you would like me to join them, Lily.'

Lily jumped up in a rage and struck out at him. Kasie held her tight and forced her down on the bunk. As he began to kiss her she fought back like mad. 'You swine! You rotter!' she cried. 'Now you're trying to rape me. I hate you, I'm sorry we met, I'd already forgotten you.'

Kasie let her go and sat down. He closed his eyes and put his head in his hands. 'Go home, Lily, I cannot stand any more. You have not changed one bit, you're still trying it on.'

'Trying what on?' yelled Lily, getting more worked up.

'Trying to use me as you always did. I can't resist you, but you only destroy me. I'd better stick to the dockside whores in future.'

'You do just that,' said Lily, pulling on her jacket and tidying herself. 'You won't get me any more, I'll tell you that. And I'm leaving this place, I'll go home in the morning.' She stumbled her way out onto the deck wondering how she was going to get down to the shore.

But he was beside her. 'This way, madam,' he said in a sarcastic tone.

Lily tried to brush past him but his arms came out and held her tight. His head went down on her shoulder and Kasie wept dry hard sobs. 'Lily, Lily, don't leave me. Stay with me, my lovely.'

Again her anger left her. She put her arms around him. 'Oh, Kasie, why do we quarrel?' she asked plaintively.

'I'm not sure,' he said, 'but life for me is hell without you, Lily, and hell with you, so what am I to do?'

'Honestly, Kasie, I don't know,' Lily said sadly. 'Come, walk home with me.'

They walked hand in hand through the deserted streets. A full moon sailed over the sea. 'Remember Pompey, Lily?' said Kasie. 'It seems so long ago.'

'I don't think it's possible to go back down that road, Kasie,' said Lily. 'I have my daughter and you have your son—that's all that's left for us.'

'Yes, my son. He's being educated at a good English school. That is why I sail to Gravesend to visit him, I make the voyage every three weeks.'

'How are your folks?' asked Lily.

'Mother died a year ago and Father has gone to live in Rotterdam with Rica. She is a widow now and has gone ashore. A lot has happened in a few years,' he said sadly.

'What about Wrenska?'

'She divorced me,' he replied flatly. 'I should never have married her, she was still full of hate and could not forgive nor forget. So I sailed off to the deep sea, and then bought this old cargo boat. I don't go home very often except for business. The passenger service on the Rhine brings me a good profit, but it is not enough for me. I shall only be content when I'm a millionaire.'

Lily laughed. 'Oh, Kasie, still full of dreams. Why don't you come down to earth?'

'Why, Lily?' he asked. 'What is there for me on earth but money?'

'That's one thing that doesn't mean a lot to me,' she said. 'I never had any money of my own.'

'Lily, sail with me, you and Avril,' he urged her again. 'I will give you everything, your heart's desire. No one will find us, we'll sail to the Mediterranean or the Far East, anywhere so we can be together.'

Lily shook her head. 'No, Kasie. I will not uproot Avril. And I never liked living on a ship—I'm afraid of the sea.'

'Oh, nonsense, you would soon adapt. Look how I taught you to sail in the tacking races across the harbour.'

'Yes,' she agreed, 'that was fun and I had such confidence in you, Kasie. But it's all gone and I'm afraid of what our love will do to us both. I must go home tomorrow.'

'Please stay and finish your holiday,' he begged her. 'Just one night and I'm off anyway. Tomorrow we'll go out and hit the town just as we used to, I'll wine and dine you, and I promise I'll behave myself.'

'I'll think about it, Kasie,' said Lily.

They stood in a dark doorway and she reached up to touch the curls at the nape of his neck as she used to do. They were still there. A deep thrilling sensation rushed through her and Kasie pressed his lips down on hers.

She pulled herself away saying, 'Oh, no, Kasie, never again!' Then she ran along the road to the boarding house, leaving him standing in the street. She put her key in the door and crept silently upstairs to her room where Avril lay sleeping. The girl's face was fresh and rosy and slightly tanned by the sun.

'Oh, darling,' she whispered, sinking down beside the little white bed. 'I cannot do it to you. Please God, make me brave enough to send him away.'

The next day Lily took Avril to the beach. It was a lovely day again. Avril's cough had gone and she looked very fit. Lowestoft was a dry, bracing windy spot; there were no damp mists like those on the Yorkshire Moors. They sat in the same spot in the sands. Wearing her bathing suit, Avril played with a bucket and spade. 'I want to go in the water,' she said.

'No, definitely not,' said Lily severely. She was sitting in a low-cut dress sunbathing, and hiding behind a pair of huge dark sunglasses, trying not to look concerned. She knew that Kasie would find them somehow.

Sure enough, he came running nimbly along the sands. He was wearing just an old pair of flannels and was bare-footed. He wore no shirt and his fine fair skin and muscular body were exposed to the hot sun.

She saw him coming but pretended not to. He sank down beside her, a little breathless. 'I'm not the man I used to be,' he joked, kissing the back of her neck. He slid his hand over her bare back.

'Oh, who sent for you?' Lily said acidly.

'Avril sent for me,' he replied. 'I'm going to take her swimming.'

'Oh, no you don't.' Lily tried to get up but Avril had already seen Kasie and came running.

'Papa! Papa!' she cried, giving him a grand welcome.

Kasie swept Avril up in his arms. 'I came to go bathing with you, *leiblin*,' he said.

'She won't let me,' Avril glared fiercely at her mother.

But Kasie slipped off his flannels and stood in his swimming trunks. Grabbing Avril by the hand, he ran with her down towards the sea.

'Come back!' yelled Lily in sheer terror. Kasie just laughed at her as he had done in the past.

Father and daughter galloped into the sea jumping up and down. Avril shrieked with glee. Lily hung her head, unable to watch her child in such danger, convinced that something would happen.

Kasie bounced Avril up and down in the water. 'You are a big girl now. Do you go to school?'

'Yes,' said Avril, 'a convent.'

'Where is it?' asked Kasie, holding her young body up so she could float.

'It's near Barnsley.'

'Is that where you live?' asked Kasie.

'No, I live at Hill Drop,' replied Avril in her open manner.

'Oh, great,' said Kasie, 'and I'll bet you know your name.'

'Of course I do,' gasped Avril, shaking the water out of her eyes. 'I am Avril Clegg.'

'Good for you,' said Kasie. 'Come on, we'll have a race back to your Mama.'

Lily sat staring at him with suspicion in her eyes as she wrapped Avril in a big towel. 'Idiot!' she hissed. 'She has been very ill. I'm taking her home straight away. I don't want her to get another cold.'

Kasie just grinned. He had got what he'd wanted now. Turning to Avril, he said, 'Now watch me, Avril, I'll swim right out to that big ship.' He ran back down to the beach and into the water. Lily could see his curly head bobbing about in the sea but she got to her feet in a terrible huff and took Avril home to an early lunch.

'I like Papa,' said Avril as they walked along the promenade.

'He's a bleeding nuisance,' said Lily, caught off her guard.

'You're swearing again,' said Avril, 'and you promised not to.'

That evening after Avril had been put to bed, Lily sat looking out of the bedroom window. Her heart was in her mouth for she could see him standing under the lamp post across the street and occasionally whistling 'Lili Marlene'.

'Oh, Kasie, you bastard,' whispered Lily to herself. 'Go away.'

He looked nice, she thought, dressed in a grey suit, collar and tie, and his hair was brushed flat. 'I am not coming out,' she muttered. 'You can stay there all night.'

Avril was reading in bed but suddenly her small voice called out, 'Mama, why don't you go out and see Papa? I'll ask Cousin Edie to read to me.'

Lily's legs went weak. 'Go on,' cajoled Avril. 'You know you want to.'

Lily went over and kissed her just as Cousin Edie came up with an egg custard and another picture book for Avril. 'How's my little one?' she asked.

'Read to me, Cousin Edie,' said Avril. 'Mummy has got a headache and wants to go for a walk.'

Trying to stay her tears, Lily put a mack on over her summer dress and went out to meet her man. As soon as he saw her, he pulled her into the shadows and kissed away her tears.

'Did someone upset you, my lovely? he asked in his gentle way.

'Don't ask me to explain. I'm here, ain't I?' she replied.

'Come, let's hit the town, Lily, it's a long time since we celebrated.'

They went to a pub along the front, sitting close together, as lovers do, drinking beer and gin. Lily's head swam. It had been a long time since she had indulged in a lot of booze. They left when the pub closed, and went to a hotel for a slap-up meal. Time meant little to them, and even conversation was limited. Later still, they walked along the front, stopping now and then to kiss with long passionate embraces.

When almost home, Kasie said: 'I have kept my promise, Lily. As much as I need you, I will never force myself on you.'

She pressed closer and closer to him. All clear thought had gone from her mind. 'It's goodbye, Kasie,' she said. 'We may never meet again.'

'It need not be. I come to England almost every month and often stay on in London. Tell me where to find you, my lovely.'

'No,' she shook her head. 'I can't do that.'

His tongue probed her mouth, his hands caressed her breasts. 'Oh, my love, let's go down to the beach. Let it be a real last farewell.'

Down into the darkness and on to the sands they went, and under the shadow of the promenade they said goodbye in their typical passionate manner. It was two in the morning when they finally parted.

'Farewell, my love,' said Lily.

'It's just till we meet again, my lovely,' said Kasie. 'I will be in London next month. Take my telephone number. Ring me, come to me. We are meant for each other, Lily. Please be sensible, I can well take care of you and Avril.' He pushed a slip of paper into the pocket of her raincoat as they went over the road and at the front gate of the boarding house, the tears fell like rain.

The house seemed very still, for Cousin Edie slept heavily and Avril cuddled her teddy in her arms with a peaceful smile on her red lips.

Lily bent down and kissed her. 'Oh, darling, forgive me,' she whispered. 'I know he would have made you such a good daddy.'

The next morning there was a gap in the harbour where Kasie's ship had been anchored. He had sailed for Holland. But Lily stayed in bed with a terrible hang-over, and Cousin Edie stared at her with uneasy suspicion.

While Avril played with her ball in the garden, Lily got up and packed. They would go home the next morning; she had had enough of the seaside.

Next day Norman met them at the station. He looked very

pleased to see them and remarked on how fit Avril looked. 'But you still look a bit under the weather, Lily,' he said in a concerned voice.

She stared at him with her dark-ringed eyes. 'It was all right,' she said mournfully, 'but I don't think the air suited me, it was always so windy.'

'Well, Avril looks blooming, so it was worth the expense,' beamed Norman. 'We'll soon get you back in trim, Lily, work's the best thing to keep the body healthy.'

Lily just gave him a wry grin.

It was nice to see her home again and inspect her flowers in the garden. The dogs welcomed her noisily while Avril tore off to visit her pony. Even George was pleased to see her, and came trotting up with tea and biscuits on a tray.

Lily lay on the settee and closed her eyes. No one is getting me out of my house anymore, she said to herself. It was safer inside the comfy cage than out.

CHAPTER THREE

A Trip to London

Overwhelmed by a deep sense of guilt, Lily kept her nose to the grindstone for two weeks. Once Avril was back at school, Lily spent most of her time helping Norman load up boxes of tomatoes and cucumbers onto the old truck for him to take to market. She weeded the garden and hoed the big field, which was planted with winter cabbages. She had plenty of energy and got through plenty of work in one day, but by the time she had prepared the evening meal as well, she had just about had enough. It was late autumn and the sunsets were glorious. A mist lay out on the hills most of the time and rainbow colours floated over the horizon. The big coal stove was lit and in the sitting room there was a log fire in the evenings. It was cosy and warm, and the evenings were spent in a very leisurely way, reading or sewing, and Lily had a renewed contentment. The ache in her heart was not there any more. She often thought of Kasie but in a dreamy kind of way as if that holiday had fulfilled her needs.

One evening after she had taken the dogs for a walk she hung up her raincoat. She noticed a piece of paper sticking out of the pocket, and pulled it out. 'What's this?' she thought. There was a London telephone number and beside it was written: Cumberland Hotel, November 6. Immediately, memories came racing home of Kasie and herself close together on that lonely beach. She made as if to tear the paper into shreds but instead she rushed upstairs and hid it in an old handbag at the bottom of the wardrobe.

Later she made a big meat pudding for dinner and took great care with the cold sweet. She still liked to cook but her mind was disturbed. Why should she worry? Kasie could never find her, he did not know where she lived. Then another worry flashed up. What if he had made her pregnant again? She sat down as her knees went weak at the thought. That would put the cat among the pigeons. She was Mrs Brown legally but neither George nor Norman was capable of making her pregnant. How would she ever get out of that one? She didn't know what to think, her mind was in a muddle. Perhaps she ought to see Kasie one more time to tell him that it really was over, that he should never raise his hopes again. Yes, she would do that, it was necessary.

'Why so pensive, Lily?' Norman had noticed how quiet she was being. 'Got fed up with your magazines?'

'No,' said Lily, 'I was thinking of going to the sales in two weeks' time. There's Selfridges and then one at C & A's.'

'In London?' asked Norman, a little amazed.

'Where else?' replied Lily.

'It's a good long trot in one day, and the money you save at the sale would be spent on fares,' returned Norman in his practical manner.

'Oh, there you go,' cried Lily irritably. 'You put a price on everything, you do.'

'Sorry, love,' said Norman, 'but I'm not taking you back to London just to go shopping. You can go to the sales in Barnsley when you get your allowance. I'll take the day off and go with you.'

'No, thanks,' Lily said ungraciously. 'I think I ought to have a break, I've worked like a galley slave these last two weeks.'

Avril had her head down in her homework on the sofa. She looked up suddenly with those steady blue eyes that were Lily's colour, but the stern look she gave was Kasie's. Lily turned her head away, feeling a little ashamed. 'Oh, forget it!' she cried in a bad temper. Norman shrugged and went outside to attend to his car, and Lily set about laying the table.

Soon Avril was beside her. She picked up a piece of bread, slowly buttered it and began to eat it in silence.

'Can't you wait a minute till supper's ready?' grumbled Lily.

Avril looked at Lily in a strange secret way. 'You are trying to go and see Papa,' she whispered, 'and if you go without me, I'll tell on you.'

Lily dropped the cutlery, she was so shocked. 'Be quiet, you little bitch,' she muttered.

But Avril got up and walked back into the sitting room munching the bread and butter.

'Don't drop bloody crumbs all over the carpet,' yelled Lily.

Red-faced and angry, Lily slammed the kitchen door and sat down biting her nails till the tears came. She could not believe that Avril, not quite eight years old, was so astute. She had to be very careful of her.

Over the next two weeks, Lily was very niggly to everyone. Once she slapped old George for bringing in mud from the garden on his boots, and he blubbered like a baby and went crying to Norman.

Norman said to her: 'Please leave him alone, Lily, I can't get an hour's work out of him when you upset him.'

'Bloody slave driver,' growled Lily.

But Avril was a different problem. She just closed up tight and would not talk about the proposed trip to London.

I expect I'll have to take her with me, thought Lily, but that way I'd sooner not go. She spent many sleepless nights tossing and turning. One night Norman put an arm about her. 'Can't you sleep, dear? Come, I'll cuddle you,' he said gently.

And Lily leapt out of bed, saying, 'Leave me alone! I've done my bloody day's work. You don't want me to work all night as well, do you?'

Norman was extremely shocked and a little bewildered. He didn't know it but it was as if the shadow of Kasie lay heavily between them.

At the end of the month Norman counted out his profits which he then shared out with the family. This was all done slowly and carefully—so much went as wages for the casual rural labour he employed and so much for housekeeping. Then he shared out so much for pocket money, for George, Lily and Avril. He rarely spent anything on himself.

George would squander his money on sweets and picture shows, for he had begun to like going to the films, though no one knew if he understood what they were about.

Lily was quite intolerant. 'What's the silly sod wasting his money for? He can't understand what's going on.'

Norman would reply gravely, 'We all have our pleasures, Lily, and that is his.'

So the pocket money was distributed once a month and if anyone ran out of cash before the end of the month, Norman would allow them to borrow on their next month's money.

'He's like a bleedin' money machine,' Lily would complain.

But this month was the beginning of November and Norman said, 'There's an extra ten pounds, Lily, for you to have your shopping day in London. I've heard that there is a special cheap fare and the outing will do your nerves good.'

Lily's face flamed scarlet and Avril's blue eyes looked in her direction with a mocking stare.

'I've changed my mind,' she said. 'Avril wants to come with me and it's too long a day for her.'

'Oh, no I don't,' Avril said brightly. 'Not if I can have that new saddle for Pamsie. That old second-hand one rubs her coat.' Then with a sweet smile on her face, she went forward to collect some extra money from Norman for a saddle for her beloved pony.

Lily looked at her warily. How perverse she was, she thought. That was the kind of reaction she got from Kasie. He would torment her but then give her everything she wanted. How like her father Avril was.

On November 6, looking very spruce, Lily was dropped outside the station by Norman. There had been a big firework party the previous night, and Lily had entertained Avril's schoolfriends with a bonfire and fireworks, and lots of goodies. The dogs were shut in the house and Pamsie the pony had been taken over to a local farm for the night.

'Fireworks upsets them,' said Avril, very concerned with her pet, and quite unconcerned with Lily's intention to go to London.

The next morning, when Lily left, Avril had been still in bed.

Norman remarked, 'Now, Lily, see you get on the right train for coming back. It leaves at six and gets in here at ten. I'll wait at the station for you.'

'Oh, don't do that,' said Lily. 'I'll get the taxi.'

'I'd feel better if I was waiting for you,' he insisted.

'Please, Norman, your chest is still wheezy after that bad cold. Stay at home in the warm, I can assure you I'll be all right.'

In her heart Lily knew that once she saw Kasie she would not be home until the morning. That deep longing for him had returned. That made her feel guilty about Norman but when the train moved out and she saw those misty mills disappearing, a feeling of relief came over her. She spread out her arms like wings of a bird. 'Well, smoky old town,' she said, 'here I come—it's a long time since I have been back.'

At the station she rang the number on the piece of paper and asked if Mr De Fries was staying there. The man on the other end of the line seemed to know him quite well.

'Yes, Captain De Fries arrived last night. Would you like us to find him so you can talk to him?'

'No, thank you, I'm on my way,' said Lily.

Lily remembered the Cumberland Hotel from her clippie days, but it had been given a facelift to remove the shrapnel scars left over from the blitz. It now looked very posh and a big, red-coated doorman stood outside. She felt a little nervous wondering if this was the right place after all. It looked very expensive—surely Kasie could not afford such a posh hotel. But once inside those big swing doors, her courage returned. She went up to the reception desk to ask for Captain De Fries and the receptionist had barely put down the receiver before he bounced sprightly out of the lift and came hurrying towards her.

'Oh, Lily, my lovely, you came.' He kissed her warmly and guided her to one of the deep luxurious armchairs in the front room while he returned to the desk to talk with the receptionist. Then he came back and took hold of Lily's arm possessively while he piloted her towards the lift. So far Lily had not uttered one word. They just stood gazing at each other until the lift jolted to a stop and Kasie had opened the door of his suite. 'Enter, Mrs De Fries,' he said gallantly, 'or shall I carry you over the threshold?'

Now Lily spoke for the first time, collecting her wits quickly. 'Turn it up, Kasie, what's the idea? I'm not stopping. I only came to talk to you.'

But Kasie had slid off her jacket and put his arms about her. His lips were hot and passionate, his hands sought her breasts.

'Oh, Lily,' he whispered. 'How I have longed for you!'

Still protesting, she moved closer to him, muttering, 'Now, Kasie, no funny business. I'm through with all that now.'

He guided her towards the bed with its silk bedspread. Rolling her gently onto the bed, he said, 'Lily, Lily, don't chat, it's time for lovemaking.'

Lily was lost. The magic of his strong sweet body and his passionate kissing had overwhelmed her. He bent her back over the bed pressing himself between her legs and with one hand he slipped off her panties. Moments later they had slipped down and down into the deep darkness, caught up by the swift hot passion that always carried them away.

Later, she sat on Kasie's lap in the deep armchair wearing only her white silk slip. He stroked her bare, outstretched legs with his strong hands. 'How I love your beautiful legs,' he said. 'Sometimes I think I will go crazy when I think of that Limey you live with who might be touching them.'

Lily started to laugh heartily. 'Oh, gor blimey, Kasie,' she said. 'What makes you think that Norman has the time to sit and admire my legs?'

'Okay, okay, laugh at me,' he said. 'But I'm not letting you go, Lily. My mind is made up on that score.'

'Oh, yes,' said Lily, wriggling off his lap. 'Let me make up my own mind, if you don't mind.'

'Then why did you come here?' he challenged her.

'Because I wanted to get it right once and for all, Kasie. I can't afford to break up my home. I have known what it is like to be

homeless when you deserted me for that Dutch woman . . .'
She paused. The thought of Wrenska still made her feel jealous.

'Oh, come, *leiblin*, don't let us spoil this lovely weekend.
We'll go out and see the town.'

'I've promised to return tonight. I'm supposed to be at the
sales at Selfridges.'

'We will go to the sales, then,' he said gaily. 'And I will buy
you all your heart's desires.' He kissed the back of her neck and
nuzzled behind her arms.

'Oh, don't, Kasie,' she cried. A strange quivering rippled
inside her at the close touch of his body.

She freshened up and tidied her hair and then they went out
onto the wet streets. Outside, a thick fog seemed to hang over
everything. All the shoppers were bustling about, trying to get
on the big red buses which cruised past, and taxis dashed madly
in and out of the traffic. Lily breathed in the atmosphere, the
hubbub and the hullaballoo of her own town. 'Never ever
thought I'd miss London so much,' she said.

'It's my favourite place,' said Kasie. 'Wherever I am in the
world, I think of you and London Town, and long to be with
my lovely.'

Lily looked directly at him. 'What the bloody 'ell is the matter
with you tonight, Kasie?' she asked. 'I've never known you to
be so soft and so excited.'

'Well, let us find a restaurant and over dinner I will tell you all
my secrets,' said Kasie mysteriously.

They went to a small, expensive French restaurant in a back
street in Soho, where they ate braised veal cutlets and drank
French wine. They sat in a corner and looked only at each other.

'I cannot understand all this sudden prosperity,' said Lily,
'that posh hotel, for instance.'

'I've been there several times recently. Had a good business
deal and met my contact there. Did you like it, Lily?'

'It's all right, but where are you getting all this money from?'

He grinned and took out a fountain pen from his top pocket.
'That's it, Lily, and there's plenty more inside that little pen.'

She giggled. 'Oh, give over, Kasie, don't kid me,' she said.

'Stay with me tonight, darling,' he said, 'and in the morning I promise to tell you.'

'I can't stay,' she insisted. 'Norman will be furious.'

He suddenly got white and looked very angry. Holding her wrist in a vicious grip he hissed: 'Don't you ever talk about that man in my company, not unless you want me to murder someone.'

'Let go, Kasie,' whimpered Lily, 'you're hurting me.'

Immediately he let go and pressed her fingers to his lips. 'Just don't provoke me,' he pleaded. 'Stay just for tonight and in the morning you can decide if it is the last time for us. Come, let's go and get drunk as we used to.'

And they did just that, and went to nearly every pub in Soho, to pubs which had acts, ones that had strippers, and some that had loud roaring music and lots of young folk twisting and gyrating on the floor. But it was all the same to Lily and Kasie. They drank and danced and talked of old times, of London in the blitz, they fell in and out of taxis and ended up in an all-night cafe. The dawn was breaking over the Thames when they got the final taxi back to the hotel. Lily's mind was very befuddled and Kasie was falling about all over the place. Clasping each other tight, they fell into the silken bed and slept till midday. Lily woke up with a terrible hang-over and went under the shower. When she came back to dress, she found her clothes strewn all over the place.

'Christ!' she said, holding her head, 'we was in a state last night, wasn't we?'

But Kasie smiled in his half-sleep.

As Lily remembered Norman and realised what she had done, she could have kicked herself for being so weak. Kasie was still sleeping when she wrote out a note: 'Farewell, my lover, I'll never forget you. But I *have* to go home.' She pinned this to the mirror.

Kasie awoke just as she was creeping towards the door. He was out of bed like a whippet. 'So, you will sneak off and leave me once more, my lovely,' he accused her.

'But Kasie, I must go,' she pleaded. 'I said I'd be back last night.'

'Yes, you will go to this northern town and I come with you. We will tell this man that he has my child and my woman and he is to let them go or to reckon with me.' He said all this very slowly in a cold voice.

'Oh, don't talk wet, Kasie, you're still drunk.'

'No, Lily, I am very sober and very determined not to be made a fool of by you anymore. You go home and get Avril and we are going to fly to Sumatra.'

'Where the bleedin' 'ell is that?' asked Lily.

'In the Dutch East Indies,' he replied. 'Remember Jack and Easi? They live there now and we will stay with them till I get my new business established.'

Lily looked at her watch. 'It's past midday and I've got to go,' she said.

'I will never let you out of this room alive,' Kasie said dramatically.

Lily sighed and sat down. 'All right, Kasie, get it off your chest. What is this big secret business and why would you suddenly give up the sea?'

'I have not given up the sea but my ship is now sailing to Amsterdam with its last cargo before being put up for sale.'

'But why?' she asked. 'I won't be able to take Avril out of England just like that—after all, George is supposed to be her father.'

'It's the wise child that knows its own father,' grinned Kasie. 'But I've made enough money in six months to look after us out there. I smuggled quicksilver from Germany. It is very hard to come by so I got a good price for it.'

'Oh, smuggling,' said Lily, 'back to your old bad habits, then.'

'Well, it proved worthwhile.' Kasie was shameless. 'Mercury is used in thermometers and industry is very short of it. So, Lily, my lovely, come with me, if we can't get Avril out immediately, send her to boarding school—there are plenty in southern England. My son is in one in Sussex. I will pay for this opportunity, and I am going to the Indies because I am interested in oil tankers—they are the coming thing.'

'Oh, Kasie,' cried Lily, beginning to get depressed. 'Don't bug me with all that. I know nothing about business, let me alone. I'll see you when you want me, but don't make me leave my home. I've got George to think about even though he gets taken good care of by Norman.'

Kasie collapsed into a chair and put his hands over his face. 'Oh dear God,' he cried, 'first there's Avril, then George, then this bloody fellow Norman, and then there will be the cat and the dog. Where the bloody hell do I come on the list?'

'Don't be silly,' cried Lily. 'You know it's only you I really love.'

'Then bloody well prove it,' he yelled, jumping up and holding her tight.

She stroked his head and kissed his cheek. 'Kasie, darling, just be patient. Let me sort it all out my own way. I promise on my honour I will try, but let me go home.'

'Why did you come?' he asked.

'I was thinking you might have made me pregnant and I was worried.'

He gave a wry grin. 'I see, so you needed me then, Lily.'

'Well, if you have made me pregnant, I will bloody need you,' she said sharply.

'Well, let me put you out of your misery,' he said sarcastically. 'Since I have put two bastards into this lousy world and I have no intention of doing it again, I have had an operation.'

'An operation?' cried Lily, puzzled.

'Yes. With enough money, you can do many things.'

'Well, I'll be blowed,' said Lily. 'Then that means I've got three old crocks, it don't seem feasible.'

'No, Lily, I'm no old crock, as you must realise, and without you it is only the whores for me in future . . .'

'Let me go home, Kasie, I'll write to you and tell you I promise.'

He got up and put on his jacket. 'You have won once more, Lily,' he said. 'I'll put you on the train.'

They walked very sombrely along Oxford Street towards the station. 'I am supposed to have come up here on a shopping trip and here I am without a bleeding thing. I've lost the heart to go to Selfridges now.'

They paused just where a Stone Martin cape was displayed in the window.

'Like that?' Kasie asked.

'It's forty quid,' said Lily. 'I can't afford that.'

'Come on, darling, have a farewell present from me,' he said in a strange tone.

Lily's eyes lit up but she checked herself. 'I can't take that from you, Kasie, not after the way I've treated you,' she said.

He edged her into the shop. 'Come on,' he said, 'last night you earned it.'

When they came out of the shop with the cape wrapped up in a box, Kasie said: 'What about a doll for Avril?'

'She don't like dolls,' said Lily. 'Ponies are the only thing she worries about.'

'Okay, let's get her some chocolates.'

So with a big box of chocolates for Avril and her smart fur cape, Lily was well pleased with herself.

Kasie's mood seemed to have changed. He held her hand and they strode along and he whistled a song she remembered called 'Let us be sweethearts.'

'I'll always remember that song,' she said, 'it will remind me of this lovely time.' She suddenly felt quite sad.

Kasie said dryly, 'It will take me a long time to forget it. In fact, I'll never get over it.'

Lily waved him goodbye, dreading the thought that she had to face Norman now. That was not going to be easy.

CHAPTER FOUR

The Stone Wall

On the train up north, she had been able to control her worries but she began to feel a little nervous when she got out of the train at Barnsley and waited for a taxi. Suddenly she was alarmed by the sound of a motor horn and there, large as life, was Norman sitting in the old truck outside the station, his face the colour of death. She hurried over the road towards him, babbling half-thought-out excuses about missing the train and meeting an old friend in town and staying overnight with her. 'She was on the buses with me, her name was Ivy,' she gabbled on.

'Get in, Lily,' Norman said coldly, 'and don't stand there chattering.'

She climbed into the seat beside him. The old truck smelled powerfully of cabbages. She sniffed and then she kissed him on the cheek. 'It's good to be home,' she said brightly.

The little muscle in Norman's cheek twitched spasmodically as it always did when he was disturbed. He's upset, she thought, I must be careful. So they lapsed into silence.

Suddenly Norman spoke in a gloomy voice. 'I've been back and forth all night since ten o'clock. I really thought something terrible had happened to you. Don't you ever do that again, Lily,' he said sternly.

'Sorry, dear,' said Lily almost overwhelmed with guilt. 'It was not a very good idea altogether, I did not like Selfridges.'

'So you didn't do your shopping?' he asked, somewhat surprised.

'Oh, yes,' said Lily. 'I'll show you what I bought when we get home.'

'I won't have the time,' said Norman. 'I have to catch up on jobs. I'll see you tonight.'

He dropped Lily off outside their home, and she went upstairs to change into her slacks and a woolly jumper. She put the little fur cape about her shoulders and paraded in front of the mirror. She stroked the fur. 'Thank you, Kasie,' she said out loud, 'you always know what pleases me.' Taking it off, she put the cape in the wardrobe.

It was back to her chores downstairs. She cleared up the breakfast debris, then sorted out the mail, vacuumed the sitting room and prepared the evening meal. There was little time to stand and stare once she got back home, she now had a daily routine.

As the sun set over the misty moors, Avril came home from school on the school bus. She ran to the house on long legs, her pigtails flying in the wind. As she reached the house, she was breathless, her eyes glowed and her cheeks were rosy.

Lily thought how lovely she was and thought how she would never do anything to spoil her happy life or take away that youthful exuberance.

'So, you're back,' Avril said, giving Lily a sly look. 'I can't stay, I've got to feed Pamsie. Brought me anything?'

'Yes,' said Lily.

'I'll see it when I come back in,' said Avril. Taking a cake from the tin on the dresser, she dashed off.

'It seems she didn't miss me,' sighed Lily, beating up the Yorkshire pudding expertly and rapidly, concentrating her mind on domestic matters again to ward off thoughts of Kasie.

After the well-prepared dinner of roast beef, Yorkshire pudding and coconut pudding, Norman, with full tummy, pushed back his chair. 'That were great, Lily. We really missed you last night.'

'I made eggs on toast, didn't I, Daddy?' exclaimed Avril in a rather possessive voice.

'Yes, darling,' said Norman giving her a kiss. He disappeared into the sitting room to do his daily accounts.

As soon as he left the room, Avril bounced up to Lily. 'Come on, what did you bring me?'

'Only some chocolates,' said Lily glumly, retrieving them from the sideboard.

'Mingy thing,' said Avril, pouncing on the lovely box, but her eyes lit up when she saw the size of it. She prised off the lid. 'Oh, yum, yum, who bought these?' she asked, 'Papa?'

Lily's heart missed a beat. She had begun to feel a little jaded and alone. 'Avril, stop this nonsense! I don't know what you are talking about, I got those at the Lyon's Corner House for you and I got lost in London. It was all very confusing with the traffic and bustling crowds.'

Avril's mouth was full of chocolate. 'Want one? They're scrumptious.'

'No, thanks,' said Lily. 'I'm going to lie down. I've got a headache.'

'I'll do my homework, and then go to bed,' said Avril nonchalantly.

'Don't eat all them bloody sweets at once,' cried Lily, losing her temper.

'Don't worry,' said Avril calmly. 'I'm saving them to show my friends at school, not everyone gets such a huge box of chocolates like this. It was kind of Papa, wasn't it?'

'I told you, I bought them!' screamed Lily, and she marched off to bed. She felt as if she had met up with a stone wall. Norman had not even questioned her about the trip. Perhaps she ought to think herself lucky, but somehow it made her feel so depressed. She took some aspirin and went to bed.

The next morning, she knew for certain that she was not pregnant. She was relieved because she had doubted what Kasie had told her. Now she was regretting that she had made that trip, for the longing for him seemed to be greater than ever.

Over the next few weeks, she tossed restlessly night after night remembering and savouring in her mind, those lovely moments of that London weekend.

Norman made no more reference to it except to remark that

the fur cape was a waste of money. He did not like women in furs, he said, for he thought that they looked tarty.

Lily felt very depressed, and no matter how she tried, she could not cheer up. An apprehensive feeling hung over as if she imagined Kasie would pop out of the wardrobe at any minute. When she made the beds, her heart was often in her mouth at the slightest sound. They had made no arrangement to meet again, and why had he given in so easily? Had he changed his mind about going to the Dutch East Indies? Was he lurking about in London in all the seedy places and getting rid of that money he had come by dishonestly? Knowing Kasie, this was probably the case. In the afternoon she sat recalling how in the blitz they had toured all those sordid back street joints, from the Chinese gambling dens where they played mahjong, to the squalid crooked clubs in the East End and the back of Petticoat Lane where Kasie seemed to be well known.

Lily tried to fight off her depression by working hard in the house and the nursery. She packed vegetables for the market, baked cakes for the ladies' social nights, anything to keep her occupied and her mind away from worrying thoughts.

One morning, she sorted out the mail as usual, separating the important letters from the circulars. She noticed one addressed to Norman in handwriting that was vaguely familiar, but she did not think about it too much. She put the letter up on the mantelpiece in the sitting room for him. Then she went about her chores, and took in the tubs of geraniums for the winter. There was a frosty warning in the air; winter was not far away. She was making the coffee after dinner when Norman picked up his letter and began to read it. His face became very red and angry, and his hands trembled. Lily knew that something was very wrong.

'Who's that from?' she asked innocently.

But Norman thrust the letter rapidly into his jacket pocket. 'I'll go and see if I turned the heaters on,' he said quickly.

Lily knew he was serious and began to worry. She put Avril to bed and gave her a story book to read. 'I'm going down to the greenhouse to see if Daddy is all right,' she said.

Lily, My Lovely

She put on her coat and went looking for Norman. She found him huddled in a heap in the greenhouse, his hands over his face. He was really crying.

'Oh, God!' she cried. 'What is it, Norman, not bad news?' She thought it must be some financial disaster, for she knew this was Norman's main obsession, and she was quite unprepared for the shock she got when he thrust the crumpled letter at her.

'It concerns you, Lily,' he said. 'Read it!'

Her hands were trembling as she read it.

I am writing to you as a friend and not your enemy, as I have been through the gates of hell and know exactly what a woman can do to a man. Your wife is continually unfaithful to you. She spent the weekend in London with a man who is the father of her child. Do not be put off by her lying to you—she is very good at it.

A friend

'Oh Christ!' yelled Lily, 'a bloody anonymous letter. Is that what's upsetting you? Throw the filthy thing on the fire.' She aimed it towards the boiler fire but Norman held her arm and stopped her. 'Is there any truth in that letter?' he demanded. 'Tell me, for God's sake, and put me out of my misery.'

'Of course not,' snapped Lily. 'It's some malicious dirty cow from the village, I expect.'

'But it was posted in London,' said Norman disarmingly.

'Well, it must be that girl I met. You can't really trust anyone these days,' said Lily, trying desperately to be casual about it all.

Norman looked her straight in the face. 'Lily,' he said, 'I never probed or pried into your past, I said I never would. But Avril is now part of my family and I regard you as my wife. For God's sake, don't do anything to destroy our relationship,' he begged.

Lily put her arms about him. 'Oh, Norman,' she said, 'I'll never desert you. You have given me and my child the only peace and happiness I have ever known.'

White-faced and distraught, Norman held her close. He was so emotional that Lily did not know him. She responded to his kisses in her efforts to placate him and shut out the grim truth from her mind.

A slight movement in the corner revealed George crouching there with tears rolling down his poor old scarred face. He was crying in sympathy for Norman.

'Oh, darling, we've got company,' said Lily as they pulled apart. Old George got up and ran out of the greenhouse, spitting at Lily as he rushed past her. 'Cow! Rotten dirty cow!' he muttered.

'Come,' Norman said to Lily, 'let's go inside. I do believe you and I'll ignore that filthy letter on condition that if you get any problems in that direction you will come and consult me. Promise me that, so I can protect you.'

Lily sighed. 'All right, Norman, I promise.'

'That's not enough,' he said. 'I want you also to swear that on the life of that child you will not desert me.'

Lily was heartbroken. 'Yes, Norman,' she said humbly, 'I promise.'

They went in and went to bed. Norman was more sexually excited than he had been for a long time and while he made love to her, he said: 'Lily, I love you. I'll die if I lose you or little Avril.'

Afterwards, she stifled her sobs and tried to sleep but uppermost in her mind was that letter. Only one person could have sent it, and that was Kasie. How could he do that? Tomorrow, I'll get the bastard, she thought, her temper slowly burning inside her. She could not imagine what he had hoped to achieve.

In the morning when Norman had gone off to work and Avril left for school, Lily drove down to the town and went into the main post office to telephone. She dialled the number he had given her. With any luck, he would still be in London—no doubt waiting for the results of his rotten filthy letter. She felt her ire rising within her when the hotel switchboard answered, but her legs trembled when the telephonist said: 'I'll put you through to the room.'

'Hullo,' came that cool soft voice, 'who's speaking?'

'You know, you bleedin' mean stinking bastard!' yelled Lily.

'Calm down,' Kasie urged. 'I don't know what you are talking about.'

'The letter, you bloody liar. You wrote a letter to Norman,' she gabbled on. 'I don't know how you got my address, but you and I are through. That's the last dirty trick you will ever play on me.'

'Lily, Lily my lovely,' he called. 'Get on a train and come to me. I am waiting for you. And bring Avril.'

'You got some bloody nerve!' she screeched down the phone at him.

Suddenly his voice hardened. 'All right,' he said, 'then I'll come to you.' There was a click as he put the phone down.

Lily stood stunned with the phone still in her hand. She was too shocked to think for a second but then rummaged in her handbag for some more coins. She had none so she dashed over to the counter to get change. As she waited, her temper cooled. He wouldn't dare come, he was kidding, she thought. Surely he was kidding. She had enough on her plate at the moment, commiserating with Norman, and having to cope with that bloody frustrating George who had taken to sulking and would not even look at her.

Oh Christ, she thought, I need a drink. She went over to the local pub and bought herself a gin and tonic. She sat in the saloon bar trying to think what the next move should be. If Kasie really was coming she might wait at the station and stop him but she could be there all day and he might not come at all. All these harassing thoughts she turned over in her mind. She did some shopping, and met Avril from school, fearing all the time that she would see Kasie's dapper little figure as he came searching for her.

In fact, it was later that evening, after supper was over and she was about to clear the table, when he arrived. She happened to look out of the window and see a figure out there in the darkness. It could only be Kasie, walking slowly and deliberately up to the front door.

'Oh,' she let out a cry of consternation, causing Norman to raise his head from his newspaper.

'What's the matter, Lily?' he asked. Outside, the dogs had begun to bark. Kasie had reached the front door.

White-faced with terror, Lily panicked. 'It's him!' she said woefully. 'He's come, Norman.'

Slowly Norman got up, took her arm and sat her down in the armchair. 'Keep calm now, Lily. I will handle this situation.' He walked across the room into the hall and opened the front door.

Lily could hear the murmur of voices.

Moments later, Norman showed the very stern-looking man into the sitting room. Kasie seemed almost alien to her, Lily just sat rooted to her chair staring at the big hefty Norman and small dapper Kasie and wondering where it was all going to end.

Casually Norman showed Kasie a chair. 'Sit down,' he said. 'Like a drink?'

'Well, it would be welcome,' returned Kasie, that sarcastic grin hovering about his lips as he looked at Lily crouched in the armchair.

He raised his glass. '*Prost*,' he said in his continental way.

Norman acknowledged it and then added: 'Have you got business with me, sir?'

'Well, you could say that,' replied Kasie. 'I've come to collect my daughter, Avril, and Lily, too, if she will go with me.'

Lily rose from her chair. 'You swine, Kasie!' she yelled. 'How can you do this to me?'

'Lily,' said Norman severely, 'sit down. I'll handle this situation, just be quiet.'

'Well,' said Norman, 'I have no intention of parting with Avril and as far as I'm concerned, she's my daughter. So what are you going to do about that? Now, Lily, tell him you do not want him and have no allegiance to him, and we will all settle this matter peaceably.'

That hard look came back into Kasie's brown eyes. He stepped towards Lily. 'Lily, my lovely, don't back out now, I came to get you both and I will not leave without you.'

Lily put her hands over her face and began to sob.

Norman put out his good arm very firmly in front of Kasie as he went towards her. 'Look, mate, I said we would settle this amicably, but if you want it another way I'm quite game,' he threatened.

Kasie went white. There was a look of murder in his eyes.

Then suddenly Avril came dancing into the room. 'Oh, what is going on?' she asked them sweetly. 'Hullo, Papa, what are you doing here?'

Everyone just looked at one another in the tense silence.

'Take Avril to her room, Lily,' Norman said in a very authoritative way.

Lily grabbed Avril and ran. As she passed Kasie she could see he was trembling visibly.

'Don't leave me,' he called to her. 'I'm sorry about the letter.'

'You betrayed me,' sobbed Lily as she ran. 'You stabbed me in the back, Kasie. I'm finished, it's over.'

She lay on Avril's bed with tears pouring down her cheeks. Avril sat on the bed beside her looking confused. 'What's the matter, Mummy?' she asked. 'I thought you liked Papa. What has he done to you, and why is Daddy quarrelling with him?'

Downstairs voices were raised. 'Will you kindly leave my house, sir,' Norman was saying. 'You have had your answer from my wife. Go now before I do something we will both be sorry for.'

'She is not your wife,' declared Kasie, 'that poor wretch over there is her husband.'

George stood in the kitchen doorway with his mouth agape, staring at the two men. He seemed overcome by emotions.

'I said leave,' said Norman giving Kasie a push.

Caught off guard, Kasie lost his balance, but he was quickly up ready to attack Norman.

Suddenly, a whirling, biting and scratching tornado rushed at him mowing him down again, it was George running amok.

'Oh Christ!' cried Kasie, 'call him off! I'm getting out of here.' He dashed out of the front door.

Norman quickly slammed the door and put on the bolts.

Lily could hear Kasie calling out to her: 'Lily, my lovely,

don't desert me.' He was standing out on the garden path, but she did not answer, she just held on desperately to Avril. Through the window she could still hear him. He was crying, and she could hear his sobs. Part of her wanted so much to get up and go to him, but something stronger held her back. It was as if it was all happening to someone else.

After a while, Avril opened the window. 'Now Papa has really gone,' she said.

'Oh, come away, darling,' cried Lily. 'What puzzles me is how he found me,' she muttered.

'I told him,' said Avril, 'when we went swimming. He asked me my name and where I lived.'

'Oh, Kasie, you swine,' sobbed Lily.

'It's a pity,' said Avril whimsically. 'I think he was rather nice.'

Despite his reception at Hill Drop Farm, Kasie was still not ready to give up, as was clear from that last dreadful letter which burned a hole in Lily's heart. She did not tell Norman about it but carried it around in her pocket where it felt like a lead weight. She was to re-read it many times over the years to come:

Lily, my lovely, I sent you my last final appeal. Now I am going home with a broken heart, I just cannot believe what has happened to us, I am so hurt and unhappy. God knows why I write this, there must be a reason somewhere. I have looked at all the possibilities and I came to the conclusion that I have not lost everything in life because I am beginning to think I never had anything except my imagination. You are not capable of giving a man what he wants. You could not keep your promise to the one man who was willing to keep and defend you. Nor could you give me what I think I own—my daughter. I am now beginning to doubt whether she is mine. Perhaps there is another one somewhere who knows the God-damned truth, for I cannot live with it any longer. So, farewell, my Lily, I will try and forget you and wish you to be happy without me. But you and I know that it will not be easy. I am just getting on the ferry now, about to drown, not myself, but my sorrows.

Always yours, Kasie.

'Oh, God, Kasie, you bloody devil,' Lily would cry every time she read it, 'how can you be so cruel to me? But one thing is certain—I'll never trust you again.'

CHAPTER FIVE

Those Mellow Years

Kasie bothered them no more except in Lily's imagination. Every night she could hear his heartbroken sobs drifting in through the window. Sometimes she could hear them in the day as well, and she found it difficult to sleep or eat.

Norman watched her with concern, but no mention was made of that fateful evening again.

Lily's worries began to show on her face. Her wide smile appeared infrequently and her face started to show lines. But she still had a ferocious energy for hard work. She cleaned and polished the house, and sowed seeds by the thousand for bedding plants for next spring. She made pots and pots of jam and tried out all kinds of new recipes; only when she was cooking could she lose herself. At Christmas she was up to her neck with children's parties and social occasions. She was still popular at the Ladies' Club and even persuaded Norman to attend its New Year Dance at the village hall. For the first time she brought out the little fur cape and put it around her shoulders. She trembled as she stroked the soft shiny fur. 'Where are you, Kasie,' she whispered. 'I wish you happiness, my love.'

She waltzed with Norman at the dance and they had been close. She introduced him to her friends from the Ladies' Club and he beamed with pride. Everyone congratulated him on the lovely big buffet for which she had done all the catering, and the villagers presented her with a huge bouquet of roses.

'Your pastry melts in the mouth, Lily,' one old fellow told her.

'Old Norman's no fool, he made a good match there,' someone else muttered to his friend.

After the dance on that New Year's Eve, they drove home past the snow-covered fields and the lights of their house shone out into the night. When they arrived home, Norman took the fur cape from her shoulders. 'By goom, lass,' he said, 'thee were a reet bobby dazzler toneet, Lily, I were reet proud of thee.'

Lily was hardly listening to him. As her fingers lingered on the fur cape, her memories came racing back of other New Year's Eves spent with her and Kasie in passionate embraces.

Norman noticed the look of reverie on her face and guessed what she was thinking. 'Never look back,' he said, 'it does not pay. Go forward, my love, there is everything ahead of us.'

Lily put her arms about his neck. 'Oh, Norman, you are a wonderful person. I don't deserve you.'

Kasie's name had never been mentioned but once they were in bed, Norman looked at her and said, 'Tell me, why did you love him so? Why can't you forget him? I'm trying hard to understand.'

She put her head on his shoulder. 'I can't explain. The love I have for you is of a different kind from what I feel for . . . him.' She could not bring herself to utter his name.

So began the mellow years. The cold hard winter up on the hill was very severe. Norman spent many nights out helping the farmers round up the new born lambs, and Lily ended up with these little 'lodgers', who had been deserted by their mothers. They were wrapped up in blankets and kept by the fire or put in Avril's cot. Lily fed them with a bottle and rubbed life into their cold little limbs.

The roads got snowed up and Avril could not get to school, so Lily would help her as best she could with her studying, not that Lily was much help. Norman and she both agreed that Avril was an unusually bright child. In arithmetic and spelling she could run rings around both of them.

'Didn't you go to school?' Avril would ask Lily when she had made some big mistakes.

'Yes, I went to school, love, but we didn't learn a lot—just writing and reading, not much else.'

'Why on earth not?' queried Avril.

'Well, we were very poor and in our slum district there were hundreds of kids and the teachers could not manage, I suppose.'

Avril would then want to know more of Lily's background and Lily would tell her some of it. 'Our small house was without a proper lavatory and all we had was a cold water tap.' She would tell her of the blitz and about poor old granny getting blown up in her bathchair. But that was as far as she was prepared to go, the rest of it Lily kept a close secret.

'What date did you marry Daddy?' Avril asked one day. Lily quickly made up a date.

'Did you wear white?' Avril persisted.

'No, love, there was a war on. No one wore white in those days. I had just a grey costume and white accessories.'

So during that long cold winter the alert lively mind of ten-year-old Avril kept Lily on her toes. Fortunately there did seem to be a silent understanding between them, for Avril never once mentioned Papa. It was as if she understood.

At last spring came. Green shoots started to appear on the plants in the big greenhouses and, urged on by Lily, Norman got a big bank loan and bought a tractor. He also purchased lots of chickens, and dug up new land to plant potatoes; cabbages and sugar beet, while Lily grew runner beans and herbs in the back garden. She kept very busy and was still full of energy. She grew slim and lean-looking and allowed her lovely hair to grow. She often wore it in a chignon, a deep auburn roll of hair that shone in the sunlight as she dug into the moist, sweet-smelling earth and watched the trees begin to bud. An over-whelming love of nature revealed itself within her and she revelled in the peace and beauty that this home high up in the hills provided for her.

The years flashed by and suddenly Avril was fifteen and about to leave the convent school. Her love of animals had persisted and she had decided to become a vet so she was now studying for the entrance exam for college. At every opportunity,

Norman and Lily encouraged her. Avril was big, hefty and healthy, though still obstinate and defiant, but she was a very clever and well-balanced child who had everything she ever wanted, a good education and a happy home life.

Every now and then Lily and Norman would still argue about the benefits of a legal marriage. Norman was straightforward. 'It will be easy, Lily, George will not ever be capable of making his own decisions, so you get an order out to that effect. Then you can get the divorce through on medical grounds, and we can be married.'

But such talk would get Lily really mad. 'Don't be so bleedin' daft! How can I get married to you after we have lived together for more than five years? I can just imagine what that lot down in the village would have to say about it—and what about Avril? How will I explain to her?'

'No need for her to know,' said Norman, who had clearly thought it all through. 'We can go up to London and get married.'

'No, thanks,' said Lily. 'I'll stay as I am.'

'I get worried in case anything happens to me, Lily. There is a lot of things to consider.'

'Why, where the bloody 'ell are you going?' demanded Lily.

'Well, thee can never be sure. I should really put my house in order,' said Norman, very worried.

'We're not old-age pensioners yet,' said Lily. 'What are you worrying about? Don't keep on, Norman, ain't you got enough to do without thinking of popping off every minute?'

In the end Norman gave in and stopped bringing the subject up and they settled to a lazy pattern of life. He improved the property, and ran the nursery very profitably. They indulged Avril, and Lily seemed relatively very happy and content.

That September Avril went to the agricultural college in town to study animal welfare, and still spent her free time riding at the gymkhanas on her new young filly, Morning Star. Pamsie was now put out to pasture. George spent his days working with Norman or else playing with Avril's pet rabbit and hamsters.

Each day the sun rose and set over the sweet moorland. The

small village of Hill Drop went on expanding with more council houses and a supermarket, and a big posh bungalow was built high up on the hill.

Norman didn't like these changes. 'It's getting a bit over populated, Lily,' he said one day. 'Sometimes I think that when I've paid off this bank loan, we will move.'

Lily screwed up her eyes and stared out at the blue shadowy hill. 'No, I like it here,' she said. 'It's the only place where I have found peace of mind.'

'As you wish, dear,' replied Norman, putting his good arm affectionately around her. Lily felt differently now than she used to about living with Norman. She was sure that she no longer wanted to fly away. As with caged birds, her wings were stiff and the inclination to fly to freedom had gone. She did not mind. She liked the close, domesticated scene she had nurtured during these last five years, and she loved the beauties of the sweeping countryside all around her. She enjoyed the love and great pride she felt for Avril and acknowledged the respect she had developed for the soft-spoken Norman who loved and cherished her in his homely way.

Old George had not improved much and was still as contrary as ever, but Lily could put up with him now that she had learned how to cope with him.

So Lily had learned to accept her fate, and she was sure she had found what she had really been seeking—peace and security. She was still rather extrovert and flamboyant in her ways, loving to dress up and look nice and be the centre of attention at any village social event. Norman would laugh at her proudly. 'Lily must be the belle of the ball,' he would joke.

One day when he made such a remark, Avril looked up at him. 'It's funny, you are so different,' she said. 'Why did you pick someone like Mummy to marry?'

'Because I loved her,' returned Norman.

Avril thought about this for a while and then said, 'What, the first time you saw her?'

Norman paused, his mind looking back down the road to when that pretty young girl came to the military hospital to visit her maimed husband. A strange expression crossed his face. 'I suppose you could say that,' he said.

'I'm not sure that I ever want to get married,' said Avril. 'I just want to work as an animal doctor. I've put my name down for voluntary work collecting all the poor old stray cats that get left behind when they pull down the old houses in parts of the town.'

'Great,' said Norman, 'I expect they'll all come to live up here, and that depresses me.'

'What, the cats?'

'No, the people. It was fine when I was a boy, but now it's cars along the road and buildings everywhere.'

'Never mind,' said Avril. 'Let's go and live in Australia, they say that it's a great big lonely place.'

Norman sighed. 'Don't know, Avril, I think I've left it a bit late.'

'What do you mean? You're not old.' Avril looked surprised.

'No, but I'm beginning to feel my age,' replied Norman.

She stared right at him in her forthright manner, her blue eyes hard and demanding. 'Well, you look all right to me,' she said. 'It's Mummy who wants to stay here, isn't it?'

He smiled at her tolerantly. She was an astute child.

'Well, if I was you, I would do what I wanted. After all, she always does,' added Avril.

'Now, now, cherub,' muttered Norman. 'Come on, help me to bring in that truss of hay for the horses.' He got up a little breathlessly, because he was still suffering from the effects of a bout of bronchitis he had had during that last cold winter.

Now he had a good thriving business, farm shop and nurseries, and a nice house. The years had not been wasted. His only worry was that Lily would never marry him; she was still obstinately refusing to cooperate with him in getting a divorce from George.

'I must make good provision for them both,' he told himself. 'I'll go to town and talk to the lawyer.' But he never got around to it.

The long bright summer passed and the moors were once

again covered with purple heather and during college vacations, Avril rode her horse over the hills and fields with complete abandon.

One afternoon, Lily was lazing in her garden sewing among the late roses and reading her glossy magazines. It was a late Saturday afternoon and a glorious sunset was building up. The sky had gone a fiery red as the big orange sun sank slowly behind the misty blue hills.

Norman was in the back garden messing about with his old bike.

'Norman!' cried Lily. 'What are you up to?'

'Been doing up me old bike,' he called cheerfully, going to wash the grease off his hands in the kitchen.

'Whatever for?' she demanded.

'Well, I thought I was getting too fat. I thought I'd start popping down for my drink at the inn on the bike again, like I used to. It'll give me a bit of exercise.'

'Oh, don't be so bleedin' daft,' said Lily. 'They go mad down that road after dark, especially when the pub shuts.'

Norman was still thrifty in his ways. 'It will also save petrol,' he said. 'The price has gone up again this summer.'

'Oh, Norman,' cried Lily, 'take the Mini, don't ride that old bike. It's knackered, you've had it since you were a schoolboy.'

'It's not in bad shape,' insisted Norman, 'and, anyway, I've fixed it oop and it's not far to ride to the inn.'

'Oh, well, please yourself,' said Lily, getting up to go in now that the sun had disappeared.

The Drop Inn was still the same even though the stature of the village was sadly changed. Not far down the street was a big new pub with a car park and the music from it was loud. This was a rendezvous for the youths from other small hamlets in the Dales. They usually came roaring in on their motorbikes. There was also a big new restaurant which had recently opened and cars were always parked outside it, taking up room on the narrow road.

Norman always went to the Drop Inn on Saturday evenings for a couple of glasses of ale and a chat with a few chaps he knew. Tonight, when Norman came puffing along the road on his old bike, a few cracks were made but Norman took these with his own quiet humour. 'It be a fine strong old bike,' he said. 'Can't buy them like that now.'

At ten-thirty, Norman said goodnight to his pals and pedalled off down the road and back up the hill to the Hill Drop Farm. At the top of the hill the bike's brakes went and in his efforts to stop the bike, Norman went wobbling down the hill and crashed into a hedge. Thrown backwards, he hit his head on the tarmac and lay very still in the middle of the road.

At that moment, a car came roaring down the hill, headlights blazing. With a screeching of brakes it tried to pull up to prevent hitting the still figure lying in the middle of the road. But it was too late. The car struck Norman and then turned over and over ten yards up the road.

The young driver managed to get out of his car just before it burst into flames, and he ran back to look at Norman. 'Oh, my God!' he cried as he went running into the village to get help.

Lily was about to close the bedroom window when she noticed a sheet of flames in the distance. Someone's got a bonfire going this time of night, she thought, slamming the window and climbing into bed.

When the police sergeant came, Lily was sound asleep. Poor old George crept from his bed to answer the knock on the door. He stood there open-mouthed, staring at the police sergeant who said: 'Go and fetch Mrs Clegg.'

But Lily had already leapt out of bed and was running downstairs in her nightie. 'Oh dear, what's wrong? Where's Norman?'

'Better get dressed, ma'am, we need you at the hospital,' the policeman said gently.

'It's that bloody old bike,' cried Lily. 'What happened? I told him not to ride it.'

Avril was on the stairs and George was hopping up and down in an agitated way. The policeman calmed them down. 'Now, now,' he said. 'It's all right, nought to worry over.'

But Lily knew the reason. There was a deep hidden fear inside her, the way she had felt when poor gran got blown up.

CHAPTER SIX

That Cold Hard World

Norman's death came as a terrible shock to Lily. At first she was completely numb but then gradually she realised just how great her loss was, though she was scarcely able to believe that this had happened to her.

Avril was so distressed that Lily tried to be strong in order to help her. Poor old George began to blubber like a baby every time he looked at Lily. It was as if he held her responsible in some way.

All the villagers had gathered at Norman's funeral in sorrow. He had been well liked and respected by all the locals. But then odd things began to happen. Relatives began to arrive from the Welsh valleys. There was a whole crowd of them—women dressed in solid black hats and coats of fur fabric, which, judging from the overpowering smell of mothballs, only came out at funerals. The men wore hard bowler hats and had deep sepulcra singsong voices.

Lily was amazed. Norman had often spoken of the nephew in Wales who used to be very close to him but he had never mentioned a whole family. They ate and drank a lot and treated Lily with a kind of hostility. Their attitude to her was very different from that of the village folk, who referred to her as 'the sad widow, Mrs Clegg.'

William, the eldest nephew, walked beside her to the grave-side. Lily had a creepy feeling inside her in spite of her sorrow. It was as if something nasty was brewing up and she was not sure what. After the high tea, all the mourners had drifted off, but William and his wife, a plump, red-faced woman named Madeline, were the only ones remaining.

'We will be staying at the Drop Inn until Norman's business is settled,' William announced to Lily in a threatening manner.

Very conscious of the atmosphere, Lily shook William's limp hand. 'Please yourself,' she said nonchalantly.

After William and Madeline had all gone, the house seemed cold and silent. Lily hustled the chickens off to bed and then stood staring out into the darkness away over the silent moors.

'Oh, Norman,' she said softly, 'you did not deserve to die. It's a cold hard world, I feel so lost without you.'

She closed the front door, crept upstairs and got into bed with Avril who was asleep, her face all tear-stained.

Fate was building up new problems for Lily. Two days later a letter arrived from a lawyer in town asking her to call on him. Norman had not been one for solicitor's advice, and to Lily this was just a bloody nuisance. But she decided that she would call anyway and see what it was all about.

At precisely ten-thirty, she arrived at the lawyer's office and there, in the waiting room, was William and his fat wife. They looked as hostile as ever.

'Oh, I didn't expect to see you here,' said Lily, genuinely taken aback.

'Why not, may I ask?' Madeline said with a nasty sneer.

Lily picked up a magazine and ignored her.

Then William said, 'I hope we can settle this amicably, Mrs Brown.'

Lily looked up from her magazine astounded. No one up here had ever called her Mrs Brown before.

The receptionist called them in, and over his old-fashioned, high-topped desk, Mr Mann, the wizened old lawyer, looked down at them primly. He stated that he wished to read out the will of the late Norman Clegg.

'But Norman left no will,' broke in Lily.

The old man raised a disapproving finger for silence and then proceeded to read this long document which stated that Norman had left all he possessed to his one surviving close relative William Clegg, son of his brother who had been killed in the last war, in consideration for the money loaned by the said brother to be repaid in ten years without interest, the sum having been spent on the building of Norman's new house.

William and his wife both sat with smug expressions on their faces, while Lily's jaw dropped in astonishment. 'But,' she cried out at last, 'Norman told me that he had made provision for Avril and me,' she gasped.

'Maybe so, but unfortunately there is no record of it,' replied Mr Mann. 'It has never been legalised.'

'I don't believe it!' Lily jumped to her feet, her temper rising quickly. 'Who the bloody 'ell are they? Why, I've never seen them before in my life.'

Mr Mann grimaced. 'Now, now, calm down, dear lady. Unfortunately, unless another will turns up, this is the only one, and everything will be executed to that effect.'

'You mean he will take everything I own, that Avril and I are destitute? That's not possible.'

The lawyer had come round to the other side of the desk and was standing beside her. He was a kindly old man who was really sympathetic to her claims.

William and his wife continued to sit looking very smug.

'If you wish to contest the will, I may be able to get you good advice,' said the lawyer, 'but it seems that you were only the housekeeper and your husband and daughter resided there with you, so I'm afraid I can't think that you have much to go on, unless our client here will make some private agreement with you.'

'Him? That Welsh bastard?' screamed Lily. 'Look at 'im, the greedy sod! He's loving all this. I can't stand it, I'm going!' With that Lily dashed out into the street. Getting into her car she drove madly back to Hill Drop Farm. When she burst into the sitting room where Avril sat reading, she was sobbing wildly.

'Oh, Mummy, who has upset you?' asked Avril.

'It's all right, darling,' said Lily. 'I was just thinking of Daddy, that's all.'

Avril put her arms about her. 'So am I, Mummy, but we must stick together because that is what he would have wanted.'

Lily dried her tears and gave Avril a half-hearted smile, then she went to the kitchen to cook the evening meal wondering about where she could go to seek advice? But she couldn't think of anyone. No one at Hill Drop knew that she and Norman were not married, and she was not going to make a fool of herself after all these years. She had no choice but to continue as before, so she pressed on. She got Avril back to school and brought casual labour in from the village to harvest the crops and care for the greenhouses. She chased old George around, giving him a broom to sweep the yard, and made him, under protest, do the washing-up.

All the time her mind was in a whirl. Why was this hanging over her head? Then one night it occurred to her that perhaps Norman had written another will, revoking the one the lawyer had. She went through his desk, and read all his papers and letters. There were some papers that mentioned the deal he made with his brother William, fond letters that he had written to him in the army, and letters of negotiations with the builders who built his house. It seemed that Norman had paid most of the money back but still owed twenty thousand to the bank, which he had recently borrowed to put into the farm. There were several bank books with two or three thousand pounds in them and some cash in his desk. So, in spite of his thriftiness, Norman had left very little. His life had been all hard work for very little profit. In none of these letters was there a single mention of his love life or his affection for Avril. Lily was annoyed. Norman was obviously deliberately careful not to write anything down, so he had left no evidence at all that she was his common-law wife. What chance did she stand?

'Oh, Norman,' she cried plaintively. 'Help me, advise me, wherever you are.'

The following week, William drove up in a big black car. 'Just like a bloody great hearse,' said Lily, when she saw him coming. Then she let the dogs loose. 'See him off, boys,' she called.

The dogs jumped up at William as he got out of the car, and refused to let him come up the front path.

'Mrs Brown,' he yelled, 'I must speak with you.'

'Piss off, robber!' yelled Lily back at him. Finally he drove away.

For a while it was fairly peaceful and Lily went down to the Ladies' Club and wallowed in the other ladies' sympathy, but she didn't mention her troubles to anyone.

Then one morning there was a long letter from the solicitor stating that negotiations must commence. Lily tore it up and burned it.

The winter that came down on the moorland that year was very bitter. Up at Hill Drop, it was bleak and very lonely but Lily was determined to stick it out. She ran the farm efficiently and went on with the dress-making. She played Monopoly with Avril in the evenings, and taught George to do basketwork. Her mind was uneasy and her heart so empty. Sometimes she did think of Kasie—would he come to her aid? No, her pride would not allow it. But face it she must.

When spring eventually came round again, many letters had come through the door, all of which had gone unopened. One day a very slick young man with steel-rimmed spectacles called. Handing her his card he said, 'I'm here to work on your behalf, madam, to get you a good settlement. I have a practice of my own. My father, the town solicitor, has asked me to help try and get you to fight for a fair settlement for yourself and child.'

Lily was immediately interested by this. 'Come in,' she said, 'let's have a drink.' He was someone to talk to after that long lonely winter, and if he was on her side, he was very welcome.

The young lawyer reminded her so much of Norman with his broad tone and slow manner, and he became her first friend in that cold hard world of adversity.

'My name is Steven Mann,' he said.

'You can call me Lily.'

'Right, Lily, give me your confidence and I can help you. We think you have had a raw deal. It is pretty obvious that Norman was the father of your child as your own husband being so disabled couldn't have fathered her. But unfortunately, Mr Clegg left no record of it. My father tells me that you and Mr

Clegg met in London while you were there during the war, so perhaps we could dig up a witness from there.'

'Oh,' said Lily forlornly, 'you mean take it all to court?'

'Well, I hope to win your case for you,' Steven Mann replied brightly.

Lily slowly sipped her drink. 'It's no good,' she said sadly. 'Avril was born before I met Norman.'

Steven looked dismayed. 'So he was not the father of the child. Well, bang goes our case, Lily.'

'Who bloody cares?' cried Lily. 'Let that Welsh bastard have his pound of flesh—but he's not getting me out of here so easy, I can tell you that.'

'The only chance we have is to negotiate with him,' said Steven, 'so you must do that.'

'If you like,' said Lily. 'What's the good of it hanging over my head all the time?'

Lily agreed to meet William at the lawyer's office on the condition that her affairs would not become public. 'I've been liked and respected as Mrs Clegg and as Mrs Clegg I will go away from here, if I have to go,' she said.

One gloomy April day they met William Clegg in Steven's office. Lily tried to behave but every time she looked at the sandy haired 'Welsh git', as she thought of him, her blood boiled.

'God knows, I've no desire to turn you out of your home,' William said piously. 'God forbid. It's for my uncle's sake that I am trying to reason with you. I'm a property developer and it's my intention to build a big hotel up there.'

'You bloody well won't,' declared Lily defiantly.

Steven Mann tried to keep the peace between them. 'Now, listen to him, Lily, and we might get somewhere.'

'I'm willing to give her a fair amount of the furniture and the fittings,' continued William, 'but the building is mine. It was my money that paid for it to be built on those conditions.'

'He paid you back, you bloody rogue,' cried Lily.

'Only the capital, no interest,' said William coldly. 'You may have been his mistress but as far as I am concerned, you were just his housekeeper and I am his next of kin.'

'I believe we can contest the will,' interrupted Steven Mann, 'because of the fact that Mrs Brown is known as his common-law wife and many of the village folk bear witness to the fact that Mr Clegg always referred to her as his wife in these terms.'

'It's up to you if you wish to take the matter to court,' sneered William, 'but as far as I'm concerned, I'm losing money all the time, so I want it settled quickly.'

Steven took Lily into the next room and gave her a glass of sherry. 'Now, Lily, what do you want to do? Make a settlement out of court? It will mean giving up your house but you will probably get enough to buy another house locally.'

'Oh, do as you want to. I am bloody fed up with the whole business,' said Lily, feeling defeated. 'I'll go back to London. I don't want to live up here all alone, it was terrible last winter.'

Steven patted her shoulder. 'Might be just as well. Don't worry about it. Now, you go home. I'll get the best settlement I can for you and then come and see you.'

With a bowed head, Lily left the lawyer's office, feeling beaten. Her pride would not allow them to subject her and Avril to public scrutiny, however good her case.

So began Lily's desire to go back to her grass roots and return to her old town and the teeming streets of London. She began by getting rid of everything that was saleable 'before that Welsh git gets his hands on them,' she told herself. She sold off the hens and some good pieces of furniture, and emptied out the greenhouses.

Avril was concerned. 'Why, Mummy, how will you live if we go to live in London?'

'Oh, don't you worry, love, I'll think of something else, and I can still work.'

'As long as they won't take Pamsie and Morning Star, I'm not worried,' said Avril. 'Daddy wanted to move, so I won't mind if we do.'

Lily's heart missed a beat. If they went to London, Avril would have to leave her pets behind. Well, there was little to be done about that at the moment, she would face that when she came to it.

It was well into the summer before Steven reached a final settlement with William. They agreed that William would give Lily £3,000 to buy another house with no strings attached as long as she moved out of the one at Hill Drop.

'Oh, well,' said Lily, 'it's better than a smack in the eye. How long have I got?'

'Three months,' said Steven. 'I'm sorry it's not great, Lily, but I did what I could.'

'That's all right,' said Lily, 'I wouldn't have got a penny without your help.'

'Why don't you come and live in the town?' asked Steven, looking admiringly at Lily's lithe figure and wealth of auburn hair.

'No, Steven, I'll go back to London. I've sent off to a London agent for a list of empty houses. I want to go back to my own end of the town, near the river, to Dall Road,' she said dreamily. 'It's dockland, where I lived before the war.'

'I wish you well, Lily,' said Steven, 'if you need me, just give me a ring.'

Avril passed her first year exams at college with flying colours. Lily was quite proud of her.

'If we're going to move,' said Avril, 'I might see where I can go on studying in London. I might even try for a degree in biology, that's always useful.'

Lily marvelled at Avril's level-headed approach to matters. She herself understood very little about further education but if Avril wanted it, then in Lily's books, Avril was going to get it.

Lily suggested that they go up to London for Christmas. 'Just you and I,' she said to Avril. 'I'll get someone to give eye to George and he'll look after the animals.'

Avril was delighted. 'Where will we stay?' she asked.

'In an hotel,' announced Lily proudly.

'But mother, you've never stayed in a West End hotel before,' replied Avril. 'You won't know which one to go to.'

'Oh, yes, I have,' Lily said with a sly grin, her mind bouncing back to when she and Kasie had spent that weekend in the Cumberland, but thinking about it now, it did seem rather expensive.

The local travel agent suggested that she try the Wiltshire Hotel near Victoria which, he said, gave a nice family Christmas party and was more within her means. So they decided to travel on Christmas Eve and stay until New Year's Day.

As Lily counted out the pound notes, she worried for a moment about her undue extravagance. But her worry was short-lived. 'Oh well,' she thought, 'let's live while we're young enough to enjoy it, as Kasie always insisted.' In many ways Avril was so like him, so anxious to see the world, and yet calm and full of her own importance just as he was. The touch of Avril's soft hand, her rich clean aroma and fair freckled skin, were all the same as her father's. How Lily wished she could erase the memory of Kasie from her mind, and she knew that Avril would never forgive her if she ever discovered that Norman was not her real father. No, she must be firm, she told herself, it was just the two of them now and she would make a new life for them. But now her conscience pricked her. What about old George? There was no way she could desert him, she thought with dismay, not now. He had clung to Norman who had protected him, and someone had to fend for him. Well, he would just have to come to London too, she thought, nothing else could be done.

On the morning of Christmas Eve, they set out. Avril looked radiant in a new red coat with a fur-trimmed hood. 'I don't look like Father Christmas, do I?' she asked Lily timidly.

'No, darling, you look beautiful,' Lily assured her. Lily had also treated herself to a new coat. It was made of a nice bright fur-fabric leopard skin with a neat round hat to match. Still very extrovert in her manner of dress, Lily was still slim and smart and, at thirty-six, very presentable.

They arrived at the cosy warm Wiltshire Hotel very tired, but Avril had enjoyed driving through London in the taxi and was so excited. She had loved the bright Christmas lights and the noise and the festive spirit that seemed to grip the Londoners as they did their last-minute Christmas shopping.

Lily was so happy to give Avril a good time in London. They went to Trafalgar Square to look at the big brightly lit Christmas tree, and join in the carol singing. They ate hot dogs bought from a little stand, and baked chestnuts from a man on the corner, and walked idly along Regent Street, window shopping as they went.

Avril admired all the wonderful expensive clothes in the shops and Lily told her about how she used to be a bus clippie and went along this route every day when the blitz was on. 'But then the shops were empty,' she said. 'It all looked so gloomy, there was nothing in the windows and everywhere was sand-bagged to shield the windows from the bomb blasts.'

Avril looked around in wonderment at this fairyland, from the Christmas decorations above to the brightly lit shops below. 'I can't believe it,' she said, 'it's absolutely gorgeous, it's a wonderful sight.'

For a little girl who had spent the best part of her young life up on the lonely Yorkshire Moors, it could seem nothing less than miraculous.

'I bought a hat up here once,' said Lily dreamily. 'That shop there used to be a hat shop and there was just this one hat in the window . . . It cost me a week's wages, but I simply had to have it. Yes,' she added, as her thoughts went back over the years, 'I was wearing it when I met him.'

'Met who?' Avril demanded.

'Oh, your daddy,' said Lily, coming down to earth. She then very quickly changed the subject.

Back at the hotel, they had dinner and afterwards there was a late night dance. Avril, looking sweet and pretty in a white dress, danced part of the time with Lily and some of the time with Bob, a young American boy who was also staying in the hotel with his parents.

They had a good time and Lily quickly made friends with the other guests in the hotel who included a Maltese family as well as the Americans, so it was a real cosmopolitan crowd.

On Christmas Day they walked in the Hyde Park and visited Westminster Abbey. Then they walked over the bridge to look back at the lovely Houses of Parliament from over the river, and admire the sweep of the river as it flowed through London towards the sea. Bob had accompanied them and he gasped at the sight of the dim, shadowy shape of Tower Bridge. 'My,' he exclaimed, 'we ain't got nothing like that in New York.'

'Well,' said Lily, 'that's a big surprise. When the Yanks was here in the wartime, they used to say they had everything much bigger and much better than we did.'

Bob blushed. 'We are inclined to exaggerate,' he said quietly.

Avril glared at Lily with her hard, stern eyes. 'Why don't you use a bit of tact, Mother?' she said, blushing red with embarrassment.

But Lily just laughed out loud and flashed her fine white teeth, not a bit abashed.

On the whole, they had a great weekend in London, but when the American family had gone, Avril was a little downhearted. 'Bob was such a nice boy,' she said. 'But he said he was going to write to me.'

'I wouldn't bank on it,' said Lily, a little brusquely.

Avril looked annoyed. 'Why are you so brittle and distrusting? Sometimes I just don't understand you,' she said frostily.

Lily was plaiting Avril's long hair as they got ready for bed. 'Well, darling, I expect it's life that's done that to me. You will live and learn just as I did. Now, goodnight.' She kissed her on the cheek. 'We'll be busy tomorrow,' she said. 'We're going down the East End to look at some houses for sale.'

'Why can't we live up here in this nice part?' insisted Avril.

'It's too expensive, my love,' said Lily, 'but don't worry, it's just as nice down there, only different.'

The next two days were spent travelling on buses down to the East End of London. When they went down to the dockside areas where Lily had been raised, she looked about her in dismay. It really was different. All the little rows of streets had disappeared and in their place stood high-rise blocks of flats which obscured the horizon. The dockland seemed empty and silent; the cranes were silent and not working, very few ships were on the river, and as she passed the old pub where she had met Kasie, the squalor and misery of the place seemed to exude out of it. Scaffolding was holding up the building because repairs were still being done to the damage that wartime bombs had done. The old canal behind was dreary and polluted, and there were black children playing football on a huge stretch of waste ground that, in Lily's day, had once been Dall Road. The warm community of families who had lived in those terraced houses had now disappeared.

'Is this really where you used to live?' asked Avril, turning up her fastidious nose, just as Kasie used to do.

'Well, it's all changed since the war,' explained Lily. 'My Mum and me grandparents all used to live in that same street.'

'But they are mostly black people,' said Avril.

'Well, at one time it used to be Chinese down by the river when I lived here,' said Lily. 'Never mind, there don't seem to be much in the way of property here. I've got an address here in Plashet Grove that might be all right. I'm determined to find a place before we go back to Hill Drop.'

They got a bus and wandered the street until they came to Plashet Grove, a street of tall Victorian houses with front gardens and steps up to the street door.

'Now, this don't look so bad,' said Lily consulting her estate agent's list, 'but it's only a flat. I wanted a house but they seem to be very expensive. Come on, let's go look at it.'

Avril was a little tired and fairly disgruntled. She wanted to get back to the lively West End. 'All right,' she said grumpily, 'but if you don't like this one, I'm not looking at any more.'

'All right, darling,' said Lily, always anxious to please her daughter.

It was a nice respectable-looking house facing a small park. 'It used to be quite posh here when I was young,' said Lily. 'I used to play in that park on school holidays,' said Lily as she rang the bell.

But by now Avril was sulking and not listening.

A strange-looking, long-haired young man came to the door.

Lily shivered and made as if to turn away, but with a nice smile and cultured voice he said, 'Come about the flat? Do come in.'

Lily hesitated for a second but then plucked up her courage and they went inside. The house smelled of new paint, and the hall was neat, bare and very clean.

'This is it, on the hall floor,' the man said. 'I'll get the key. I live upstairs, so when I'm not working I show people around. The owner lives here downstairs. She goes out to business every day.' He chatted in a nice pleasant manner.

Lily relaxed and smiled her big smile. 'We're moving back to London from up North,' she said, 'just my daughter and I.'

He opened up the door to the flat and showed them into a long room with big windows at each end. Midway there was a pair of folding doors and in each room a huge fireplace with marble surroundings.

'This is nice,' said Lily, 'but the room is so big.'

'You can convert it into two,' he suggested.

At the end there was a long glass conservatory which had been made into a modern kitchen. This thrilled Lily. The window overlooked an untidy garden but had a good view of London. The huge, modern block of flats in the distance shone silver in the sun and the hundreds of windows reflected back the light and warmed the kitchen.

The young man then showed her the bathroom and a very small bedroom across the hall. Lily took a look at the room and thought it was just the place for poor old George.

'I think this will do us very nicely,' said Lily.

'The owner will be here on Saturday afternoon, if you want to meet her. She is very anxious to get the right kind of tenant, and I'm sure that you'll get on with her,' said this pleasant young man. 'My name is Mike. I'll tell her you have called and will be back. Is that all right?'

'That's fine,' said Lily, glad to have a little time to make up her mind.

All the way back to the hotel, Avril complained. 'How can we live in a flat?' she grumbled. 'What about the animals?'

'Oh, dear,' sighed Lily. 'Now Avril, you must be sensible.

We have very little to live on, so I have to work, and you do want to finish your education and go on to university, don't you? So you will have to do without pets.'

'Oh, well,' Avril returned sullenly, 'why we have to be lumbered with old George, God only knows!'

Lily bit her lip, determined not to be dominated by her. 'Look, George goes with us. He has no one else, and your Daddy loved him and was good and kind to him.'

Avril pouted. 'I can't understand why, but let's face it, he's bound to show us up if we go to live in that big posh house.'

'It's not such a posh house,' replied Lily. 'It might have been years ago but now it's been converted into flats, so I think I could buy it fairly cheaply. Come on, let's go and have a slap-up tea in Lyon's Corner House at Marble Arch. I'll see the owner on Saturday afternoon. Let's hop on this bus,' said Lily. 'I used to be on this run when I was a bus clippie.'

'Oh, don't keep on about your hectic good old days,' complained Avril. 'It's getting boring.'

Lily swallowed her chagrin. She had a strong desire to slap Avril right out there in the street, but she restrained herself, and they rode back to the West End in silence.

Avril did not say a word and neither did Lily. But her mind was working hard. This was to be a new beginning for them both, and Avril was going to have to accept the fact that they were no longer comfortable, middle-class farm folk, but instead ordinary working-class Londoners.

At the Lyon's Tea House, they ate chocolate eclairs, and tea from a silver teapot, which cheered Avril up no end, and when they came out, the Christmas lights were on and they wandered down that fairyland along Oxford Street around Soho and back to the hotel. Avril had cheered up and held Lily's arm, giggling at the adverts for strip shows. They were once more very close. In a strange way it seemed to Lily that it was Kasie there clinging to her arm and chuckling at everything as he used to do when they walked the West End streets together.

On Saturday, Lily left Avril at the hotel and went off early to see the estate agent and then on to Plashet Grove to meet the owner of the house.

Lily was quite surprised by the appearance of the owner, a tall, slim young woman who could have passed easily for a young man. She wore a tailored suit with well-fitting slacks, and a white laundered shirt. Her hair was cut very short.

'I'm Jo Macy,' she said, holding out her hand. 'I understand you're interested in buying the lease of the hall floor flat.'

'That's right,' said Lily, looking amazed by the slick appearance of this woman.

'The house is mine,' explained Jo Macy. 'I used to let the rest in flats but it's no longer profitable. So I've decided to sell them off on a leasehold.' She invited Lily downstairs to the very comfortable lounge. 'Would you like a sherry, Mrs Brown?' she asked.

'Yes, please,' Lily replied. 'And you can call me Lily.'

They relaxed and sat sipping their drinks.

'I'm not sure if I understand the position exactly,' said Lily. 'What do you mean by leasehold?'

'Well, you buy the leasehold for ninety years,' explained Jo Macy, 'so it won't affect you much, but you will get the flat fairly cheap and only have rates to pay and they will be fairly small since there are four of us to share them.'

'Ah well, I'll be shooting up the daisies by then,' jested Lily, 'so it won't matter, but the property will be mine. You see, I've been done in the eye, had my home smarted off me up North, so that's why I'm moving back here. Got to make a new start.'

Jo's small, deep-set eyes twinkled at Lily's Cockney expressions. 'But you're a real Londoner, Lily,' she said.

'Yes,' said Lily, 'I came from Canning Town, not far away from here.'

So they began to gossip.

'My grandmother left me this house,' Jo told her, 'and it's become a bit of a white elephant lately. She also left three baker's shops, all in the East End. That's why I am always out at work—they take up a lot of time.'

'I'll have to get a job when I move back,' said Lily. She had to drop the bombshell now. 'You see, I have a disabled husband. He was wounded in the war, so I'll have to support him. And I want my daughter to have a good education—she's just sixteen.'

'There's a fine college up the road, West Ham College,' returned Jo. 'One of my tenants is a lecturer there—Mike, I believe you met him.'

'That's right,' said Lily, 'nice fellow.'

'Smoke?' asked Jo and passed her a cigarette. Lily accepted and lit up. She felt as if she had known Jo Macy all her life. She had a sort of compelling feeling that made Lily respond to her.

'I had decided that I would be willing to go down in price if I got the right sort of tenant, Lily,' explained Jo, 'and you seem ideal. The price was £2,500, but I'm happy to go down to £2,000, if that suits you.'

Lily was very pleased if rather surprised. 'I'm not short of money,' continued Jo, 'and I don't want to get a flock of coloureds coming in here,' she said. 'What about it, Lily? Does that suit you?'

'Done,' said Lily. 'I'll send the cheque as soon as I get back. I'll be going home tomorrow.'

'Yes,' said Jo, 'it's New Year's Eve tonight. I expect we'll have a party when they all get home from work. We're a fairly lively lot in here, I must warn you, but we're all fairly happy, and that compensates for a lot of things, I think.'

'Won't worry me,' said Lily. 'I'm pretty lively myself.'

'Yes,' smiled Jo. 'I thought you were.'

Lily returned to the hotel to find Avril busily dressing herself up in her party dress. She was in a very good mood and looked pretty in the brightly coloured dress which Lily had just bought her from C & A Modes.

'Well,' said Lily, 'we're going to take that flat, Avril, and I've been told that there's a good college just down the road for you.'

They went out to dinner and then to the dance where they joined hands with everyone else to sing 'Auld Lang Syne'. Afterwards, they joined the crowd running out into the street where they waved and cheered and threw streamers into the air. Then they went down to Trafalgar Square where the excitement was intense. The big Christmas tree was all lit up and students jumped into the fountains and climbed up on the lions. Lily was pleased to see that Avril was thrilled. 'This is my town, Avril,' she said proudly. 'It's the London I love, and I won't be sorry to leave that gloomy old North behind.'

Avril put her arms about her, 'Happy New Year, Mummy, I'm sorry if I upset you.'

A big lump came into Lily's throat as that soft cheek pressed against hers. It was as if Kasie's sweet smell came drifting by, pervading her senses, and she suddenly had visions of them both in a close embrace one New Year's Eve in wartime. 'No Christmas tree, no lights, just you and me, Lily my lovely,' he would have said.

CHAPTER SEVEN

London Town

When Lily and Avril left Hill Drop, the snow on the hills had begun to melt and rivulets of water ran down the slopes and flooded the fields. The ladies of the village had given them a big send-off the night before with a great party in the village hall and a silver tray presentation with an inscription on it: 'To Lily Clegg for all her good work done in our village.'

Lily had wept as the chairman made a speech saying how sad they were to be losing the best cook in the area. 'And who is going to make those lovely cakes for us now?' she asked. 'Lily has for many years helped and held together our little village which is now slowly turning into a suburb of the town. She has done great work, and we will always miss her lively happy manner and remember our Cockney lady for all time.'

The next morning, with a terrific hang-over, Lily did the final packing. The stripped house looked quite forlorn. She put George into the removal van, and he clutched his scruffy Yorkshire terrier. It was one of Avril's strays that she was always acquiring. George had grown very fond of the dog and let it sleep on his bed. When they tried to remove it from his grasp to leave it behind, George showed his teeth and growled just like the dog. 'It's no good,' Lily said, 'let him take Yorkie.' She just wanted to get the moving over quickly. Avril had tears streaming down her cheeks having just returned from the riding school where she had said goodbye to her two ponies. Lily gave her favourite dogs a gentle pat as she handed the labradors over to a neighbouring farmer, and then a little girl came for the ginger cat and her basket of kittens. It was all becoming a bit too much, and Lily was beginning to feel the strain of leaving. But do it she must.

Like Lot's wife she took just one look back at the farm as Steven Mann drove her and Avril to the station. There it stood, looking so lonely high up on the hill, the house that Norman had been so proud of, the one he pledged his life's work to build. Now, apparently, it was to be pulled down to make room for a big hotel.

'Goodbye, Lily,' Steven said. 'I'll come up to London if you ever need me, just give me a ring.'

Lily kissed his cheek. 'Thank you for everything,' she said. 'I'll be okay, I've made up my mind to go it alone.'

The moving van had been to Plashet Grove and gone, and all the furniture was all waiting for them when Lily and Avril arrived in London. And there was George with a smug look on his face and still clutching Yorkie, sitting in Jo Macy's flat, and eating toast and cream buns.

Lily was most apologetic to Jo. 'Take that scruffy dog outside, George,' she scolded.

But Jo smiled her charming smile. 'The dog's all right,' she said, 'and so is George. Please sit down and have some tea.'

Lily sighed a deep sigh of relief for she had worried about how they would take to George who could be exceedingly awkward when he wanted to be.

Jo soon assured her. 'Relax, Lily, I understand. We're good pals, George and I, and I think Yorkie is very sweet. It will be nice to have a pet in the house. I am always out, so I could not keep one myself.'

Avril smiled at her. 'Do you like animals? I'd like to be a vet one day.'

'I do, Avril,' replied Jo, 'but I like to see them well looked after, don't you?'

'Oh, yes,' said Avril, 'I worked for the P.D.S.A. on Saturday mornings in Barnsley.'

'Well, you can still do that here,' said Jo. 'In fact, you'll be needed more in London where there are lots of neglected animals.'

Lily sighed contentedly. It seemed she had really hit on the right spot; it was very pleasant at Plashet Grove. The rooms were big and the park opposite made it peaceful and green. The tall elms whose bare branches rose up to the sky had a hint of bud on them. There were red and yellow tulips in the flower beds in the small park that was hemmed in by old-fashioned railings. That first morning, as Lily looked out of the window, a sense of freedom came over her. She was now the proud owner of this bit of property and had almost £1,400 in the bank. That was what was left after the legal fees had been paid, so it was indeed a brand new start. She had to answer to no one, the world was her oyster. And best of all, only a stone's throw away were more of the places she knew—the East End and the markets, the West End shops. All around her were the big docks of London and not far distant, the river Thames, whose smell came in through the window as it did when she was a child.

In her thorough manner, she soon began to organise the kitchen and rearrange the furniture. 'I might have a spend-up and get some nice new furniture,' she told Avril. 'Might as well make the place comfortable.'

Avril was also full of ideas. 'Mummy, will we get rid of that old wooden bed? It's a terrible eyesore and I hate sleeping with you—you snore.'

'I don't!' cried Lily, but she listened to Avril's plans.

'Now, let's sit down and work out exactly what we need and how much we have got to spend,' said her daughter.

Lily was astounded. Avril had never had to budget her affairs before, she had been given everything she asked for by Norman and Lily. This child had suddenly grown up, she thought with delight.

'Now,' Avril continued, 'we will buy a new bright modern carpet for this front room and two modern divans so that if we want to entertain we can open up the doors and have one big room.'

'Well, I never!' declared Lily, 'that's a good idea.'

'We will buy heavy drapes to fill that big window and keep out the draughts, and have matching bedspreads and cushions, of course,' she said. 'Some of this nice old furniture will be fine, like the sideboard and the table, but I expect you'll have to chuck out a lot of that old stuff. Now, let's work out just how much it will all cost and see if we can afford it.'

There was a very warm feeling inside Lily. She felt as if Kasie was there with her and giving and spending generously, covering her with that cloak of love. 'Let's go shopping, darling,' she said to Avril, 'because we never know what we might need.'

At the shops, Avril picked out smart, modern things that were not as bright and colourful as Lily would have liked.

'No, Mummy, not orange,' Avril would say, 'beige, I think, will be easier to match.'

So Lily squandered five hundred pounds but the results were good. By the end of their spree they had a smart modern bed-sitting room, with a standard lamp which shed a pretty light, heavy, wine-coloured velvet curtains and two divans, and plump cushions all made of the same material.

They painted the kitchen and installed a new stove. Avril was so happy; dressed in a pair of old slacks she white-washed the ceiling. All the other occupants of the house came one by one to introduce themselves and offer help. It took a little time to realise that they were rather an odd lot and, although Lily was a little concerned at first, because of Avril, she took it all in her stride.

There were Ray and Andy on the top floor. They arrived together and their conversation bounced off each other like a musical comedy. Andy seemed rather effeminate and worked in a West End bar, while Ray, a civil servant, was stocky, wore big owlie spectacles and had a gruff voice. At weekends, Andy painted his nails red and shampooed his hair, and wearing a long flowered dressing-gown he would walk around the house with a turban wound around his head.

Avril liked Ray and Andy. 'They kill me,' she said. 'They're queer, you know.'

Lily was a little worried. 'You mean they're nancy boys?'

'Oh, don't be so quaint, Mother,' said Avril. 'They call them queer these days.'

The couple were very entertaining and frequently quarrelled violently when Andy would flounce about the house sulking, visiting the other tenants, and threatening to commit suicide.

Jo Macy would reassure Lily. 'Don't take them too seriously, Lily,' she would say. 'It's all an act, but they are good tenants and it takes all kinds . . .'

Lily was soon to discover that Jo was not quite normal in her way, either. On the school vacation, a young student called Jill occupied Jo's bed. She had lovely long black hair and she spoke in a slow Suffolk drawl. She had been a drama student and had played at the local theatre before going to Leeds University.

Lily was amazed one night to meet Jo and Jill in the hall. Jo was dressed entirely in masculine attire—a white shirt, bow tie, and man's suit. She looked very smart with her hair slicked down and swept up away from her face. Jill was wearing a long dress with a fur jacket and held possessively on to her arm. Seeing the look of surprise on Lily's face, Jo seemed a trifle sheepish. 'We are off to a theatre party, Lily,' she said.

'Jo is also the other way,' remarked Lily to Avril later. 'We're living in a house of oddbods.'

Avril shrugged. 'Who cares? They're nice and easy to live with, and Mike's okay. I've been talking to him about the West Ham College, he is going to help me with my entrance papers.'

Lily did not worry much more about her neighbours. As long as Avril didn't mind, she didn't either.

One bright spring Sunday morning they strolled down to Petticoat Lane, the famous East End Sunday market, where it is rumoured one can buy anything from a needle to an elephant. There were as many people there as ever before but Lily was very struck by the absence of uniformed men who used to throng Petticoat Lane when Lily had walked there with Kasie. They had drunk in every pub and swallowed Dutch herrings whole and had lunched in Jewish restaurants. As Avril toured the stalls for bargains, Lily's mind revolved wistfully around those past happenings. Meeting up again, they stood listening with amusement to the Cockney patter of the stall traders. The crowd pushed and shoved as the voices rose in a high-pitched buzz. To Lily the excitement was so stimulating that she felt young again, and kept hoping that she might see a familiar face in the crowd. But in this sea of faces there was not one that she knew. When they came to Club Row, Avril was appalled by all the wistful looking animals waiting for someone to take them home and love them. Seeing some tiny, underweight puppies in an overcrowded cage, Avril rushed up to the vendor, protesting loudly. 'Young man,' she said, 'you should be shot putting all those puppies out there in the cold. And it's unhealthy having them all in an overcrowded cage like that.'

'Piss orf, if yer ain't goner buy,' said the cloth-capped young man.

Avril got very aggressive and wanted to continue with the argument, but Lily quickly intervened. Grabbing her by the arm, she hustled her away, saying: 'It don't do to stir up trouble down here, they're a funny lot.'

Avril had tears in her eyes. 'Oh, what a dreadful place,' she cried, forgetting the fun she had had earlier. 'I'll never go there again.'

On the whole their life in Plashet Grove was fairly pleasant—Lily was really quite surprised by how quickly she was getting over the loss of poor Norman. And, it appeared, so was Avril.

Avril spent a lot of time with Mike. He helped her swot for her examination papers for the West Ham College and on Sundays they went to the tennis courts together while Lily stayed in her lovely kitchen and made grand Sunday lunches, to which she often invited one or two of the tenants. Always Mike was there. He loved Lily's cooking of roast beef, Yorkshire pudding and baked spuds, and always gobbled plenty of her farmhouse cake for Sunday tea.

There were times when Lily worried what Mike and Avril were doing when they were upstairs together. She wanted to dash up and find out what was going on, but she always checked herself. Something told her that Avril was a very capable girl and that Mike was not actually interested in one so young and innocent. Nonetheless, she did say to him one day, 'Mike, don't be offended but young girls like Avril are easily influenced . . .'

Mike laughed. 'Lily, dear, don't worry about Avril or me. I know we live in a house of odd fellows but I'm quite normal. I've been divorced and have a girlfriend who is studying law. One day I will marry again. Avril is all right with me. She's bright and so intelligent, it's a pleasure to be able to help her.'

'Thank you, darling,' said Lily with her wide smile. 'Let me know when your girlfriend will be here and I'll bake you a cake.'

'Good show, Lily, I must say you're a super cook.'

'I thought everyone could cook,' said Lily, 'but it's one thing I do like doing.'

'Why don't you take an advanced course at evening classes?' suggested Mike. 'If you can get a diploma, Lily, it often helps to get a good job.'

'That's a good idea,' said Lily.

'Join up when they open in September.'

Those first six months in Plashet Grove passed by very quickly. On Saturday nights someone usually had a party and all sorts of way-out people arrived—boys with long hair, and girls in bare feet and long, old-fashioned dresses.

Lily always joined in the fun. The music was loud and the cheap wine was drunk by the bottle-full. Lily made sausage rolls and little fancies for the buffet and laughed riotously at the strange antics of the young folk, but she also always watched Avril very carefully.

In fact, she need not have worried about Avril, for she was a rather stiff and prudish young girl whose hard blue eyes stared with disdain at any young girl who had drunk more than enough and was making a fool of herself. 'Leaping all over the blokes,' Avril would declare distastefully.

Lily often felt a little jealous when she saw the youngsters kissing and cuddling. How different her life was now, she thought. She seemed suddenly to have grown old. That romantic nonsense had no part in her life now, and she felt it never would again.

George lived in his little room across the hall with Yorkie, the dog. He helped with the housework and often did the shopping. Lily would give him a long list to take to the shop and soon all the other tenants would give him a list of purchases to get for them, too.

George had come into his own. By doing these errands, he made a lot of pocket money which he still spent on sweets and cinema. Gradually, he seemed to be coming out of his shell. He had learned a few choice swear words from the quarrels between Ray and Andy and would often open his mouth very wide and pronounce them with care. This made everyone else laugh, but Lily hated it and would slap him, whereupon George would snarl at her. 'Rotten cow,' he would mutter. 'Murderer!'

Lily knew that in his poor old warped mind, George thought she had killed Norman, and this really used to annoy her.

George enjoyed taking his little dog for a walk in the park where he would try to talk to the old men who sat on the benches. For the first time in years, George was free to come and go as he pleased. It wasn't long before he had taken a dislike to the little gangs of youths who hung about in the park at weekends and school holidays. He would shake his fist at them and say, 'Yobbo.' He had had a similar attitude towards village boys up North, but these Londoners were a different kind of lad. They were the products of the post-war world and the descendants of the old-time villains of the East End. They lived in the high-rise flats and did not want for much in the way of pocket money or nice things to wear. Yet they were bored and very vicious, and often got into fights with gangs of the new immigrant families. They wore leather jackets and kept flick knives down their socks, and one of their amusements was to prowl around the park tormenting people like George as he sat with his little dog on his lap. Usually he would be sitting on a bench beside one of the old men who, when they saw the boys coming, would say: 'Watch out, George, here comes the yobbos. You'd better go home now.' But obstinately George would stay on and stare aggressively at the boys, making faces at them.

'Hi, barmy sod,' the boys would say. 'Ger movin', or we'll carve up yer mongrel an' eat 'im.'

Some of them then jumped on the flower beds and pulled up a few park railings and continued to taunt George until the police, called by the keepers, appeared. Then the gang dispersed as the boys fled.

George was most incensed by it all. 'Yobbos!' he cried, screwing up his fist.

Avril had now entered the college at West Ham and was exceedingly happy and very studious. She spent all her spare time with her books or attending museums and art galleries with her fellow students, and there were times when Lily felt a little lonely. She said to Jo one day: 'I'm at a loose end. Also, money is getting low. I'm determined not to break into the capital. I can just get by on the interest but I ought to get a job.'

'Well, it don't do no harm to keep busy,' said Jo. 'It takes your mind off your problems. I've always had to work hard but sometimes I feel it's not worth it.'

'You've got a good business, Jo, you are lucky,' said Lily. 'Me, I've always had to do unskilled jobs and they are often very hard graft.'

'But you're such a marvellous cook, Lily, surely you had some training.'

'Only in the wartime. I was at one of those training centres learning how to make meatless pies.'

Jo began to laugh. 'Well, that's something, a vegetarian cook. I never eat meat because they have to kill animals to produce it.'

'Everyone to their own perversion,' jested Lily.

'Now I could take that two ways,' Jo replied, with equal humour. 'I feel I know you, Lily, and can trust you.' She hesitated but then continued. 'Sometimes I do wonder why you, a good-looking woman in her thirties, put up with the life that you have with poor old George. But I admire you for it.'

Lily smiled, lit a cigarette and passed one to Jo. 'That's not all the story, Jo,' she said. 'There have been other loves in my life.'

Jo's eyes twinkled. 'I thought so,' she said, eager to hear more.

'But I'm off men at the moment,' said Lily, 'and any other kind of sex. I'll get myself a job, that's the best answer.'

'Why not work for me, Lily?' asked Jo. 'I'll teach you to ice the wedding cakes in a very professional manner. I was brought up on this kind of work so it comes easy and the East Enders, in the area where my shops are, have terrific weddings. I cater for most of them and I could do with some reliable help.'

'Well!' cried Lily, 'that don't seem a bad idea. I like cooking and the extra money will be handy.'

'Done,' said Jo, reaching out and grasping Lily's hand in her firm, mannish grip.

Once Lily started work with Jo Macy she never looked back. Every morning when Avril went off to college, she would tidy up the flat, and remind George to look after the place. She would tie the latch key about his neck, and say, 'Don't let no one in, and if you go out shut the door, sweep the path and do the potatoes, and just you behave your bloody self.'

George would stare at her with that hostile look he had especially for her, and his mouth would turn down at the corners as he muttered defiantly under his breath.

Ignoring his growls, Lily would put on her old mack and flat shoes and walk down to the High Street to Jo's main shop. Lily was really interested in her job and extremely glad to get away from George for five hours each day. It was a busy shop with two young girl assistants. Lily relieved them in the shop when they went to lunch or had coffee breaks, but most of the time she spent out in the bakehouse with Jo where the cakes were cooked.

'This is a very old-fashioned shop, Lily,' Jo told her. 'It was started by my grandfather, a German Jew you know. He changed his name in the First World War because they used to persecute them. I would like to have a modern place and I'm losing trade all the time because the big industrial bakers with all their cut processed breads are causing me losses.'

The huge ovens were operated by two large coloured men who did the baking. They started work at night and were usually on their way home just as Lily got to the shop in the mornings. She loved the smell of the newly baked bread and the cheerful chat of the customers. In the afternoon she would work with Jo preparing the food for various receptions. Jo had a small van and delivered the orders herself. It was a cheery, busy life, decorating lines of pastries and icing the huge cakes for birthdays, anniversaries and weddings. Lily enjoyed it and really came into her own, and there was also that nice fat wage packet at the end of each week. By Friday, she felt weary, but could relax contented at home on weekends.

With her well-earned money, she bought Avril a record-player, and a television, which pleased George very much.

The cold chill of winter came down on London and yellow fog obscured the streets. Often it was only possible to see a few inches in front of your face. It reminded Lily of those bad foggy days in wartime but then they had all been grateful for the fog because the bombers could not come.

'Bloody fog,' complained Avril, 'it gets right up your nose.'

'Avril, watch your language,' scolded Lily.

'Well, watch yours,' Avril returned. 'That's who I learned it from.'

'Avril's getting saucy,' complained Lily to Jo as they walked home in the fog one day. It was too foggy to drive the van.

'Oh, she's a good girl,' said Jo, who liked Avril. 'I'm sure it's not serious. Teenagers are always cocky.'

'The government is talking of doing something about these fogs. They're going to stop us using coal because they reckon it's the coal fires that cause the fog.'

'I shouldn't wonder if they're not right,' commented Lily. 'We don't get fog in the summer, do we? And it's time they did something. This bloody smog gets into your chest.'

'We'll be getting very busy soon,' said Jo, 'making Christmas cakes.'

'That'll be nice,' said Lily, 'I look forward to that.'

In this friendly relaxed manner they often chatted as they walked home from the shop. So Lily's life began to revolve around her friends in the house and her work with that very business-like Jo. The hurts and the hardships of the past years seemed very far away.

CHAPTER EIGHT

That Gloomy Christmas and After

As time went by, the relationship between Jo Macy and Lily deepened. But they were nothing more than friends, as Lily firmly told Andy one evening after he had hinted at there being a lot more to it than that.

'Oh, don't mind me,' Andy said with a laugh. 'I'd understand, being queer myself. I've always been effeminate. When they put the first long pants on me I knew it should have been a frock.'

He was lolling on Lily's settee bed, clad in a long, frilly dressing-gown. His hair was in bobby pins which he frequently fiddled with as he complained endlessly about Ray's treatment of him.

Lily was ironing Avril's white shirt blouses, which she wore for college. Andy's conversation usually amused her but tonight it did not.

'Now, mate,' she said viciously, 'don't start the rest of the house thinking things like that about me. Suppose it got back to Avril?'

'Sorry, dear,' apologised Andy, 'but one often wonders about your sex life. You never seem very anxious to discuss it and we all know that poor old George ain't up to it.'

'Well, you can all mind your own bloody business,' said Lily, banging down the iron. 'Now, get going, I'm off to bed.'

'Sorry, old gel,' replied Andy in a fluster. 'Don't get shirty, I like to come down here for a little chat with you. You know, what with Ray being out so much these days, my own love life is not what it used to be.'

'Well, that's your own bloody concern,' snapped Lily, 'but

don't go imagining things about Jo and me because it's a purely business relationship. Now, goodnight.'

Andy flounced out of the flat looking a trifle peeved, and Lily banged the door after him. She set the alarm for the morning, laid Avril's supper tray and went to bed. As she lay there she thought over Andy's snide remarks. They had hurt her, for she had become very fond of Jo. They had done many things together that last year, working in the shop and the bakehouse, organising weddings and parties. They had also done several terms at evening classes together.

'It's all right to say you can cook,' Jo had said, 'but often they need some formal proof of your abilities if you want to open a business.'

So they had both worked to get diplomas for cake decoration and fancy cooking. Lily really loved studying, for it filled in those long dull evenings while Avril was immersed in her studies at the college, or out with her many new friends. So in the company of the cool, calm Jo, Lily matured further. She also became more aware of herself and was more careful about her appearance again. She bought a smart tweed jacket and swinging skirts. She became alert and lively and was a very popular person wherever she went.

She often went with Jo to the theatre to see all the new plays, for this was another of Jo's hobbies. 'I'd like to write plays,' she confided in Lily one day. 'But ever since I was very young I've had to work in that bloody old baker's shop. I was trained to the yoke by my grandparents at a pretty early age.'

'What about your parents?' Lily enquired.

'Oh, I'm illegitimate,' replied Jo. 'I don't think my mother even knew who my father was. And she died an alcoholic when she was only forty.'

'That's sad,' replied Lily. 'But I'm surprised, you seem to have come from a comfortable background.'

'That was the trouble, the comfort, the money. If my mother had been poor it would have been a straightforward case but it seems that my grandparents never thought anyone was good enough for her.'

'Life is strange,' said Lily. 'I don't think anyone really gets what they want.'

'Some do,' sighed Jo, 'but you see, Lily, I'm not one thing or the other. I don't like men. I love cuddly, effeminate women and they bloody well take me on.'

'Not to worry, Jo,' Lily said, passing her that ever-lasting fag—they both smoked very heavily. 'It will all come out in the wash.'

'What a kinky lot live in this house,' Lily remarked to Avril the next day at breakfast, 'but in no way would I have it otherwise because I'm truly happy here. It's the kind of freedom that I never had before.'

Avril was quickly gobbling up her food. 'I just haven't got the time for them,' she said, 'I've a lot to do with my life, and I've no intention of getting mixed up with sex of any description. I'm off, bye.' With that, she sped off to college on her sturdy legs, her flat shoes plonking down the pavement as she went.

Watching her through the window, Lily thought that Avril was no longer very like Kasie at all, except for the colouring and those stern blue eyes that glowed so angrily if she did not get her own way. Kasie had been slim and gentle, and always so neat and smart. And Lily could still picture those fair curls that grew from his high forehead. Avril's hair was quite straight and had turned a kind of dung colour, and she had a strong physique, with broad shoulders and big hips, which were unlike her father's.

Lily pulled back the velvet drapes and looked out towards the park where she could just see old George loping about exercising Yorkie. She sighed. Was this all there was left in life for her? She was not yet forty and still slim and fairly good to look at, but so far no other man had shown any interest in her. Perhaps that was because she went around with Jo; she was probably classed as an odd-bod, men were like that. But she didn't really care too much; hard work had managed to cool her ardour. And sometimes if she did give any thought to what she and Kasie used to get up to, she felt a little ashamed of herself.

Oh, well, life must go on, I suppose, she thought wearily as George came in with his dog and went straight to his own little room. He always stayed out of Lily's sight if she was alone.

'Oh, well, back to work,' she sighed, pulling on her mack. As she arranged her blue beret on her head, she called out to George: 'Don't forget to wash up and lay the table, and to put out the rubbish.'

George did not answer. He never did.

As Lily went off to get the bus, she thought about the lucky escape she had had recently. The greatest dread in her life was that Avril would find out the secret of her parentage and then despise her. When Avril first entered West Ham College, she had asked Lily for her birth certificate. 'They say they need to see it,' Avril had said.

Lily's heart had leaped in terror. It had never occurred to her that this might happen. 'Oh, I don't know where it is,' she said impatiently, trying to cover up her concern. 'It probably went astray in the moving. Don't worry, I'll sort it out,' she added, hoping that it wouldn't be mentioned again.

The reason why Lily had been worried was that Avril's name on the certificate was Avril Brown but she had grown up as Avril Clegg. This was a problem that Lily could not find a solution for and she never knew whom to ask advice from.

Avril had continued to pester Lily for the certificate until Lily had felt quite sick with worry about what to do, but then suddenly a few days ago, Avril had said: 'Oh, by the way, Mike said not to bother about my birth certificate. They got my records from the convent apparently, so it will be all right.'

Lily had breathed a deep sigh of relief. Her secret was safe once more. But always in the back of her mind was this worry about how she would face it one day. At least while she lived in this house, she felt safe about it; everyone there seemed to have a secret of some sort. She never had any letters and everyone called her Lily, not Mrs, and as for George, he would not let the cat out of the bag. After all, he was not sure of his own identity and lived only for his little dog and sweets and the local picture house. But she was afraid it would come out some day.

Christmas Eve that year was cold and misty. With a big shopping bag and his little dog on a lead, George went to do the shopping. In his hand he held a large purse with a list of provisions needed by everyone in the house. They tended to be a little lazy about shopping nowadays and they relied heavily on good old George and his good associations with the local shopkeepers, who would serve George and tick the items off his shopping list and put his change back into his purse before giving him a stick of liquorice and seeing him off down the road.

Because it was Christmas Eve, the shop was crowded and the shopkeeper busy. Very nervous, and knowing that he was not allowed to take his dog inside the shop, George waited patiently outside the shop, hoping that the shop would clear a little. As he stood there clutching his purse, a large group of local youths came down the road. They were all a little high, as it was the festive season, and they had drunk a few beers. They larked about, pushing and jostling the shoppers on the street. Then suddenly a tall youth in a leather jacket spotted George standing placidly on the corner with his little dog on a lead. 'There's ol' barmy!' he cried, 'come on, lads, let's give 'is arse a roasting.'

The youths all gathered around George, edging him around the corner into the darkened street.

''Ere, wot yer got there? Look at that scruffy mutt!' someone yelled. They made a grab at Yorkie, who snapped and snarled at them. George was very concerned and bent down to pick up his little friend but a terrific whack on his head sent him spinning. As his purse went rolling in the gutter, the silver coins rolled out.

'Oh, look! 'e's loaded,' one cried, as George scrambled about to get his money.

In the meantime, Yorkie went tearing off, his tail between his legs in fright. A big youth grabbed George's legs, while another aimed a kick at George's head with a big, iron-shod boot. George was screaming in terror but they gave him a good beating and then, dragging him by his legs, chucked him over a low wall. Then they tore off down the road. Poor old George, thinking only of his little dog, literally crawled home and collapsed on the front step, bleeding profusely. His little dog lay against him, whimpering pathetically.

At six o'clock Lily came swinging along the road. It had been a busy day and she had finished much later than usual. Jo had gone to park her van as Lily saw the little dog Yorkie running towards her.

'What are you doing out here? You'll get run over,' she said. 'Where's that George?' She grabbed hold of the hairy little dog. He felt very wet. 'Why,' she said, 'what have you been up to?' In the light of the street lamp she looked at her hands and saw that they were bloody. 'Oh blimey,' said Lily. 'You are hurt. Let's get you home.'

With the dog in her arms, she hurried to climb the steps and almost fell over George who lay moaning and groaning just outside the street door. 'Jo! Jo!' screamed Lily. 'Come quickly!'

Jo had just reached the gate. She dashed up and caught hold of George in her strong arms. Lily opened the door and together they carried him to his room.

As Lily staunched the bleeding as best as she could with towels, Jo said; 'I'll ring for an ambulance. He's badly cut about the head.'

Lily wiped George's face. Her tears were falling fast. 'Who done it, George?' she asked.

'Yobbos,' whispered George, as he lost consciousness.

The police were called to the hospital because of the bruises.

The doctor spoke to Lily as she sat in the casualty department of the hospital. 'He has been badly beaten and seems to have been kicked in the head where he had already had a bad injury. We'll do what we can but he is still unconscious.'

The attack on George soon became a local issue when the newspapers picked it up and made a big thing of it. Thus George, who had been a nonentity in his life, shot to fame as he died on Boxing Day. The whole house in Plashet Grove was devastated.

Lily was very upset about it all and became violently angry with the police. 'What can they have achieved?' she cried.

'There wasn't much more than a fiver in that purse and he was harmless, poor old George. If you get those young bastards, they deserve hanging.'

The policeman tried to calm her. 'Well, we are now living in violent days,' he said. 'It gets worse all the time. This was once a select area but now with the council estates and the problem families, it's slowly deteriorating and there is not a lot we can do about it.'

'Well, do your bloody job and catch them,' said Lily, 'that's all I ask.'

But no evidence was forthcoming and no one came forward as a witness. Soon the whole affair was forgotten and only the odd-bods in the house remembered George. They missed him very much. Yorkie, George's little dog, attached himself to Lily and slept on her bed as he had done on George's.

Not long after George died, Avril, rather solemnly, said: 'I was very upset about old George even though he aggravated me.'

Lily said, 'Yes, poor George. He never got much out of life, and I feel very guilty sometimes.'

'The papers said he was your husband,' said Avril. 'Is that true?' Her voice was cold.

Lily hesitated as she felt the colour rising in her cheeks.

'Look, Mother, don't try to treat me like a child,' Avril said impatiently. 'I know that Norman was my father and I can understand that I am a bastard. I can take that. But please don't try to tell me that poor old fool George fathered me, will you?'

Lily clasped Avril close in her arms as tears fell fast. Was now the time to tell the truth? But did she need to tell? Avril seemed content to suss the situation herself, so why try and explain further?

'George did not always look like that,' she said in a heart-broken voice.

'Perhaps not,' Avril said in a matter-of-fact manner, 'but seeing as I was born at the end of the war, I don't blame you for living with my Daddy. But for God's sake, why didn't you divorce George and marry Daddy? That is what I do not understand or forgive.'

'Darling, it might sound easy but life is a very complicated business as you will find out before you are much older.' Lily tried to guide the conversation onto something else.

'Oh, well,' said Avril impatiently, dismissing the subject. 'I'm certainly not going to let it interfere with my life. I'll go on to the polytechnic to get my degree in biology and chemistry next year, if it kills me.'

'That's right, my love, get a good education and you'll never have to rely on a man to support you.' Lily relaxed a little as they talked of other things.

Because it had been such a gloomy Christmas, Jo decided to try and cheer everyone up by giving a supper party up West and to follow that with a show. She was very generous about it: 'It's all on me,' she said. 'We need something else to think about and there's a great show at the Palladium this year.'

When getting ready to go out that evening, Lily opened the wardrobe and got out the little fur cape that Kasie had bought her so many years ago. It had been carefully wrapped up, for she had not worn it for a long time, never having the occasion to. But tonight, wearing a nice new dress of dark-blue chiffon, she put the soft cape over her shoulders and admired herself in the mirror.

Avril had been stomping around the flat getting herself ready when she suddenly noticed Lily. She stood staring at her in horror. 'Oh my God, Mother, take that thing off, it terrifies me!'

For a second Lily blushed guiltily, feeling sure that Avril had guessed the secret source of the little fur cape. But then she realised that it was not possible. 'Why?' she demanded angrily. 'What for? I've not worn this for years, and I think it's just right for this occasion.'

But Avril's dark eyes glowed in anger. 'Do you know how many poor little animals were slaughtered to make that thing?' Her voice was hard and stern.

Lily couldn't help herself, and began to laugh very loudly.

'Take it off at once!' yelled Avril rushing at her and taking hold of the fur.

But Lily held on tightly, saying: 'Oh, is that all that's bugging you?'

'Take it off!' said Avril. Her face red with anger, she stamped her foot. 'It makes me want to puke. I'll not go out with you while you have that repulsive thing hanging about your neck.'

Lily snatched the cape back from her grasp. 'You can please your bloody self,' she said. 'This is mine and I am wearing it. Your Daddy bought it for me.'

'You're a bloody liar!' yelled Avril. 'You came back with that one afternoon after one of your mysterious trips to London. Don't think I can't remember, because I do.'

Lily's face flamed scarlet and her eyes filled with tears. 'Why, you nasty little bitch!' She struck out at Avril impulsively.

Ducking away from the blow, Avril snatched the cape and threw it up on top of the wardrobe. 'That's that, you try and get it down,' she challenged Lily aggressively.

Lily stood white-faced and bewildered. Never before had Avril defied her and now she was positively violent.

On hearing the yelling Jo came dashing upstairs. 'What's up?' she demanded. 'You two having a quarrel? Get it over with. The taxi's here, and we'll be late for the show if you don't hurry.'

With a sullen expression, Avril watched Lily without saying another word. Lily opened the wardrobe, put on her tweed coat and said quietly: 'It's okay, Jo, we're ready.'

But it had put a damper on what might have been a good evening, and they also had to put up with Andy who was in a neurotic state because Ray had gone off at Christmas and so far had not returned. After his second glass of wine, Andy was being very temperamental, and weeping and complaining about Ray. 'My dear,' he told Lily, 'I've practically kept that fellow and now he goes off without a word. When he comes back I'll tell him what I think of him, the big ponce.'

In fact, on their return home Andy started screaming hysterically because Ray, it seemed, had been in while they were out, packed all his things and left for good. Lily and Jo finally calmed Andy down and gave him some aspirins and lots of sympathy. When he had finally gone up to bed Lily said, 'Gor blimey, I feel bloody exhausted. What a night it's been!'

'I did my best, Lily,' said Jo. 'Too bad the show wasn't so good, either. What's the trouble between you and Avril?'

'She won't let me wear my fur cape. She says it's because of all the small animals that are being killed.'

'Oh, well,' said Jo, 'she's at an impressionable age. You'll have to go along with her, Lily.'

'I don't see why I should,' Lily said obstinately. 'She's just like all those other cranky college kids. She won't eat meat now, either.'

'You'll have to learn vegetarian cooking, Lily,' said the practical Jo. 'I'll teach you. I've been a vegetarian for years. In fact, I'd quite like to open a restaurant just for vegetarians. I think there'd be a market for that sort of thing now.'

Lily sighed. 'I suppose I'll have to learn to live with it. After all, she is all I've got left now and I can't afford to fall out with her.'

Once more Lily wrapped up the fur cape and put it out of sight. The next day she cooked chestnut cutlets and egg flan and she invited Jo to eat with her and Avril.

Avril looked pleased. 'That was nice, Mummy, I can see you're getting some sense at last.'

Lily felt decidedly small and humble. She was not sure she liked the feeling but she made a face at Jo, as if to say, 'Anything for a quiet life.'

That term Avril started at the polytechnic and was quite thrilled about it. She made a host of new friends and spent less time than ever at home.

Lily would lounge in front of the television set and, to her surprise, often found herself thinking about old George. She actually missed him, she realised. In fact, she thought about George more than she had ever thought about Norman, and now she often tried to recall her own wedding when George had been a bright Cockney lad and had turned up at the church in a light grey suit and his cloth cap still perched on his head. Lily had asked her grandfather to snatch it off George's head as he went into the church wearing it. That had given the family a real good laugh. Yes, she reminisced, they were the good old days before the war, days that would never come back. Full of such nostalgia, she spent many lonely hours that spring. Jo had gone off on a specialised course for catering management down in the south, so Lily kept the shops going and coped with the whims of Avril who got more and more domineering than ever.

Andy was in the throes of a nervous breakdown and full of pills. He was always on a visit to the hospital or the doctor's. He was on the dole and was always hard up and never paid his rent. Every day he scrounged around the house for fags and money.

'I'm bloody fed up with you,' Lily told him one day when he came to cadge some cigarettes. 'Go out to work like the rest of us have to.'

'Oh dear, don't nag me, love,' cried Andy. 'You don't know what I'm going through. Look at the pills I have to take—some to make me sleep, some to pep me up and these are special, they are hormones. I'll let you into a secret; I'm going to have a complete sex change. I'm going to be a woman, my doctor has advised it.'

Lily stared at him in disbelief. 'Don't kid me,' she said warily.

'Look dear,' he opened his dressing-gown to show her his chest. 'It's already working, isn't it exciting?'

Lily stared in amazement at Andy's well-developed breasts and pink nipples. Her eyes travelled downwards. 'And how the bloody hell are they going to do that?' she demanded.

Andy flushed. 'They operate, dear, my nerves being in such a state, the doctors have advised it for medical reasons.'

'Well, what a bloody waste of money,' Lily said irritably.

'Oh, don't be like that, dear,' pleaded Andy. 'And from now on, I wish you all to call me Anita. I want to get used to my new name.'

Lily could hardly believe it. She shook her head and gave Andy the cigarette he wanted.

That spring, Avril was eighteen. Lily decided to give her a

nice party in Jo's flat which was larger and more convenient than hers.

Of late, Avril had become quiet and dreamy, and all she could talk about was the new young language teacher who was called Neil. Lily had seen him bring Avril home in his little red sports car and wondered if this was a romance. It would be Avril's first. For so far, Avril had only been interested in her social activities. Now it was all 'Neil said this' or 'Neil said that'.

Lily decided that it was time to meet some of her friends and a birthday party would give her the opportunity to do so. Jo did the catering, with Lily's help, and they cleared out most of the furniture in Jo's flat, leaving only some comfortable seats in the sitting room, a big buffet table in the hall, and a bar in the kitchen. It was quite a splendid affair with pop music and dimmed lights.

The guests arrived in droves, and the food disappeared rapidly. As the music became louder and louder, the young bodies twisted and turned in the dim lights. No one was introduced to anybody else, they just marched in and out or lay about in the dark corners kissing and cuddling. Some of them smoked evil-smelling cigarettes which they passed from one to another.

Lily was disappointed by the way it turned out, for she had planned a more select affair.

'That's the kids of today,' Jo said, when Lily complained. 'They smoke pot and make love in public—it's not our scene anymore.'

Lily was forced to agree. Across the room she could see Avril dancing very close with Neil, her fair-haired boyfriend. The sight of them made her feel suddenly disgruntled and for a moment she thought there was something familiar about him, but perhaps it was just that she had seen him bring Avril home in his car.

As the evening wore on, the party quietened, and the young students sat in groups on the floor to cool down. Then Neil pulled a chair into the middle of the floor and began to strum on a small banjo. When he started to sing, Lily suddenly felt as if she had received an electric shock. She felt paralysed as Neil sang the popular numbers in his soft, sweet voice. The red light over his head formed a kind of halo, his hair, straight-lined features were clearly defined, as was the sensitive mouth moving in rhythm to the music. Suddenly Lily was back in the East End in Charlie Brown's pub and Kasie was crooning beside the piano. She covered her eyes with her hands and then looked around again. She was dreaming, it was pure imagination, but she moved a little closer. The glint of mother-of-pearl on the small, old-fashioned banjo convinced her. It could only be Kasie's old banjo which he had brought from his homeland and humped around the world when the war was on. It had to be the same old banjo that Kasie had received as a gift from his father and with which he had entertained so many folk in those war-torn times. Lily knew that she was not mistaken. She had to get closer and find out how Neil got it. Excitement was mounting up within her.

Neil had started to sing folk songs. His clear voice rang out across the room: 'Oh Shenandoah, I love your daughter . . .'

Lily's heart almost stopped dead. Shaking a little, she went and sat out on the garden steps and began to cry. In the chill night air, she shivered as if the ghosts of the past were right there beside her.

'What are you sitting out there for, Lily?' Jo called. 'You'll catch cold. Come on, I believe they are at last packing up to go home.'

Lily went back in and watched the youngsters go trooping out rather unsteadily, clinging to each other as they fell against the corridor doors.

Avril stood close to her boyfriend and they kissed a passionate goodnight. He had left his banjo on the settee. Lily went over, picked up the familiar old instrument and smoothed her fingers over the mother-of-pearl handle.

'It's nice, isn't it?' Neil said proudly. 'It's very old, you know.'

'How old?' asked Lily.

'I'm not sure. My father gave it to me when I was twenty-one and his father gave it to him. It has been in London before, you know, when my father was in the British Navy during the war.'

'Oh,' said Lily dreamily, still holding the banjo. 'And where is your home?'

'In the Netherlands,' Neil replied, 'but I have spent most of my life over here at boarding school. That is why I have no accent.'

Through a veil of tears, Lily saw that he was tall and slim with tight fair curls, and she knew she had seen him before. It was the little lad at the Heeg from so many years ago.

'It's nice to meet you, Neil,' she said, putting out her hand. As he clasped it, she knew the feeling was there. That soft warm skin was just like Kasie's. Her heart thumped hard, and Avril stared at her suspiciously.

'Give over, Mother, he's my boyfriend, not yours,' she cried.

Lily released Neil's hand. 'Well, that's your birthday party over, goodnight all.' She went up to her own flat where she sat thinking hard. Could there be a mistake? Was it really possible that the first boy Avril had fallen in love with was her own half-brother? Lily felt sick with fear. 'Oh dear God,' she prayed, 'let me be mistaken.'

The next day was Sunday and Avril lay in bed most of the day. Lily took her nice meals on a tray and pampered her. Then she began to question her. She was determined to find out if her fears were well-founded or not. Had Avril really got a crush on Neil, she asked tentatively.

'Oh, Mummy,' Avril exclaimed joyfully, 'I think I have fallen in love with him.' She looked radiantly happy.

'Wait till you know him better,' Lily advised, 'it's too soon to know that.'

'No, my mind is made up, if I can get him, I'll be extraordinarily happy.'

'Perhaps he's already married,' ventured Lily.

'Don't be silly, he's only six years older than I am and when he's done this course he is going up to Oxford, I might even try for the university myself,' she added complacently.

'What's his real name?' Lily enquired.

'Oh, it's a funny one. It's Cornelius De Fries, it's Dutch, or something.'

Lily was speechless. So it was true. She felt stunned. Whatever should she do?

Avril nudged her. 'Wake up, Mum, I'll have another cup of tea, if you don't mind.'

'I'm tired,' said Lily. 'I'll give you your tea but then you must get up and get dressed, there's a good girl. I might have a doze in the armchair.'

She took Avril a cup of tea and then, sitting in the armchair, she closed her eyes, and turned over these problems in her mind. She was still battling against the truth. It could be a mistake, she thought, there must be plenty of Dutchmen with that name. It was just a coincidence. Yes, she would ask Neil to tea next week and probe a bit more. In the meantime, she prayed that Avril would cool off so she would not have anything to worry about.

But every evening when Neil brought Avril home from college, they would sit outside in the car chatting for some time before she came in. And every time, Lily would spy on them from behind the curtains, with anxious gaze, her eyes dark rimmed through lack of sleep and worry.

On Sunday evening Neil came to tea. Lily made some fancy cakes, and got out her best china. Neil was polite and charming and seemed much more mature than Avril in his ways. And Avril was on top of the world. She cuddled close to him, and held his hand looking blissfully happy while Lily's face got longer and longer with anxiety.

When Neil told Lily that he lived in Amsterdam and that his father and mother had separated when he was young, she knew that she could deny the truth no more. Her face was frozen as Neil chatted openly about himself and his family.

'We get on fine, Papa and I,' he said. 'He is a sea captain and recently made a lot of money on a big oil deal for the Middle East. He's not often at home. My mother divorced him and remarried, and now she lives in a flat in Amsterdam.'

Lily looked more mournful than ever. 'Has your mother got a nice name?' she asked in a weak voice.

'Yes, she is called Wrenska,' he replied politely. This made Lily positively shudder and she did not say anything more.

'I don't know why you have to give Neil the third degree,' grumbled Avril when he had gone. 'I thought you were positively rude. I don't think I'll ask him here again.'

But Lily did not answer; she was too preoccupied with her own thoughts.

CHAPTER NINE

Facing the Consequences

Thus a new and massive problem had arisen in Lily's life, just when she thought everything was under control. The ghost of Kasie had appeared large and formidable in the form of this blond young man called Neil.

Not knowing what to do immediately, she prayed that Avril was not going to make any sudden, rash decisions, and she threw herself even more into her work and her cooking classes, for she now helped the teacher at the adult centre, teaching the younger ones how to make good cakes and serve nice meals.

'I think you are wasted working in my bakery,' Jo said one day. 'Let's open a restaurant together, you and I, this vegetarian restaurant I've wanted to run for so long.'

Lily looked worried. 'Not yet, Jo,' she said. 'The money I have saved is for Avril's education, I don't want to break into it.'

'You'd soon get it all back if we are successful,' said Jo. 'Besides, Avril might decide to get married and give up all this education. She seems very keen on that young tutor from college.'

'Oh, please God, no,' muttered Lily.

Jo looked at her very curiously. 'I didn't know you felt so intensely about marriage, Lily, but you'll have to face it if it comes. The young ones today will make their own decisions.'

One evening Avril came home very late and her hair was all untidy. Unable to bear the strain, Lily flew into a rage. 'Where have you been? It's gone ten o'clock,' she cried.

Avril threw down her mack and bag on the floor and faced her mother. She was not quite as tall but she was much broader.

Her eyes glowed with temper and her lips were set in a thin straight line, just as Kasie's used to be. For a second, Lily felt a twinge of fear as she often had when she lined up for battle with Kasie, but she did not retreat this time.

Avril started to shout at her. 'Mother! I've had about enough of your cranky ways, holding a bloody post-mortem on me every time I get home.'

'Well, I worry over you,' said Lily firmly. 'Don't forget that you are still very young and know nothing of the world.'

Avril started to grin. 'Oh, Christ!' she said. 'How corny can you get? I'm eighteen and I've got a regular boyfriend but I still have not yet been to bed with him. I'd like to but he hasn't asked me, but if he does, I will. Does that satisfy you?'

A lump came into Lily's throat, she was wounded by Avril's hard, contemptuous tone. 'Darling,' she said, 'don't be hasty, he might not be the right one for you and then you'd be sorry.'

'Sorry? Why should I be sorry?' asked Avril. She poured herself a big mug of coffee and sat down beside the fire to drink it.

'Well,' said Lily, 'because if another man comes along who is your true mate, it will spoil things for you, dear,' she tried bravely to explain but she knew it was a losing battle.

'Oh, what the bloody hell is wrong with you, Mother? Why this propriety all of a sudden? No one worries about being a virgin any more—that's all old hat.'

'Well!' cried Lily, 'then it will serve you bloody right if you get left in the cart, like I was.' The moment the words were out, she immediately regretted them.

Avril banged down her mug. 'That's nice!' she yelled, 'remind me I'm a bastard! But that's your bloody fault, not mine, and I can assure you, I'll not be as bloody daft as you were.'

These last words were too much. Lily began to cry. Avril got up and cuddled her. 'Oh, don't cry, I can't bear it,' she said. 'Look, Mother, I promise that if I do indulge, I'll tell you, how's that? Anyway, Neil is a very respectable young man and I can't really see it happening. But I'll still keep trying!'

Lily dried her eyes and looked at Avril in amazement. There was no nonsense about her. She faced the situation with a clear mind and Lily knew that Avril would give all for love, just as Kasie had done.

'Let's be friends, darling,' said Lily hugging her tight and kissing her on the cheek. 'You know I would never ever hurt you, but because life has not been kind to me I'm afraid for you sometimes.'

'Okay, Mother,' said Avril. 'Come on, let's make some toast and have some more coffee.'

Mother and daughter sat together around the fire very close and very warm. As Lily stared into the artificial log fire, her memories flowed back to the East End during the war days, back to when Kasie came on leave and they made love on that old rug beside the coal fire in the house in Sewell Street, beside the Limehouse Churchyard. At least for the time being she could be satisfied that Avril had not completely involved herself with Neil. But how long could that last?

For many days, Lily struggled to find a solution to her problem and in the end she decided that there was only one answer; she had to sort it out with Kasie. How she would contact him or what his reaction would be after all this time, she could not bear to think. According to Neil, his father was not often at home because he was mostly away at sea. How was she to find him on her own? She turned these problems over and over in her mind and spent many a sleepless night as a result.

Jo noticed the change in her. 'Aren't you well, Lily? You look very tired. Perhaps you had better have a week off on the sick list.'

'I'm all right, Jo, but something is worrying me.'

'Can I help?' offered Jo.

Lily shook her head, but then she said: 'If you wanted to contact someone you hadn't seen in years, how would you do it?'

Jo looked at her curiously but made no comment.

'I know the place and the town where this person sometimes lives,' added Lily, 'but not the address.'

'How about the personal column of the local newspaper?' suggested Jo.

'It's not in England,' replied Lily.

'That doesn't matter. Just write to the town hall, or send a letter to the local newspaper. They'd print it, I'm sure.'

This sounded like a good suggestion and so Lily, convinced that this was her best move, wrote to an Amsterdam newspaper asking them to insert her advert. The message was simple: 'Kasie, if you still remember me, I must speak with you. Lily.' But she had no success.

The college broke up for the Easter holidays and Avril was very disgruntled. 'Neil has gone off to meet his father somewhere out East. He didn't ask me if I'd like to go, too, and I don't know what I'm going to do without him.'

'Never mind,' said Lily. 'I'll take a few days off and we'll go up West to do some shopping. I'm sure you will soon forget him,' she said hopefully.

'Not on your life, Mother,' Avril said sharply. 'He and I have such a lot in common but he does not want to be tied down. He hopes to go up to Oxford this year, and he said I would stand a good chance too, if I get a good pass in chemistry next year. He thinks I should spend my time and energy on humans, not animals, but you know I don't really like human beings, I prefer animals.'

Lily smiled. 'But what about Neil?' she asked.

'Oh,' said Avril, with a smug look on her face, 'now that is very different.'

So Lily's hopes fell. It was not really over at all. And she knew that she had to try harder to contact Kasie.

'Where have Neil and his father gone?' she asked.

'They've got a ship, an oil tanker I think, and Neil is flying out to meet his father. Then they will go back to Amsterdam. It seems they have some other interest, a passenger line on the Rhine. Neil has promised me a trip on it later this year. They say it is very lovely along the Rhine, with lots of grand castles.'

Lily was pondering. Yes, that was how she could contact Kasie, through his passenger service on the Rhine.

The next day, Lily went to all the travel agencies stating that she wanted to go on a trip along the Rhine. She was handed several brochures, and eventually the right one cropped up. It was the D & K Line sailing from Rotterdam to Basle. She wrote a letter to Kasie addressing it to the shipping line, asking it to be forwarded to him. Then with sweat on her brow she sealed up the envelope. Surely this time she would find him. In her letter, she had asked Kasie to meet her in London and to wire her confirmation of the time and date. She stressed that it was very important to them both. She posted the letter with trembling hands and waited anxiously for a reply.

Three weeks later it came. The telegraph boy was waiting on the step when she came home from work. The telegram just read: 'Cumberland. April 15. Kasie.'

Her breath came out in a loud sob as she screwed up the message. 'That's just like him, it had to be some posh hotel,' she thought with irritation. Then through her mind rushed the memories of that last weekend they had spent together. Well, this time she would not be soft with him, all that had gone out of her life. All this was for Avril's sake and hers alone.

As April 15 drew near, Lily began to get nervous. She went out and bought herself a new navy blue suit and smart black court shoes. She would look the part, she decided, he would see a marked change in her. And she wondered just how he would look.

'What's going on, Mother?' Avril was curious. 'Got a date or something, buying all this gear?'

'No, it's just a new suit for the spring. I didn't have one last year.' Lily made excuses. 'Is Neil back?'

Avril looked a little crestfallen. 'Yes,' she mumbled, 'but he's been a bit busy lately studying for his finals, but we have had a couple of dates.'

Lily wondered was she being too hasty, the affair might already be over, but she could not change her plans now. 'I need a day off,' she told Jo, 'on April 15.'

'That's okay, Lily,' said Jo, 'going anywhere nice?' she asked.

'No,' said Lily. 'I'm meeting a very old friend in town but please don't tell Avril.'

'A man friend?' enquired Jo very surprised.

'Of course not, silly,' replied Lily. 'It's a girl I was on the buses with in the wartime.' As always, when she resurrected poor old Ivy, Lily felt a little guilty about this but Ivy had been the only real friend she had ever made.

At lunch time, looking very trim in her new suit, Lily got on the bus to Oxford Street and, without hesitation, walked into the lounge of the Cumberland. As she did so she wondered if she would recognise Kasie, or he her.

There was no need for her to worry, for there he was propping up the bar, lounging against the ornamental column, he had a big fat cigar in his mouth and a full glass of beer in his hand. He was much stouter and wore a light tanned suit and open-necked shirt.

Lily pulled herself up sharply and then went straight over to him. She stared at him very intently without smiling. 'Hullo, Kasie,' she said. 'Long time no see.'

Kasie grinned and there was a flash of gold teeth and the twinkle in those brown eyes. He took her arm. 'Come, sit down,' he said warmly. 'I'll order some drinks.'

In the shady corner behind the potted palm, they looked into each other's eyes and neither one liked what they saw; there were lines and crinkles around his eyes and the line his lips formed seemed harder than ever; and Lily's chin jutted out obstinately. Like two armed vessels, they lined up for battle.

'Well, Lily,' he said at last. 'I must say, you haven't changed much.'

'I don't know what you mean exactly,' said Lily haughtily, 'but you look like a bloody barrel of lard. I never thought you would get so fat.'

Those teeth flashed a gold smile once more. He raised his drink. 'It's good to see you again, Lily,' he said.

As she raised her glass, his hand came out and covered hers. It was that same, warm tender skin. A strange emotion coursed through her veins. 'Hullo, my lovely,' he said softly.

She looked down at her lap. 'I came for one reason only, Kasie. Something has cropped up concerning Avril, and only you can help me.'

His face changed. 'So, now I have a daughter, you say. Have you forgotten that you stole her from me and gave her to another man?'

Lily's eyes filled with tears. 'Oh, don't drag up old sores, Kasie,' she pleaded. 'This is very serious.'

Cautiously, he looked around them and then back at her. 'Let's go up to my room and talk,' he said with a sly grin.

'No, thanks,' she returned abruptly.

'It's quite all right,' he said cajolingly. 'I promise not to rape you.'

'I'll see you bloody well don't,' retorted Lily

'Well, *leiblin*, one advantage for you would be that up there you can yell your head off at me. Down here they'll all be listening.'

'Oh well, I'll come—but no funny business,' decided Lily.

Quickly he guided her towards the lift. There were other people in it so they were still not alone. As the lift started to move, they stood very silent, yet close together. Lily's heart began to beat madly. So there was still that old magic, some unspoken bond between them. They got off at his floor and she watched his well-manicured hands as he put the key in the door. A little voice in Lily's head was urging her to leave. 'Go now,' it warned. 'Soon it will be too late and you will never escape.' But she obstinately ignored it. She had to get this business of Avril and Neil over and settled once and for all.

As usual, Kasie had taken a very big, expensive suite. Lily noted the large double bed and the separate bathroom. She sat down in an armchair while Kasie went to the beside cabinet and out came the inevitable bottle of Bols gin, and two glasses. So he had been expecting to entertain her, she thought cynically, as he handed her a drink.

'You haven't lost the taste for this, I hope,' he murmured.

She shook her head. 'A little water, please, if you don't mind,' she said.

'Tonic?' He handed her a small bottle.

Cradling his own drink in his hands, he sat facing her, running his eyes over her, all the way down to her long slim legs. 'Well?' he asked suddenly. 'What's all this news you have to tell me?' His lips twitched and that mischievous grin hovered there just as it used to.

'Kasie,' Lily said, suddenly angry, 'what I came to tell you is not a joke. In fact, it's very serious.' Although she had rehearsed this speech many times, the actual words now stuck to her tongue.

Kasie held up his glass to her. '*Prost*, Lily, my lovely,' he said, and then put his hand on her knee. 'And how are my lovely legs?' he asked in that low, sweet tone.

'Pack it up!' yelled Lily, springing away from his touch. 'I did not come up here for that.'

'Well, what do you want of me?' he queried.

Lily resented the way he was playing cat and mouse with her. She got up from her chair and declared loudly, 'I came because your son Neil is having a love affair with our daughter.'

Kasie now stared at her in amazement. Then he took a large swig of his drink. 'I don't believe it. How does she know my son?'

'He's the student tutor at her college,' replied Lily. 'I only discovered by accident that he is your son. They seem to be very keen on each other, and I'm really worried.'

To her astonishment, Kasie began to laugh. 'Well, Lily,' he said, 'let's hope they are not as we were.'

'Oh, don't joke about it,' she snapped. 'Even if you want deformed grandchildren, I don't.'

Now he did become very serious. 'I see what you mean,' he said soberly. 'And it will not be easy to tell them that they are brother and sister if they are so much in love.'

'I beg you to advise me,' said Lily. 'And let's please see eye to eye on this matter, it's so very important for me. I live for Avril—she's all I've got left.'

'Well, I can take care of my son, but you seem to have

forgotten, my lovely, that you took my daughter away from me. Perhaps now is the time to tell her the truth.'

Lily gazed at him very forlornly. Kasie reached out and pulled her into his arms. She went willingly, resting her head on his shoulder and weeping. He kissed her gently and held her close. Strange tremors went through her, and that old passion overcame her again as she allowed him to sit beside her on the bed and kiss her passionately. As though beyond her control, her arms locked around his neck.

'Oh, my Lily, my lovely, come back to me,' he whispered. He slid his hand up and down her legs as he used to do and Lily, so long without a man, found it almost impossible to resist him. His head nuzzled her breasts and she grasped his curly head as he guided her to the bed. He rolled on top of her and the heat of his body as it stiffened made her gasp for breath.

'Oh, Kasie, don't, don't!' she cried. 'Please, you did promise.'

He got up swearing a little, and poured himself another drink. 'Why do I always make a bloody fool of myself with you, Lily?' he demanded. 'I can never forget how you sent me packing like a whipped dog with my tail between my legs.'

Lily sat up and pulled down her dress. 'Open the door, Kasie, and I'll go. But promise me you'll do something about your son.'

'Oh that,' he grumbled. 'It so happens·that I'm about to set off for South America. Neil had wanted to come with me but I didn't want him to miss his studies. I'm quite sure he will still want to come if I say I've changed my mind.'

'I will be eternally grateful to you, Kasie,' said Lily tearfully. 'And I'll never trouble you again.' She picked up her handbag and went to the door. But Kasie barred her way and stood looking at her with a strange expression on his face.

Suddenly their lips were locked in a passionate embrace, his tongue probed her mouth as his hands roamed up and down her body.

'Lily, you need me,' he whispered in a hoarse voice, 'just as you did that first night when I took you against that garden wall.'

Lily was lost. He carried her to bed where he took off her blouse and unzipped her skirt. As he then undressed himself, she stood beside the bed, naked. 'Oh, God, Kasie,' she said, 'if I get into bed with you, I'll never let you go again.'

He lifted the sheet for her to enter. 'Come, darling,' he invited her. 'Look at him, he has waited a long time for you.'

When the dawn light rose over London town and the slow roll of the traffic could be heard outside, Lily sat up in bed and looked down at Kasie sleeping like a child beside her. 'Wake up, Kasie.' She gave him a prod. 'We've been here all night, and I must go.'

He smiled in his sleep and turned around and clasped her tightly around the waist. Unable to stop herself, she kissed him and snuggled down again beside him. She did not want the day to begin. It was as if she had been reborn. They were together again and it was as if it was only a dream which she never wanted to end. But at ten o'clock the cleaners were outside the door. Lily got up, took a shower and ordered some coffee. She roused Kasie again. 'It's ten o'clock, I've been out all night. Avril will be very worried.'

He sat up to drink the coffee. 'Oh, she's a big girl, Lily, stop worrying about her.'

'But I've never done this to her before. I have never done this before,' she repeated.

He grinned. 'Yes, I can well believe it. It was like sleeping with a virgin.'

'Oh, Kasie, don't jest,' she begged him. 'I know I love you and I want you, I always have. Now I am free to make up my own mind but I'm still afraid to face Avril.'

'She has to be told,' said Kasie. 'I will take Neil to South America, and I'll be gone three months. That will give you time to think things over, but remember, I'll stand no more nonsense from you. I can well take care of you and Avril now, so let's be wed while we are both free. Just promise me that, or I won't let you out of this room alive.' His eyes glowed with that murderous glint that Lily had seen many times before.

'Oh, Kasie,' she pleaded, 'don't spoil things by losing your temper.'

'There's the phone. Ring up and tell Avril that you won't be home until tomorrow, and that you are very busy entertaining her father.'

'Well, I suppose I could ring Jo,' Lily said reluctantly.

'Go ahead and then we'll go out and have a good time like we used to.'

Jo was most surprised when she got the message from Lily. 'Tell Avril I'll be back in the morning. My friend got tickets for a show,' Lily said.

'Have a good time, Lily,' said Jo. 'Avril will be okay.'

Having got her phone call over, Lily felt unusually happy. Kasie was in the shower singing to himself, and she suddenly felt carefree as if nothing was important anymore. It was a very wonderful feeling.

They went down to lunch in the hotel restaurant and she heard Kasie explaining how his wife had arrived late last night as he registered her at the reception desk.

'I must go home tomorrow,' she told him, over their lunch of crab salad and white wine.

'That's fine. I also go tomorrow, so let today be today.'

They went for a walk in Hyde Park and fed the ducks. For most of the afternoon, they sat on a park bench talking and kissing, and catching up on that space of ten years.

'I lost poor old Norman, and George got mugged,' she told him.

'So all's well that ends well,' said Kasie with confidence. 'I'll not let you escape me this time. I've made a lot of money in the past three years, Lily,' he informed her. 'Do you remember the mercury that I used to smuggle? Well, it got me a good stake and then I got interested in oil, which so far has really paid off. If this South American deal comes off I might retire. Then just think—you and me in some quiet spot. I'll buy a sailing boat, you remember Amsterdam harbour?'

Lily grimaced at the idea of spending any time on a boat again.

Kasie laughed. 'It's all right, darling, you can live ashore as long as I can find you when I want to love you.'

'It sounds great,' said Lily, 'but what about the kids?'

'Kids? They are not young children but a grown man and woman,' said Kasie. 'We will tell them the truth. Besides, Neil is actually engaged to a girl in Holland. She is from a good family and Neil will probably want to get married and come into the shipping line.'

It all sounded so easy. Lily knew life never was like that, but there Kasie was, warm and happy, right beside her. How many times had she longed for this moment? She would not spoil it now.

After tea in the Lyons Corner House, they went to the cinema and then on the usual pub crawl around Soho. They ate dinner in a late night restaurant, and returned to the hotel in the early hours very unsteady on their feet but exceedingly happy. That night they spent in each other's arms vowing to love one another till death do us part.

In the morning, in the best of spirits, they parted, Kasie went to the airport and Lily caught the bus to East London. But then, as she rode on the top deck of the bus, Lily's worries returned. She smoked one cigarette after another, and her head ached after last night's big session of drinking and loving. How was she going to face Avril? She could not think of any way to do it. Would she honestly be able to tell her the truth? Avril believed that Norman had been her father. How could she, Lily, suddenly disillusion her now? The more she thought about it, the less she felt she was able to face the situation.

When she eventually arrived home, Avril was out in the park feeding the army of stray cats she had adopted.

'Morning, Lily, had a good time?' Jo called to her.

'Fine, thanks, Jo,' replied Lily, but she retired to her flat and kept out of sight. She did not feel like facing any of her neighbours just yet.

Half an hour later, Avril bounced in, her coat flying open, her hair all over her eyes. She gave Lily a venomous look, 'So you made it, you got home at last,' she declared scornfully.

'Oh, I'm sorry, dear,' stammered Lily, 'but my friend Ivy so wanted to see this show and had booked the seats.'

'Bloody liar!' yelled Avril, 'don't try to kid me. That friend you keep digging up died years ago. You told me that yourself.'

Lily felt a lump rise in her throat, and a kind of fear gripped her.

'I know you've got a fancy man,' confirmed Avril. 'You used to pop off to see him when poor Daddy was alive. Don't think I can't remember, because I can.'

Now was the time to tell her, Lily thought, trying to be decisive, but as usual her tongue clove to the roof of her mouth. Her head swam dizzily as she tried to control her feelings.

Avril banged noisily about the flat getting ready to go out. 'I don't care what you do,' she said at last, 'but I'm a grown up adult, Mother, so don't try no fairy stories on me.'

Lily put her hands over her face as Avril finally swept past her, saying sarcastically, 'I presume we have your company for tea. I'll be back at six o'clock.'

When Avril had gone, Lily sat down in the armchair feeling utterly defeated. Once more she had lost the opportunity. Now it might never be said.

Hearing Avril banging the front door shut, Jo came creeping upstairs to hear the latest news. She looked sympathetically at Lily's white, strained face and passed her a cigarette. 'Don't let Avril worry you,' she said comfortingly. 'I think she's just jealous. Her boyfriend didn't turn up last night, you know.'

Lily listened with interest. Perhaps, she thought, getting in touch with Kasie had all been for nothing. Perhaps it was only a platonic friendship between Avril and Neil, and perhaps would stay that way.

'I'll be in the dog house with her for a while but I'll make it up to her.'

'You must live your own life, Lily,' warned Jo. 'Old age comes very quickly and it's better not to have too many regrets.'

Lily wanted to tell her all about her meeting with Kasie, to explain how wonderful it had been with his warm, loving arms around her once more, but she was afraid to trust anyone, even such a loyal friend as Jo. Jo began to tell Lily of a young girl she had met while she was on her cooking course. 'I might ask her to come and live here. You won't mind, will you, Lily?'

'It's not my business, Jo,' replied Lily. 'Everyone has their own way of living, but I would like to think that you would not be too lonely if I leave here.'

Jo looked alarmed. 'Don't say you're going to leave,' she protested. 'I'll never stay in this big house without you. And why are you thinking of leaving? Is it because you have a lover?'

'Well, it's someone I used to know a few years ago. That's all I can tell you. But he's abroad now and will not be back for three months.'

Jo relaxed. 'Well then, in the meantime let's not worry,' she said. 'I think you will like Rene. She's a waitress but has got ambitions of owning a restaurant, so we might all get together. I'm certainly going to close down two of the bakery shops. They're just not doing so good, now that most of the East End population has moved to the new towns.'

'Let's see what this year brings us, Jo. At the moment I don't know whether I'm on my head or my heels.'

'Bad as all that, was it, Lily?' smiled Jo.

'Oh, a lot worse! But somehow it was worth it,' Lily replied with a smile.

CHAPTER TEN

The Nutcracker

Andy still claimed to be in the throes of a nervous breakdown and pestered everyone with his troubles. And he still sat around in Lily's flat in the evenings trying to probe into her sex life. 'Don't try and kid me you ain't had it lately,' he would announce dramatically. 'Didn't you pop off for that crafty little trip to God knows where, and come back looking ten years younger?'

Lily smiled knowingly. 'Keep your long nose out of my affairs,' she said.

This remark immediately made Andy worried. 'Oh,' he cried, 'my nose isn't that predominant, is it, love?' He dodged over to the mirror to examine his nose. 'Don't tell me I got to get a nose job done as well.'

Lily started to laugh heartily, 'Oh dear, you'll be the death of me,' she said. 'I meant don't be so nosey.'

Andy was offended. 'I tell you all my secrets, so why are you so stingy with yours?' He had gone over to her wardrobe. 'Look at the smart dresses you've got,' he said, fingering the material. 'What I'd give to own a smart outfit like that! When I have my operation, I'll really get spruced up.'

Lily looked a little sorry. Andy was so kinky but perhaps he could not help it. 'Okay, take one of those at the end. I don't often wear any of them nowadays.'

'Oh, Lily, you darling,' gasped Andy in delight. Quickly stripping off his floral dressing gown, he began to try on Lily's dresses. 'How's this?' he asked, parading up and down before her like a mannequin.

Lily remembered how she used to make her own dresses

when she lived with Norman and often longed for someone to admire them when there was no one.

Andy finally left with a floral two-piece, a handbag, stockings and sandals. For days afterwards he paraded delightedly all around the house, letting everyone see him as he wanted to look.

'It's kind of pathetic,' Mike remarked. 'I don't know whether to kick his arse or kiss him.'

Not long afterwards, Andy bought a blonde wig and crept surreptitiously up to the wine bar wearing it one Saturday night. The other inhabitants of the house watched him from Lily's window as he set off mincing along, swinging his shoulder bag. Even Avril was amused. 'Oh crikey!' she cried. 'How kinky can you get?'

But Andy returned later that night after the bar had closed with a black eye and missing his nice blonde wig. He wept on Lily's shoulder. 'It was such an expensive wig,' he wailed. 'Oh dear, they are philistines, these East End people, they don't understand about art or beauty. When I have me op I'll move to somewhere nice, where they will accept me.'

'Oh, poor dear,' Lily said to Jo the next day, 'it must be terrible to be born that way. I can't understand it, I only know one kind of sex—never thought about anything else.'

'What about me, Lily?' Jo asked sadly.

'Oh yes, Jo, I sometimes forget about you. You know I don't mean anything nasty, and to me, you're a good pal.'

'I don't understand it either,' said Jo. 'All I can say is that there must be a kind of third sex. We are just born that way and the rest of humanity will not accept us.'

Lily put her arm around her. 'Never mind,' she said. 'You'll be happy when that little friend comes to live with you.'

'I hope so,' said Jo, a little doubtfully, 'I'm looking for true affection, Lily, and so far I've never found it.'

Then Lily in her generous way gave out love and little things that mattered to her companions.

Not long afterwards, Lily discovered that Neil had left Avril's college. Lily had watched her daughter for a while when Avril was glum, pale-faced and very silent. The only thing she told Lily about Neil was that he had left the poly. 'He was supposed to be writing to me,' she added sadly, 'but somehow I think I've had it.'

'It's always hard to lose a first lover,' Lily said philosophically, 'but someone else will take his place.'

'I am not like you, Mother,' Avril said rather bitterly. 'I've got no sex appeal, men don't run after me, and I'm well aware of it.'

Lily blushed guiltily. 'Oh, darling,' she said, 'you're a lovely girl with a great brain. I've not got the brain of an ant and never read a book in my life.'

'But I don't think you've missed out on a lot,' Avril said dryly.

Mother and daughter drew closer once more and Lily was very happy, but she vowed that she would never upset Avril again. And thank goodness the relationship with Neil had gone no further.

She often looked at herself in the mirror and recalled Kasie's remarks at their last meeting. He had commented on how rough her lovely hands had become after working so hard in the bakehouse. And he had suggested that she let her lovely hair grow naturally and take the cosmetic red colour out of it.

So Lily left off that henna rinse and brushed her hair each night to help make it grow. She cold-creamed her hands, and began to wear gloves for the heavy duties. She frequently looked at herself in the mirror and noted with pleasure that the sallow look was beginning to leave her face, and her eyes looked brighter. Often she sighed, thinking of that night. It had been wonderful, but she was lost when he was there, she had no defence against him. Just the thought of his strong body near hers gave her many sleepless nights.

One morning a letter arrived for Avril with a South American stamp on it. When she saw it, Lily's heart missed a beat as for a moment she thought that Kasie might have sent it. But when she examined the writing, she was relieved. It was not Kasie's big untidy scrawl, it was a much neater, educated hand, possibly from Neil.

When Avril came in she snatched the letter from the table and hid in the bathroom to read it. When she came out, her eyes were filled with tears but she had a very determined look on her face.

Lily poured out the tea. 'Been a nice spring day, hasn't it?' she said cheerfully.

Avril scowled. 'Don't hedge, Mother. If you want to know about the letter, why don't you ask?'

'Well, I don't want to probe into your life, dear,' said Lily.

'It's from Neil, giving me the elbow, if you must know. He's gone to South America with that father of his. He's given up his studies and is going into business. So, does that satisfy you?'

Lily nodded glumly. Deep inside she felt the hurt. The knife turned in her heart. She knew she was responsible, and it was hard to bear.

'It's Sunday tomorrow,' she said brightly. 'What about going down the lane and treating ourselves?'

'No, thanks, I'm going on a hike with some girls from school,' replied Avril. 'Might go to Epping Forest. I've got this friend who's very interested in wild life.'

'A boyfriend?' quizzed Lily with interest.

'No, it's not a bloody boyfriend,' shouted Avril, 'I'm through with men. I expect I'll end up like that kinky Jo downstairs.'

'Don't raise your voice, someone might hear you,' warned Lily.

'And a bloody good job too!' cried Avril as she flounced out, wearing her Wellington boots and a big anorak, all of which made her look enormous.

Lily sighed. If Avril wanted to, she could make herself very attractive but she never seemed anxious to spend any time on herself and rarely looked in the mirror. She's not like me in her ways, Lily thought, and not even like Kasie, either. He had always been smart. She recalled his dapper little figure in naval uniform, with the shiny black shoes and bright brass buttons.

Ah well, she thought, Avril was young and very brainy, so perhaps it did not really matter.

Avril seemed to get over Neil quite well. Sometimes Lily thought that it would have been better if she had left well alone. The affair would have ended anyway. But now, in a couple of months, Kasie would be back and know exactly where to find her. She could not bear to think about how he might try to change her life. Should she run away once more? But where would she go? Life was smooth and happy in this house of odd-bods and Lily had no wish to start again. But she was so happy that the danger had passed with regard to Avril and Neil, she decided that she was not going to start worrying about Kasie now.

Jo had been making changes in her bakery shops. She and her new girlfriend now ran the shop in Aldgate which also had a restaurant attached to it, but she had decided to sell the shop Lily worked in because it just wasn't making a profit. As the high-rise flats took over the East End, people began to shop in the supermarkets and buy manufactured bread. The nice hot spicy loaves Lily sold in the little shop were no longer popular.

'When I get a buyer for the shop, you can come and work with us,' suggested Jo. 'What I'd really like to do is get a new slant, and open a modern restaurant in a smart town position—possibly a late-night place, for that's where all the money is now. But at the moment, I'm not sure that I can afford the stock and fittings. And I certainly don't want to sell this house. Never mind, something might turn up,' she added optimistically.

After Jo had told her this, Lily began to think about the possibility of investing her savings in Jo's business. She would need a job till Avril started earning and it seemed like a good idea. It was a bit of a gamble but she would take a chance if Jo wanted her.

Soon Jo had a buyer for Lily's shop in Canning Town and Lily had to say goodbye to the other shopkeepers and the old customers and then move on to Aldgate and help the other chef in Jo's restaurant. She helped serve the business lunches and high teas.

Lily came to like Jo's friend, Rene, who waited on the tables in the restaurant. She was tall, slim and dark-skinned, and now lived downstairs in Jo's flat. Rene told Lily her life story of being put in foster care and then Council homes followed by approved schools. It had not been an easy road for her and she hated the male sex for some reason that she never disclosed.

Jo was happy with Rene, so on the whole it was a good sort of relationship and now the idea of opening another restaurant was being discussed seriously.

'I've seen a place in Woodford,' said Jo. 'It's a posh area but the business is a bit run down. Some old couple have run it for years and now they want to retire.'

'Take a chance, Jo,' said Lily, 'and I'll come in with you. I've got three thousand in the bank and I'll work for a while without wages till we start to make a profit. It will do us all good.'

'Are you sure, Lily? I thought you weren't anxious to spend that money because of Avril.'

'I am not quite so worried now,' said Lily. 'Besides,' she added with a laugh, 'we might make a fortune.'

So Jo bought the restaurant and Lily helped with the cleaning up and redecorating.

Lily went with Jo to the solicitors and signed an agreement to the effect that she was to be half owner of the business but Jo owned the property. They both seemed equally satisfied.

'You know,' Lily confessed to Jo, 'I feel sort of free. That money actually used to bother me. I've never been used to a lot of money—I used to live for each day.'

'We'll have Rene to work with us. We'll give her a small wage and support her,' said Jo. 'She won't mind, and she's a good worker.'

So it was that the alert, business-like Jo made her plans.

They worked for several weeks getting the restaurant ready. When it was finished, it was all painted arty crafty gold paint with old pictures on the walls, and candles in bottles. They were thrilled. There were red cloth covers over the tables and old

French wine bottles hanging up on the walls. With the red shaded lights, the atmosphere looked extremely cosy. The menu in gold embossed covers gave the final touch.

'Who wouldn't want to be wined and dined here?' said Lily, 'and made violent love to afterwards . . .'

'Lily!' said Jo, pretending to be shocked. 'I wonder who you are thinking of.'

They called the restaurant the Nutcracker and they opened in August after advertising in the local paper. There was a special menu for the vegetarians and the usual dishes of the day for the rest of the customers. In the first week they did very well. Avril brought her friends from the poly, several people rang up booking tables for birthday and anniversary celebrations, and everyone worked late and was very tired.

It took very little time for the Nutcracker to become established. It was started up at the right time and place, for the fashion for eating out among the working classes was just beginning.

Lily was so busy that she hardly had time to protest when Avril announced that she had decided to spend the summer vacation abroad. 'I'll be all right, Mother. We're going to hitch-hike across the continent,' she said.

Lily was horrified. 'You can't do that!' she cried. 'You don't know what it's like.'

'Well, neither do you,' retorted Avril, 'but I intend to find out.'

So Avril went off with her equipment piled high on her back and wearing a pair of strong walking shoes. 'Don't worry, Mother,' she said, 'I'll be gone about a month. I'll send you a card.'

Lily engrossed herself in her work. She served the tables and organised menus, and spent most of the day and weekend at the restaurant wearing a smart black dress. With her hair piled up in a modern style, she was a gracious and charming hostess.

The money poured into the till and Jo was thrilled. It was nice and clean in this little town far away from the noisy city and the

East End. They did not mind the hard work and they were all happy and relaxed.

'Best idea I ever had,' said Jo as she checked the month's takings at the end of August. 'It won't be long now, Lily, before we get a bit back.'

Lily was not worried. She had her food and a roof over her head. The rest did not matter.

In September, Avril returned home tired and extremely grubby. But she seemed very relaxed, and told Lily about her new friend who lived out in Epping and whose mother had a riding stable. 'Might take up riding again,' she said. 'I did a bit out in France—I'd forgotten how great it is.' She returned to the polytechnic for her last term very happy and quite invigorated.

'I don't know why I worry over her so much,' Lily said to Jo. 'She seems quite capable of making her own decisions.'

'What did I tell you, Lily?' said Jo. 'You must live a bit yourself.'

Occasionally Lily thought of Kasie. She had not heard anything from him in more than three months. He never meant a word he said, she thought angrily. Well, he can go to hell, she decided, I don't care.

One misty evening in early October it was Lily's night off. Earlier she had been out with Avril shopping, and now Avril had gone off with her pal to some disco party. Lily walked home slowly, carrying the heavy shopping bag, when she noticed a figure standing under the light of the lamp post. He leaned casually with his hands in his pockets as if waiting for someone.

Lily stopped in her tracks, feeling very nervous. It was so easy to get attacked in London, and things had been getting worse lately. To her horror, the figure came towards her. Then she saw that it was him, Kasie, coming out from the shadow. He was wearing a soft hat and dark suit.

'You gave me a fright,' she said in a whisper.

'Sorry, darling.' As Kasie swept her into his arms, she struggled from his embrace.

'You've got some cheek turning up like this,' she grumbled. 'How did you find me?'

'Oh, I have my means.' He smiled and took her shopping bag as he walked beside her.

At the door to her house, she said, 'I can't ask you in, Kasie, Avril might come home.'

He looked annoyed, but he said: 'Please yourself. I'll wait for you at the pub down the road. Don't be long, I've plenty to talk to you about.'

He turned abruptly and as she watched him swinging down the road, her face was scarlet with suppressed anger. She banged the door as she went into the house and bumped into Andy who was about to go out. 'Is that your fancy man, Lily?' asked Andy. 'He's been hanging around all day.'

'Mind your own business,' cried Lily angrily, marching into her flat. She threw her shopping down on the floor. 'Well, of all the nerve,' she muttered, 'turning up just like that out of the blue . . . I won't go. He can knock the bloody door down, but I won't go!'

But as she rinsed her face and made it up, brushed her hair and changed her dress, she knew that she would have to meet him; she could not help herself.

When she arrived at the pub, Kasie had removed his hat, and his hair shone in the electric light. It was now almost platinum blond and his skin was very tanned. Lily's heart missed a beat. How attractive he still was, and he must be past forty. His sweet smile greeted her and his soft warm hand covered hers.

'Oh, darling, I've missed you,' he whispered.

'I'd never have noticed it. I didn't even get a dirty postcard,' scoffed Lily.

That mischievous smile wreathed his lips. 'So,' he murmured, 'we are not in a good mood, are we?' Putting his arms around her, he cuddled her up close.

Kasie passed her the large gin and tonic he had ordered for her. Join me, *leiblin*,' he said. '*Prost*,' He raised his glass in his usual manner.

But Lily did not return the toast. She just sipped the drink dolefully. 'I do wish you had given me some warning, Kasie,' she said.

Kasie stared at her in amazement. 'I don't believe you are very pleased to see me, Lily,' he commented.

'Oh, I am, but I have to live my life when you are not here.'

'How many husbands or lovers have I to contend with this time?' he asked in a jesting tone.

'Oh, shut up,' she said petulantly, 'I'm not thinking of that, it's Avril.'

'It's time she was told the truth,' Kasie said firmly. 'Now, come on, don't spoil our meeting. Tell me how you are and if you still love me.'

She put her head on his shoulder and that same magic crept between them. That wonderful feeling of closeness of their bodies was always there.

'Don't explain, Lily,' he whispered. And as he pressed his lips to her neck, she gripped his hand tight.

'Let's get out of here and go somewhere,' he said suddenly. 'Come, drink up, Lily, where would you like to go?'

She looked thoughtfully at him. 'Let's go and have something to eat,' she said.

'That wasn't exactly what I had in mind,' grinned Kasie, 'but if you're hungry, darling, that's what we'll do. You're the boss.'

Quite suddenly Lily got the idea to go to the Nutcracker as a guest, and take Kasie with her and face the world with her lover. 'Let's go on the bus,' she said.

'No,' said Kasie. 'We wait for a taxi.' He hailed a passing cab and once they were inside he kissed and cuddled her passionately. 'Oh, Lily,' he whispered, 'come to a hotel for tonight if you won't invite me into your home.'

'I can't,' said Lily. 'Avril will want to know where I am.'

'Oh, for Christ's sake, does everything have to have her permission?' he complained.

'We'll go to a restaurant I know for dinner. I have got a friend there who might have some ideas about what we can do,' she said. Jo was very surprised to see Lily arrive with this good-looking man, and she smiled at Lily's tousled appearance. Jo gave them a secluded table and, asking no questions, sat at the cash desk watching them.

They drank plenty of wine and enjoyed the well-served meal but most of the time they said very little, and just sat with their heads almost touching.

When Lily went to the ladies' Jo met Lily half-way. 'You did spring a surprise on me,' she said. 'Who's he?'

'He's my old friend,' said Lily.

'Bit more than a friend, I think,' smiled Jo.

'He's been abroad. It's the first time I've seen him in four months,' she explained to Jo a little lamely.

But Jo gave her a hard thump on the back. 'Great work, Lily, he's obviously mad about you. I'll have your coffee served in the back room, and leave the keys for you to lock up,' she added tactfully.

On her return, Kasie was still drinking and looking around him. 'Nice place, this, Lily. Got a continental air about it. How did you find it?'

'It belongs to a friend of mine. She's just suggested that we go out to the back room and have coffee and liqueurs. She might join us.'

'Please yourself,' said Kasie, 'but, Lily, I want us to go home to bed, darling.'

'We can't do that. Come, let's go and meet Jo.'

In the comfortable back room, Jo had laid out the small table with a pot of coffee and a bottle of liqueur.

When Lily introduced Jo to Kasie, they shook hands. 'We're good friends, Lily and I, and I'm pleased to meet you. Please make yourselves comfortable, I have a few chores to do before I go home.'

On leaving, Jo switched off the main light and left on just a small lamp. There was a large comfortable settee for them to lounge on. They sat drinking the heavy liqueur, getting very close and very sleepy. Lily heard the front door click and the restaurant lights go off. Good old Jo, she thought, that's what I call a pal. She slipped off her pants and pulled Kasie down beside her. 'Oh, my love, my darling love,' she gasped. 'I need you, I must have you.'

'Oh, Lily, my lovely,' he cried, as they went down and down into that world of passion and made love until they both fell asleep.

At dawn light, Lily heated up some coffee then woke up Kasie. 'Come on, love,' she said, 'I'll ring for a cab. The chef will be here early, so we have to go.'

'But why? What is the set-up, Lily? What is the secret life that you have? I cannot understand why we must spend the night like two fugitives.'

'It was better than out on the common,' said Lily abruptly. She had a hang-over and her head throbbed.

'But nothing has been said. I don't know what you're up to,' he complained. 'I want to trust you, Lily. I came back to ask you to marry me and come back home with me—you and Avril.'

Lily looked away. 'It can't be done at the moment,' she said. 'Avril has to finish college.'

'Oh, damn and blast Avril!' cursed Kasie. 'It seems that not one decision can be made without consulting her.'

'Well, now, that's nice,' returned Lily, losing her temper. 'Don't you dare say that.'

In the cab they said little. When the taxi slowed down outside her flat, he held her hand tight. 'When do I see you again?' he asked.

'Ring me at work,' she said. 'There's the number.'

'Where do you work?'

'In that restaurant,' Lily said with a grin.

'Ah, so that is the set-up . . .'

He seemed relieved to be in the know at last, and he put his arms tight around her waist and kissed her until the cabbie said: 'Are yer gettin' aht or ain't yer?'

'Bye, darling,' said Lily, climbing out, and the taxi went back to the West End taking Kasie to his hotel bed to recuperate.

Lily crept quietly upstairs, praying that Avril was still asleep. But there was no need for her to worry; Avril was snoring away with the healthy sleep of youth. Lily pulled on her dressing-gown on over her dress, dived quickly into her own bed and dropped off into a deep sleep of exhaustion.

At eight o'clock, Avril made the tea and got ready for college. 'Are you on late turn this week, Mother?' she asked. 'You weren't home when I got in at eleven o'clock.'

'No, darling, I didn't finish till late because there was a birthday party going on.'

'Will you be late on tonight?' Avril asked a little suspiciously.

'I expect so,' Lily replied sweetly. 'I might be, darling, you don't mind, do you?'

'No, but I'd like to know when to expect you. I get worried in case something happens to you.'

Lily gave a little shrug saying, 'How's your new friend? What's her name?'

'Laura,' replied Avril. 'She's quite well off, and drives her own car, a little Mini. Her mother has riding stables and she did suggest asking her mother if I could go over to Epping and stay the weekend. She was quite surprised that I was interested in riding.'

Lily's heart leaped high. 'This weekend?' she asked sleepily.

'Could be, why, what's the problem?'

'None whatever,' said Lily. 'In fact, it would make a nice change for you.' She crossed her fingers hopefully under the bedclothes.

That afternoon Kasie rang the restaurant. Jo answered the call and was quite excited. 'He has a real sexy voice, Lily, where *did* you get him from?'

'It's a long story,' said Lily, going to answer the phone.

Kasie sounded impatient. 'What's happening?' he asked. 'Do we meet again or do I go home today?'

'Don't be like that, Kasie. I'm trying to find a way to get Avril off my back this weekend.'

'We're not discussing Avril,' he said, 'but you and me. I will not hang about this lousy town waiting for you. I'll book my flight home.'

A voice inside her told her to let him go, but Lily said

sweetly: 'Oh, Kasie, it was so good to be with you again last night. Maybe we could do it again tonight.'

'No thanks,' he replied dryly. 'I think I did myself a permanent injury on that settee last night.'

Lily began to giggle. 'Where are you now? At the Cumberland?'

'No, I couldn't get in, I'm at a crummy hotel in Portland Place. Lily, I want to say so much to you, we have to talk. It might be for the last time. I'll not come back again.'

'All right, darling,' she agreed. 'I'll come and meet you at our old spot—Aldgate Station at four o'clock.'

'I hate to ask you,' she said to Jo after she had rung off, 'but can I get off this weekend?'

'Off for a dirty weekend, Lily? I'm surprised at you,' jested Jo.

'Well, he's very fussy, he likes his comfort and he's going away again in a few days.'

'What is he?' asked Jo, 'a commercial traveller?'

'No, he is a sea captain.'

Jo laughed. 'You certainly know how to pick them,' she said.

Lily went home early that afternoon and Avril had just got in from college. She was throwing a few things into a bag. 'Laura's waiting for me,' she said. 'See you on Monday.' With that she rushed out of the house.

Lily was overjoyed and did a little dance around the room with sheer delight. Then she sorted out her best nightie and a nice dress for evening wear and put them in a suitcase. When Kasie arrived at the underground station, she was waiting for him with a beaming smile on her face.

But Kasie looked solemn and a little disgruntled.

'Cheer up,' said Lily. 'You've got me for the whole weekend.'

His face brightened up at this news. 'Good, where shall we go?'

'Let's go down to the seaside,' said Lily.

'We'll go to Portsmouth,' he said decisively. 'It will revive old memories.'

Soon they were speeding away in the train from Waterloo Station leaving London rapidly behind them. They sat very close together recalling the first time they had gone down to Pompey and Lily had spent the summer down there with him while he was on the minesweepers.

It was late autumn and the weather was cold and windy, but they booked in at the Havant Hotel just to relive old memories of the days when they were both young and in love.

Over dinner, Kasie looked at her approvingly. 'You look very nice, Lily. I didn't think a black dress would suit you but you just seem to be growing more and more beautiful.'

Lily smiled lovingly. She felt great with the wine and good food inside her and no one to bother them. It was like a dream come true.

'Shall we go for a walk along the promenade, like we used to after dinner?' she suggested.

'If you want to. Tonight is ours—let it be our honeymoon,' he said romantically.

'Oh, Kasie, I wonder if we will ever really marry.'

'No reason why not. I'm willing to take a chance but it's up to you, Lily. I think it's strange that it's always you who finds a good excuse not to. First it was George, then it was Norman, now it is Avril. At the end of the line comes poor old Kasie, still sitting waiting with his tongue hanging out.' He laughed and lolled his tongue like a puppy dog.

Lily stroked his cheek. 'Don't mock me, Kasie. It hasn't been so easy. Because of you I have been down to the gates of hell and back, and it's still not over.'

'Let's go for that walk,' he said, catching her hand.

As they strolled hand in hand along the deserted promenade, the huge waves beat against the sea wall and the wind swept the heavy spray over them. For a while, they stood in the shelter saying nothing as Kasie looked out gloomily at the stormy sea. 'It's a pity that I did not go down on one of those stormy nights out there. I've got fat, and I've got nothing in life. The only woman I ever loved, I'm still chasing and that was twenty years ago.'

'Why, what an old misery you are,' cried Lily, putting her arms about him. 'Come, Kasie, let's enjoy ourselves. I know we're almost middle-aged but we're still alive. Come on, let's go home to bed.'

Their lovemaking was kind of subdued that night as they were both almost sober. Kasie, for once, had not been in a drinking mood. But they were close and happy just to be together.

Afterwards they lay in each other's arms. Kasie seemed very pensive. 'What is wrong with me?' he asked. 'I am forty-three, I have enough money to retire on, yet I cannot go ashore and live in a city with other human beings. Without you I am lost. Only when out at sea can I find contentment.'

'You have your family and your son,' replied Lily. 'And one day I will be with you, but not yet, I cannot upset Avril, I want her to finish her studies.'

Solemnly, he stroked her body, running his hand over her large breasts and along her slim legs. 'Your body is still lovely, Lily, but your mind is all screwed up. You don't trust me, so what chance do we stand of happiness?'

'Oh, Kasie, do cheer up,' Lily said irritably. 'I'm beginning to wish I never came.'

Kasie nodded. 'I'm not sure that I should have come either. I ought to have taken my flight to Rotterdam. This goes on and on and gets us nowhere, Lily.'

'Oh, shut up, for Christ's sake,' she said, turning her back on him and going to sleep.

The next morning when she woke, Kasie was standing and looking down at her. All he had on were his short pants.

'What's up?' she murmured sleepily.

'This,' he said with that mischievous grin. Jumping into the bed, he pressed his hot dry lips to hers. 'Oh, Lily, last night we were like an old married couple squabbling all the time,' he said. 'Let me love you now as we always do.'

Lily smiled and moved towards him. 'Kasie, dear, you know I can't resist you.'

After a long session of lovemaking, their good humour had

returned. Later that day, they wandered along the sea front and visited old familiar bars. They ate a good lunch and then dined on the train journey back. At Waterloo they parted.

'I don't know when I'll be back,' he said, 'but be faithful to me, even if you mean to be my mistress and not my wife.'

CHAPTER ELEVEN

Possession

Having decided again not to accept Kasie's offer of marriage, Lily had a feeling of relief. She did not know why, but as much as she loved Kasie she never really trusted him. She had some strange fear that he would eventually come between her and Avril.

'But why, Lily?' asked Jo. 'You're missing out on the chance of a good life.'

Lily tried hard to explain. 'It's something I don't really understand myself. I know he is a good catch and a lot of women of my age would grab at him, but I can't let go of my independence. I have struggled a long time on my own and I will not give up.'

Jo nodded approvingly and accepted that answer. But Lily had not been completely honest with Jo, for she still hung on to her secret that Kasie had fathered Avril and that she had known him for twenty years.

The restaurant had begun to pay its own way, and every night it was full. Jo had been very shrewd to start it when she did. Jo had recently made lots of new friends who were interested in the vegetarian menus. Many were like Avril, who would not tolerate the killing of animals, while some were slimmers or good health enthusiasts. In her off-duty hours, Jo began to compile a book on calories and diets.

'You're so clever, Jo,' said Lily. 'I can't even read a complete book and here you are writing one.'

'Oh, I always have to have something going on,' replied Jo. 'I used to write little plays, but I could never sell them. But this interest in vegetarian cooking is a coming thing. Perhaps we could get together on some recipes, you and I, Lily.'

So for a while, Lily's life settled to a regular, busy routine. Everyone was busy, including Avril who was about to do her final exams at the polytechnic. She spent most of her weekends away from home with her friend Laura riding in Epping Forest or off on some wild goose chase protesting about fox hunting or vivisection.

It was during this quiet period that Andy went into hospital for his sex change operation.

Lily went to the hospital to take him some flowers from everyone in the house. As she walked down the ward carrying the flowers, Andy spotted her. Throwing off the sheets, he spread his legs wide crying out loud, 'Look, Lily, I'm a woman at last!'

Lily was so embarrassed, she stopped dead in her tracks. A nurse came rushing forward and covered him up. 'Now, Esme, behave yourself,' she said.

'Esme? What's all this?' asked Lily when she eventually sat beside the bed. 'I thought you wanted to be called Anita.'

'I prefer Esme,' said Andy. 'It's short for Esmerelda. Do you like it?'

'Well, it's not such a bloody great mouthful,' jested Lily.

When Esme came home a few weeks later, she really looked the part. She waved gaily to the other occupants of the ambulance which had brought her home, and walked up the path slowly leaning on a stick. She was dressed in a neat suit, her hair had grown quite long and henna rinsed. Huge dangling earrings hung from the lobes of her ears, and nylon stockings and high-heeled shoes completed the ensemble. Andy, or Esme, really looked the part of a woman.

The other members of the household stood in the hall to greet her singing, 'For she's a jolly good fellow.' They all agreed that Esme was very good looking and seductive.

'Give us a kiss, Esme,' laughed Mike.

Esme replied loftily: 'I'm convalescing at the moment but I

can assure you, Mike, that when I'm well, you'll have to take your place at the end of the queue.'

'Well, I'm blowed,' said Lily. 'I hope she's not going on the game.'

'If she is, perhaps she'll pay some of the rent she owes me,' remarked Jo dryly.

Esme spent all her time making herself beautiful, frequently popping down to get advice from Lily. 'Tell me what you think of this petunia shade of lipstick, Lily. Do you think it's too dark for me?'

'No, duck, it's fine. You're really beautiful,' Lily would say, and meant it. For Esme seemed to be growing very lovely, no one would ever have believed that she was once of the male sex.

But Esme lazed about all day and only got herself up in the evening to go to a rather seedy wine bar. Jo would be very disgusted. 'Why can't she take a secretarial course, or something useful?'

But Lily would be sympathetic. 'It's a bloody shame. It's such a waste, now she's such a good looking woman, she finds it hard to keep a man.'

And she would try not to notice Esme creeping upstairs with a young man, both full of booze and unsteady some nights. These furtive youths never stayed long, and Esme's blue eyes grew wide with anxiety and her full red lips drooped in petulant sorrow. Being a woman was not so easy, after all. The next day she would sit around with Lily and weep. 'Oh dear, my trouble is I'm so much in love with love.'

'Poor cow,' Lily would mutter. 'Blimey, what a state to get in!'

Avril was doing a course on sociology which seemed to include politics. Lily was completely baffled by her interests. Lily's understanding of politics was summed up by her comment the night President Kennedy was assassinated. 'Oh, what a pity,' she said. 'He was so nice-looking, too—and Irish, just like me.'

Avril stared at her aghast. 'You're not Irish,' she exclaimed.

'Well, my mother was,' admitted Lily.

'What happened to her then?' demanded Avril.

'Oh, she went home at the beginning of the war and we never heard of her since.'

'What a funny lot,' commented Avril.

For a while Lily had no communication from Kasie, but then suddenly one day there arrived a crate of French wine and a bottle of Chanel perfume. They were delivered to the Nutcracker, with a note saying that the wine was for Jo and the perfume for Lily.

'Oh, what a nice thought,' said Jo.

Lily looked worried. This meant that he was not far away. 'Like a bad penny, he'll turn up one day,' she told Jo.

'Don't you mind these long absences, Lily?' asked Jo.

'No, I've got used to them but if I thought he was with anyone else, I'd go mad with jealousy,' Lily admitted.

'Well, how can you know?' she probed.

'That's the trouble, I can't,' said Lily.

'They say that a sailor has got a girl in every port,' replied Jo.

'But what can I do about it? He'll never settle ashore, I know that. Last time I heard he was sailing to Africa from Rotterdam.'

'If he's dealing in oil, he must be making plenty of money,' said Jo.

'It doesn't bother me,' replied Lily. 'Thank God I can support myself and my daughter on my own. He hasn't always been well off—but that's all I can tell you, Jo, so don't ask me any more.'

Jo nodded understandingly. 'We'll have a party for him when he does arrive—how's that?'

'Oh, that will please him all right, he's very anxious to get his feet under my table, but I have to think of Avril.'

'She's away most weekends, take a chance,' suggested Jo.

'I'll think about it,' said Lily.

About a week later, Kasie arrived at the restaurant late on Friday night. He was accompanied by another seaman, a big and burly man with a full beard. Kasie looked a little drunk. Jo served them a meal as Lily was busy in the bar, but Kasie came and kissed her in full view of the customers. Those cool dry lips on hers sent a shiver down her spine.

'I'm not staying long,' he said, 'I got a lift into London by a pal of mine. I'll ring you tomorrow, *leiblin*,' he said. 'Goodbye.'

Lily felt slightly annoyed by his sudden disappearance, and wondered what he was up to. No doubt boozing and womanising with that other wily sea captain.

Lily was a little irritable the next day, not knowing what plans Kasie had made for the weekend. 'Will you be staying with Laura?' she asked Avril.

'I expect so. Why do you ask?'

'I might go to a party after the restaurant closes, with Jo and Rene,' lied Lily.

'Please yourself,' said Avril, without much interest.

When Avril left, Lily busied herself by cleaning up the flat. While she dusted, she wondered what bed Kasie had slept in the night before. It was time to make a proper decision about this affair at last. She knew she took a chance, really, sleeping with him after he had been romping about London all night.

On Saturday, late in the afternoon, she went off to work. Kasie rang her at five o'clock asking her where they should meet.

'I'm not sure that I want to see you,' declared Lily. 'You've wasted most of our weekend,' she accused him.

'Oh, Lily, my lovely, you know I will make up for it.' He smooth-talked her till she gave in.

'All right, pick me up here. It's very busy and I'll not be finished work until after ten o'clock.'

Tears poured down her cheeks as Lily laid the tables for the evening meal.

'Oh, don't cry, Lily,' said Jo, trying to comfort her. 'No man is worth it.'

'I'm not crying over him,' she snivelled. 'I'm crying because I'm such a bloody fool for him. He has got me just where he wants me.'

'But he did ask you to marry him,' said Jo.

'But that don't make him stay away from other women,' wept Lily.

'Oh, I see, it's jealousy that's eating you,' said Jo. 'Well, why don't you take a chance and take him back home tonight? Avril won't be back till Monday after college.'

'Shall I, Jo?' queried Lily, brightening up at the idea. 'It would solve one problem—at least we could have a bloody good fight without anyone listening.'

'And the rest,' added Jo dryly.

Kasie arrived at exactly ten o'clock, spick and span, neat and smiling as usual. Lily's earlier misery disappeared at the sight of him. Each time she met him she loved him more. Kasie chatted with Jo and treated her to double brandies. Then he and Lily left in a cab.

'Where to, Lily my lovely?' he asked, beginning to embrace her as soon as they entered the cab.

She stared at him suspiciously. 'Why? What have you got laid on?'

'I always leave such arrangements to you, my lovely.'

'Well, this time we're going home to my flat. Does that inspire you?'

'What pleases you pleases me,' he replied. 'I look so much forward to being with you. I would sleep in a dust heap as long as I was with you.'

'I don't believe you,' declared Lily, 'and where were you last night?'

He covered her face with kisses. 'Lily, Lily, don't start a quarrel,' he said. 'Let us be happy, you and I.'

She knew he was right and snuggled close to him as his hands travelled over her.

They held hands going up the stone steps to her house, and as they crept into her flat she did not turn on the lights. Kasie's arms were around her instantly, and the swift passion encircled them likewise. For minutes, they embraced, lost in another world. Then Lily switched on the light. 'It's a bit of a dump,' she said apologetically, 'but it's my home. Avril will not be back till Monday.'

'Oh, thank God for that,' said Kasie, looking around with interest.

'We might as well make ourselves a bit comfortable,' said Lily, pushing Avril's bed up close to hers. She switched on the bedside lamp. 'There's some booze in the cabinet, Kasie. Pour out some drinks. This weekend is ours. How do we sleep?' she asked, unzipping her dress.

'In the raw, of course,' cried Kasie pulling off his clothes and jumping into Avril's bed.

Lily was soon snuggling up beside him, and they hugged each other tight. They kissed, drank gin, and talked of old times, and then they lay close together, their bodies becoming one.

Early the next morning Lily got up and made the coffee. Humming happily to herself, she put the coffee and some biscuits on a tray which she brought back to bed. They sat up in bed eating their Sunday breakfast like any old married couple. They talked softly and sipped their coffee, perfectly happy and relaxed.

Their quiet solitude was suddenly shattered by the unexpected arrival of Avril, who burst in through the door, long hair flowing wildly. In horrified astonishment she stared, openmouthed, at the sight of her mother in bed with a man.

Kasie did not seem put out. He simply put his hands behind his head and stared at her nonchalantly, but Lily was appalled. She sat up abruptly, forgetting that she was naked, but put her hands over her breasts when she saw the look of horror on Avril's face.

'So that's it!' screeched Avril. 'A bloody fancy man! And in my bed, too!'

Trying to remain composed, Lily pointed at her dressing-gown which lay on a chair just out of reach. 'Pass me my gown, Avril, I'll explain when I get up.'

'No, I bloody won't!' roared Avril. Her temper was really up now as she opened the wardrobe and started pulling things out onto the floor. 'Look at you!' she sneered. 'You're disgusting, in bed with nothing on. I'm off. I'm leaving this rotten dump, you won't see me again.'

'Don't be silly, Avril,' implored Lily. Her eyes were on her dressing-gown and she wondered if she dared get out and face Avril as naked as the day she was born, but a strong sense of propriety prevented her from getting out of bed.

Avril bounced a big suitcase down from the top of the wardrobe and started to ram things into it. 'I just popped in because I forgot my riding boots, and this . . .' she glanced at them, her nose twitching with disgust, '. . . is what I find.'

'Don't be silly, Avril,' pleaded Lily tearfully.

'Silly! Silly! You're the one that's silly, a woman your age acting like a whore! I'm fed up with this bloody kinky dump. I'm going to live with Laura.'

Kasie grinned and lit a cigarette. He offered one to Lily but she pulled the sheet up over her bare breasts and ignored him. Her face was as pale as death as she watched Avril ranting and raving, and banging the suitcase shut.

'Get on with what you were doing,' Avril shouted scornfully, 'don't let me stop you!' She marched out to the bathroom to grab her toilet things, and then she was out of the flat door. A moment later Lily could hear Jo coming up the stairs and saying something to Avril outside the flat door.

'Mind your own business!' Avril yelled at her. 'I'm getting out of this rotten, stinking house. None of you are any good.' And bang went the front door.

Lily jumped out of bed and slipped on her dressing-gown. She heard a car start up outside just as she looked out of the window, and she saw Avril's friend's Mini car speeding off down the street. Lily burst into tears.

'Come here, darling,' said Kasie, pulling her to him and cuddling her. 'There's nothing to get upset about. In my opinion, it's time that big fat blackbird tumbled from the nest.'

'Oh, Kasie!' cried Lily. 'How can you talk like that?'

'Quite easily,' smiled Kasie. 'In fact, I wonder if I could really father such a fiend.'

His remark made Lily very angry. She beat him with her fists. 'Oh, you beast! You always do it to me. How can you say such things when you see how upset I am?'

He pulled her back into bed. 'Darling, be sensible. The time has now come to face the truth. You belong to me, let Avril find her own way of life now.'

'No, no!' sobbed Lily. 'I'll never desert her.'

Avril's arrival and abrupt departure had put a real damper on their weekend together. While Lily cooked the Sunday lunch, Kasie lounged around trying to make Lily see reason.

'One thing puzzles me,' he said, 'and that is how you manage to live in this dump—eating and sleeping in the same room, with no privacy, surrounded by the other inhabitants who keep popping in to hear the latest news.'

'I like it here, Kasie,' Lily replied quietly. 'This is the home I made for myself and here I'm my own boss.'

He grinned. 'Except when Avril's around.'

Immediately Lily lost her temper. 'Don't criticise my daughter! She does try to get on with everybody. Compared with her we're all cabbages—she's had a good education.'

Kasie roared with laughter. 'And filthy manners,' he said.

Now Lily showed where Avril's bad temper came from. She strode up and down the flat, ranting and raving, and banging things about as she puffed madly at her cigarette. 'Why, you swine! You bloody evil sod!' she cried. 'How can you say such things about your own flesh and blood?'

Kasie began to pack up his shaving gear. 'Very easily,' he replied, 'because I see her as a thoroughly spoiled brat and if I had any say in the matter, I'd put her across my knee and give her a good spanking.'

'Don't you dare interfere!' screeched Lily.

'No, darling, I won't. I'll let you get on and finish the job,' he said sarcastically.

They faced each other, both livid with rage. Then Jo tapped gently on the door. 'Can I come in?' she called, putting her head around the door. 'Pipe down, you two,' she said. 'Everyone in the house is listening in.'

Lily burst into a flood of tears and Kasie smiled in his charming manner. 'Morning, Jo,' he said. 'I was just leaving.'

'No, you're not,' announced Jo. 'We've arranged a party for you tonight.'

Kasie looked apologetic, and Lily stepped forward. 'Sorry, Jo,' she said. 'Call it off.'

'No, I bloody well won't, so pull yourself together,' Jo said firmly. 'It starts at eight o'clock in my flat.' She made for the door. 'He's right,' she whispered to Lily as she went. 'And young Avril is a bit much.' With that, she disappeared very quickly.

Kasie came forward and, as he often did, put his hand under Lily's chin. He kissed her gently on the lips. 'Do I go or stay, Lily? It's for you to decide, my lovely.'

She put her arms around him and pressed her face close. 'Oh, Kasie, forgive me. I know what a bitch I am when I get in a temper.'

He stroked her hair. 'Who knows you better than I, Lily?' he said sadly. 'What about a cup of coffee?'

They went into the small kitchen, where Lily made some more coffee. They drank this and ate some of the very delicious nut cookies that Lily was so good at baking.

She sat at the table dressed in her red dressing-gown which hung untidily open, her long wavy hair falling over her shoulders. Kasie looked at her intently and thought how smooth and white her skin was and how her long graceful body did not seem to age. 'Lily, darling,' he said, 'I believe we have come to the crossroads, you and I.'

'What do you mean, Kasie?' she queried, a little puzzled.

'Come with me, there is nothing to hold you here. I sail for the Dutch East Indies next week. You can be a guest aboard the ship—the captain is a friend of mine. I have bought a new tanker and intend to sail it home to Rotterdam. Come with me,' he begged, 'forget the rest of the world, let us live or die together.'

She stared at him in a melancholy sort of way. 'Don't tempt me, Kasie, you know that I won't go with you, not until Avril is settled.'

He got up impatiently. 'Here we go again. Avril must be

consulted. Why not leave her alone? Give her this damned poky flat and I'll give her an allowance. Let her find herself.'

'Oh, Kasie,' cried Lily. 'I don't think I am brave enough to do that.'

He held her tight. 'I'll give you courage, darling, promise me that you'll think about it anyway. I shall sail in one week from now. Once out there, we will stay with Jan and Easi—remember them? They now have a family, and Jan and I have business together.'

Lily smiled as she recalled Amsterdam harbour.

'This is the address to wire me,' he said, handing her a piece of paper. 'But I warn you, Lily, this time if you let me down I'll never come looking for you again. This time you come to me or it is all over between us.'

Lily had heard this threat many times before and did not take it too seriously. She avoided saying yes or no, and was just glad to clear the air. With their quarrel over, she began to wash her hair and get ready for the party in the evening. 'We'll go down to Jo's and forget our troubles,' she said.

Jo's party that evening was a party to end all parties. Jo always gave good entertainment. In Jo's spacious flat, a big buffet was laid out with all sorts of good things to eat and drink. Esme was there in full war paint, rolling her eyes at Kasie. Mike and his girlfriend were also there, as well as Rene and several people from the restaurant staff. It all went with a swing.

Lily had made up her face and wore her favourite navy blue dress with sequins around the heart-shaped neck line. Her hair was piled up with sparkling combs, and her long, blue dangling earrings matched the colour of her eyes.

'When you are dressed up, Lily,' Kasie had said to her, 'you are really something.'

They drank and ate, sang songs and danced. Jo and Esme did a funny act together and then sang old favourites such as 'As time goes by'. They were very good, and everyone clapped.

Kasie took Lily's hand. 'It's a long time since I sang for you,' he whispered, 'but tonight, just to prove I still can, I'll do it.'

Jo played her piano and Kasie's voice filled the room. It was still sweet and low and had that kind of charismatic tone of his youth. With his eyes fixed on Lily, he sang: 'You'll never know just how much I love you, You'll never know just how much I care.'

Lily hung her head and the tears coursed down her cheeks as the words swept her back to the East End and Charlies Brown's pub.

'Is there no other way to prove that I love you? Because you'll never know if you don't know now,' Kasie continued singing.

Two long streaks of black mascara ran down Lily's cheeks as everyone applauded, and Kasie smiled as he came towards her. As he got out his hanky and wiped her face, a kind of quiet embarrassment pervaded the room.

Then Esme sprang up. 'Come on,' she said, 'let's put some records on.'

But Lily felt rather depressed and sat huddled on the settee drinking, while Esme danced rock and roll with Kasie who, for his age, was very agile and light on his feet. They put on some smoochy records, and Esme pressed herself close to Kasie who, much to the amusement of the rest of the company, ran his hands up and down her back.

But the sight of them dancing close together like that drove Lily wild. Getting up from the settee, she gave Esme a great push. Esme landed on her backside, as Kasie waltzed Lily out into the garden, saying to her: 'Lily, calm down.'

It was a full moonlight night and the garden wall was covered with Virginia creeper. 'It's just like that time we first met,' whispered Kasie as his arms went around her.

That party to end all parties was over for them. Still clinging to each other, they went inside and upstairs to bed.

Early in the morning, Kasie packed his travelling bag ready to catch his plane. 'I'll be waiting for that telegram next week, Lily,' he said gravely, 'so don't forget your promise to me.'

'Bye, darling,' murmured Lily sleepily. It was the start of another day, she had a hang-over and she was going to climb only one mountain at a time. Kasie closed the door quietly and crept out of her life again for a very long time.

Lily slept through until teatime and then got up and lazed around. She knew that she had drunk too much gin the night before and sincerely hoped that she had not upset too many of her friends. She wasn't sure what she was going to do about Kasie, or joining him. Whatever happened, however, he would be back. She was sure of that. He always turned up. All that talk of not coming back was nonsense. Kasie was no different to Avril, he was just trying to get his own way. Avril would bounce in from college tomorrow full of the good weekend she had spent with her friend Laura. No, there was no need to worry, Lily decided. She would go down and chat with Jo and help her to get her flat straight after the party.

Downstairs, Jo was busy typing the manuscript of her cookbook and the sitting room was still strewn with unwashed glasses and scraps of uneaten food. Lily started to clear up a little, and chatter away to Jo, who was very engrossed in her work.

'Just like me to make a bloody fool of myself,' Lily muttered. Jo did not answer and Lily just continued. 'I seem to have had quite a hectic weekend. He does that to me, Kasie, always disturbs me mentally and physically, he always has done. And poor little Avril, she got such a shock seeing her mum in bed with a strange man. If she knew the truth, I wonder what her reaction would have been then!' She rambled on but then suddenly shut up, afraid that she might have said too much.

Jo took off her specs and put the lid on her typewriter. 'Let's have a drink, Lily,' she said. 'I think we need a livener after all that excitement last night.'

Lily couldn't agree more, so the two women sat around the fire and relaxed without saying much. Jo had a kind of peaceful effect on Lily, which always calmed her down.

Contrary to what Lily had assumed, Avril did not return on Monday night, and Lily lay in bed worrying about her until she fell asleep in the early hours. The next morning she went up to the college to find her and was informed by some students, who were hanging about in the foyer, that Avril was absent and that she and Laura hadn't come back after the weekend.

'Are you sure?' said Lily, very worried.

'Yes, I'm in her class,' chirped a young man. 'You can leave a letter in the rack for her and I'll tell her it's there,' he said.

Lily sat down and scribbled a note and the young boy went and got her an envelope. She wrote:

> Avril, darling, I am so worried over you, please come home and tell me you forgive me.
>
>   Love Mum.

Then with tear-filled eyes, Lily went off to work until ten o'clock that night when she returned home very exhausted. She fell into bed. Throughout the day, she had not given one thought to Kasie, her mind had been completely occupied with the disappearance of Avril.

The next day she rang the college from the restaurant to talk to Avril's tutor. He told her that after being absent for two days, Avril had returned that morning.

'Thank God!' cried Lily to Jo after putting down the 'phone. 'Avril's such a wild one. I was so terribly worried something had happened to her. So, she'll come back tonight.'

Jo tut-tutted. 'Really, Lily, why are you such a fool with her? At fourteen we went out to work, no one cossetted us. And she's eighteen. Leave her alone, Lily. Your boyfriend was right, it *is* time you pushed her out of the nest.'

Lily looked amazed. It was obvious that Jo did not miss much. 'Did you know he asked me to go away with him?'

'The Dutch East Indies?' said Jo with a smile.

'He told you?' asked Lily.

'He did pop in before he left,' Jo admitted. 'He told me that if I kept an eye on Avril he would be very pleased and the flat was to be kept on as long as she wanted it. As far as I was concerned, it was all settled, Lily.'

'Well, of all the bloody sauce!' cried Lily. 'Who does he think he is telling me what to do with my life?'

'I believe he means it, Lily,' Jo said encouragingly. 'I'll miss you but it's your decision to make.'

'It's made!' declared Lily. 'If Kasie wants me, he knows where I live and that's at 10 Plashet Grove. I'll leave the restaurant early tonight, Jo,' said Lily once the discussion had come to an end. 'Avril will come home if it's only to collect the rest of her belongings—her books and all her sports stuff are still at home.'

So Lily went home and arranged a big dish of salad with little spikes of asparagus all around it and a big plate of sweet pastries from the restaurant. She sat down and waited for her errant daughter, who did finally arrive. Avril came in very slowly and cautiously. Her face was pale and looked kind of woeful, as she looked suspiciously around the room.

'It's all right,' said Lily brightly, 'he's gone.'

Avril did not answer. She took off her duffle coat and put it on a chair. Still standing up, she began to pick up bits of the salad and nibble at them while Lily poured out the tea.

'Come on, darling,' Lily cajoled her. 'Sit down and enjoy the salad. Look, I got rum babas and chocolate eclairs for afters.'

Avril pulled up her chair and glanced sulkily at her. 'Don't try to get round me,' she warned, but never the less, she tucked into her meal. Afterwards, they sat round the fire while Avril scoffed the cakes. Lily looked down at her daughter sitting on the rug like a twelve-year-old, her fat legs tucked under her, and stroked her silky hair. Avril's head went down and rested on Lily's lap. Lily did not cry but she felt choked up.

Those hard, sad brown eyes looked up at her. 'Oh, Mummy, how could you do that with a man, and at your age, too?'

Lily began to laugh. 'I'm not that old, Avril,' she said. 'And it's a long time since I was made a widow.'

'It's no excuse,' declared Avril. 'Why, animals have more finesse than that. You were in bed with nothing on and there he was grinning like an ape. I think it's disgusting. I don't know who he is, but I hate him and if he comes in here again, I'll go out for good.' Having said her piece, she folded her arms and stared into the fire with her mouth in an obstinate thin line, just as Kasie used to do when he was in a foul temper.

Lily sat thinking quietly. Did she have the courage to tell Avril the truth? She might upset her so much that she would lose her once and for all. Well, she had to say something but she could not rush it. 'I have known him a long time,' she said gently.

Avril stared at her keenly. 'I thought so. I faintly remember a night when you and Daddy quarrelled and Daddy fought with him downstairs. That man stood in the garden crying bitterly. I was kind of sorry for him.'

Lily stared at her wide-eyed. The memories of that fatal night were hard to bear.

'I just don't understand it,' continued Avril. 'Daddy was a good husband and wonderful to me. Why did you have to be unfaithful to him?'

Lily swallowed the hard lump in her throat. 'Life is very funny, darling, it never goes the way you think it should and remember, I was not like you, I had a poor home and a mother who never cared a jot about me.'

'Poor old darling,' said Avril, giving her a kiss. This caress was unusual coming from the reserved and undemonstrative Avril. 'If you have to see him,' said Avril, 'let me know and I'll stay out of the way. But don't ever spring surprises like that on me any more.'

'He's gone,' said Lily. 'He's a sailor, and I can't be sure if he will come back again.'

'Well, don't be so bloody silly,' Avril cried impatiently. 'Find yourself someone nice and respectable to take you out, not someone who will just sleep with you and then disappear.'

Lily smiled sadly. Avril was practical and there was a lot of good sense in her advice. 'I promise to behave myself in the future,' she said softly.

By Friday of that week, Avril and Lily had resumed their old relationship. Avril went happily off to college saying: 'I might not go and stay with Laura this weekend. I'll come home and we can go to the pictures if you get the afternoon free.'

'Great,' said Lily, 'then when I go to work you can come up and have a slap-up feed on the house.'

After Avril had gone, it was only then that Lily began to think of Kasie. She got out the piece of paper with his address on it. It was a shipping office in Rotterdam. What should she do? Phone him? Send him a wire? She did not know what to say or do, and she sat nibbling her pen for a good half hour before deciding not to do anything. If he heard nothing, Kasie would know she was not coming; it had happened so many times before. 'Oh well, Kasie,' she muttered. 'See you next trip.' Putting the address back in the drawer, she got ready and went off to work. She felt quite happy-go-lucky that day. Avril had cleared the air. Lily knew the way she was heading, and it was not to some God-forsaken island, she was sure of that. On Saturday they went up West to see a terrible film all about rock music. Lily hated it but it made Avril happy and that's all Lily cared about. In the evening Avril brought her friend Laura to dinner at the Nutcracker and Lily was so happy to see her laughing and joking with her best friend and consuming sweet foods that would play havoc with her already plump figure.

In Rotterdam, Kasie, very drunk, leaned on the bar in a dive. Staggering to the phone booth, he dialled the Nutcracker.

A very pale-faced Lily was called to the telephone by Jo.

'To hell with you, you bloody bitch!' cursed Kasie down the line. 'I've waited a week to hear from you.'

'Now mind your language,' Lily replied acidly.

'It's goodbye, Lily, I've had enough. Where I'm going, no one will find me.'

'Oh, Kasie, you're drunk,' said Lily. 'Go home and sleep it off.'

But he banged down the receiver.

CHAPTER TWELVE

Liberated Women

Lily worked hard for the rest of that summer to try and forget Kasie. Not once did she allow herself to admit that she missed him. Avril had now left the polytechnic having got good enough grades in 'A' levels to apply for a place at university.

Lily was delighted and bought her a new set of riding clothes and Avril spent the late autumn at Laura's mother's riding stables earning her own pocket money by helping to instruct the very young children to ride.

With Avril out of the house, Lily dived into her work at the Nutcracker which was still thriving, and in her free time she worked with Jo helping her with her second book of vegetarian cooking. The first book had been published and was selling quite well. When Jo took a late vacation to visit Israel with Rene, Lily took over the restaurant and coped quite well. She was surprised that during all this time there was neither sight nor sound from Kasie. And occasionally she would worry. He must be in some kind of trouble, she would think. Surely he would not just drop me like that . . . Their relationship had become too deep and so necessary to them both. She spent many sleepless nights and began to look very pale and wan. Finally, she decided that Kasie was just trying to punish her with his silence, so she would not give in to him.

When Jo and Rene returned, they were both very sun tanned and full of life. They had had a great time and were very relaxed. 'Now, you take a holiday, Lily. Take Avril abroad to the South of France or some place where the sun is still shining.'

Lily looked doubtful. 'I've never been on a holiday,' she added.

'Stay in a nice hotel and be waited on,' suggested Rene with her warm affectionate smile.

But Avril made up Lily's mind for her. 'I'm sorry, Mum, we're still too busy at the riding school. I can't afford the time there, and I want to stay put till I hear about the university. You see,' explained Avril, 'places are not easy to get even if you have got the right qualifications. It also depends on your background, and mine is a bit dodgy.'

Lily stared at her aghast. 'I don't understand,' she said.

'Well, I will have to get a grant because we are a one-parent family. It will be all right, but I'll have to depend on you for extra pocket money.'

'But, darling, I'm only too pleased to help you,' insisted Lily.

Avril stared back at her with those stern brown eyes. 'It's a three-year course, so I will be away a long time if I go to Leeds.'

Lily was shocked. It had never occurred to her that Avril's advanced education would take her away from her. 'Why can't you stay in London?' she demanded.

'Mother, Laura is going to Leeds and they are trying to pull strings for me to go with her. I'll be very happy if it comes off.'

Lily sat biting her lip.

Suddenly Avril said, 'What happened to the money Daddy left you?'

Lily sighed. Poor Norman had only left her a lot of trouble. 'What I had left after buying our flat, I put into Jo's business. It's coming back quite nicely.'

'Well, hang on to that,' said the practical young Avril, 'because I'll need it for the vet's college when I get my degree.'

Lily felt slightly annoyed at Avril's attitude that what was Lily's was hers, too, for Lily still worked very hard and had always been careful with her money. But she said: 'It's all right, darling, it's there to finish your education. There's nothing to worry over.'

'Better keep it dark about the business,' said Avril, 'for when I applied for a grant I made out you were a poor widow,' she grinned.

Lily had seen that same self-satisfied smile on Kasie's face whenever he had pulled off a smart deal in the old days, when money was so important to him. She was no fool, this young girl, and as hard-headed as Kasie when it came to getting her own way. But unfortunately, like Kasie, she would give her all for love.

During the day, Avril would ride out through Epping Forest with her young charges, and the evenings she spent with Laura at the animal clinic doing voluntary work. She was placid, happy and nowadays very good to Lily. No other mention was made of Lily's indiscretion, and still Avril showed no interest whatever in the opposite sex. The fat little blackbird was a lot slimmer now from all the horse riding but she clearly didn't have the slightest intention of allowing herself to be pushed from the nest. For the time being, Lily was quite content and happy to indulge Avril's whims, but deep down she dreaded the approaching day when Avril would go away to university.

That day came in mid-October when Avril and her friend Laura set off together for Leeds University. Lily cried for a whole week and in those lonely sleepless hours she often longed for Kasie. One night she had a dream that he was drowning and calling out to her to save him. Waking up, she got out of bed and prowled about the flat. 'Blast you, Kasie,' she cried out, 'if you are dead don't try to reach out from your grave. Leave me alone!'

A few weeks later, however, she sat down and wrote her first long love letter to him and sent it to the shipping office in Rotterdam. In it she had tried to explain how hurt she was at not hearing from him and that Avril was now away from home for three years and she could not bear to think of the lonely days ahead.

It was many months before she received a reply, but it did come—a blue envelope with a foreign stamp lying on the mat one day. She snatched it up but as she read this strange, disjointed epistle, a cold feeling came up from her toes, it hurt her so much.

Lily my lovely,
It made me happy to get news of you. I often wondered did you

forget me and that wonderful love we shared. So, Avril has deserted you like you deserted me.

Well, how are you faring after this long year of parting? I have sailed into a safe harbour. The thought of life without you became so unbearable to me that I gave myself a long vacation. I have found a paradise island and I am perfectly happy here and very lazy. You did not want to come with me, Lily, but you and I could have been so happy here together. There are blue skies and warm seas with lots of sunshine, it is very like my own home in Heeg. My old friends Jan and Easi have settled here and raised a large family. Jan and I own a fishing boat and take tourists out shark fishing. There is not much money in it but I do not need money as I have no one and nothing to spend it on, except my Bols gin, and there is plenty of that around. It is very cheap and, as always, I am still thirsty. I cannot promise to come to you and I know you will not come to me. I still miss you and love you dearly, but you have ruined both our lives. I must be getting old. I do not care quite so much about anything. I just live for each day and grow fat and lazy. Neil, my son, and Fritz, my nephew, run the business in Holland and are very successful. So there is little left for me to do but enjoy myself. I still think of you and wish you and Avril every happiness.

Yours always, love Kasie.

That letter really hurt because it was so unlike him. Lily was horrified by the thought of her healthy, virile man giving in and just vegetating in some God-forsaken island. It was not like him at all, Kasie had so much drive, he always had some scheme for making money, always had someone to love. So this really was the end of it all, she thought. She still could not believe it, he was only forty-three. He seemed to have lost his deep sense of humour. And she could not believe he was on his own. Surely someone had taken her place, Kasie would not remain long without a woman, not if she knew him right.

She wrote back a very impersonal letter telling him that Jo's cookbook had been published and well received, that Avril had done very well on her first year at Leeds University, and that the Nutcracker was still going with a swing. 'I miss you, darling,' she wrote, 'but we have both found our own way of life, so it was not to be. I have never met anyone else that I love as I love you. So I will always be here in case you need me. Love, yours always, Lily.'

Quite a lot went on that year, though it seemed to Lily it was one of the worst times of her life. She felt unloved and unwanted in spite of getting involved in Jo's new book which also contained recipes by Lily Brown. Together they did a short television series on vegetarian cookery and they were very popular. Lily looked very smart dressed up with lots of beads and bright dresses, Jo was neat and smart in male clothes, her dark hair short cropped. They even became known as Mr and Mrs for extra publicity, but the platonic friendship between Jo and Lily remained the same, it never wavered. Jo and Lily were only best friends. Rene was Jo's true lover. But because Lily went around in the company of an obvious lesbian, men always shied away from her so she was never able to establish another stable relationship.

'I don't bloody want to,' she grumbled to Mike one day. 'I'm okay by myself.'

One night Avril turned up unexpectedly at the restaurant. She looked very nice and had lightened her hair which was now cut into a short bob with a smooth fringe hiding her high forehead. She wore lipstick and a smart dress and looked kind of excited.

Lily felt proud of her. Almost twenty, Avril was at the peak of her maturity and was mentally and physically in top form.

Avril dashed up to her. 'Hullo, Mumsie. We just want a coffee, we're not staying. We're on our way to see Laura.' Behind her was a dark shadowy figure who had a wide grin on his face. Straight away, Lily noticed his green calculating eyes which did not smile.

'This is Jonny, my boyfriend,' said Avril, introducing him.

A muscular hand shot out and gripped Lily's, pumping her arm up and down. A true Cockney voice said: ''Ow do, Ma? Pleased ter meet yer.'

Lily felt quite stunned. She gave them both coffee and did not say much until they had gone. She was quite unable to believe what she saw.

'Well,' announced Jo, 'our Avril has perked up, hasn't she? Didn't she look smashing?'

Rene raised her lazy eyes and said, 'She's really got a nice figure now, hasn't she?'

'Well, she's not quite such a fat lump,' said Lily crossly. 'But where the bleeding hell did she get him from?'

'Not from Leeds, that's for sure,' replied Jo.

'No, he's a bleeding Cockney,' cried Lily. 'I know that kind of East Ender a mile away.'

The mystery of Avril's boyfriend was not solved until August of that year when she came home for the summer vacation. She seemed a little subdued but generally was completely different from the wild, woolly, thick-legged, dark-stockinged animal campaigner of the old days. She was now quite mature and had a glint in her eyes as if she carried some dark secret.

Lily was delighted to see her home and immediately set about making plans for the summer vacation. 'We'll have a few days up West shopping, then maybe some Sunday we could take a few coach trips down to the seaside,' she informed Avril, who gave her a quick look with those hard brown eyes.

'Well, Mother,' she said, 'I've got good news and bad news for you. The good news is that I'm still with Jonny and the bad news is that I am off to spend the hols with him, so don't try to organise me as I won't be around.'

'Doing what?' demanded Lily.

'He's got a council flat in Stepney and that's where I'll be staying.'

Lily was astonished, but like a drowning man, grabbed at straws. 'Well,' she said, trying to remain calm, 'that's not far away. Why can't you come home?'

'Because I don't want to,' Avril replied obstinately.

'What about his parents? You can't do things like that if you're not married,' cried Lily.

'Oh, don't be so bloody corny,' Avril retorted rudely. 'You didn't marry my father, did you?'

'There's no need for that,' replied Lily, very shocked.

'Face reality, will you? And don't keep feeding me with all that old-fashioned stuff,' replied Avril.

'Oh, Avril!' Lily almost sobbed.

But Avril's expression remained hard. 'Look here, Mother, I love Jonny and he loves me. We sleep together weekends up in Leeds, so why not spend our hols together? I'll pop in occasionally,' she added, putting some clothes into a small bag.

Lily begged her to listen. 'Don't be so hasty, darling, you know nothing about life and you cannot afford to get involved if you are to finish your education.'

'Who said so?' yelled Avril. 'They're all at it up in Leeds, I don't sleep around. I've got one boy and I'm in love with him. You should be very pleased,' she said, zipping up her bag.

Now Lily lost her temper. 'Bloody well get on with it, then,' she cried. 'And don't come crying to me if he leaves you in the cart.'

Avril gave her that quiet, amused smile. 'I'll need some money,' she said. 'Jonny is out of work.'

Lily took some notes from her purse and threw them at her. Avril picked up her bag and then her expression softened a little. 'Look, Mother, don't start being ridiculous after I've gone. I'm only a bus ride away, and I'll bring Jonny in to see you.'

'Don't do me any bloody favours,' yelled Lily. 'I've not worked hard to make you somebody just for you to throw yourself away on a guttersnipe.'

'Well, thank you,' said Avril. 'I must say that's charming. Well, so long, I'll see you in a week's time, perhaps you'll have calmed down by then.'

'No, I won't, you can bleeding well get on with it,' yelled Lily at Avril's disappearing back.

She heard the front door shut and realised that she was shaking. She could not believe that this was really happening to her. Not knowing what else to do, she ran down to Jo for consolation.

'Whatever have I done to deserve it?' she complained.

'It's just a phase, Lily,' Jo said wisely, 'it won't last. Avril's always been a little wilful, so try not to worry so much.'

'I hope you're right. But what puzzles me is how she could pick on someone like that after the careful way I brought her up.'

'She'll find out for herself,' said Rene quietly. 'We all do in the end.'

Lily shook her head. 'I just can't think how she met him. I'll not rest till I get to the bottom of it.'

That Sunday evening, feeling very lonely, she wrote back to Kasie on his remote island.

> Dear Kasie,
> I hope you are still happy in your paradise, but frankly I think you must be mad to drop out at your age and probably drinking your head off, if I know you. You accuse me of ruining your life but it could be that the boot is on the other foot. I still love you, and so I cannot settle to find anyone else. It's all work and no play for me these days. Still, I wish you well.
> Love, yours always, Lily.

Her bitter disillusionment with life showed through in that letter, much as she tried not to let it. Come Monday and it was back to the grindstone. She worked late duty at the restaurant and a number of regular customers asked Jo, 'What's up with Lily? She's in a vile mood.'

Jo just smiled. 'Oh, she got out of the bed the wrong side,' she would explain, but knowing Lily better than other people, she knew it was more.

A week passed and Avril arrived on the Sunday evening accompanied by her beloved Jonny. Lily swept her into her arms. 'Oh, darling, how are you?' she cried. 'I've been so worried about you.'

Jonny stood behind Avril looking like a naughty schoolboy. His face showed that he was quite unsure of his reception.

Lily wiped away her tears and smiled at him. 'Hullo, Jonny,' she said, 'like a cup of tea?'

Jonny looked pleased. 'Yes, please, Ma,' he replied brightly. Once he relaxed he had a fair amount of chat in him and talked about the East End of London that Lily knew only too well.

'I'm out of a job at the moment but as soon as I get a little stake I'll get meself a yard and buy ol' cars and sell scrap. There's plenty o' lolly in it.'

Lily suddenly had a mental picture of old Dutchy and the burning of old iron in the yard under the railway arches so many years ago. She smiled at Jonny, confident now that he had relaxed. 'How did you two meet?' she asked casually.

Avril was busily scoffing up the last of the cakes. 'We met at a horse fair, didn't we, Jonny?'

'That's right,' said Jonny. 'I was dahn there stayin' wi' me cousin,' he told Lily.

'I'll tell her,' Avril said bossily, so Jonny shut up. 'I went with Laura to this fair outside Leeds to look at some piebald ponies for sale. Her mother was interested in buying them. We started chatting up this gipsy chap who owned them, and he invited us to have a drink in the refreshment tent and that was where I met Jonny.'

A vivid memory of the black-and-white ponies that Dutchy was so fond of flashed in Lily's mind. She felt dizzy. What was happening?

'Me ol' man bred piebalds,' broke in Jonny. 'It's me cousin wot breeds 'em nah. There's a strain of the ol' mares that we 'ad dahn the West India Dock Road.'

A sob broke from Lily's lips. She got to her feet trying to smile. 'I'll put some hot water on the tea,' she said sweetly, and disappeared into the kitchen. There, she leaned against the sink, her knees trembling. No, it was not possible, surely her past was not catching up on her again. She had to find out, she had to be sure. She refilled the tea pot and took it back to the room. 'Did your foals come from that area?' she asked blithely. 'My home wasn't far away, in Canning Town.'

'Well, we was born there but me ol' man came from 'olland. 'E was a well-known East End character and made a good livin' dealin' in ol' iron just after the war. He was known as Dutchy and, believe it or not, me Ma was a real gypo. She left her own folk to settle wi' 'im.'

Lily stared vacantly in front of her, and Maria's green hazel eyes flashed in her mind's eye. 'Are your parents still living?' she asked quietly.

'Nah, both dead. The bloody council drove 'em off that bit o' land beside the railway. It killed 'em. Dutchy set abaht the coppers and got time, so me Ma 'itched up the two piebalds to the 'riginal gipsy van and took all the kids dahn to Wiltshire to join 'er own family. They never got back togevver. Unfortunately I was in trouble wiff the law and when I was fourteen I was away in Borstal, so I couldn't 'elp 'em. When we got aht, the ol' man and me gorrus a council flat and 'e lived there wiff me till last year.'E was always full o' bloody booze and was a bloody nuisance in the end,' said Jonny with disgust.

'That's a sad story,' said Lily.

'It's me cousin, Steve, who I was brought up wiff who got the piebalds. They say they're becomin' popular again, use 'em for these toffee-nosed blokes wot go trottin'.'

Lily's mind was in a whirl. There was no mistake. This was one of those little ragged-arsed urchins who used to play in the yard under the arches when she had lived with Maria and Dutchy. She felt her heart torn both ways.

Jonny cheerfully said goodnight and Lily found herself kissing him on the cheek. Avril smiled and whispered, 'He's not so bad, my Jonny, is he, Mum?'

Lily smiled back a little indulgently. 'Take care of yourself, darling,' she said.

But once Avril and Jonny had gone, she sat down and gave vent to her feelings. Once again fate had brought her past back to punish her. What was she going to do? It was pretty obvious that Avril was in love with this lad who could not, after all, really help his background, any more than Lily could help hers. Was there no way out? Who could she confide in? Perhaps it would be all right, perhaps Jonny would turn out a decent lad, but one could never be sure. And clearly Avril was not going to be dislodged from him at all easily. Like Kasie, she was passionately attached to the things she loved, and Jonny was her man.

That night Lily dreamed of Maria. Those clear hazel eyes

came up so close to her and Maria held a bunch of roses under Lily's nose. Lily reached out to touch them knowing they were made of crêpe paper . . .

After that, every Sunday afternoon during the vacation Jonny and Avril came to tea, and Lily found she could not really dislike this lad. In spite of his rough ways, he was happy and generous and Avril seemed so content with him. And every weekend, Avril would say, 'Got any money, Mum? I'm broke.' Whereupon Lily would part with another ten pound note in a half-hearted way. It was obvious to her that Jonny did not like work.

At the end of the vacation Avril came home to collect her text books then went off back to Leeds with Laura in her Mini car. Lily breathed a sigh of relief. At least for a time she would not be seeing Jonny and perhaps she would meet a different young man, Lily thought hopefully.

'I don't know why I got so worried,' she said to Jo. 'Jonny wasn't too bad when you got to know him.'

'Oh, well,' commented Jo. 'Give a dog a bad name and it sticks.'

'He can't help his background,' Lily defended him. 'But he is inclined to be lazy, and I don't think he's the type to be tied down, though neither is Avril.'

'So all's well that ends well, Lily,' smiled Jo.

The restaurant was still doing well but Jo was beginning to find life very irksome. 'I've been grafting since I was a kid,' she said. 'If I don't break away soon I'm going to be like some donkey dying in harness.'

'Oh, don't talk like that, Jo,' pleaded Lily. 'You're not old.'

'I won't tell you how old I am but I can assure you it's more than I look,' Jo replied. 'And I'd like to travel around and see the world while I'm still fairly active.'

'Well, why not?'

'I've got too much on my plate,' said Jo, 'what with that damned house, this restaurant and my ambition to make a career as an author. It's all a little too much, I feel something has to go.'

'I don't really understand,' said Lily. 'I'm a real stick-in-the-mud, I can't stand change of any description.'

Life at the house was rather quiet nowadays. Mike had gone to Canada for a few months to do an exchange teaching job, so his flat was empty for the time being, and Esme was being very moody and kept very much to herself.

'Esme's quiet these days,' Lily commented to Jo one day. 'She hasn't been to visit on Sunday for weeks.'

'What do you expect, out all night and in bed all day?' Jo said unsympathetically. 'I haven't seen her this week at all, and she hasn't paid her rent for three weeks,' she grumbled.

'I'll go and sort her out,' said Lily, 'I'll ask her down for a drink. I haven't made much effort with her lately, I feel a bit guilty about her.' Getting up, she climbed the stairs to Esme's flat on the top floor. It felt very cold and kind of creepy as she passed Mike's empty flat and then on up the narrow flight that led to Esme's flat. There was a silent, brooding atmosphere—no warmth or light, no cooking smells or even the cheap perfume that Esme used—just a cold depressing sadness.

'Esme!' called Lily. 'Come down for a drink.'

No answer.

'Come on,' she said, peeping through the keyhole, 'why are you in the dark? Put the light on.'

Still no reply.

'Esme, you silly cow!' she screamed, banging hard on the door. But all she got was a dull echo.

Running back downstairs she called to Jo. 'I'm sure she's in there, but she won't answer. Perhaps she's ill.'

'I'll get the spare key,' said Jo decisively. 'I'll move her, she's playing up.'

With Lily behind her, Jo banged on the door. 'Esme, it's Jo. It's time you paid some rent.'

Not a whisper was heard, so Jo turned the key in the lock. Lily hovered outside, as Jo went in. Her nostrils curled as a strange aroma wafted out of the flat. Seconds later, Jo rushed out holding her hand to her mouth and heaving as if she was about to vomit. 'Don't go in, Lily, run down and phone the police. Something has happened to Esme.'

Lily dashed down to the hall to dial 999. In no time at all, police cars came screeching up the street followed by the ambulance. As a doctor dashed upstairs, Lily handed a glass of brandy to Jo, who had just come downstairs looking very white.

'What is it, Jo?' begged Lily.

Jo shook her head urgently. 'Esme's dead. She's been there a few days.' She sat on the stairs with her head in her hands. 'Oh my God, and I think she was murdered. She was all bruised and twisted, and the smell was terrible. I don't want you to see her, Lily. It's going to take me a long time to get over it.'

They took Esme's poor distorted body away and the police questioned Jo and Lily. Did they see the pills all over the floor? Jo said she never looked, she was too shocked, and that Lily had stayed outside.

'There will be an inquest,' the police said. 'It might be misadventure. There was a nearly empty bottle of pills by her bed and some all over the floor.' Jo told them that she wasn't sure if Esme had been on drugs, but she did drink.

There was an inquest and the verdict was death by misadventure. It was decided that Esme had been knocked about and beaten, by someone unknown outside the house somewhere, and tired and depressed, she had crawled home, taken too many sleeping pills and never regained consciousness.

It was tragic. Poor Esme, it was only four years since she had obtained her heart's desire to be a woman, but it had given her little happiness.

Only Jo and Lily attended Esme's funeral. Where she came from or who she really was no one ever knew, and that was the end of a very sad story from which the house at Plashet Grove never seemed to recover.

CHAPTER THIRTEEN

Moving On

Lily was in a very depressed state as she sat reading Kasie's letter:

Lily, my lovely,
I have just received your bitchy letter and am sorry if you are feeling downhearted, it is not like you. You have always been my sunshine—remember the song I used to sing for you? I know life has not been all that kind to us but now we are both doing what we wanted, or are we? I ask myself this question very often but I could not stand another rejection from you. Either we sail the rest of life together or not at all. So often I think of your lovely white body and those long slim legs. How are my lovely legs? We did have some good times together, yet I am learning to face the future without you. I hope you can do likewise. You are still young and have Avril to live for; I have only my selfish drunken self. You asked if I had found another bedmate. Well, no one will take your place in my heart, Lily, but as for my bed, who knows? Who cares?
I love you for ever, Kasie.
P.S. Easi has a beautiful young sister but I am not that desperate yet.

It was an ironic letter with an underlying tone of bitterness which Lily keenly felt. She had been feeling downhearted since the tragic death of Esme, which had brought back memories of poor old George. The house always felt creepy to her now, and she hated being alone in it, which was sad after she used to love it so much. Mike was still away and Jo had not got around to re-letting Esme's flat yet. With Avril back in Leeds life was lonelier than ever. Lily spent most of her time at the Nutcracker diving into her work with terrific energy, but she always waited for Jo and the end of each evening. 'I won't go home alone,' she said.

Jo was gradually losing interest in her large house now that the warm, sociable atmosphere was no longer there. There were changes outside in the neighbourhood, too. The high rise blocks of flats had replaced the small slum houses, and were inhabited by strangers who came from far-away places, like Jamaica, India and Africa to replace the cheerful Cockneys. A new hazard outside was the football hooligans—young lads who came to see West Ham play. They swept through the high street knocking down everything before them—old folk, babies in prams—pinching from the shops, breaking windows and smashing car windscreens as they went. After getting caught in this holocaust one Saturday afternoon, Lily was not only alarmed but truly angry. 'Whatever's wrong with all the bloody kids?' she demanded of Jo when she got home. 'They've got the best of everything yet they act like bloody cannibals.'

'Well, as long as they don't cook and eat us, Lily . . .' replied Jo with her dry humour, 'but no doubt that will be the next thing on the agenda. To tell you the truth, I'm getting a bit fed up with it also.'

One night they arrived home to find the house ransacked. The electric meters had been raided and all their personal trinkets taken. The house looked as though a bomb had hit it.

'Now I've really had it!' declared Jo. 'I'll sell the bloody house and put my name down for one of those new service flats that are going up in Woodford.'

Picking up the debris from the floor, Lily said, 'I've been happy here, Jo, I don't think I want to move.' When it came down to it, her old stick-in-the-mud attitude remained the same.

'You might as well, Lily, it will save a lot of time and expense to be nearer the Nutcracker.'

Lily sighed. 'I'll talk about it with Avril when she next comes down from Leeds.'

'I shouldn't depend too much on her, Lily,' Jo warned, 'you might find she has ideas of her own.'

That night Lily replied to Kasie's letter. She did not mention her troubles, she just told him about the affairs of the day. She could feel herself weakening, she was in no doubt about it, but her pride would not allow her to let him know how much she really needed him. 'Let him stay on his bloody desert island,' she muttered angrily as she sealed the letter.

As Jo had warned her, Avril did not come down from Leeds when Lily expected her, she made some excuse about going to the Yorkshire Dales with Laura.

'I can't make up my mind,' Lily told Jo, having given up waiting for Avril. 'Will it make any difference to you if I stay on here?'

'No, Lily,' said the business-wise Jo. 'You have bought the lease so therefore you are entitled to stay until the lease runs out. It will just mean a change of ownership of the house, that's all, but remember it might be entirely different to what it has been with us these last years. We have all lived very cosily together.'

'You mean there will be new tenants?' asked Lily, a little bewildered.

'Who knows? It's a run-down district now, and could get worse in time. If you come with me, I'll put your name down for a flat next to mine. They'll be ready this year and I'll sell this place to a development company—like that, I'll get a good price.'

'I'll think about it,' said Lily who got very depressed. She would never be one to like changes.

That Christmas they were extremely busy at the restaurant and spent long hours there. Avril turned up one evening late and all alone. 'Not with Jonny?' asked Lily hopefully. She had noticed that Avril looked pale and wan.

'He's gone to a party and I didn't want to go,' Avril replied, none too cheerful.

After the restaurant closed they all had a celebration meal together. 'You're putting on weight again, Avril,' Rene said gently.

Avril scowled and looked at Rene in a very glum manner.

'Remind me to write you out a diet sheet, Avril,' said Jo.

'Don't bother,' grunted Avril. 'I'll eat what I fancy.'

When they arrived home to Plashet Grove, Lily bent down to light the gas fire. Avril threw off her coat and said sullenly, 'I got fed up with their nasty cracks about my figure. I bet they wouldn't be so chirpy if they knew I was having a baby.'

Lily sat up abruptly, and quickly threw away the match which was beginning to burn her fingers. 'Why, you silly bitch!' she cried.

'Thank you very much,' Avril returned nastily.

'Now, Avril, don't fool around, don't joke about things like that,' pleaded Lily.

'I'm not,' replied Avril, patting her high tummy. 'What do you think this is? Scotch mist? No, it's true life.'

'Avril!' cried Lily, 'why didn't you tell me sooner?'

'What difference would it have made?' replied Avril. 'If you think I would destroy a new life, you have made a big mistake.'

'Oh dear, what will we do?' sighed Lily.

'It's not your problem, Mother,' said Avril. 'Jonny and I have decided to get married.'

'But Avril, what about your education? You will have to leave the university and you were getting on so well.'

Avril kicked off her shoes and toasted her toes near the fire. 'That's the last of my worries, as long as I get my Jonny, I don't really care.'

'Oh, it's such a pity,' sighed Lily.

'Pity? We don't need pity!' snapped Avril. 'We need help, but not pity.'

Now Lily began to get angry. She resented Avril's truculent attitude. 'Surely there's some other way. Have I spent all this time and money to see you got more out of life than I did, just so you could throw yourself away on a bloody barrow boy?'

'If you are thinking of abortion, cut it out!' yelled Avril. 'You're supposed to be a Christian, yet you want to end the life of a tiny baby. Jonny and I both agree that there is only one way and that is to get married. It's a pity you never thought of that idea and married my father.'

Lily's face flushed scarlet but she held in her temper. 'How will you live?' she asked. 'I don't suppose Jonny's got a job yet.'

'Jonny fiddles a living,' said Avril. 'And he's got a flat. We'll be quite content. The only problems we have are the ones you're making.'

This made Lily feel extremely guilty. 'All right,' she said, 'make your own arrangements and I'll pay for the wedding.'

'Now you're talking a bit of sense,' Avril said with a satisfied smile. 'What about something to eat? I'm starving again.'

So even though it was well after midnight, Lily made Avril some eggs on toast which she scoffed very greedily.

Lily wept many bitter tears that night. This was her punishment, she was quite sure of that. Again, Maria's face loomed in her mind, holding that bunch of paper roses under her nose.

Three weeks later, Jonny and Avril were married in an East End register office. Avril made no fancy preparations, she just allowed Lily to buy her a big dress. It was navy and white with a full front, maternity style. 'It'll do for later on,' she said.

When Lily offered to lend her a small white hat, Avril protested. 'I can't abide hats, ' she sniggered. 'Well, just wear it for the ceremony,' suggested Lily.

Lily took the day off and kept it secret from Jo and Rene. For some reason, she was a little ashamed to tell them.

When Jonny arrived, Lily was relieved to see him very smartly dressed in a grey suit and a white carnation in his buttonhole. He had a wide grin on his face as he greeted Lily. ''Ow do, Ma? Glad yer came.' His eyes were red-veined from the effect of his stag night with the boys, who now stood around outside the register office waiting for the celebrations to begin. 'Over the boozer,' Jonny informed them.

After the short ceremony, Lily stood outside the register office while Jonny's friends threw confetti and made crude jokes. Then it was a general exodus to the pub over the road.

'I'll not come, Avril,' said Lily. 'I have to be at work this evening.'

'All right, Mother,' Avril said, quite unperturbed.

Lily kissed her. 'I wish you happiness, my love,' she said.

Avril looked radiant with happiness. 'Mind how you go, Mum, you're welcome to stay and come back to the flat later on,' she said.

Still Lily declined and as they all disappeared into the pub, she turned and walked a little wearily down the road. Never before had she felt quite so alone and so dejected. She had reached the crossroads of her life. She had lost Kasie and now Avril. What was there to live for? She had a stunned, alienating feeling as if this were happening to someone else and she wandered along the road without noticing where she was going.

After a while she realised that she was in the West India Dock Road, and then the square tower of the Limehouse Church came into view. She lingered to touch the spot on the old wall, the place where she and Kasie had fallen over into the graveyard, having been so drunk on Victory Night. Then she crossed the main road to where the old coffee stall used to be nestled down under the railway arch and, way behind it, where old Dutchy's scrapyard and the gipsy camp had been. She felt very strange, almost high, as if she was running a temperature. She tottered at the kerbside, just as a big red bus bound for Aldgate flashed past. It would be so easy to wait for the next one, she thought, and throw herself under it. No one would know, and it would be regarded as an accident. Then it would all be over. She had found little happiness in life; surely there was some other place than this hell on earth.

With these grim thoughts in mind she waited for that other bus for five minutes. Then it was too late. Reason returned. With a deep shudder, she pulled herself together and, on unsteady feet, walked further down the road to the tube station where she bought a ticket to Woodford. She reached the Nutcracker looking like death and ten years older.

Jo was most concerned when Lily told her what had happened that morning. 'Oh, Lily, Lily, why didn't you share this burden with me?' she cried. 'You know I am your friend.'

But Lily just laid her head on Jo's shoulder and cried.

The effect of Avril's hasty wedding stayed with Lily for a long while. Her face had lines where there had been none, and she did not laugh so often or so heartily. She told Jo to put her name down for a new flat and go ahead and sell the house. 'There's very little left for me there now, Jo,' she said. 'Might as well move on, and you and Rene are the only friends I've got left.'

'Oh, you won't regret it, dear,' returned Jo. 'It's time you started living for yourself, Lily. I have lots of plans for the future. We're not finished, my love, we're just beginning.'

After a few weeks, Avril arrived one Sunday afternoon to visit Lily. She came alone and looked a little scruffy, but she had put on more weight and looked very fit and happy.

Lily embraced her. Then, feeling a little guilty, she asked: 'Where's Jonny?'

'He won't come over, he's a bit scared of you,' declared Avril.

Lily smiled. 'Well, I never! A big fellow like that scared of little me?'

'You know what I mean,' said Avril, searching in the larder for something to eat.

'There's a tin of biscuits on the top shelf,' said Lily dryly.

'I get starving hungry. Hope I'm not having twins,' said Avril, setting about eating the biscuits with gusto.

'I'll get the tea ready,' said Lily. Tears filled her eyes as she poured the hot water into the teapot. How casual Avril was about it all. Still, she must try to avoid a scene. No good could come of a quarrel and she might lose her altogether.

'Got a cat and she had four kittens,' said Avril, 'a ginger, a black and two tabbies. She had them under the bed.'

'Oh, Avril, it's a council flat. You're not supposed to have animals,' Lily protested.

'Jonny and I don't let little things like that worry us. He's getting me a little dog, just like Yorkie.'

George's old pet had eventually died of old age and despite all of Avril's protests in the past, Lily had refused to get another dog, saying that they made the house smell. But now Avril was her own mistress, she was filling her home up with animals and thoroughly enjoying it.

Lily sighed. 'Jonny got a job?' she asked.

'He's all right doing the markets. We get by. He's down the Lane Sunday mornings.'

Lily recalled Jonny's mother and the insecurity of Maria's day out in the worst of weathers, roaming up and down the market with her basket of paper roses and lucky charms. 'Well, no one ain't going to get very fat on that,' she said a little spitefully.

But Avril just stared at her with those dark hard eyes. 'No need to get bitchy,' she said. 'Mother, it's not my fault you couldn't hold onto a man. But I've got my Jonny and we get by, so you can keep your funny remarks to yourself.'

It was hopeless. There was no way Lily could get through to her own lovely daughter. She felt as if her heart would break. 'If you are short of money, just tell me,' she said because she didn't know what else she could say.

'Well, now you are talking sense,' returned Avril. 'You can lend me twenty pounds till Jonny gets on his feet, and I'll go and do some shopping.'

Lily opened her purse and handed her the notes.

Immediately Avril brightened up and smiled. 'Thanks, Mum. I'll pay you back, I promise.'

Lily smiled resignedly. 'Don't worry, Avril, I'm still able to earn some money.'

They parted good friends. Lily told Avril to buy some wool and start knitting for the baby.

'Oh, I can't be bothered,' said Avril. 'I've got enough to do with the cat and her kittens and Jonny to look after.'

'All right,' sighed Lily. 'I'll buy some wool. I expect Jo and Rene will help me out in their free time.'

Avril left and went off very happy with a big bag of food and one of Lily's best blouses.

When Lily told Jo and Rene about the knitting, Rene was delighted. 'Oh, I'd love to knit for the baby,' she said. 'I always wanted to knit but could never think of anyone to knit for.'

'Well, here you are,' said Lily, taking a bundle of white wool and patterns from her bag. 'Start right now, because I'm not too good at it and Avril is too lazy. That poor little sod, his mother won't have a shirt to put on him when he's born.'

The business of the baby's wardrobe was well taken care of for Rene loved to sit and knit. Her long slim fingers worked swiftly and soon she had turned out lots of little vests and matinee jackets. In addition, Jo made little nighties by hand and embroidered pillow cases with the word 'Baby' on them.

The excitement of the women was great as they prepared for the arrival of Lily's grandchild.

The house went up for sale and Lily's name went down on the list for a new flat in a Woodland setting and containing every modern convenience available.

So quite a lot was going on in those last months of Avril's pregnancy, and Lily hardly realised that she had not heard from Kasie for quite a while. When she did, she saw that her life was becoming full once more as she was getting by without him. At home, they all began to pack their personal belongings after Jo had sold the house to a builder who was going to pull it down and re-develop the area.

'At least I shan't have to see it decaying and empty,' said Jo. 'There is, after all, a bit of sentimental value attached to it. I lived here with my grandparents, a wonderful old couple.'

'I've had many happy days with you all,' said Lily, 'and I wonder if they will miss us. They say that spirits hang on to places they like.'

It was less than a month before they were due to move. The china was packed already and Lily had paid the deposit on her new flat which was one floor below Jo's and Rene's flat. It had a pretty balcony looking out towards Epping forest, and was in a very nice neighbourhood, just a ten-minute walk away from the Nutcracker. It had not been easy for her to decide to leave the old house, and Lily was quite pleased with her new strength and determination to make a life of her own. Then one morning the postman handed her a letter just as she was going off to work. She stopped in the hall to read it while Jo impatiently revved up the van outside.

It was from Kasie.

Lily my lovely,
    I know it is a long time since you have heard from me but I hope
this letter finds you in good health. You will notice that I am back in
my homeland because I suddenly got very homesick. I also wanted
to be back with my family. I am now a grandfather, as Neil's wife
just had a little girl. They have called her Neilte after my mother and
I could not wait to see her. I was determined to sail my own ship
back across the Atlantic and it was a long heavy haul. I bought an
old ship and had it refitted, as labour is cheap out here. The ship is
now in Amsterdam harbour and I intend to live aboard her until the
winter when I will sail to sunnier climes. I came home with a
coloured crew—all islanders who wanted to settle in Holland—so I
was well taken care of. I still miss you, *leiblin*, but I know you won't
come to me, so I am resigned to my fate. All my love to you and
Avril. If you need anything just let me know. I am at least a
thousand miles nearer to you if it makes any difference.
                    Yours always, Kasie.

Lily's heart missed a beat as she read this. So he was back once
more. Was she sorry? Her feelings were mixed. As much as she
longed for his kisses, she was afraid he would possess her, and
overpower her again, just when she had reached a very independent stage in her life. She thrust the letter in her pocket, saying
to herself: 'Oh no, Kasie, I'm here if you really need me but
somehow I don't think you do.' She shut the door behind her
and ran down the steps to the van. 'Sorry, Jo,' she apologised.
'Got a letter from Kasie and stopped to read it.'

'And how is he?' Jo asked.

'As full of his bloody self as ever,' declared Lily, '*and* he's back
home.'

Just one week before the move, everyone was in a good frame
of mind and looking forward to the future. On Sunday
morning, Avril arrived at the house looking very dishevelled
and out of breath, being only one month from her time and
extremely heavy.

'Oh Mummy,' she cried, almost collapsing on Lily as she
opened the door.

'What's wrong, darling?' cried Lily with some alarm.

'It's Jonny,' Avril sobbed. 'He's been arrested and they won't let him out.'

'Oh dear,' Lily sighed, and sat down as her knees went weak. She cuddled Avril close. 'Calm down, love,' she said gently, 'and tell me all about it.'

'I don't really know, but it's something to do with a lorry that's been stolen. I went up to the police station but they said he has to stay there till Monday and then he'll be in court and charged.' Childishly she wept, holding on tight to Lily.

'It's not so bad,' Lily said comfortingly, 'he'll get off on Monday, in the meantime, you'd better stay here.'

'Oh, I can't do that,' wailed Avril. 'What about my cats and my little dog? They'll starve.'

'All right, I'll come back with you to your place,' sighed Lily. Knowing Jonny's background it came as no surprise to her that he was in trouble.

'They're always in trouble with the law, these market boys,' she said to Jo when she went to tell her what had happened. 'It's a way of life, I'd better go back and stay with her, I think, or she might have the baby prematurely with all this fuss and worry.'

'Oh, Lily, Lily!' sighed Jo, 'where will it all end?'

Lily said farewell to Jo and Rene. 'I'll be back next week,' she said. She packed a few things and then went with Avril down to Canning Town to stay with her in their council flat. The flat was on the fourteenth floor and you travelled up to it in a lift that smelled of urine. Then you had to walk along a seemingly endless corridor past lots of front doors that all looked the same. It was quiet that Sunday evening and the sky was heavy with an air which threatened to be a thunderstorm any minute. No one was about. All the inhabitants were behind locked doors, no doubt staring at their television.

Inside, the flat was chaos. Avril had never been a very tidy girl but apparently Jonny surpassed her. Clothes were strewn everywhere—on the backs of chairs, and hanging up on the picture rails. Playing cards and bottles covered the table and the smell of cats almost knocked you flat. A scruffy little bundle of

hair came racing out snapping at Lily's legs. Avril swept him up
into her arms. 'Oh, Yorkie, darling,' she cried, 'our Daddy is
gone away and left us.'

Lily looked in horrified disgust at the sight of the kitchen:
there were cats in a box under the sink which overflowed with
filthy pots and pans and crocks caked with food. Saucers of milk
were all over the place, most of them half-spilt over onto the
floor.

'For Christ's sake, Avril,' cried Lily, 'don't you ever clean
up?'

'Oh, don't start,' snivelled Avril. 'I haven't felt like doing it
and besides, Jonny was going to help me this weekend.'

'Oh dear,' said Lily running the hot water. 'Get them bleedin'
cats out from under my feet.'

'I'll put them on the balcony,' said Avril, 'but they must come
back in at night in case it gets cold.'

'Take them to the bleedin' cats home,' grumbled Lily, diving
into the washing-up.

Avril put the cats and their box out on the balcony and then
started weeping once more. 'I feel terrible,' she wailed.

'Go and lay down,' Lily swept the debris from the settee to
allow Avril to lie down, and covered her over. Within minutes,
Avril was asleep like a child with a tear-stained face. The scruffy
little dog at her feet snapped and snarled at Lily every time she
passed the settee.

Lily washed the crocks, cleaned the stove, and the kitchen
floor. Sweat poured from her brow as she scrubbed up the
grease. She disposed of empty beer cans and whisky bottles,
tidied up the sitting room, and last, she made a cup of tea and sat
waiting for Avril to wake up.

Supper that evening was bought by Lily from the Chinese
take-away down in the street below. When she went out to get
it, she felt very strange and nervous. This East End used to be
her home but now it was an alien place. Crowds of young lads
larked about and slithered past her outside the flats. They had
loud voices, wore big boots and leather jackets. It was a

frightening world there now, and one she was sure she could never get used to.

'You really ought to get out of this place, Avril,' she said as Avril filled herself with the Chinese food which Lily could not even touch.

'Why?' Avril wasn't bothered. 'Jonny likes it here and no one interferes with us.'

So Lily closed her eyes and said a silent prayer. 'Please, God, let Jonny come home.'

On Monday morning, Lily and Avril sat in court waiting for Jonny to appear before the magistrate, who was a woman. At first Lily was pleased, a woman will be more lenient than a man, she thought hopefully, but she was wrong.

Jonny was looking a bit under the weather as he stood in the dock with two other lads, but he shot a grin in Avril's direction and mouthed something. Avril smiled sweetly back at him.

'What's he say?' asked Lily.

'He said, "How are yer, toots?"'

'What's that in aid of?' asked Lily.

Avril smiled dreamily. 'That's what he calls me, he don't like Avril, so he calls me tootsie wootsie.'

Lily looked at Avril in amazement and wondered where she had gone wrong.

The court read out Jonny's previous convictions which amounted to four, and a suspended sentence hanging over his head. On hearing this, Lily knew there was no hope for Jonny or his mates.

It all happened quite quickly. Avril insisted on going up to plead for her husband and Lily hung her head as the old hag of a judge gazed unsympathetically at Avril and muttered loudly, 'Oh dear, they are all pregnant.' And she ignored Avril's efforts to plead for Jonny's character. 'Your husband is a habitual criminal,' she said, 'and you have nothing to worry about, the State will take care of you and your baby.'

Lily rushed forward to hold Avril as she came sobbing from the dock. 'Vicious old cow,' she muttered, glaring at the honoured judge at the bench.

Jonny was sentenced to one year, with remission for good behaviour. This came as a terrible blow to Avril who had not expected it at all. She was completely distraught.

For the next week, Lily stayed with Avril in that crummy old flat, trying to get her to take exercise for the baby's sake. But Avril slouched in front of the television, hugging the dog or one of the cats, and moving about very little.

As Jonny left the dock, he had said to Avril, 'Take care, toots, look after him. I'll be back soon.' And it was clear that she was just waiting for that day.

One night Avril woke up calling out and Lily ran to call the ambulance. Lily went with her in the ambulance to the Bancroft Maternity Hospital, recalling how she had walked alone through the darkened blitzed East End streets to this same hospital on the night that Avril was born. Well, history seemed to have a way of repeating itself, she thought bitterly. But in Lily's case, she had not had a loving mother to care for her, as Avril did. And Lily was glad that she was able to be there beside her.

Next day Avril gave birth to a bonny boy. He was ten pounds in weight and was doing well. Lily had spent all night at the hospital and went to see the baby since the father was not available. As she looked down at the little bundle of love, her first grandchild, she was overcome by a wonderful feeling of warmth. She smiled at Avril who just sat up in bed snivelling. 'I want my Jonny,' Avril cried.

But Jonny had been sentenced and JonJon born. Lily knew that her independence had gone, that there was no escape for her now.

Back home, Jo pleaded with her not to be foolish, but Lily would not listen. 'It's no good, Jo,' she said. 'I can't leave her alone with a young baby to cope with.'

'She'll get by,' Jo insisted. 'Girls do these days. You were just getting independent and happy about it. Allow yourself to develop, otherwise you'll grow old and lost.'

'Okay, Jo, thanks for cheering me up,' returned Lily dryly. 'But nothing you say will make me change my mind.'

'Then bring Avril and the baby with you. We'll help Avril with him and she can earn her keep working at the Nutcracker.'

So for a while Lily saw a glimmer of hope but when Avril came home from the hospital, she immediately squashed the idea. 'No!' she said emphatically. 'I'm staying here till Jonny comes home. You can do what you like.' She stared defiantly at Lily, holding little JonJon in her arms and looking so much as Kasie used to in moments of extreme tension.

Guiltily, Lily reached out for the baby. He was dressed in all the nice white woollies Rene and Jo had provided for him, and was so fair, so tiny and cuddly. Again she felt a rush of love for him, her own grandchild. 'All right,' she said. 'Get your coat off and make him a bottle. We'll stay here.' So rather reluctantly, Lily settled for Jonny's slum flat and cancelled the modern one in Woodford.

When Jo and Rene moved out to that nice country town, Lily saw very little of them, but it was not so bad when she got used to it. There were often squabbles between her and Avril, but always JonJon helped to bring them together again. On Lily's insistence, homes were found for the kittens and the cat was neutered. Yorkie was taken out for a walk twice daily by Avril so that the flat had a chance of being kept clean and free from animal smells. When her own home was dismantled, Lily brought extra comfort in the form of beds, linen and crockery, and they lived fairly well. Avril proved to be an excellent mother and kept her baby clean and well fed. All the meticulous attention she used to shower on animals was now spent on little JonJon who thrived and grew bonny. He had lovely golden hair and blue eyes, and a toothless grin for his grandma and loud chuckles as Lily walked around the patch of green grass attached to the high flats, pushing him in the pram. It always seemed so cold and windy there. The high blocks picked up the breeze from the river and whirled it around those estates. Sometimes the lifts did not work and Lily would be forced to leave the pram down below and carry JonJon up fourteen flights of stairs. But apart from these hazards they managed to get by. She did not dare venture out at night, for the streets around them were pretty dangerous, but all in all they got by exceedingly happily together, and enjoyed shopping in the supermarket or turning over the stalls in the market for bargains.

Avril lived only for Jonny's letter every few weeks. He was now in an open prison and had quite settled down.

'Take care of JonJon, tootsie,' he would write. 'I'll make it all up to you when I get out.'

His were not passionate love letters but they were written in a genuine tone as if he really meant what he said. Lily would listen glumly while Avril read bits out to her. In her heart she wished he was not so genuine, for with Jonny's background it was not going to be easy and she had wanted so much more in life for her only child. But there was nothing she could do about it, so she decided not to let it get her down. She cooked and cleaned and poured her own money into the home, and forgot about everyone else. It occurred to her one day that Kasie did not have the faintest idea about where to find her now even if he wanted to, but she closed her heart to this fact, and went on with the little that life had to offer. She took care of JonJon when Avril went to visit Jonny at the prison. And when Avril came back starry-eyed and full of chat about their future plans, Lily knew that come what may, Avril would stick by her Jonny forever.

Each week Avril would cross out the days on the calendar. 'Seven days nearer to my Jonny coming home,' she would say.

'Why don't you ring up Laura?' Lily suggested one day. 'You could go out together. I'll mind the baby.'

Avril stared scornfully at her. 'Mother, Laura's the last person I'd want to have know that Jonny is inside. I don't need friends, I'll wait for my Jonny to come home.'

In some ways Lily secretly admired her for her determination and independence. At Avril's age, she, Lily, was going out with her mates having a good time during the war, and she had needed their company.

One Sunday she persuaded Avril to go with her to visit Jo and Rene. Avril agreed because she was proud of little JonJon and wanted to show him off. So they got the bus out to Woodford with JonJon looking sweet and smiling, wrapped up in all his best attire. Avril spent most of her money on clothes for dressing him up.

Jo and Rene welcomed them heartily and made an awful fuss of the baby. They had tea sitting out on that wide balcony overlooking the forest. It was very high up on the Essex weald and the air was sweet and fresh.

When Lily commented on how nice it was, Jo agreed. 'Well, Lily,' she said, 'you could have had the same down below, but it's been sold now.'

Avril stared sullenly at Jo, who changed the subject and told them that she had been asked to tour America with her latest diet cookbook. 'It's all the rage out there, this slimming business,' she said. 'I'd like to go but I haven't quite made up my mind.'

'How's the Nutcracker going?' asked Lily.

'Well, we all miss you but have survived. If I do go to New York, I'll put in a manager. By the way, Lily, I've paid your share of the profits into the bank for you. You'll be surprised by how well we did. Come out to my office and I'll show you a copy of the accounts.'

Lily left Rene and Avril fussing the baby and went with Jo to her small office at the end of the hall. 'It's not as roomy as Plashet Grove,' said Jo, 'but it's all nice and handy, and easy to keep warm.' As soon as she closed the door, she sighed. 'Thank God, I never thought I'd get you alone,' she said. 'I have a letter for you, and he's rung me several times. I didn't let on. I pretended I didn't have your new address but told him that should I get it I'd forward the letter on.'

'Oh, you mean Kasie,' Lily said a little wearily. She had a strong feeling that she did not want to face any more problems. 'Thanks, Jo,' she said, putting the letter in her pocket. 'I'll read it later when I'm on my own.'

Jo looked surprised at Lily's casual attitude, but she said, 'Your secret is perfectly safe with me. I'll not tell him where you are if you don't want me to, but Lily, do think about the future. What will you do when Jonny comes out? The time will soon pass, you know.'

'Oh, I'll cross my bridges when I come to them,' said Lily. 'At the moment I've got enough on my plate.'

'You can come back to live with us, and I'd be so pleased to have you back at the Nutcracker,' Jo assured her.

That night after she returned home, Lily sat reading Kasie's letter. It had been posted in Rotterdam three months ago.

Lily, my lovely,

Have not heard from you since I came back home. Hope everything is all right with you and Avril. I came back to see my new granddaughter and she is very lovely. She looks like Avril when she was a baby. Always in my mind are those lost happy days we spent together in London. I have become interested in another kind of business here in Rotterdam. It's to do with tugs and salvage, but I know that it will not interest you. Darling, maybe we could plan a meeting later this month. You could fly out to me or would you prefer to meet me in London? We are still not too old to paint the town a brilliant red. We are not too old to live it up as we used to and it would be so wonderful to hold you in my arms once more, *leiblin*. Let me know soon. My regards to Avril.

Always your lover, Kasie.

Lily's tears dripped down onto the letter. So he had capitulated and agreed to meet her and continue their affair but fate had decided otherwise. It was three months since he had posted that letter. He was back to normal, full of drive and back in the rat race of making money. 'Oh, well, Kasie, sorry darling,' she whispered, 'it was just not to be.'

Each day passed by. Jo wrote to say that Rene and she were flying off to New York the next week and that there was now a manager at the restaurant. And as the time drew nearer for Jonny's release, Lily wondered how smooth life was going to be when he came home again.

JonJon was seven months old when Jonny came home, looking very fit and well. Avril was ecstatic and the two of them sat mooning over each other like a honeymoon couple. Lily kept out of his way as much as possible, for she had a strong feeling that he did not expect to see her there. And then one morning she overheard Jonny's loud voice demanding, 'How much longer is she going to be here?'

'Oh, don't be like that, Jonny,' she heard Avril reply. 'Mum has nowhere else to go. She gave up her home to take care of me.'

'But now I'm around once more, toots, you don't need anyone to look after you. I'll do that,' Jonny told her.

'I know,' simpered Avril, 'but I feel awful. Mum put twenty quid into the home every week while you were away.'

'Right,' said Jonny, 'now I'll give her twenty quid to stay out of it.'

Avril giggled and Jonny roared with coarse laughter. Lily could hear them larking about and Jonny humming his favourite tune: 'Toot to tootsie, goodbye, Toot to tootsie, don't cry.'

Lily stopped eavesdropping. Her face was very white. 'Well,' she muttered, 'that's all I bleedin' need.' She decided that she would leave that very day, but where would she go? A desolate feeling came over her. There was no place for her. Avril did not need her any longer, it was time to go. As she began to put some things into a suitcase, she noticed Kasie's letter in the bottom. Suddenly she had an idea. She quickly went down in the lift to the post office and sent a telegram to the address on the letter: 'If you still want me, Kasie, I'll come to you now. Please reply.' She added her address and then went back to the flat to finish packing her suitcases.

'What are you doing, Mother?' Avril asked.

'I might go on a little holiday, now that Jonny's home,' Lily replied.

'But where are you going?' asked Avril, looking rather concerned.

'Only over to Jo and Rene,' lied Lily. Fortunately, Avril did not know that they were in New York.

'We're going down the Lane and taking JonJon,' said Avril. 'Be back later.'

Lily sat on the edge of her bed in the tiny box-like room where she slept, and waited anxiously for the reply to her telegram. At six o'clock the telegram boy arrived at the door. She tore it open with trembling hands. 'Meet you at the Hook Monday evening. Love Kasie.' Lily kissed the paper and smiled joyfully.

She snapped shut the suitcases, put a few other belongings into her travelling bag, and went down in the smelly lift for the last time. Her eyes filled with tears as she thought of little JonJon, but this time she must never ever turn back. This she vowed at forty-two years old as she went off to the arms of her lover who had waited such a long time for her to come.

CHAPTER FOURTEEN

Till Eternity

The wheels of the train seemed to pound out a rhythm as the express sped over the rails. 'I am coming to you, I am coming to you, Kasie.'

Lily was feeling harassed, for she was already beginning to regret her hasty departure. Would Avril look after JonJon as carefully as she herself had done? So obsessed was Avril with Jonny that she might even neglect Lily's grandson. All these concerns rose in Lily's mind as she began to worry. What about money? What would they live on? Jonny had not shown any intention of getting a job, and he was still only out on parole. One false move and he would be back inside. She closed her eyes. A cold sweat had formed on her brow. Was she burning her bridges? She had not liked Kasie's country before, it was cold and flat, and the language was so difficult. And had he changed much in the last two years? He was getting on a bit but then they both were getting on a bit. She was forty-two and he was forty-eight.

Taking out her pocket mirror, she examined her face. 'Oh dear, what a bloody mess,' she exclaimed to herself. She had to make up her face, and she should have gone to get her hair done. She cursed herself. What would Kasie think when he saw her now? She looked so much older, with dark rings around her eyes and deep lines around her mouth. A very depressing mood possessed her and was still with her when she got out of the train at Harwich. There was still time to turn back. All she had to do was cross the bridge to the other side of the track and wait for the train home. But what home? She had no home now, nowhere to go except where she was going now.

So she didn't turn back, she walked on with the crowd to the Cross-Channel Ferry, and all the time Kasie's sweet smile was with her. It was almost as if she could put out her hand and he would be there, his hot dry lips on hers and she could hear that gentle voice with its soft accent whispering sweet nothings to her.

On board, she booked a cabin, found it, and lay down on the bunk waiting for the ferry to sail. She dropped off into an exhausted sleep, but then woke to the thump of the engines as the ferry pushed out across the cold Channel. She got up, tidied her hair, made up her face and went to find the bar. With several drinks inside her, she soon calmed down and amused herself by watching the antics of the excited young boys and girls out on their first trip abroad. They were singing and dancing, and getting drunk. Their happiness suddenly made Lily feel very much alone. Miserably, she went back to her cabin and slept until dawn brought the big ship to the shores of Holland.

A grey mist lay over the coast line and the kids, all tired after their all-night revelling, lay around the deck amid a confusion of kit bags and haversacks. Lily drank some early morning coffee, feeling very shivery and rather afraid of that huge grey expanse of North Sea. It was high tide and the water was very choppy. As the waves raced towards her and dashed themselves against the bows of the ship causing it to roll about, Lily's stomach heaved. The screeching gulls escorted the ferry in alongside the dock and she was suddenly reminded of that dreary old landing barge where she had lived with Kasie when Avril was a baby. They had lacked most comforts then, but had had lots of love.

She waited with the long queue of passengers to go ashore, and looking shorewards to the dockside, she saw him. There he was, that same dapper little figure chatting nonchalantly to some harbour official just as if he owned the place, she thought ruefully.

As she came down the gang plank, Kasie came forward to meet her.

'I'm not supposed to be out here,' he said, 'but the harbour man is an old pal of mine. Come on, my lovely, I'll get you through very quickly.'

She walked beside him silently. She felt unable to speak, so deep were her emotions at the sight of him. She waited with him for the rest of her luggage and once through Customs he pulled her close to him. 'Lily, my lovely, I never thought you meant it, but welcome again to my land.' He pressed those tender lips to hers as she closed her eyes and a deep sob rasped in her throat.

'Now, *leiblin*, don't cry. Are you happy to see me? I have been up all night waiting for you.'

She smiled up at him a little wanly.

'Oh, dear, you are tired,' he said. 'We're going to stay here at the Hook for a few days while we get back together.' He hailed a cab, they sat close together in it without uttering a word.

The cab wended its way along the coast until they came to a small seaside town with a white sandy beach. Tall houses of all different sizes stood higgledy-piggledy all over the place. They drew up at an odd-looking hotel that overlooked the sandy beach.

'It's not a hotel, Lily,' explained Kasie, 'but a small pension, or guesthouse. It's here we will spend our honeymoon. Cheer up, Lily,' he cajoled, 'I've never seen you so down.'

Once they were settled in the bright little room with its high windows looking out to sea, Lily relaxed and put her arms about his neck. 'Oh, Kasie, it's been so lonely,' she murmured and her body melted close to his. That old magic was still there, she thought as she stroked his face which now had deep rugged creases where there had once been soft pinky flesh. She took off his hat and looked at his hair which was now cut very short and was sprinkled with grey. They stood looking closely at each other.

'You've changed, Kasie,' she said. 'Your hair is going grey and you're much thinner.'

'That was the hot sun in the Indies, *leiblin*, but I confess, I'm not the man I was.' He smoothed his hand down her body and slipped off her coat. 'Now let me look at you. You still have that lovely slim, supple body.' He kissed her neck softly. 'But, Lily, you seem so sad. I feel it has not been easy for you this last two years.'

'It's been bloody awful,' cried Lily, regaining some of her old spirit.

They sat on the bed and as he fondled her Lily felt the swift passion rising within her. She lay back on the bed.

'Want me, darling?' Kasie whispered.

'You know I do,' she replied.

'Well, let it be love first and eating after,' smiled Kasie, gently coming over to lie on top of her. His hand slid up her leg to remove her tights and his hot lips kissed her abdomen. He rolled up her dress. 'Oh, Lily, my lovely,' he whispered hoarsely.

Lily gasped and shivered with passion. 'Oh Kasie,' she moaned, 'love me, love me like you used to.'

His tongue probed her mouth and his hands ran over the curves of her body. His body stiffened and he entered her. They were so hot for each other, it did not last very long, and lying back on the bed afterwards was one of the supreme moments for them. 'Oh, Lily,' he said, 'we are like wine, we have matured with age.' He lay beside her, slightly exhausted.

'Oh, Kasie,' Lily said. 'You don't know how miserable I have been without you.'

Time was endless. Each day sped on golden wings. They lay in the hot sun on the little beach of very white sand, and ate good meals at the guesthouse. They talked very little about the past and almost nothing about the future. It was just a time for love and lovers, and both made the most of it. Lily's pale face assumed a golden tan and her wide happy smile came back again.

'How foolish we have been to spend most of our lives apart,' Kasie said one day. 'Let us end all that and get married.'

'No, do you really mean that, Kasie?' Lily asked cautiously.

'Many times I have asked you, Lily, and there was always some reason not to. Surely we have reached the age of consent by now.' He grinned at her in that mocking way.

Lily was lying on her back wearing just a brief sunsuit. She sat up and looked steadily at him. 'You know, only just recently have I realised what a fool I've been. I don't know if anyone took my place with you but, quite honestly, no man but you has owned me since that night in the blitz, and still I'm always hungry for you. If that's not true love, what is?'

Kasie pulled her to her feet and clasped her tight in his arms. 'Oh, Lily, Lily my lovely, so long I have waited to hear you face the truth. So now, my darling, there is no turning back.'

They stood in a tight, passionate embrace until the giggles of some nearby teenagers brought them down to earth. Hand in hand they walked slowly back to the guesthouse for lunch.

As they ate, Kasie told her of his plans for the future. 'Tomorrow we will go back to Amsterdam and I will introduce you to my family. Then we will get your papers in order for a permanent residency and I'll put up the bans and we'll have a slap-up wedding. I will be so proud of you, darling.'

A little frown appeared on Lily's brow. 'Do we have to? Couldn't we be married secretly?' she asked.

'That's up to you, darling,' he said. 'Quite frankly, as long as I keep you with me I'm not worried. I only came back to see Holland to see the *leiberkin*, my Neil's new daughter. It was as if she called me across the sea, and now my return has brought you to me, darling. I cannot believe my luck, so you can do anything you like and spend as much money as you want, as I am not short of money. But my family would be rather hurt if I took the step of marrying without including them. You can send for Avril and her family so they can be present too.'

It all sounded like a dream. Kasie was very excited and his eyes glowed with a fierce brightness. Lily looked away. Some strange feeling deep in her heart seemed to be telling her that this was the beginning of the end. Something would go wrong. Kasie was still talking in that kind of excited manner; she looked uneasily at him.

'I've planned to sail my ship around the Mediterranean for about a year until we find a place to settle down. I know you do not like to live aboard ship, Lily, but this is not the old landing barge, just wait till you see her.'

A little tug of fear pulled at Lily's heart. Kasie was so intensely happy. This was a lover she never knew; he had always been independent of her yet he had changed, and now seemed to clutch at straws to keep her with him. She wished fervently that she could feel the same, for in the back of her mind the matter of Avril and whether she could cope without her still gnawed at her. But she said nothing and reached out her hand across the table to gently stroke the deep creases on both sides of his mouth. Kasie kissed her hand passionately in response. No word was uttered between them but she knew she had committed herself to staying with him.

At the end of the week they packed and went off to Amsterdam where they stayed in a rather more commercial hotel that lacked the intimate atmosphere they had enjoyed at the pension. Soon Kasie got busy once more with his own affairs and, with a very generous allowance from Kasie, Lily spent her time shopping in the big town stores. She had told him: 'I have my own money, Kasie, I did not come to you broke.'

Kasie had kissed her. 'My *leiblin*, while I live it is my money we will spend, not yours.'

So Lily bought herself some very smart suits and tiny hats with eye veils to match, long, graceful negligées and nighties galore. Everything was charged to Kasie's special account, which seemed inexhaustible.

At the end of each afternoon, Lily sat outside the cafe under the striped canopy, sipping coffee or consuming pastries and ice-creams.

Kasie always came looking for her, and he often carried a big bunch of flowers bought at the flower market in the town centre.

'This is the life,' said Lily, and she thought how surprised Jo would be to see her now. Then she thought sadly of Avril and JonJon, and Jo and Rene back in England.

So far she had not been able to understand a word of what was spoken around her, and so she had not made the acquaintance of anyone. She had refused to meet Neil again or even see

Rica, Kasie's sister, saying, 'Oh, leave me alone, Kasie, I'll see them all when we are married.'

At night they would lie in bed and talk of the past and the plans for the future. 'I'm truly sorry that Avril let you down,' Kasie said one night, 'but it does not surprise me really. You spoiled her, Lily.'

'Oh, don't tell me I was wrong,' Lily pleaded. 'She was all I had.'

'She had a father but you disowned me,' he grinned.

'Oh don't dig up old sores, Kasie, tell me what I should do. I left without explaining anything to her. She's probably frantic with worry about me by now.'

'Well, *leiblin*, there is nothing to hide. As soon as your papers are in order we will be legally wed, so I suggest you write and ask her to our wedding.'

'She's a strange child,' said Lily, 'I just cannot face it.'

He sighed. 'Well, send her money, then, if what's what's worrying you. Then later you can give your grandson an allowance, as I will do for mine.'

'Okay,' said Lily. 'I suppose it's that affair Avril had with Neil that makes me feel funny. You know, I have always felt so guilty about breaking them up, and then she went back down the road and married that barrow boy.'

Kasie smiled. 'Don't condemn them just like that, Lily. Think of us, we were of very different backgrounds.'

'And look at the bloody trouble we caused,' said Lily.

'But our love has lasted.' He kissed her bare shoulder. 'It faded occasionally but was evergreen, like a rose bush full of prickles but ready to bloom again.'

She laughed at last. 'At times you are so funny, Kasie,' she said more cheerfully.

'I can be much more amusing,' he said wickedly, pulling her to him.

As each day passed they got closer in their relationship. One day, Kasie said: 'Lily, will you come and see my other lovely lady?'

She stared at him with suspicion.

Kasie laughed. 'No need for jealousy, it's my ship, the *Leiber Frowen*, she's anchored over there in the harbour not far from our old place where we lived in those old happy days.'

She hesitated as her old fear of the sea surfaced once more. She tried to pretend it was not there but it showed in her face.

Kasie saw it and looked disappointed. He said gently, 'I had hoped that when we were married we would live aboard her and sail to summer climes, just you and me, Lily, and my lovely lady.'

Lily relented. 'Yes, darling,' she said, 'you know I'd love to,' she lied.

The next day, Kasie went off for hours on some mysterious shopping expedition. He rang Lily at the hotel to say he would pick her up at five o'clock.

Lily sat in her room making herself beautiful. She still had a flamboyant flare for making herself up and dressing, and the finished product was always great, she thought. Her mane of auburn hair shone like burnished gold and the long earrings matched the bright rows of chunky beads around her neck and big cheap rings on her hands.

This jewellery started their first argument which was so fierce that it was like old times in that hotel room.

When Kasie came in, Lily paraded up and down the room in her finery. 'How do I look?' she asked, a little vainly.

'Like a bloody Zulu,' said Kasie dryly.

'Oh, you sod!' she shouted, throwing the hairbrush at him. Kasie caught it deftly and threw it back, making Lily jump up and down with rage. But he grabbed hold of her, pulled off the beads and then tried to get the earrings off. She bit and scratched, and they fought each other, until they finally fell onto the bed with Kasie laughing his head off.

'Oh, you rotter!' she cried, looking in dismay at the beads all rolling about the floor. 'I'm not going out with you, I'll go back home in the morning.'

He held her hands tight. 'Calm down, *leiblin*, I'm sorry, but to see you looking like a tart makes me angry.'

Lily began to weep and all her heavy make-up melted down

her face. Kasie wiped her tears away with his hanky and then began to wipe the make-up from her face. His gentle voice cajoled her as he did so. 'Come now, my lovely, calm down. Look what I have brought you—a real orchid. We will pin it on this nice dress and if you have just a little make-up on your face and roll back your hair, you will look like the Queen of Amsterdam.'

Quietly she sobbed but knew he was right. This was a different world, with customs she was not sure of. Perhaps all that war paint would not go down with these dreadfully respectable people.

'I want to be proud of you, Lily, and we have two guests aboard our *Lovely Lady*, one of whom has met you before.'

'Who?' she asked suspiciously.

'My son Neil and his wife.'

'I'm not going,' she cried.

'Oh, yes, you are,' he said firmly, picking up the hairbrush and beginning to smooth the frizziness from her hair and brush it in a roll at the back of her neck. His smooth gentle touch soothed her.

'Okay, Kasie, I'm a bitch,' she said, 'but you always get me in a temper.'

His lips caressed her neck. 'Come, Lily, get up and put your face to rights, otherwise I will get in bed with you and no one will be going anywhere.'

She washed away her tears, and put on a sprinkling of powder and a light dash of lipstick.

'Show me your hands,' he ordered.

She spread out those well-kept hands and he began to take off the cheap rings.

'Oh, no, Kasie,' she entreated him.

'Oh, yes, Kasie,' he mimicked her. Then he took out a small box from his pocket and slipped on her finger a lovely three-stone diamond ring. 'It's the best in Amsterdam for the loveliest lady,' he said.

'Oh, Kasie!' cried Lily, throwing her arms about his neck. 'I really don't deserve you.'

'Come, *leiblin*, let us go. Put on your nice white fox jacket and we'll be off. Now you look so fabulous I want to show you off, I am really proud of you.'

They went by cab down to the harbour, and then in a smelly motorcraft they crossed the harbour. It was almost dark and the lights of the town twinkled in the smooth, calm water. When the ship came in sight, Lily could see that she was a big white craft, all smart and modern and recently painted. 'Take care, Lily,' Kasie warned as she balanced precariously in the rocking boat. 'Be careful,' he said as he guided her up the gangway, 'you're not a skipper's wife yet.'

Lily was conscious of the size and the luxury of this craft as they went down into a large saloon. The table was laid for dinner with white starched tablecloths and table napkins. Pink carnations were tastefully arranged in the centre of the table and the silver gleamed in the reddish light from the lamp.

'Oh, dear, isn't it posh!' exclaimed Lily.

'I warned you, didn't I? This is my other lovely lady and I am very proud of her, too.' He helped her off with her coat and they sat in the main saloon on a very comfortable leather-covered seat. Kasie went over to the cocktail cabinet and poured them some drinks.

'Like it, Lily?' he asked. 'Look, that's our honeymoon chamber.' He slid back a door to display a well-fitted bedroom.

'It's great, Kasie,' Lily said with genuine enthusiasm, 'it's just like a house.'

'I know, darling. You roughed it on the old landing barge but this is our dream home, the kind of home I always planned for us. We will sail away and live just for each other.'

It sounded great but Lily still wished that all that water was not around her. She would have felt much happier and safer on dry land, but she made no comment. She sipped her drink and lay back looking at the luxurious fittings of Kasie's other lady.

They heard the guests arrive and Kasie got up to greet them. Nervously Lily gripped her glass hard as she watched them come towards her. With his father's charming smile, Neil gripped her hand warmly. 'Hullo, Lily,' he said, 'so we meet again. This is a great pleasure.' Behind him stood a short, stout woman with a fresh complexion and snub nose. She could only be Dutch. She looked shyly at Neil. 'This is my wife, Jante. She speaks a little English so you will be able to get on together.'

Excitedly Kasie talked to them in Dutch and they chatted back. The cabin seemed full of noise and Lily's head swam but she sat back and smiled even though she felt strangely out of it all. Kasie refilled their glasses and they all seated themselves at the table and waited for the dinner to be served. To Lily's amazement, a very young coloured girl brought in the dishes. She spoke rapidly in her own tongue to Kasie who replied with a whimsical grin. The girl's dark eyes flashed in Lily's direction with a hostile expression, before she exchanged a quick word of greeting to Neil and his wife. Acutely conscious of atmosphere, Lily wondered what the hell was going on.

They ate a good dinner and all began to relax. The meal was roast pork and all kinds of strange vegetables and plenty of wine with each course, followed by sherry trifle, cheese, sausages and various breads. The others all seemed to eat and drink a lot and thoroughly enjoy their food. Silently Lily ate, conscious all the time that this was to be her future way of life, and she wondered if she would be able to cope.

The coloured girl served them throughout the meal. She had a sad face, with dark, soulful eyes and long black lashes. Her black hair was shiny and coiled into plaits around her head, and her smooth, coffee-coloured skin was set off by the neat pink cotton dress with a white lace collar. She was certainly beautiful, Lily thought.

Once the table was cleared, it was folded away to give much more room in the saloon. Kasie proudly showed off his record player and all the modern records he had collected. Lily looked around this neat fitted place which was to be her home in silent wonder, observing the golden shine of the wood panels, the neat curtains at the portholes, and the numerous places for books. Kasie's possessions were all around, including a big photograph of Lily when she was younger, just after Avril was born, placed next to another photograph of his family group, including Oma and Opa, taken at the old island home in Heeg. As she examined them, Kasie came up and stood beside her. 'Well, Lily, does my *Lovely Lady* meet with your approval?'

'Yes, it is very nice,' she admitted looking up at the wall. There in its place of honour, was the little old banjo.

'Remember this?' said Kasie, taking it down very gently.

'That has been to your home in England, Lily,' said Neil.

'Twice,' Kasie corrected him. 'It went with me all through the war.'

That was the first reference anyone had made to the fact that Lily had been around a long time.

The little coloured girl brought in a tray of chocolates and a bottle of sweet liqueur, then left hurriedly looking as if she was about to cry. As she passed Kasie, he cajoled her with sweet words in her own tongue and she raised a wan smile.

Neil spoke hastily in Dutch to Kasie and Lily knew that he was talking about Lala, the coloured girl.

Kasie replied in Dutch and seemed to be warning him not to say too much, Lily thought. She looked suspiciously at Kasie, who passed her a drink, and Jante broke in with her meagre English, offering Lily a sweet. 'The trouble with us,' she said haltingly, 'we eat and drink too much that we lose our figures.'

Apparently this was something they all agreed upon as their laughter was long and infectious. Kasie slowly put a gentle arm about Lily's waist and said, 'Not my lovely lady, she doesn't.'

The ice was broken at last. Lily forgot Lala and began to enjoy herself.

Neil held her hand and spoke sincerely to her while Kasie sat looking at them, strumming softly on the old banjo.

'Lily, it is my great pleasure to meet you once more,' said Neil, 'and also to be best man at your wedding. I am happy, for now Poppa needs you more than ever. I know you have always been his woman and that Avril whom I loved was my sister. It was indeed a blow to me to discover that, but now there is no reason why we cannot all meet and be as one family, Lily.'

Lily's dark-blue eyes looked sombre. 'It's not all that easy,' she said, gazing into Neil's cool grey eyes.

'I see very few problems,' Neil said with a smile. 'You are both free and the family will be so happy to accept you. But if you want to be married quietly, your secret is safe with Jante and me.'

'Thanks, darling,' Lily said gratefully, giving him a little kiss on his cheek.

'I always admired you,' returned Neil, 'I wish we had known about each other sooner. But that you are Poppa's woman, we have now all acknowledged and are happy to support you either way.'

With a grin on his face, Kasie still strummed on his old banjo singing in his sweet voice that was no longer so tuneful but still had the graceful charm of his youth. 'I whistled and sang till the green grass rang, And I won the heart of my lady.'

After much more liqueur had been consumed, they became a little drunk. Neil and Kasie began to sing very noisy sea shanties until Jante, who did not drink alcohol, said rather primly: 'Now coom. Time to go, anough is anough.'

'I think we stay aboard tonight, Lily,' said Kasie.

'No, certainly not! I will drive you home,' insisted Jante. 'My car is down at the harbour.' With Jante, respectability came first. 'You have plenty of time for all that, Poppa,' she said primly. 'I will take you back to your hotel.'

Neil lay almost unconscious in the back seat of the car, his head on Lily's shoulder. Kasie sat in front with Jante who nagged him continuously in Dutch so that not one word could Lily comprehend.

Once back in the hotel, Kasie continued to drink. He was in a sort of maudlin mood, and soon well into his bottle of Bols gin. Lily got ready for bed feeling quite relieved to get off that ship which had rolled about too much, and away from the hostile looks of that lovely young Indian girl, but she was determined not to argue with Kasie tonight about her.

'Lily,' he said, lolling in the armchair with glass and bottle. 'You got on so well with Neil, which pleases me. We could have had a son together if you had not gone off and left me the first time you came to Holland.'

'Oh, don't start, Kasie,' begged Lily, getting into bed. 'Stop drinking and get some sleep.'

'Don't try to shut me up, you know it's true,' he argued. 'We could have had so many sons and daughters, but because of you I destroyed my powers of reproduction.' He slurred on that last long word.

'Not me, Kasie!' snapped back Lily. 'It was you who could not keep out of those stinking brothels. That's why.'

Kasie got to his feet and staggered about the room waving the bottle. 'I dispute that,' he slurred drunkenly as he came towards her. He stopped for a moment and then fell flat on his face and lay still. The bottle of gin rolled away from his hand, spilling gin everywhere.

She got out of bed, and turned him on his back. 'You got to knock off all this bleeding booze, mate,' she muttered, putting a cushion under his head, 'that is, if you want to marry me.' Then she went back to bed, leaving all the lights on.

A long time later, Kasie crept into bed with her. He was cold and miserable. 'Put your arms about me, Lily,' he said. 'I'm too drunk to make love to you, but hold me close. I dread to wake and find you have left me once more.'

'Oh, you silly old fool,' said Lily, wrapping herself around him. 'Now, get to sleep, or you'll be fit for nothing in the morning.'

Kasie awoke with a terrific hang-over in the morning, and lay late in bed while Lily went down to the foyer to collect the mail. She seldom did this, because the busy hotel disturbed her, with its constant flow of people coming in and out with their avid chatter, not one word of which was she able to understand. The other guests gave her wide grins of greeting but she did not respond, she just went glumly about her own business.

Generally, the hotel was very pleasant. There were huge bowls of coloured tulips everywhere, and the whole place was spick and span, with shining brass and sparkling china. But it was just not her scene. Lily had never felt so alone as in that big commercial hotel in the centre of Amsterdam. Outside, the city street thronged with faces but there was not one familiar one amongst them. The beautiful buildings, the slow-moving canals and even all those fascinating little restaurants had all lost their appeal. To Lily, a fish-and-chip shop, a jellied eel stall and the cries of the Cockney traders would have made her feel at home. When she returned to the room, she told Kasie what she thought. 'Even their rotten breakfast gets on my nerves,' she said. 'Why can't they eat eggs and bacon like civilised people?'

Kasie was still in bed. He grinned as he sorted out his letters. 'All you have to do, *leiblin*, is order an English breakfast,' he told her.

'Oh, they never understand me,' she complained.

'Everyone in the hotel speaks English, Lily. What are you making such a fuss about?'

Then suddenly he waved the letter he was reading. 'Hurrah! Your troubles are over Lily, my lovely, you'll soon be leaving this place you detest so much.'

She stared at him suspiciously.

'Look!' he cried. 'At last our permit to marry has arrived. Our papers are in order and we can get wed tomorrow in the town hall at twelve thirty.' He jumped out of bed and waltzed her around the room.

Lily hung her head dolefully.

'What's wrong, *leiblin*? Don't you want to marry me?'

'Oh, yes, I do, Kasie, but the thought of living all my life in this dull country drives me crazy.'

He sat down and took her on his lap. 'Now, Lily, no tantrums at this last minute. I have worked very hard to get your papers cleared so that we could be wed. I had to stay here for a while but we can now sail away to any place on earth.'

'That's what I mean,' Lily cried impatiently, 'we will have no settled home.'

'Why not? If you find a spot where we can both live happily, I will go ashore, but first we sail in my *Lovely Lady* on that long honeymoon that I have promised myself.'

'What about that girl on board?' she said sullenly.

'Who, Lala? She is all right,' he said. 'She's a great sailor and a good cook, you'll soon get used to her.'

'I won't!' declared Lily. 'Because I won't go while she's there.'

Kasie got up abruptly, almost pushing her onto the floor. 'So, that's what's wrong with you!'

'What is there between you?' she cried. 'Even I could see she was in love with you.'

His eyes blazed now with temper. 'Lily,' he said firmly. 'She is the younger sister of my friend Easi. I am responsible for bringing her from her home because she wished to sail with me. There is nothing between us. She is very young and, as far as I know, still a virgin. Yes, she loves me, but I have been good to her and watched her grow to womanhood. What sort of a friend do you take me for?'

'I don't believe you,' cried Lily. 'Why was she crying? And why does she hate me? I could just feel her hatred.'

'Lily, until you decided to come, I had no intention of being married. I am as she had always known me—a lonely bachelor—and she has been very good to me and very useful. I also brought her aunt and uncle over with me and they are staying with a family in Amsterdam, but Lala wanted to stay with me, and I say she can stay with us.'

'Well, that's that!' declared Lily. 'It's her or me. You have given me an answer.'

His lips tightened, and he crashed his fist violently down on the table. 'You try the patience of a saint,' he cursed her. 'At this last minute you find a reason to leave me. I must be a bloody fool to waste my time and money on you.'

'Oh, you bloody devil, I don't want your favours,' she cried, endeavouring to pull off the ring he had given her.

But Kasie stepped forward briskly and caught her hands. 'Oh, Lily, for Christ's sake, let us see reason. Don't destroy this love we have built up. We are not children, so why must we squabble?'

White-faced and a little afraid, she stared at him for a moment, but then collapsed, weeping, on his shoulder. 'I can't help it,' she wailed. 'I'm so jealous of her, I cannot share you, Kasie, I'm too independent.'

'Who is asking you to share? Lala is not yet sixteen and in this strange country I am responsible for her. But I promise I will do my best to make arrangements for her to stay with Neil and Jante, as a nursemaid for his children. We have already discussed it.'

'I'm sorry, Kasie,' she wept. 'I want us to be married, I can't live without you.'

'Or with me,' he added dryly. 'Now, dry your tears and go to the beauty parlour because tomorrow is your wedding day. I have to go out and I won't be back tonight. But I will send Janta in the morning to help you get ready and bring you to the town hall.'

'Oh, don't leave me alone, Kasie,' Lily snivelled.

'I have to take care of several things,' Kasie said firmly, 'and one is a crew. If you will not sail with Lala, I shall need at least two others to help me sail the ship because she is a very heavy craft. And you will not be much use to me, except in bed.' He laughed and kissed her. 'Don't let me down, Lily, will you?' He picked up his hat and went on his way.

After he had gone, Lily stared at the door for a long time. Then she got up and started to pack her bags. It would be easy to run and she felt he had given her the chance to do just that, it was Kasie's way, but who else in all the wide world wanted or needed her?

He did.

'No, Kasie,' she murmured, 'you are not getting rid of me as easy as that.' Her attitude to Lala had hurt his feelings, she could tell, but that was something in him she would never understand—his pride and his generous acceptance of the love of this young girl.

Lily spent the rest of the day in the hotel beauty parlour. She got her hair fixed after having a facial and a manicure. This expensive beauty parlour amused her, filled with rich women, well past middle-age. Some had thick and heavy features and all wore lots of jewellery. Some were even having their toes manicured as if they had nothing else to do all day but sit and look at themselves in the mirror and watch themselves grow old.

'Oh, dear,' sighed Lily, 'will my life be like that?' It did not bear thinking about. When her sex life was over, would Kasie still be the same? Life was never dull with him around, that she must confess, yet she was still full of misgivings about giving up her freedom. She thought of Avril and little JonJon and wondered if Avril had got her letter. Then she returned to her room and took some aspirins and went to bed.

All through that partially sleepless night, whenever she dropped off for a few minutes the face of the gipsy Maria was there waving the paper roses in front of her. 'Oh, don't put a curse on me, Maria,' Lily begged. 'I know I've been bad but let me be happy with Kasie.'

In the morning Jante was there very plump and jovial. She sorted through the wardrobe passing comments of admiration on Lily's smart clothes.

'Did you see Kasie?' asked Lily.

'Oh, yes, he is at my house with Neil and Fritz, his nephew, a beeg party eet vas.'

'A stag party?' asked Lily, and thinking dolefully that once more Kasie had been full of booze while she lay crying her eyes out.

Jante chose a nice grey ensemble for Lily to wear—a smart plain dress with a frilly jacket. While Lily dressed, two corsages of flowers were delivered: freesias for Lily and carnations for Jante.

'Poppa is a fine man,' said Jante. 'A goot thinking man.' She pinned the flowers to Lily's jacket, and they went down in the lift. Outside the hotel, Jante hailed a cab to take them to the town hall.

Kasie was waiting at the top of the steps with his tall son Neil beside him. He looked so spick and span in a navy blue suit and a light felt hat. Nervously Lily climbed those steps, looking up at Kasie who had that same whimsical smile hovering on his lips as he watched her. When she reached the top, his arms went around her, and she felt safe and secure once more.

It was a short solemn ceremony conducted in Dutch and English, and they went to a restaurant afterwards with Neil and Jante for lunch. Then they all parted with fond farewells and Lily and Kasie went back to the hotel to get their luggage and check out.

They soon began to laugh in their old carefree way as they gathered their bags together.

'Well, we did it at last, Lily,' said Kasie with a deep chuckle. 'I suppose I should have carried you over the threshold, but honest to goodness I'm not the man I was. I think you have made a very bad bargain, Mrs De Fries.'

Lily started to laugh heartily. Kasie emptied the remains from his bottle of Bols into two glasses and handed her one. 'Well, Lily, here's to us.'

'Till death do us part,' cried Lily, still giggling.

CHAPTER FIFTEEN

The Long Honeymoon

When Lily began that long honeymoon with her new husband, Kasie, it was a lovely April day with sunshine and light showers, and a few patches of cloud in the bright blue sky. Everywhere in the streets of Amsterdam there were hosts of spring flowers in pots on every house balcony, and golden daffodils and a myriad of coloured tulips in every window box of the tall block of flats. To Lily, this town, which she had always disliked so much, suddenly seemed to have taken on a new beauty.

As they waited outside the hotel for the cab to come and take them to the harbour, Lily said, 'How nice all these flowers are. I never noticed them before.'

'Oh, they were always there, Lily, especially in the spring,' said Kasie with a gentle smile. 'As we pass the flower market we'll collect some to take aboard the *Lovely Lady*.'

Lily felt a nervous tremor go through her at the mention of what was to be her new home, but bravely she resisted the feeling. Here she was burning her boats to go and live on Kasie's boat, but now it did not seem to matter quite as much as it had before.

Kasie moved in a sprightly manner towards the cab as it slowed down, and heaved the suitcases up with an easy grace. She thought how young he was in his movements and even though his hair had faded, he was still good looking, and he was in such a happy mood. From now on, she decided, she would try very hard not to quarrel with him as they had done over the last twenty-odd years. And having made this resolution, she sat holding his hand in the cab.

'The *Lovely Lady* is out in the bay,' said Kasie. 'I've had her shifted from the dock ready to set sail when we want to. I have been very lucky and managed to get a crew—a man and his teenage son. They had been on a cargo vessel but got stranded in Hamburg, and they were working their way down the river to get back home. They're Scottish, so you will find no difficulty in getting along with them.'

'I wish we were on our own, Kasie,' Lily said sadly.

'So do I, *leiblin*, but this way we will have more time together. There will be plenty of room because the crew have their own quarters and will not bother us. Also, when we take trips ashore, as I intend to show you the wonders of this world, we will not have to worry about the *Lovely Lady* because they will take care of her.'

As he had promised, Kasie stopped the cab at the big flower market. He got out and in a few minutes returned with a huge bunch of daffodils, tulips and sweet-smelling freesias.

'To my lovely lady to take aboard the other lovely lady,' he announced brightly.

Lily pressed her nose among the blooms to hide the tears of emotion in her eyes.

When they reached the harbour, a small motor boat was there to take them out into the bay to where the *Lovely Lady* was anchored. She was a smart white ship with a red-and-white painted funnel bobbing up and down on the briny. This was Lily's new home.

A middle-aged man with a small pointed beard and a strange accent let down a ladder for them. Kasie held it steady saying, 'Now, Lily my lovely, show them what you can do now you are a skipper's wife.'

Her legs felt like jelly but, holding her breath, she grabbed the ladder and painfully climbed aboard, her high heels slipping on every rung. As soon as she was near the top, another pair of strong hands grabbed hold of her and helped her on to the deck.

Kasie dismissed the boatman after he had handed the luggage aboard and Lily stood looking around her a little bewildered. A

tall fair-haired lad put out a capable hand to steady her; already
the sight of the vast expanse of water had upset her nerves.

'Take off your high-heeled shoes, madam,' the young lad
said, 'and then you won't slip on the deck. Now I'll take you
below.' He took the flowers and shoes from her, and then
escorted her down the companionway into a cosy cabin. Lily sat
down with a deep sigh of relief. She felt as if she had just
conquered Mount Everest.

'I'll put the flowers in water, madam,' said the lad, and
promptly disappeared.

Lily could hear Kasie talking up on deck. It was rather
comforting on board, she thought, and a peaceful air pervaded
the cabin. There was a table with a pretty white lace cloth on it,
and on the sideboard were bone china tea cups and plates. There
was also a tea-light with a slim teapot on it. This tea-light was,
she knew, a type of spirit lamp which was used to keep the
beverages hot.

'Shall I pour you a cup of tea?' asked the young lad as he
returned with the flowers in two large vases.

'Yes, please,' said Lily. She glanced anxiously at the flower
vases, afraid that they might tip over with the movement of the
boat.

Noticing her anxiety, the lad pointed to the little brass rails he
placed the vases behind. 'They'll be all right there,' he said.

Lily tried to smile. This boy must know that she was a
landlubber, but he was certainly a polite, patient kind of person.
She was grateful to him for that.

'Thanks,' said Lily, taking the cup of tea from him. 'What do
I call you?'

'Just Jock, Mum, that's what they always called me out there.
And my Pa they call Tandy. We're from Glasgow. I understand
that you are from London.'

'That's right, Jock,' said Lily, gratefully sipping the tea.
'We'll get on fine, you and I.'

Soon Kasie arrived and immediately searched in the cupboard
for his bottle of Bols. 'So you've met the lad. Like him?'

'Oh, yes,' replied Lily, 'and he speaks my own language.'

'Yes, I was lucky to find them. They both also speak Dutch, German and a little French having been to sea nearly all their lives. Jock will help you with the chores and his father Tandy will assist me at the wheel and with the engines. All being well, we'll set sail in the morning.' He came over and sat beside her. 'Lily,' he said, putting his arms about her, 'I really believe that this is the happiest day of my whole life, my dream come true.'

She leaned her head on his shoulder, a feeling of tranquillity possessed her.

He kissed her neck. 'After dinner, Lily, we'll go straight to bed and no one will disturb us.'

Lily looked around at the shining brass fittings and the immaculate modern kitchen, or galley, as she should think of it now, and the cosy bedroom with its two deep bunks side by side. 'It's nice,' she said, 'just like a little house.'

'It's our little house, the one we have waited so long for,' replied Kasie. 'Jock will serve the food. I have sent ashore to the restaurant tonight for our dinner, but, darling, it will be your duty to cook for me in the future, and I know you will like that.'

'I thought you could not stand my cooking?' said Lily.

'Well, you will learn to please me, won't you?' replied Kasie, grinning, 'because I will be with you now for ever and ever.' He swept her into his arms. 'Let's go to bed now and to hell with dinner,' he said with a fiery gleam in his eyes.

Lily laughed and pushed him away. 'Now, Kasie, behave like a respectable married man and wait until after dinner.'

But Kasie had slid the door shut. 'You know that's not going to be possible,' he said, coming towards her.

Lily felt the mounting desire within her and bent her body to his. 'Oh, Kasie,' she said, as he picked her up and deposited her on the soft downy bunk. 'I can't, and never could, say no to you.'

Kasie slipped down her blouse and buried his head in her scented bosom. 'Lily my lovely,' he murmured, 'don't ever say no to me, because now we are one we really belong.'

The next day when they set sail, the sea was calm and the sky cloudless. 'From now on,' said Kasie, 'it's old slacks and flat deck shoes for you, Lily. It will be very windy up on deck, so you should wear a warm jersey and put something on your head.'

Lily laughed out loud in her usual merry way. 'Dear God, Kasie, have I joined the bloody navy?'

Kasie was in the wheelhouse with maps spread out before him. His yachting cap was perched on the back of his head, and his brown eyes were bright and alert. 'Come, I'll show you the voyage I have planned for us. We will sail into the sunshine, so first we head for Gibraltar then go through the straits in the Mediterranean Sea. After that, you can choose Malta or Majorca, any island you please.'

'It sounds great,' said Lily, 'but everything's so far away. How will you know you are going in the right direction?'

He kissed her indulgently. 'Leave those sorts of worries to me, Lily,' he said. 'It might get a bit choppy once we are in the Bay of Biscay, so if you feel sick at all go and lie down. There are some tablets in the cabinet beside the bunk.'

'Oh, I won't be sick,' declared Lily with great confidence. 'I've been on boats before.' She was still lounging about in her red dressing-gown.

'Now, go and dress yourself, there's a good girl, or you'll catch cold. I'll be down later when Jock takes the wheel.'

Reluctantly Lily went below and put on the warm clothing that Kasie had instructed her to wear. Then she began to wonder what on earth there would be to do all the long day. Everything was so spick and span, and there would be no hoovering or dusting for her to do. She lay down, on the long settee and read a magazine but her mind began to wander a bit and returned to thoughts of Avril and little JonJon.

Avril had still not answered Lily's letter, which she had sent from the Amsterdam hotel, and now here she was going away into unknown places without having made contact. She choked back her tears. They might never meet again. What had she done? She poured some coffee from the pot which was always kept hot on the small spirit-lamp. They had met the heavier seas and the ship was now swaying about quite violently at times. At one point, Kasie sounded the siren in greeting to a passing ship, and Lily almost jumped out of her skin. After drinking the coffee, she began to retch. Her stomach seemed to turn over and she staggered to the lavatory, then returned to lie down on the bed with a bowl and some towels beside her. There she rolled around in agony, vomiting and retching wretchedly. Never before had she felt so bad. Every time the ship rolled over, it threw her sideways, knocking her head on the wall. She felt totally helpless.

Soon Kasie came down to the cabin. He bathed her head and gave her a stiff glass of brandy to drink. 'Now, *leiblin*,' he said gently, 'do not panic, it will pass off. We'll soon be in calm waters.'

'Oh, Kasie,' she wept. 'I want to go home, I want to die. I knew I could not live on the sea, I've *always* known it.'

'Nonsense,' he said firmly, patting her forehead with a pad soaked with cologne. He emptied the bowl and brought her some clean towels, remaining all the time, calm, sweet and gentle, 'You'll be all right by the morning once we get round the coast of Spain.'

'Oh,' howled Lily. 'I want to go home. I want my little JonJon and my Avril.'

Kasie gave a wry grin. 'Try to sleep, Lily. It will soon pass.'

Soon she was fast asleep, and she woke in the early morning to feel the warm sunshine on her face. The ship was still, calmly anchored in a peaceful bay. She rose, took a shower and dressed in her slacks and woolly. Then slowly she went out into the clean, sweet, salty air.

Kasie was in the wheelhouse still drinking his bottle of Bols. He looked tired and there were whiskers about his chin but he greeted her with his lovely smile. 'Well, well, here comes my lady. And how are we this morning?'

Lily looked very wan. 'Don't ask me, Kasie, don't remind me, I've never felt so ill.'

He sat on the steering-hatch beside her. 'I'm sorry, my *leiblin*, I did push it a little, I wanted to get out of the heavy weather before morning. Look out there—you can see Oporto, on the coast of Portugal. We'll sail into the harbour when the tide is right, go ashore and celebrate.'

Lily looked out at the high mountains that seemed to ring the coast and felt a little lonely. It was yet another strange land. Without Kasie it would have had no appeal for her at all, her heart was really still with Avril and JonJon in smoky London town.

At six o'clock that evening, a jubilant Kasie sailed into harbour. He had not slept for two days and was a little drunk, but he was also very excited. He insisted that Lily dress up and come ashore with him into the brightly lit town where they dined on a meal of lobster and salads and drank lots of wine. As they danced very close to one another, Lily commented on how quickly she had recovered from last night's bout of seasickness.

He smiled and hugged her close. 'Now you will be fine, Lily,' he said.

They didn't stay long in any port. They gave themselves enough time to get a quick look around the markets and to buy some extra food and, once Jock and Tandy came back on board, they would set sail again. Now the weather was fine and they lay up on deck in shorts and sun shirts, enjoying the hot sun which streamed down on them.

With Tandy at the wheel and Jock doing the chores, Lily and Kasie just lazed about all day. 'This is the life,' said Kasie. 'What do you think of it now?'

Lily shielded her eyes from the hot sun and smiled. 'It's very nice, Kasie,' she said, but her answer lacked enthusiasm.

He put an arm around her and gave a sort of sigh. 'I hope you're not going to disappoint me, Lily. I have hoped so much that you would adapt to this kind of life.'

'Oh, don't be silly,' she said dismissively. 'We are married now, Kasie, I go where you go. But I can't help it if I prefer my feet to be on solid ground.'

'No, I suppose not,' he replied. 'But I so much want us to be happy together, darling, I'll try not to expect too much.'

As the day wore on, Lily settled down and prepared a meal of the special Spanish salad which Kasie had liked so much, with lots of oil and vinegar in it. He was fastidious about his food and she was often a little nervous about being able to please him. But she was generally happy and they grew very close on this part of the voyage as they sailed around Portugal to the Straits of Gibraltar. They often sat up on deck talking of old times.

'You were a little devil,' he said. 'I will never forget that fish you slapped me with, and all over my service pants. I had to have them dry-cleaned.'

'Oh yes, that haddock,' giggled Lily. 'Well, it was your fault, you should not have complained.'

'But, *leiblin*, it not only looked repulsive, it smelled disgusting, too.'

Thus they spent their days, reminiscing about this and that of the past. In the evenings they lay on the deck looking up at the brightly lit sky. Kasie pointed out the Milky Way with its millions of tiny bright stars, and Lily marvelled at the sky which was like a dark-blue velvet. Kasie would bring his portable record player up on deck and they would sit listening to all the old records which brought back such sweet memories of their youth. Lily's body took on a lovely deep tan. They both wore very little now and often on the hot afternoons they would go back down in the cabin to make love.

When they reached Gibraltar they stayed there a week, going ashore ever day and sightseeing. Lily liked Gibraltar because everyone seemed to speak English. She bought coloured postcards to send home, little souvenirs and some little paintings to hang in the cabin. She sent the cards to Avril and Jo, telling them that she would send an address for them to write to as soon as possible. At the moment, she wrote, she was on a cruise.

'Why not leave well alone,' Kasie said, 'and let Avril find her own direction?'

'No, I cannot desert her completely. Sorry, Kasie, I could never do that.'

'Please yourself,' said Kasie abruptly, 'but in the meantime let us continue our honeymoon. We'll go up to the Rock to see the view and the monkeys. You might prefer one of them to me,' he jested.

'Oh, Kasie,' Lily began to laugh. 'I wish you would behave yourself!'

They had a great time in Gibraltar, going to lots of late night dinners and cabarets. They got drunk most nights and always fell into bed exhausted. The wine was cheap and the entertainment fabulous.

'It was nice there,' said Lily wistfully, on the day they sailed away from Gibraltar.

Kasie put his arms around her. 'That's it, my lovely, enjoy it while you can. This might be the journey of a lifetime.'

In this happy and carefree existence, Lily had begun to relax though her fear of the sea never really left her. On stormy nights, when a summer storm sprang up, she cuddled close to Kasie's warm back listening to the howling wind and the beat of the waves on the bows. When they anchored late one night off Malaga, on the coast of Spain, every roll of thunder and every flash of lightning made her jerk convulsively.

Kasie held her tight. 'Oh, Lily my lovely, why are you so afraid of these natural elements?'

'I don't know,' she said, her teeth chattering. 'It could be the aftermath of the blitz, I never did like storms after that, but being out here in this wide ocean really terrifies me.'

'Tomorrow we will go in to dock,' said Kasie. 'I need to refuel and make some telephone calls to Neil. Is there anything special you want to do, Lily?'

'Yes,' she said a little tearfully. 'I want to post my letters to Avril and Jo, though mind you, I don't know why I bother, I never get any answers.'

'Oh, how stupid of me,' said Kasie, 'I should have explained that if you address your letters *post restante* for our next port of call, your letters will be there waiting for you.'

'Oh, so that's why I never got an answer from Avril,' said Lily. 'I gave her the address of the hotel in Amsterdam.'

'It's all right, tomorrow I'll sort out your mail and it will catch up with us. I'm truly sorry, darling.'

Lily stared at him a little suspiciously. Was he truly sorry? Or had he deliberately allowed her to think she could not be found? She was not sure.

'If you don't want to go ashore,' he said, 'Jock will keep you company. I'll be gone most of the day. I'm taking Tandy with me because he has to help me get a new spare part for the engine.'

Lily did not mind. She had already got out her pen and pad and was busy writing a long letter to Avril and a very newsy one to Jo Macy.

Kasie addressed the envelopes for her and took them with him to post ashore.

Lily still felt strangely content and lazed about on deck chatting to young Jock who, as usual, was busy with his mop and bucket.

'You don't know how relieved I am to learn that I can get my letters,' she told him. 'I felt so isolated.'

'It's all right, ma'am. I correspond with a girl in East Berlin and I still hear from her although it takes a long time for her letters to reach me.'

'Is it serious, Jock?' asked Lily.

'Could be, but she's behind the Berlin wall and it's difficult for us to meet. That's how Pop and I got stranded in Berlin and missed our ship in Hamburg.'

'That's a pity,' said Lily. 'Why do they do these things?'

'Don't ask me, ma'am,' said Jock, 'it's all to do with the last war.'

'Oh, well,' said Lily, lying down in the sun. 'We can all bloody well forget about that. When you go ashore on Sunday, Jock, will you see if you can get me the *News of the World*? I miss the old Sunday papers.'

'I will, ma'am, certainly. I get the English magazines in most places, so I'll probably be able to get a newspaper.'

From that day on, whenever Jock went ashore he brought back copies of the *News of the World* for Lily. Sometimes they were as much as a week old, but she did not mind, it kept her in touch with London and she was a much happier woman.

Jock was a very nice boy and seemed something of a loner. He told her that he had been at sea with his father since he was thirteen, after the death of his mother. He was a sturdy-looking lad. It seemed such a pity to Lily that he was being lugged around the world by his sea-going father. Tandy was a typical ship's engineer and had lived aboard so many ships since the war. Like Kasie, he was a heavy drinker, but he was always completely sober when on duty. His Glaswegian accent was so heavy that Lily often couldn't understand a word he said.

That Kasie and Tandy should return that night very drunk, was a foregone conclusion. She heard them staggering up the gang-plank singing: 'I belong to Glesga,' in their slurred, drunken voices. Quietly Jock came from his quarters to help haul them aboard and Lily got up and made some fresh coffee.

Kasie was so happy having had a complete day of freedom. He had lost his cap, but he clutched a parcel which he now handed to her. 'For you, my lovely,' he drawled.

Lily took off his shoes and offered him coffee but Kasie just got up and wandered off to bed.

Lily unwrapped the parcel. Inside there was a lovely silk Spanish shawl—white with scarlet embroidery and long fringes. She had so often admired the Spanish girls in their best Sunday shawls. They were so beautiful with their dark hair and flowers tucked in the smooth shiny roll of black hair. She looked at Kasie who now lay on his back snoring with his mouth open and had a sudden pang of regret that she had not gone ashore with him. Deep in her heart she knew she could never be sure of him, not as far as beautiful women were concerned. She folded the shawl and put it in the drawer. She had just started to hang up Kasie's clothes when she noticed a wad of letters sticking out of the jacket pocket. She removed them and looked through. They were mostly business letters for him but there was one addressed to her, as Mrs Brown. There was only one person who knew her as such: Avril. The envelope as covered with various postmarks so it had obviously travelled around quite a bit. With trembling hands she tore the envelope open, muttering, 'Darling, darling!' Her knees felt weak so she sat down to read the letter.

Dear Mother,

I was not surprised to know that you had married that man. He has been around long enough, but at least you could have been a little more straightforward with me about it instead of going off and leaving us just like that. Little JonJon cried for you for days. You will be pleased to hear that Jonny has got a yard of his own now and we are living fairly comfortably. I have put my name down for a council house. I am expecting another baby. Let me know when you will be coming back or are you going to live abroad? If so, I wish you well and don't worry about me, Jonny takes good care of us. A kiss from little JonJon, he will be a year old soon. I am enclosing a letter that came for you from Jo Macy.

Keep in touch, love Avril.

The tears fell from Lily's eyes down onto the letter. 'Oh, Avril, thank God you are coping so well, but I really miss you, darling.'

Then she read the battered-looking airmail letter from America which was dated three months back. It was from Jo and Rene in New York, a chatty, happy letter, describing the noisy city of New York and their hotel in Broadway which, Jo said, was fifty storeys high. 'We are travelling on to Los Angeles so I am becoming very interested in this new health and beauty culture which seems to be making lots of lolly.' Just like Jo, thought Lily, all business. She would never stand still. But Lily felt so happy and not quite so far from home.

She covered Kasie up and kissed him. 'I hope you appreciate what I have given up for you,' she whispered. Then she climbed into bed and put the letters under her pillow.

In the morning all hell broke loose with Kasie saying that his head felt like a pumpkin, and grousing and complaining about everything and everyone, and Jock and Tandy having a shouting match.

Lily lay up on deck in the hot sunshine and let them all get on with it. She was feeling happier than she had been since she had left England.

That afternoon, Kasie set sail again, insisting that he had enough of Spain and complained that they were all thieves and lechers. He headed for the Greek Islands. So, soon they were off once more slowly cruising around the coast. The weather was good and peace was restored once more.

Jock confided in Lily that he hated strong drink because of his heavy-drinking father. Even the smell of it irritated him, he said.

'I think you're a grand lad,' said Lily. 'I'd like to have had a son like you.'

'Did not you and the Captain ever have a family?' enquired Jock.

'We only just got married,' laughed Lily, 'but I have a daughter from a previous marriage, and a fine grandson. I miss them very much.'

Jock's blue eyes looked sad as he pushed a lock of his fair hair off his forehead. 'I have warned Tandy to stay sober, or else,' he said a little impatiently.

'I wish I could say the same to my husband,' replied Lily, 'but I would be wasting my breath.'

They remained very good friends, this virile young man and Lily. Kasie often eyed the young man with suspicion, and ordered him back to his own quarters, but in spite of these little hazards, the voyage progressed peacefully.

They had a few days ashore in Malta, where it was very hot, and Kasie seemed tired. Of late he had slowed down and lost a lot of weight but the Bols bottle was always on hand and he continually puffed at his little black cigars after dinner.

'You seem a bit under the weather, Kasie,' Lily said one day. 'Are you all right?' she asked. That night they had stayed in a hotel, and Kasie had slumped wearily off to sleep with just a goodnight kiss.

Lily had had a great day out shopping and sightseeing. The golden sands, the blue sky, and the lively town had pleased her. It was British, with British goods in the shops and English-speaking locals.

'I'll be all right when we get back on board, Lily,' said Kasie.

'I can't stand these foreign hotels and the hot climate I have found a little stifling.'

Lily had never seen Kasie under par before; he had always been so healthy and full of life.

But once back on board, Kasie seemed to get back to his old merry self. Wearing only a pair of white shorts, he dived off the deck to inspect under the ship. Lily held her breath, afraid he would not come up again. Soon, however, he was climbing back on board and shaking himself like a wet dog.

'Oh, Kasie!' Lily exclaimed, 'Why do you do that?'

'I like to take a look at the old girl's bottom occasionally,' he jested.

Lily was still afraid of water, and no power on earth would get her into the sea.

'You really should learn to swim,' Kasie told her.

'Not me,' said Lily emphatically. 'If I fall in, I'll drown, but who cares?'

'We'll stay at sea now till we get to the Aegan,' said Kasie, 'and there is a business acquaintance I have promised to visit in Crete. We'll stay there, drift around the islands for the rest of the year and then go back home in the spring. What do you think of that, Lily?'

But Lily was engrossed in an out-of-date copy of the *News of the World*, reading all the lurid details of various court cases, and about a huge, loud-mouthed American boxer called Cassius Clay who had challenged Freddie Mills. Reading this brought her closer to her East End home of many of London's sportsmen.

'Are you listening, Lily?' demanded Kasie a little crossly.

'Oh, yes, I heard,' Lily replied casually.

'Well, for Christ's sake, take some interest, will you? How you can wallow continuously in those bloody filthy newspapers, I'll never know.'

'It's not filthy,' Lily defended her only link with home. 'And I don't really care where I go, it's all beginning to look the same to me.'

'Well, that's nice,' Kasie declared, getting up and storming

out. 'Well, we're going to Crete, I've got business for Neil to do
and surely you can get *some* pleasure from this trip. I just don't
understand you.'

When he had gone, Lily felt a bit guilty. He was not his usual
old self at all. Although he would never admit it, she thought he
was also a little lonely for his home and family. But for her a
long time at sea would mean no letters and a long time to wait
until she heard from Avril again. She sighed. Oh well, better
not quarrel with Kasie. She decided to go up on deck and make
peace.

She stood beside him at the wheel fondling the back of his
neck the way he liked her to, and soon they were kissing as
passionately as they always did. She stood close to him, her
breasts sticking out firm and hard through her translucent silk
shirt. Kasie blew the whistle for Jock to come and take the
wheel, and they stood for a while on deck looking out at the
blue sea and the lines of white foam as the waves struck the
bows of the ship. With his arm about her waist, they watched
the long shaft of sunlight that came down through the clouds
from the setting sun. The sky glowed orange and gold and the
sunbeams danced on the water. 'That sight always reminds me
somehow of a ladder to Heaven, that long shaft of sunlight from
the sea to the sky,' Kasie said.

This was an unusually fatalistic thing for Kasie to say, but
Lily put her arms around her protectively. 'Come on, darling,
let's go down to the cabin. We'll climb on our bunks, I've no
intention of letting you climb up to Heaven yet.'

He laughed heartily. 'Oh, Lily, my lovely,' he cried. 'You are
my sunshine, my sun and moon, my Heaven.'

They sailed on through the Mediterranean into the long hot
sunlit days of the Aegean Sea, arriving at the island of Crete a
little eager for the sight of land. They sailed into harbour short
of food and fuel but very fit and very happy.

'Would you like to stay ashore for a week?' he asked Lily at
breakfast that morning.

'Yes, that will be nice. I'll get my hair done and do some
shopping.'

'Okay, I have some business calls to make, so pack a few things and when Jock gets back this evening, I'll book us in at an hotel in the town. We'll go sightseeing like real tourists,' he jested with that dry humour which was always there. 'You will be all right. Tandy will be on board and I won't be long. I'll be back at about six o'clock.'

Lily contentedly packed her bag with her make-up and an evening dress. It would be nice to dress up for dinner, she mused, she was fed up with wearing shorts and swimsuits.

Jock was ashore. She had asked him to buy her some English magazines and, of course, the *News of the World*. Happily she lazed around. For once, her sky seemed cloudless but she had an inner feeling that it was not right to be so happy.

CHAPTER SIXTEEN

Dark Clouds

In the harbour of Canea on the island of Crete, it had been a long hot day. Towards evening a cool breeze had sprung up and the sea got a little choppy. With a blue cardigan around her shoulders, Lily waited on deck for the return of Kasie. She was really looking forward to the promised week ashore.

Jock came back on board at five o'clock bringing with him a bundle of magazines and he handed her some old issues of the *News of the World*. 'Best I could do, Lily,' he said.

'Oh, thanks,' she cried. 'It's getting chilly, I'll go down and catch up with the news of England.'

She made herself comfortable on the settee and began to read eagerly. The first copy she read was three weeks old. She opened it and there, on the front page, was a big picture of a youth spreadeagled on the pavement outside a well-known London store. The caption read: 'Man shot dead by police today in a crowded London street as he ran from a bank hold-up'. Lily stared intently at the picture. Poor devil, she thought, so the coppers were using guns now. It must be getting like Chicago. She was about to turn the page when his name in the story caught her eye and she gave a frightened gasp. 'Oh no, it can't be!' But there it was: 'Jonny de Loos, a man known to the police, had threatened them with a firearm as he tried to make a getaway. The police were armed because they had been tipped off about the raid.'

'Oh my God! Jonny, you poor silly fool!' she burst out. 'Oh dear, what about Avril? I must go to her immediately.' She got up and feverishly put more things into her case. Finding her passport, she pushed it and some money into her handbag.

Kasie was whistling merrily and in a very good humour when he finally came back. Lily ran towards him with sobs tearing at her throat. Kasie clasped her in his arms. 'Dear God, Lily,' he exclaimed, 'whatever's the matter?'

She handed him the newspaper. Looking down at it, he said: 'Avril's husband? So that's it,' he said when she nodded.

'I must go to her,' Lily cried, 'at once.'

'Now, *leiblin,* calm down. Sit down. I will get us both a drink and then we'll sit down and assess the situation.'

'I mean to go, Kasie, whatever you say.'

Kasie barely touched his drink as he grimly read all the newspaper articles about Jonny's life and his role in the bank robbery. He was described as a gipsy boy who lived in the East End and who consorted with crooks and hoodlums. There were vivid descriptions of the defiant way Jonny had waved a gun about, not knowing that the police were armed. And, worst of all, the articles said, it had been a tragic waste of life because his gun had turned out to be a toy pistol belonging to his little son. He was further described as having been married to a London girl and the father of two children.

As Kasie finished reading the articles out loud to Lily, she sat sobbing her heart out.

'Lily,' he said gently, 'there's not a lot you can do now. The youth is dead and buried. It would be better to stay out of it.'

Lily wiped her eyes. 'No, Kasie,' she said, getting up, 'I'll ask Jock to take me ashore if you won't. Somehow I'll find my own way home.'

'Oh, Lily my lovely, don't leave me now,' Kasie pleaded.

'Kasie, I don't care what you say or do, I'm going to my daughter, she needs me.' She threw all her clothes into a suitcase, snapped it shut and got her coat.

Kasie sighed. 'All right, Lily,' he said. 'I'll sail for the mainland tonight and get you on a plane in the morning.'

She reached out and kissed him. 'I don't want to leave you, Kasie, I have been so happy with you these last few weeks.'

'Oh well,' he sighed. 'Why don't you send her some money

and sympathy,' he suggested in one last effort to make her stay, 'but do not go away now, my lovely, I need you.'

Lily stared defiantly at his white, drawn face. 'Why don't you come with me? She's your daughter, too, and she's in real trouble.'

His lips clamped down in a thin, angry line. 'Will you never understand that I have no allegiance to her? You never allowed me to be her father.'

'Well, you are, whatever you try to tell yourself, and I am her mother, she is my own flesh and blood. I also have two grandchildren, so don't try to stop me, will you, Kasie?'

He began to put on his oilskins. 'Oh well, I can't say any more about it. We're in for a stormy night by the sound of the wind but I will get you to the mainland and you can get a plane straight through to London Airport.'

'Thank you, Kasie,' she murmured.

'Don't thank me,' he replied in a hard tone, 'I'm doing this against my own will.'

'I'll come back,' she said. 'I promise faithfully I'll return.'

But he was already climbing up the companionway and did not reply.

It was indeed a stormy night and, feeling rather sick and dressed in all her clothes, Lily lay wrapped in a rug just waiting for the daylight. Each time she dozed a little, the angry hazel eyes of Maria came close to her.

Early in the morning Kasie came and kissed her. His face was all whiskery and tasted of the salty sea.

'We are in port, Lily,' he said. 'Make some coffee and we'll go ashore.'

She stared at him sorrowfully.

'It's all right,' he said with a rueful smile, 'but against my better judgement, I'm going with you.'

Lily threw her arms around him. 'Oh, Kasie, I'll always remember this sacrifice you are making for me.'

As he sipped the hot coffee, he said: 'I have discussed it with Tandy during the night. He is willing to sail the *Lovely Lady* back to Rotterdam where he and Jock will sign off because they are a little homesick for Scotland. The ship will be safe there with Neil who will take care of her. So once more we are off on our travels, and God knows why.'

They caught the night flight from Athens and landed at Heathrow Airport next morning. Feeling very weary, they booked into a hotel in Victoria and Kasie insisted that she must rest. 'Take two or three hours' sleep, and you'll feel much better for it.'

The hotel room had single beds but they held hands across the space between them as they slept, and Lily slept the deep sleep of pure exhaustion.

After breakfast the next morning, they took a cab to the East End. When they arrived at the block of flats, the locals looked curiously at this smartly dressed, middle-aged couple who stood waiting for the lift in the grim hallway with its broken windows and the walls covered with graffiti. Lily, tall and slim, was dressed in a grey, tailored dress, and a burgundy coloured hat with smart shoes, gloves and bag to match. Her auburn hair was pulled back in shining rolls and her skin was suntanned. She looked ten years younger than her age. Kasie was dressed in his best suit, and his mop of light hair was well groomed, but he had a very serious look on his face as he looked around at the poverty-stricken surroundings. 'What a place!' he muttered, shaking his head.

A small, dishevelled woman answered their knock on the door of Avril's flat. Her hair was tied up in a host of rollers and she wore a grubby apron.

'Is Avril there?' asked Lily. 'I'm her mother.'

'Hoy, Avril! It's yer Ma!' screeched the woman standing back respectfully to allow them to enter.

The flat stank of cats, and Yorkie, the little shaggy dog, snapped at their heels. Avril was sitting looking mournfully into the fire with the new child on her lap. On the old settee was a litter of baby things. Avril had grown fat again and her dun-coloured hair hung loose and greasy over her brow. With dull, lustreless eyes she looked at them as they stood in the doorway.

'What do you want?' she asked. 'It's a bit late now, Jonny's long dead and buried.'

Lily ran to her and knelt down on that mucky carpet. As she put her arms around her, Avril began to sob hysterically. Lily took the baby, put him in his cot, and then sat beside Avril trying to say the right things to comfort her. But the words were of little use.

Kasie still stood in the middle of the room looking about him in his lordly, disdainful manner. Seeing the expression on his face, Avril screwed up her mouth in temper. 'What's he want?' she snapped. 'I don't want him to pity me.'

'Now, darling, we have come a long way to help you,' Lily cajoled her.

'Well, you can go back,' said Avril. 'I'll get by.'

Then little JonJon, who had been playing in a neighbour's flat, came trotting in. He stared with puzzled blue eyes at Lily who swept him up in her arms with a kiss. Then all three huddled on that untidy settee, weeping and laughing at the same time.

While consoling Avril, Lily had completely forgotten Kasie, who stood staring forlornly at them. Then he said in a barely audible voice: 'I'll go back to the hotel, Lily. Ring if you need me.' Then he walked quietly out of the front door.

Lily was bouncing JonJon up and down on her knee and did not answer. She just gave an inclination of her head as the front door closed.

Once Kasie had gone, Avril calmed down. Lily put JonJon in his high chair and then petted the baby which by now was screaming.

'He wants his bottle,' said Avril, making an effort to rise.

Lily dashed out to the kitchen which she found in a terrible mess. There was crockery piled high in the sink and animal dirt on the floor. 'For Christ's sake, Avril,' she exclaimed, 'you had better get this place cleaned up, it's a shambles.'

'I don't care,' sniffed Avril. 'I don't care about anything now Jonny's gone.'

'Oh, don't be so bloody dramatic,' said Lily, taking off her smart hat and struggling out of her expensive dress. She got a grubby overall from behind the door and put it on. 'Oh, blimey,' she muttered, 'here we go again.'

She made the baby's bottle, opened a can of beans for JonJon and fed him with a spoon. She washed up and turfed all the animals out onto the balcony. Then she scrubbed the kitchen floor with disinfectant.

Still Avril did not move but just sat staring moodily into space.

On the mantelpiece was an array of pill bottles, some empty and some half-full. 'What's all this muck?' demanded Lily.

'They are tranquillisers. The doctor prescribed them for me, otherwise I think I would have gone mad.'

'Well, you get your bloody self together,' Lily said firmly. 'You've two children now to consider and you can't bring back the dead.'

Avril started to grizzle again. 'Oh, that's it,' she snivelled. 'I didn't expect much sympathy from you. In your eyes, Jonny was a bad man, so he deserved to be shot down like a dog.'

A guilty flush coloured Lily's cheeks. Avril had hit the right spot. 'Oh, now, come on, dear, you know that's not true, I lost two men in my life and had to get by.'

'And fell on your feet, didn't you? You got money and a bloody yacht,' sneered Avril. 'You carried on with that man and upset my own poor daddy and yet you get all the luck.'

Lily sat down beside her. 'Darling, don't quarrel with me. I'm here to stand by you.'

Wearily, Avril put her head on Lily's shoulder. 'Oh, Mother, I feel so tired, as if it's too much trouble to move.'

'Right,' said Lily, 'let's do something about it then.'

Little JonJon had dozed off in his high chair so Lily carried him into the bedroom for his afternoon nap. She then persuaded Avril to take a bath, and wash her hair. Afterwards, Avril sat brushing her hair dry, around the fire. Sitting there in her dressing-gown, she looked much more like her real self.

Lily made hot bowls of soup, and then they had tea and biscuits. Avril talked a little more rationally about her Jonny.

'We were happy, Mum. I didn't mind the ups and downs, for he made money and would always give it to me. He wanted us to move into the country to get away from all his mates because most of them were crooked. I believe that was why he got involved—it was a kind of last chance to get money to buy our own house.'

'You knew that I wasn't short of cash,' said Lily. 'Why did you write and say all was well with you?'

'Sheer bravado, I think,' said Avril. 'I was jealous of you.'

Lily stroked her cheek. 'No need to be, darling, no mother could love their daughter as much as I love you, and Kasie is a fine man.'

'Oh, don't talk about him, it upsets me,' snapped Avril. 'You will stay with me, won't you, Mum?'

Now was the time to tell her, Lily knew, but once more she allowed the opportunity to slip past. There was a lump in her throat as she replied. 'I won't leave you, not while you need me, Avril,' she said softly.

That evening, Lily went down again into that smelly lift, and out into the darkened street to find a phone box. But every one she tried had been vandalised. Eventually, very nervously, she went into a sleazy bar and asked to use the phone. Male eyes stared seductively in her direction and female eyes looked enviously at her lovely evening dress. That she was now an alien in the streets where she had been raised, she was very aware. When Kasie answered the phone, he sounded very drunk. His speech was slurred.

'I can't make it tonight, Kasie,' she said, 'so quit drinking and go to bed. I'll let you know what's happening tomorrow.'

He laughed bitterly. 'Now, that is extremely kind of you, *leiblin*.'

'Don't be sarcastic,' Lily said, feeling irritated, 'I'm doing my best. Goodnight, I'll ring again tomorrow.'

'If I'm still here tomorrow,' retorted Kasie.

'Oh, don't be so childish,' she said ringing off.

Over the following week, Avril slowly came back to life but she still leaned on Lily for moral support.

Jonny's brother had brought a charge against the police, and the day that Avril went to court to hear the legal case was an especially bad one. But the law was right, the judge pronounced. Jonny had threatened the police with a firearm. Even though it was a toy gun, they could not have known that, so the police had retaliated. There was nothing else they could have done. So once more the papers were full of this case of Jonny's life and his progress from a gipsy camp to the crooked underworld of London. And once more Avril was devastated. She continued weeping and, much to Lily's dismay, continued to swallow tranquillisers. Bravely Lily coped with the children and the housework, and she met Kasie on Sunday morning at Aldgate. He was looking really ill.

'For Christ's sake, what have you been up to?' she demanded.

Kasie smiled wanly. 'Booze, what else?'

'Oh, Kasie, don't make the situation even worse for me.'

'Well, you have the answer. Tell Avril the truth, make her leave this lousy place. We could all go home and get a house in Rotterdam and take care of her and the children.'

Lily smiled gratefully at him. 'Oh, Kasie, I don't know if it's going to work, but give me time.'

He held her hand. 'I miss you, my lovely, but tomorrow I'm going home. I cannot stand another day in that lousy hotel all on my own. I'll go to live with Neil and Jante until you make up your mind to return to me. But don't leave it too late . . .'

She held him tightly to her. She felt hurt but she could not even shed a tear. 'I promise I will come back,' she whispered.

Kasie opened his wallet and handed her some notes. 'Here's a bit of ready cash, you might need it. Write down this number so you can still ring me, but charge it to the office in Rotterdam.'

For the rest of the afternoon, they walked through the old familiar sights of East London. 'It's like old times,' said Kasie, as they stood in a deep dark doorway to say goodbye once more.

Watching Kasie's back as he disappeared down into the tube, Lily suddenly felt devastated. He had left again. Creeping back to the little box-room she occupied in Avril's flat, she cried for the rest of the day.

Avril left her alone that evening but the next morning she was full of spite. 'Some bloody husband, he is, going off and leaving you like that. If my Jonny could come back, he would never leave my side. If I were you, I'd get a divorce. I can't see why you lumbered yourself with another husband at your age.'

Lily's eyes were swollen from weeping all night and she did not reply. She had no intention of getting into a battle with Avril. The tranquillisers that Avril took were inclined to make her bitchy, especially early in the morning.

'Let's go out,' said Lily. 'It'll do us all good. We'll go down the market and buy some things for the children.'

They walked along in the weak winter sunshine to Shadwell Market and hung around the stall buying bits for the babies. Then they went on to the eel and pie shop.

'It's like the old days,' said Lily nostalgically. 'I remember when I was a kid at school, every dinner time it was pie and mash. We had no school dinners in my day.'

'Oh, quit moaning about the good old days,' snapped Avril. 'It's hard enough for us to live now without being reminded how good it used to be.'

Lily lapsed into silence. It was impossible to get close to Avril. It was as if Jonny's death had completely severed their bond of love for each other. What could she do now? Could she go on like this?

Avril filled herself with a large portion of pie and mash, and afterwards they went home where Avril lay down to sleep while Lily coped with the two small children.

This way of living continued for two weeks until Lily, at her wits end, rang Kasie, planning to ask him to come and rescue her. But the foreign voice at the other end of the phone did not seem to understand her when she asked for him. Then another person who spoke good English came on the end of the wire to explain that Captain De Fries had just gone on a voyage to the Middle East, and that if she wished to leave a message it would be relayed to him.

'No message,' said Lily abruptly, and rang off.

She wandered aimlessly along the Main Road feeling completely numbed. Well, he had not waited long to go back to sea. That was just like Kasie, she thought. All they ever did was chase each other. Where would it all end?

The sharp sound of a motor hooter brought her to her senses, and she realised that someone in a grey car was trying to attract her attention.

'Lily, Lily!' the voice yelled. It was Jo Macey. She pulled up at the kerb and her tall figure dashed out of the car and swept Lily into a terrific bear hug.

'Oh, dear,' gasped Lily as she got her breath back, 'how nice to see you, Jo.'

'I've been looking everywhere for Avril's flat,' said Jo. 'I lost the address, and it's like looking for a needle in a haystack. She's not even on the phone.'

'I'm staying with her, Jo, but let's go for a chat somewhere, shall we?'

'Sure, Lily, get in. We'll park the car and then go for a drink.'

They sat on the high bar stools in an East End local and surveyed each other.

'Must say, you look very fit, Jo,' said Lily, admiring the fact that Jo's hair was now iron grey and very close cropped. She was wearing a neat navy suit, with well-tailored slacks and a white shirt. She looked slick and smart, just like the same old Jo. But there were lines on her face that had not been there and she looked a lot older.

'I can't say the same about you, Lily,' said Jo, with concern in her voice. 'When I spotted you, you looked as if you had all the cares of the world on your shoulders.'

Lily told Jo about her marriage to Kasie and of all the trials and troubles of Avril in recent months.

'I was in the States,' said Jo, 'so I never heard. I'm so sorry, Lily, but you know what I think—you can't spend your life looking after Avril. Go back to Kasie. She'll stand on her own feet better if she doesn't have you to lean on.'

'I can't go, Jo,' confessed Lily.

Jo sipped her gin and looked worried. 'Let's face it, Lily, Avril was always a bit of a problem child.'

'I've spoilt her,' Lily admitted, 'and I did not want her to marry Jonny, that's why I feel so guilty. But there are my grandchildren to consider, as well, now.'

Jo looked concerned. She paused and said, 'Rene left me while we were in America.'

'Oh, Jo, I am sorry.' Lily put a hand on her arm.

'I'm over it now,' said Jo. 'But it was a bit of a blow. She left me for a good looking young fella who hasn't got a bean. Anyway, I made a bit of money on that last book and I've just opened a slimming club. Something else I got interested in when I was in the States.'

Trust Jo, thought Lily. She was still a very shrewd business woman.

'I was trying to contact you, Lily,' said Jo, 'because I sold the Nutcracker. You owned a third of that business and your money is in the Midland Bank. We didn't lose out. We both got out quite a bit more than we put in.'

'Well, that's nice, Jo,' replied Lily, 'but you know, I don't really need it now, unless I leave Kasie. He is very generous, you know.'

Jo's strong firm hand covered hers. 'He's a fine man, Lily,' she said, 'so don't lose him.'

Lily shrugged. 'What can I do? I'm so confused about it all. I've never felt so badly about Kasie. He's not the man he was, he seems to be so dependent on me.'

'Well, let's face it, Lily, you've got to make a quick decision and get Avril straightened out. You've got to get her earning her own keep or she'll soon go to pot.'

'I worry over those pills she takes but she won't take any notice of me.'

'Valium?' Jo said deliberately, 'she has got to get off them. I've seen some terrible cases of young women who got addicted to them. I'll come and talk to her tomorrow afternoon. She might listen to me.' Jo took out a small notebook. 'Write down the address, Lily, I'll find you. In the meantime, think over what you want to do with that money in the bank. I have a few ideas.'

After she had seen Jo, Lily felt quite rejuvenated. Her friend was so alert, bright and so concerned for Lily. Really, she was the only close friend Lily had made in all those years since Ivy had died. As always, Jo had instilled confidence in her that all was not lost after all.

Avril was a little sulky when Lily explained her long absence and told her that Jo was calling the next day.

'I might go out,' she said petulantly. 'I don't want her commiserating with me.'

Lily sighed impatiently. 'That's the last thing in the world that Jo is likely to do. She has a good business sense and she has already started a new kind of business to do with health and slimming.'

Avril ran a hand over her podgy hips. 'Oh, I've heard of that keep fit stuff. I suppose I might stay and listen to what she has to say about it.'

Lily relaxed, delighted to have found a chink in Avril's armour. Avril was concerned about getting fat again.

The next day Jo arrived bright and breezy with chocolate for the children. They passed a very pleasant afternoon with cups of tea and lots of chat. Jo talked all about America and of her new activities. Not one word was mentioned of Avril's troubles and she was more like her old self, giggling about the dry comments on the fat ladies of New York. Before she went, Jo paused to ask Avril to visit her health club in the City and gave her some hints about her diet. Avril was very interested.

'If you do the course, Avril,' said Jo, 'you take no pills, no drugs of any kind, just good, honest, healthy food.'

Thus Jo had begun to pave the way to Avril's recovery. Lily looked after the children while Avril went with Jo in the afternoon to her health club.

'Right,' said Jo. 'I don't expect to pay you, but you had a good education so you can help me out with some secretarial work in return for the slimming course.'

So Avril helped Jo run her health club by spending the

afternoons adding up accounts and typing letters for her at home in the evenings.

Lily was feeling a lot better. She wrote a long letter to Kasie asking if he still loved her or if he wanted to finish the marriage seeing as he had gone back to sea. Her feelings about him were very confused.

She received a reply from Kasie some weeks later. It was a little humble, not a bit like the proud Kasie:

> Lily, my lovely,
>   Don't ask me if I miss you. Life is hell without you. That is why I went back to work. Surely there is a way for us to be together since we have wasted most of our lives. Our love does not fade and die that easily. Come back to me, darling, I really need you.
>   Yours forever, Kasie.

'Oh, Jo,' Lily said when she told her of the contents of that letter, 'it really broke my heart.'

'Lily, you must understand that Avril is a lot better now. Why can't you go back to him?'

'Who will mind the children?'

'The Council nursery. It will be good for them.'

'Oh, I can't face it. If Avril has a set-back, what will happen to them?'

Jo frowned. 'Look, Lily, I'm about to make an offer to you. You know all about me but I can assure you that side of my life is over. Why, I turned fifty this year even though I'm told I don't look it. But do you get my meaning?'

'Yes, I do,' said Lily, 'but it wasn't even in my mind. Avril could be your own daughter, you are so good to her.'

'So, we know how we stand. I have a suggestion to make. I want to buy a house in the country and convert it into a health farm, a kind of clinic where people who are overweight and have money to spend can come and stay. I've got several people lined up who will work with me and have got my eye on the right property. How would you like to come into business with me? Better still, why don't you put Avril into it?'

Lily looked astonished. 'Why, I would never have thought of

doing that! I don't need the money that's lying in the bank and I could then go home to Kasie.'

'That's what I'm getting at,' said Jo.

'Oh, blimey!' cried Lily, reverting to her Cockney accent. 'It's a bloody good idea! I'm with you all the way.'

Within weeks, Jo had bought a big house in Sussex with a cottage attached for Avril to live in. The health farm was an instant success both for Jo, whose business acumen had worked again, and for Avril who soon had a nice slim figure and was much more confident as Jo's assistant. Also the children were settled in and looked after by the housemaids while Avril was working.

Lily had helped out at the beginning but by the end of the year, there was not much for her to do anymore. 'It's time to go,' she said to Jo one day.

Jo nodded. 'Good luck, Lily.'

'I wonder how he will greet me,' Lily said, 'after all this time.'

'Oh, in the usual way, Lily,' grinned Jo, 'if I know Kasie.'

CHAPTER SEVENTEEN

No Return

Strangely enough, it was almost with some reluctance that Lily returned to Kasie. Six months of being apart had increased her longing to be with him but some deep feelings within her told her it would never be a really smooth path. Perhaps she should settle for a life of freedom, she thought, to live with Avril and Jo Macy, and have the joy of watching her grandchildren grow up in that very peaceful part of Sussex. But she decided she had to go to him. She kissed her little family goodbye, and boarded the plane at Heathrow.

Kasie was not at Amsterdam Airport to meet her, as he had promised. A little irritated and disappointed, she got a taxi to take her to the dockside tavern where she was quite sure she would find him. Sure enough, there he was holding up the dingy bar. He looked a little worse for drink, clad in wide, untidy pants and plimsolls. Seeing her, he gave her a soft slow smile and his red-veined eyes glinted in humour at Lily's expression.

'Welcome home, Lily my lovely,' he said, giving a mock bow.

'Gor blimey!' cried Lily, 'why the hell didn't you tell me you wouldn't be there to meet me? I had to leave my luggage behind.'

He said nothing. He handed her a drink and led her to a table.

Lily stared at him suspiciously. 'What have you been up to? You look as if you're soaked in booze.'

Still the warm smile hovered around his mouth as he raised her hand to his lips. 'Same old lovely Lily,' he said quietly.

'Oh, you really exasperate me,' grumbled Lily. 'I never know how to take you. Now I wish I had never come.'

'I'm so glad you did, Lily,' he said, 'in fact, it was because I could not face another rejection from you that I lost my courage and did not go to the airport. I was afraid you might not be there.'

Lily looked at him very strangely. This was not like Kasie at all. He seemed to have lost his ability to fight with her. 'Oh well, I'm sorry.' She kissed his cheek then swallowed the fiery gin. 'Don't let's quarrel, because this time I've come home for always.'

'Till the next time,' Kasie muttered grimly under his breath.

Lily looked around at the old men sitting in the bar. They all wore big floppy jerseys and round hats and swallowed huge jugs of beer as they talked loudly in their foreign tongues. They were all old salts, men from the boats who idled their time away down in this dockside tavern. Was Kasie going to turn out like them? 'Come on, darling,' she said suddenly, 'let's go. Where are we staying?'

'Aboard.' Kasie put down his glass and pressed his face close to hers. 'Aboard the *Lovely Lady*,' he told her. 'Do you mind?'

'No, no,' she muttered, a little amazed. She had expected a good hotel for that night at least.

Kasie stroked her arm dreamily. 'I have decided that we will continue our disrupted honeymoon. I've been having the *Lovely Lady* refitted so that we can sail to the Indies to find the nice warm sun and visit Jan and Easi. Would you like that, Lily?'

'Oh well, if that's what you want,' she sighed resignedly.

'That's why we must stay aboard the *Lady*, otherwise those workmen will pinch everything. I have to keep my eye on them, and it costs too much money to stay in the dry dock.'

'Come on then, Kasie,' Lily said impatiently. 'Don't drink any more, let's go home.'

They left the bar and walked along the dock. Kasie walked a little unsteadily beside her. 'I'll send for my luggage tomorrow,' she said as they inched their way along the wooden walkway which ran between the ships to where the *Lady* was now anchored.

On the ship's deck there was a lot of rubbish—paint pots and rolls of rope. She looked a trifle neglected and the smart white paint was now quite weather-beaten. Lily's heart sank. From down below came the sound of hammering and as she went down the gangplank she heard Kasie telling the workmen to pack it in for the day. He gave the crisp orders in his own language. They picked up their tools and disappeared.

It was untidy down in the cabin which had lost its immaculate look. An oil heater had replaced the generated heat but it was quite warm. Soon Lily had brewed some coffee and Kasie lolled in his chair smoking. He talked about the ship. 'I shan't be sorry to move out to sea,' he said. 'I'm sick of hanging about in this dock.'

'I don't know why you have been,' said Lily. 'There's no need. Surely you have your business and your family in Rotterdam.'

'I told you why I am here, Lily,' he answered irritably, 'and Rotterdam is a long way from here.'

She poured out the coffee feeling very depressed. What was wrong? Something had happened to their relationship. They were like an old married couple and fed up with each other. She sat facing him as she sipped her coffee, and stretched out her long, slim legs.

His eyes caressed her legs and travelled to her face. 'You never change, Lily,' he said. 'You're still as lovely as when you were young.'

A lump came into her throat. She put down her cup and went over to kneel down beside him. Putting her head on those greasy old pants which smelled of diesel oil, she cried: 'Oh darling, what's wrong? Don't you love me any more?'

Kasie pulled her roughly up onto his lap. 'That's the trouble, I'm still crazy about you,' he whispered as their lips met. So they began to make love in that old passionate way, and ended up in bed close to each other, leaving the world outside behind them. Lily thrilled once more to Kasie's touch, and smoothed her hand over his freckled body.

'Lily,' he said, 'let us be happy together for a while. Remember the good days we had when we were young and lived in this harbour?'

'Of course we will, darling,' she cried. Trembling with love, she clung to him. 'There's nothing to stop us now. We are both free of our commitments.'

The days passed into weeks and months. The weather had got warmer but still they hung about the harbour. For some reason, the repairs to the ship were not making much headway. She was now getting a coat of paint overall, her decks had been reinforced and a new wheelhouse had been built on. Lily wasn't happy. The thumping and banging of the workmen, and the arguments she had with Kasie about his lazing about in the dockside tavern, drove her frantic. She hated the sea more than ever, she was afraid of it. On very windy nights when a force ten gale was blowing down the Channel she would huddle close to Kasie shivering with fright.

'Nothing to worry about, *leiblin*,' he comforted her, 'surely you have got your sea legs by now.'

He always gave her plenty of money to spend during the day. She would sit outside the cafes drinking coffee and eating cream pastries, thinking about Avril and her grandchildren. In the afternoons she would roam the big new stores that had sprung up in the town, buying baby clothes and lots of make-up to send home to Jo and Avril. There was no need for her to dress up, and there were no occasions to get her hair set or wear any of her nice dresses. The boat was a complete shambles and there was nowhere to get really comfortable. Kasie was more often partly drunk. He would sit outside the tavern in the heat of the sun arguing with the old men about the war, playing cards and drinking. Lily watched him with a grim expression on her face. Something was more wrong with Kasie than he seemed prepared to admit. Even his lovemaking had slowed down. But determined to keep the peace, she soldiered on, longing for home, steak and kidney pudding, and eggs and bacon for breakfast. She still tried hard to master the language but got tongue-tied when she tried to speak it.

At last the workmen had finished. Kasie was jubilant. 'The inspector is coming to pass her sound next week, and then we can get on our way. We'll go into town and stock up with good things to eat and drink. You must buy some nice shorts and bikinis, because it will be very hot where we're going.'

Lily shivered. The thought of going to this strange land and all that sea in between, really gave her nightmares.

Kasie got up a crew—all coloured boys wanting to get back home.

'Now, there will be little to do but lie in the sun, you and I,' he said, 'and make love.'

She gave a wry grin. Love had been in short supply of late. Kasie had been dead drunk most evenings after carousing down in the tavern until after midnight. However, undaunted, she began to make the cabin comfortable. She polished up the pots and brightened the galley, and then sat up on the newly painted deck writing letters to Jo and Avril. Inside, she was feeling lonely. The women aboard the other boats often wanted to gossip but Lily found it difficult to converse with them, so she stayed away from them.

It was a bright September day when they set sail, Kasie was looking a little pale and wan, for he had suffered many sleepless nights lately, sitting on the edge of the bunk smoking.

'I'll be all right once we are out at sea,' he had told her. 'It has just been a lot of worry getting the *Lady* shipshape.'

Soon a bright day arrived when they pulled out of Amsterdam harbour, Kasie's boozing pals all waving farewell from the dock side. As the ship moved out towards the deep waters of the open sea, Lily and Kasie stood on deck close together. The crew were hurrying about pulling in ropes and starting the engines.

'Here we go, Lily my lovely,' said Kasie, 'off on another honeymoon. First we go to Rotterdam to say goodbye to the family, but we will not delay, I want to make the crossing while the weather is mild.'

But they were only words. In Rotterdam they really delayed

while Kasie went visiting with Neil or entertained Fritz, his nephew. The *Lovely Lady* was anchored out in the bay, and they went ashore each day in a small motor boat. They went out to eat dinners in hotels and Lily was often very sleepy, not being able to keep up with the conversation once they all started talking and drinking. But Neil was always kind and considerate to her and tried to make her feel less left out. 'I'm so pleased you are going with Papa,' he said to her one day. 'I wanted to stop him, but you know him, he would not listen.'

'Why?' asked Lily. 'Why should you stop him?'

Neil looked at her strangely. 'Hasn't Papa told you?' he asked, looking confused.

'Tell me what?' demanded Lily, a little confused.

Neil's face quickly changed as he assumed a cold mask. 'Oh, just how fond he is of you and how pleased we all are for you both.'

The conversation ended abruptly, leaving Lily feeling that something had not been said which should have been said.

At last, one evening, as the setting sun shone over the sea and lit up the waves with golden light, the *Lovely Lady* set sail. Lily and Kasie celebrated with another drink and slept that night wrapped up in each others arms.

'I will make it up to you, Lily,' Kasie said. 'I know I was a very naughty boy, all that drinking down at the harbour tavern.'

'Right,' said Lily. 'From now on, you only drink with me and I will see you don't get too much down you.'

Kasie looked sad. 'Well, I've had a lifetime of drinking, and it's not easy to stop, so I suppose I have asked for it.'

'Asked for what?' demanded Lily.

But Kasie remained silent. Reaching out for his old banjo which still hung on the wall, he started to strum on it and hum a tune.

Lily lazed beside him listening to his soft, crooning voice. He had become a little husky but it was still pleasant to listen to.

Kasie sang, 'If I had my life to live over, I'd still fall in love with you, We wander again down that shady lane, And still do the things we once knew. I've loved you since schooldays were over, and I still fall in love with you.'

As the soft voice caressed the notes, Lily shivered. 'Oh, don't sing like that, Kasie,' she cried, 'it upsets me and makes me feel sad.'

He put the old banjo down beside him and came and held her in his arms. 'Are we going to be happy together, my lovely?' he asked.

'Of course we are,' she said, 'but I can't look back, it's all too much for me.'

They remained close in a long kiss then a discreet knock told them Kasie was needed on deck.

That night it was really stormy. Lily lay close in Kasie's arms while the gale raged outside. The *Lovely Lady* tossed wildly about pulling at her anchor. Yet bright and early next morning the sun shone and the sea was relatively calm.

Kasie got up early and when Lily awoke he was drinking coffee still dressed in his oil skins. 'Got to take a look at the old girl's bottom before we set sail again,' he said brightly. 'Never can tell if she is shipshape, it's a long and heavy crossing.' He began to undress and soon stood before her in a pair of swimming trunks. His well-framed body was not as perfect as it used to be, and he had lost a lot of weight. 'Don't do that, Kasie,' she said. 'Let one of the crew go under the ship.'

But he just kissed her and laughed merrily. 'I'm still the boss,' he said.

She heard the splash as he dived overboard, and she lay in the cabin waiting, knowing that he would soon return all wet and sprightly wanting to make love. But the time passed and there was a stillness in the air. All she could hear was the shrill cry of seagulls and then the excited chatter of the brown sailors. She lay still for a few more minutes but a strange feeling gripped her heart. Leaping out of bed, she grabbed a dressing-gown and stumbled on deck. 'Kasie, where are you?' she called.

A panic-stricken sailor rushed up to her. 'Captain, he not come up. We launch boat to look for him.'

Lily's legs trembled at the knees with fear. She stared out at the wide blue sea, and the golden ladder of the sun that came down from the sky caressed the white-topped waves.

'Kasie! Kasie!' she cried. 'Where are you?' There was only silence. Surely he was playing some trick. 'Come out, Kasie!' she yelled, looking wildly around her.

The sailors had launched the boat and were rowing around looking into the water. One dived under the bows but by their gestures she knew that they could not find him. She gave one last wild cry, 'Kasee!!!' And then she sank down in a faint.

Kasie's body was found in Rotterdam harbour. The tide had brought him back to his own land that he was so proud of. Lily spent most of the next few days in a daze. She was taken back to Rotterdam to stay with Neil and Jante. Everyone was very kind to her but she hardly noticed anything.

Kasie was buried out at sea, his ashes thrown from the deck of his ship, the *Lovely Lady*. Lily did not attend, she was still in bed, sedated by the drugs given to her by the doctor.

Jo Macy and Avril arrived from England to see her. 'What will you do now?' asked Jo.

'I'll come home with you and Avril,' said Lily. 'I hate this place, and there's nothing to hold me here now.'

Avril stood sullen-faced at the end of the bed. Her face portrayed little emotion but Lily knew she was thinking: 'So, you have lost your man. Well, I lost mine and he was only half his age.'

Lily wiped her tears. 'I have to go downstairs,' she said. 'For some reason the relatives insist on reading Kasie's will, it's a kind of custom. Stay with me, please, both of you.'

They went down into the large sitting room where black-clad folk sat around drinking.

In the centre a wizened little man sat at the table preparing to read out Kasie's will.

Neil came forward to greet them. He put an arm around Lily and also around Avril who stared at him curiously but there was no time for comment.

The old lawyer began to read out the will in a cracked voice. There was a lot of legal jargon and then the list of businesses and properties that Kasie owned. They were substantial. The Rhine Line was to go to Fritz, and the salvage and oil tankers were to be divided equally between Neil and Avril. This gave everyone a bit of a shock, but the lawyer's next words shocked them even more: 'Avril is my natural daughter by her mother, Lily. She never knew this fact in life, so perhaps she will appreciate me in death.'

A loud gasp ran around the room, and Avril put her hands over her face and began to cry.

Lily stared dumbstruck as the lawyer continued. 'The cash in the bank, the property in Amsterdam, the house in the Indies and an annual gratuity from all three businesses go to Lily whom I have loved more than life. I was told that my end was near, and I wanted just six months of happiness with you, my darling, so I would not mind. Goodbye, my lovely. The *Lovely Lady* I leave in the capable hands of Neil, my son, who I hope will look after it and keep it in trust for my grandchildren to enjoy for as long as they live.'

The family wiped their eyes on black-bordered handkerchiefs as the lawyer rose and gathered up his papers. Then someone came in with a tray of drinks. It was all over. Kasie had had the final word.

Neil came up to Lily. 'I'm sorry that we did not warn you but Papa had been told by his doctor that his heart was failing. He refused to have any treatment but insisted on sailing to the Indies instead.'

Avril was staring hard at him. 'How strange,' she said, 'that we are brother and sister, and I used to be so much in love with you.'

'And I with you, little Avril,' said Neil gently.

Then Avril turned to Lily. 'Well,' she said, 'it would have been nice to have known my own father in his lifetime but at least my kids will not want for money.'

'Let's live together as a family, Lily,' said Neil. 'You are very welcome.'

'Oh, no,' wept Lily. 'I want to go home, back to England.'

The next day Lily left for England with Jo and Avril. She was still in a daze and she looked out of the window of the plane with a faraway look in her eyes. Kasie was gone; she hoped that he was at peace. Suddenly a very serene feeling soothed her. He had gone but her love for him remained. No longer would they love and leave each other, or torment each other as they had done for a lifetime. Perhaps it was for the best.

Avril had fallen asleep with her head on Lily's shoulder. Lily kissed her head and smiled at Jo who had caught her eye. Life had not come to an end, after all, she thought. She would go back and live and work with Jo and Avril and her darling grandchildren, and enjoy the peaceful existence in Sussex. She would live in her beloved England but have Kasie in her memory and her heart. A quiet smile lit up her face. Life was hard but she knew that she was a survivor, and perhaps now, with no alternatives, she could be at peace with herself at last.

All Futura Books are available at your bookshop or
newsagent, or can be ordered from the following address:
Futura Books, Cash Sales Department,
P.O. Box 11, Falmouth, Cornwall.

Please send cheque or postal order (no currency), and
allow 55p for postage and packing for the first book
plus 22p for the second book and 14p for each additional
book ordered up to a maximum charge of £1.75 in U.K.

Customers in Eire and B.F.P.O. please allow 55p for
the first book, 22p for the second book plus 14p per
copy for the next 7 books, thereafter 8p per book.

Overseas customers please allow £1 for postage and
packing for the first book and 25p per copy for each
additional book.